TEGAN JAMES

MIX AND MATCH

SCARLET

Enquiries to:
Robinson Publishing Ltd
7 Kensington Church Court
London W8 4SP

First published in the UK by Scarlet, 1998

A copy of the British Library Cataloguing in
Publication data is available from the British Library

ISBN 1–85487–593–0

Printed and bound in the EC

10 9 8 7 6 5 4 3 2 1

.... james, rich,
.... yachtsman Jet Diamond is unique.
Or so Aberdeen thinks when she falls in love with him. But
.... before she .... his twin brother, film-maker Jasper
Diamond Identical in looks but with very different
personalities, the Diamond twins bring double trouble to
the women in their lives. So what does that mean for
Aberdeen? In Stacy Brown's regency novel, *Heaven
Sent*, rebellious bluestocking Celeste Wentworth is determined to escape from the dreary life that her stern grandfather is planning for her – a suitable marriage and a
family. She resolves to be 'ruined' and falls for notorious
rake Simon Barclay, the Earl of Dragonwood. As their
relationship develops, they become caught up in the
strange web of a secret society responsible for the corrup-
tion of society girls, including Simon's own stepsister.

Don't forget that the second *Scarlet* hardback, *Finding
Gold* by Tammy Hilz, will be available next month. To
reserve your copy, send us your details now!

Till next month,

Sally Cooper

SALLY COOPER,
Editor-in-Chief – *Scarlet*

About the Author

Tegan James was born and educated in Tasmania. She began writing while still at school and had her first book published in 1977. In 1979 she married, and now has two children – a boy and a girl.

With her husband, Tegan has travelled around Australia, and has visited the Queensland Gold Coast, one of the settings for her first *Scarlet* novel *In Search of a Husband*. Travel is always tied in with research for future projects.

The author has received and been short-listed for many awards.

Apart from reading and writing, Tegan is interested in music, travel, embroidery, social history and animals: she and her family have a number of pets, including four cockatoos.

In the future, Tegan and her husband hope to travel to the UK and also to drive the Alaskan Highway.

Other *Scarlet* title available this month:

HEAVEN SENT – Stacy Brown

CHAPTER 1

'I've lost my *job*?' Aberdeen couldn't keep the incredulous squeak from her voice.

'The committee has decided not to confirm your reappointment.' Brian Cooper met her gaze squarely. 'I did try to warn you, Ms Shawcross. I did suggest you should take the long view.'

So, he was implying it was all her own fault. Typical Cooper-speak! And Ms Shawcross? He'd always called her 'Aberdeen' before.

'I *did* take the long view,' she said sharply.

'The financial statement isn't good.'

'So? I might have refused a quick dollar in favour of long-term commitment to our goals, but the underwear display was a smash!'

She was sure of her ground here, for 'Colonials Undercover' had certainly caught the public imagination. There was something extremely erotic about the display of tightly laced waists, crotchless drawers, basques and hoops and corsets that had once surrounded the female form. Bad for the health, and darned uncomfortable, but Aberdeen found costume fascinating. So fascinating that she planned to buy a terraced house and set up her own costume museum;

the definitive collection for the twenty-first century.

She mustn't think of her goals now. She was in deep water if she couldn't get herself reappointed; deeper than Sydney Harbour. Without her job, there would *be* no house, no definitive collection, no winter study trip to see the great museums of Europe. Without her job, her future was dead in the water.

Her sense of injury deepened. Dammit, she had earned that job! She had been meticulous in her work. Patiently she would unravel silk threads, starch high collars and halt the depredations of moth, rust and mildew. Shattered silks were stitched patiently to backing; only in extreme cases would she use the iron-on net as a restorative. Net would support the brittle fabric but, once applied, it was permanently bonded. She had demanded proper humidity control, dust filters and acid-free tissue. She had refused to use plastic pouches for fragile documents in case the chemicals reacted badly with the paper. She had made the conservators' department of the Pitt Gallery an active, innovative part of the organization, and this was her reward.

'I'm good at my job!' she persisted. 'You know I am. You even approved my study trip next year!'

There was a short, charged silence, which she broke by slapping her hand on the desk. 'I'm *good* at my job!' she repeated.

'No one denies your dedication,' said Cooper. 'The fact is, Ms Shawcross . . .' He paused, and twisted his pen between his fingers.

'What?' she snapped.

'You're *too* dedicated. The committee finds you over-conscientious. Your exhibition cost nearly as much to stage as it brought in, and as for the group who wanted to hire those old ballgowns for the pagcant – '

'It would have put an unacceptable strain on the fabric,' said Aberdeen hotly. 'The seams would have been ripped, the trains trodden – '

'Clothing is made to be worn,' said Cooper.

'That's like saying a ninety-year-old woman is made to dance the can-can! Maybe she could have, once. Maybe she could do it still, but what doctor would advise it?'

'Minor damage can be repaired.'

'The surrounding cloth is too fragile to hold the stitching . . . oh, why am I talking to you?' Aberdeen thrust a hand through her cascade of curly fair hair. 'I know the publicity would have been good, but it wasn't worth the risks to the specimens. As for the cost of the exhibition, we're in this business to *conserve*, not damage the goods by using shoddy mountings!'

'You are entitled to your opinion, but it isn't one the committee shares. I'm sorry, Ms Shawcross, but there's no point in continuing this discussion. The decision is out of my hands.'

'Brian – ' began Aberdeen impulsively. 'Please! You know I'm committed to the eyeballs – I've put down a deposit on the study trip – dammit, you let me think the re-appointment was a mere formality!'

'I'm sorry,' said Cooper again. 'We're going to have to let you go.'

A few days before Christmas, Aberdeen cleared her office. She was still shell-shocked. Her exhibition had garnered praise from many unexpected sources, praise for its novelty, for its professionalism, for the witty and informative taped commentary. So much praise that

3

she'd have bet her life on retaining the position for another term. She'd certainly bet her future. First the study trip to Europe, then two more years at the Pitt Gallery while she built her own collection. She had chosen the venue and put down a deposit. Her plan was ambitious, and she knew it would need an accomplished balancing act to get the timing right. It didn't have a hope now she was unemployed.

She and her accountant went over the figures of income and expenditure.

'Savings?' asked Hugh Cornwell.

Aberdeen gave a hollow laugh. 'I've ploughed everything into the deposit for the terraced house and the trip – and now I'll have to cancel both. I don't even get severance pay, since the position was never permanent. Don't tell me, Hugh. I'm badly over-extended.' She bit her lip hard. 'Someone up there hates me.'

Fate, having withdrawn her favour from Aberdeen, certainly made a job of it. Or perhaps it was simply the house-of-cards effect. A month ago, she'd had security and ambition; now, she had nothing. And all because some blinkered, myopic committee members couldn't see further than their own sharp noses.

Christmas carols tinkled and pealed from every shopping centre; Sydney Harbour Bridge was lit up like a promise. A giant glittering tree appeared in Martin Place, and even the pigeons in the little park near the Glebe Library seemed to coo peace and goodwill. The magpies carolled in the trees along Glebe Point Road, ignoring the buses that thundered up and down and the taxis that trawled the streets like hungry sharks. Glebe was full of restaurants, flower shops and ethnic chic cafés. *Ergo*, it was also full of traffic. Glebe was the place she'd chosen as a venue for

4

her museum. Glebe was the place where the estate agent had pulled the plug. He wouldn't hold the option any longer.

'Merry Christmas,' said Aberdeen bitterly to the pigeons, and stepped over a lump in the pavement; the tree-roots laughed at asphalt and tar . . . She went back to her flat in Blaxland and telephoned her mother.

Kate Shawcross commiserated, and did *not* say, 'I told you so'.

'Come and stay with me,' she suggested. 'Get things into perspective.'

'I don't want perspective I want justice.'

Kate chuckled. She had married late in life and had been well over forty when Aberdeen had arrived, a mid-life surprise packet for herself and her astonished husband. Literally a surprise packet, since Kate hadn't even realized she was pregnant. 'I put you down to the menopause, then to middle-age spread,' Kate had told her daughter. 'In the end, I thought you were appendicitis, so I went to the doctor. Luckily he had more sense.'

'Only you, Kate, only you,' said Aberdeen, but unorthodox reactions were typical of Kate. Her husband had been her rock and stay, but he had died when Aberdeen was eighteen and already living in Sydney. Six months later, Kate had left her home in Melbourne for an extended holiday in Tasmania, had rented a cottage in Battery Point and had somehow forgotten to return. That had been five years ago.

'I've been watching *Top End – In the Rough*,' Kate announced, apropos of nothing.

'What's that?'

'A documentary,' said Kate. 'He goes to interesting places.'

5

Aberdeen sighed. 'Who's "he"?'

'The presenter, darling. Jasper something . . . Jasper . . . Jasper . . .' Aberdeen could hear Kate snapping her fingers as she sought the elusive name. 'You must know who I mean.'

'I don't have TV,' Aberdeen reminded her. 'I don't – didn't – have time to watch it.'

'I'll show you the video when you come for Christmas. I'll be away for New Year, but that won't bother you.'

Aberdeen, aware that the alternative was making excuses to avoid the round of jollification in Sydney, agreed that it wouldn't bother her at all.

'You can see the Sydney-Hobart yachts come in,' said Kate.

'I'm not interested in boats.'

'This isn't *boats*, darling. It's champagne and streamers and lots of glistening muscles. Yachties with sexy baggy eyes. I'll book you a flight.'

Tasmania was cooler than Sydney, thought Jasper Diamond. And much, *much* cooler than the top end in Arnhem Land, where, fourteen weeks before, he had been engaged with file snakes, mangroves, a mysterious shipwreck and three helpful tribal elders. And Tam, of course.

Arnhem Land had certainly had its moments (especially Tam's face when faced with a shell-roasted mangrove crab), but the rough-cut edit and the post-production sound had been exacting as ever, and the Sydney Diamond/Spellman studio lacked aesthetics.

Tasmania was pretty and peaceful, but filming wasn't going well at all. There seemed to be strings of disasters, and one was happening now. You'd think a rock that had survived millions of years could survive one roadie with small neat boots, but it hadn't. It had snapped off, bounding down the cliff-face to land in the valley and stranding Rod Bowen on a inconvenient ledge.

Grist for mills, Jasper reminded himself grimly. Unconsidered trifles. Whatever happens, can it for future use. *In the Rough* could use it however rough it got. Barring murder.

The thought amused him, but there was no reflexive ripple on his strongly-carved face. No sparkle at all, which was why he had resisted suggestions that his own name be used as a title for the series. Diamonds ought to sparkle. His brother Jet sparkled. Jasper didn't. Maybe he was a *Diamond in the Rough*. Or an *Uncut Diamond*. That amused him too, but he couldn't stand there thinking. He had to rescue Rod and *try* to inject some life into this project.

Rod wouldn't have fallen if only Tam had come. The disasters wouldn't have happened, if Tam had come.

'You're part of the team. Everyone loves you,' he'd protested when Tam had dropped her bombshell.

'They can love someone else. Let them love *you* for a change.'

'The punters like the team as it is. Why fix what isn't broken?'

Tam had accepted the compliment without a blink. 'Because *I'm* broken, or at least severely bent.' She had grinned wryly. 'Ask Jet to co-present if you need someone to hold your hand.'

'I'd rather have you. And Rod's offered to stay behind – '

7

'Bother Rod! I've had it up to here with Rod, and I'm not having it any further!'

'Your father is expecting you to stay with him while we're there.'

'Look,' Tam had said tightly, 'I can't take any aggro right now. Officially, I'm ever so busy; unofficially, I can't take Rod and I can't take my father. I had enough of his little homilies after Chris died. So please, Jasper, in the name of all that's merciful, *leave me alone.*'

Tam's outburst had been atypical, so Jasper had dropped the subject. The truncated team had come to Tasmania, but things weren't going well. The weather hadn't been kind and now Rod Bowen had fallen off a cliff.

'Lower away,' said Jasper. The harness bit into his armpits and tilted him back as it took his weight. He had a light camcorder strapped to his helmet, and another on his belt. Stew, the number one cameraman, was filming the background shots while whatever footage Jasper achieved would be spliced in at intervals to give a feeling of immediacy to the material. If it was used at all. Rescuing his colleague might have a piquancy, but there would be plenty of viewers who would think he'd been bloody careless to let Rod get stuck in the first place.

Bloody careless? He'd been asleep! And what the hell was Rod up to, prowling the cliff in the dawn light?

'What the heck were you up to?' he yelled.

There was no reply, save the echo that rebounded from the cliffs on the other side of the ravine.

He wasn't scared of heights, but this part was not much fun, even for a bloke who'd spent most of his eighteenth year leading climbers up a Norwegian mountain. Jasper's boots scrabbled for traction on

8

the convex side of the cliff, but he had to allow most of his weight to sag from the harness. He felt like a spider on a thread.

Rod was uninjured, but the bulge in the cliff had made it impossible to get a rope to him in the ordinary way. Jasper's boots dropped below the bulge, and he fended himself away from the rocks with his gloved palms. The rope slid down another couple of metres, then he gave a warning tug and ducked to assess the situation.

Rod was crouched on a lip of rock. Behind him, the crumbled ledge shone clean and silver-grey. He stared out at Jasper, his face a white, smudged oval. 'What kept you, Diamond?' he asked. 'Did you stop off for a full telly make-up on the way? I warn you – that's staff exploitation.'

'I was perfecting my script,' said Jasper with irony. 'Do you want to be rescued?'

'I'm thinking, I'm thinking. What's that row up there?' said Rod as sobbing wails were heard above.

'Dottie thinks you're dead.'

Rod arched one eyebrow, then rose to his feet, wincing as his cramped calves twinged. 'Petrifaction has set in,' he intoned. 'I am officially ossified.'

'I'm going to chuck you the rope,' said Jasper. 'Pull me in so I can pull you out. And don't fall off, or Tam will sue me.'

'Tam would *thank* you,' corrected Rod grimly.

Jasper unhooked one end of the weighted line from his belt, then tossed the coil towards the ledge. 'Lower away!' he called to Ellie and Steve as Rod snapped the line to his own belt and began to draw it in.

Slowly, the winch above let out the slack. Jasper's boots crunched as he joined Rod on the ledge. 'You go

9

up first,' he said, and helped Rod into the second harness.

'Yes. Right.' Rod swallowed as he glanced at the sheer wall below.

'As soon as you're ready!' called Jasper, then, to Rod, 'What the heck were you doing down here, anyway?'

'Birdwatching. I slipped.' Rod watched the tension gather on the rope and harness, then stepped off into space. Slowly, he rose from sight. Jasper turned about to let the sweep of the view sink into his camcorder, moving quickly to increase the effect of vertigo. Might as well make a bit of drama for the punters. But it was peaceful, in its way, and after a bit he squatted down to enjoy the solitude. The chance to do so came too rarely these days, save when he managed to steal a day or so on his island. Lovely Allirra Island, purchased out of his almost unacknowledged need to have something of his own. A place where no one ever went but him.

'Don't think much of your taste,' his brother Jet had said in amusement. 'Tropical beaches are all the go, not piles of rock and trees.'

Tropical beaches had their place, but Jasper preferred soul-silence on Allirra, an echo of which he felt on the mountain now. Peace and silence – and a film-crew waiting for him above. Rod, and Stew, Ellie and Steve and Dottie, who was a dog of few brains but much thwarted mother-love. He hoped she'd lavish some of it on Rod. The strain that had been incipient in his friend throughout the trip so far had been jolted to the fore. Jasper had a safety valve for himself in Allirra Island. Rod had nothing much, since he'd split with Tam. He'd been depressed, but his concentration must be really shot if he'd fail to take normal precautions on a cliff.

10

Rod's state of mind was a problem, but it wasn't that that stirred Jasper suddenly. The touch that came was from somewhere outside himself as his gut told him something was missing. Not Tam this time, not Rod's usual cheerful mien, but something, someone, some part of Jasper Diamond.

It was blasted Jet again, he supposed. Pulling another blonde or risking his neck in a high-speed car. Doing something that made his adrenalin surge; a surge that echoed in Jasper's gut and in his loins as well.

Jasper Diamond wasn't psychic, wasn't fey, resisted any such notion. That was Tam's department, looking beyond the horizon, but he couldn't deny the itch of inner knowledge that sometimes came to unsettle him. He wasn't crazy. Just a genetic freak, a natural clone.

Jasper and Jet, identical twins, but which was the original, which the copy? They'd never agreed on that. And what was Jet up to that resonated so strongly in Jasper's mind and guts?

Last time this had happened, Jet had been romancing Grete Fischer – a beddable blonde from Bonn and Jasper's current lady. Jet had won her away from Jasper, who shivered now as a goose walked over his grave. He hadn't loved Grete, but they'd shared some good times. Then Jet had entered the equation, and Grete had been fascinated by the implications of mix and match.

Too fascinated.

Jet had known at once, damn him, and had set out to exploit the knowledge.

'May the best man win!' he'd said. 'Or maybe we could share.'

Like hell.

Another twinge of borrowed excitement; what was

11

Jet up to now? Appropriating something else that concerned his brother?

Down came the rope, and Jasper drew in his line with relief, and ascended the cliff. Stew's camera followed the last of the action as Jasper took off his harness and helmet, and switched off the camcorders that still whirred softly. Rod was drinking coffee, his handsome profile sharp against the sunlight. His hand was shaking, and his expression was strained.

'You OK, mate?' said Jasper, but Rod shrugged him aside so coldly that Jasper felt a shock of dismay.

'We've got to go,' said Rod abruptly, 'or we'll miss the yachts.'

Constitution Dock was swarming with tourists and locals, all in a holiday mood. Tasmanians loved the Sydney-Hobart, loved to fête the winners of the race, loved to lay informal bets on the line-honours and revel in the euphoria of the victorious crews. Salt water and champagne blended to dampen the shirts and oilskins of the sailors, sun-flushed faces beamed, teeth flashed and the air resounded with the pop of corks, the blare of music and the high-octane buzz of conversation. Streamers and balloons abounded, and the city had put on a fresh gentian sky to welcome its day of days.

The wind-riding field had left Sydney on Boxing Day, and now, almost three days later, the front-runners had arrived at Constitution Dock. The handicap winner hadn't broken the race record for the 1167-kilometre run, but she was by no means disgraced. *Lou Galah*, her name was, thirty-five feet of sleek grey and pink, and her young crew was just about delirious at the win.

Jet Diamond, the navigator, was mildly amused at the fervour of his crewmates. With them but not quite

12

of them, he was standing in for a friend who had suffered a compound fracture. Not only had this accident taken Nick Green out of the race, it had also upset Jet's plans for the summer. The pair of them had been set to sail clear across the Pacific.

'We can leave as soon as I've finished the Sydney-Hobart,' Nick had promised, but Nick had broken his leg. Trying a six-car jump on a motor-bike indeed . . . Jet shook his head. Risks were acceptable, but *that* risk, at *that* time – Nick must have rocks in his head. He'd lost his chance on the *Lou Galah*, and he'd thrown Jet's schedule out of whack. Finding another crewman at short notice would be difficult, so Jet had decided to wait for Nick to mend.

The end of March, he decided. Nick would be out of plaster and they could be on their way. First to Queensland to suss out an opportunity there, then off wherever the winds might blow. Meanwhile . . . he'd leapt at the chance to take Nick's place in *Lou Galah*. And here he was in Hobart, at Constitution Dock. And here he was with a free twelve weeks to fill with whatever adventure came his way. Pity about Grete Fischer. He'd said goodbye to her a few weeks ago, when she'd knocked back a chance to join the epic voyage and expected him to stay with her instead.

Herzlos, she had called him in her Wagnerian German accent. He shrugged. He wasn't heartless really, but he'd seen that wedding-ring gleam in her eye before. And Grete, while warm and sexy, and spiced with the satisfaction of taking her from Jasper, wasn't quite the kind of woman he wanted to marry.

He drank champagne, and his natural ebullience rose with the bubbles. His expertise had helped to win the Sydney-Hobart race. He needed a woman to help him celebrate. He needed a woman, and with his usual optimism he had no doubt that one would come along. Today, he was a winner, and winners had a certain magnetic attraction. Add that to his natural charisma and how could he miss?

The thought of it brought a grin to his mobile face, a grin which faded suddenly to a look of astonishment as a stalwart figure, dressed in a faded shirt, rubbed old denims and a broad-brimmed hat, appeared in his path. The man's face was in shadow, but Jet's mind's eye supplied the auburn hair, the dark horse-chestnut eyes. And the way the warmth of the colouring warred with the naturally still expression.

His brother was here, at the docks.

It figured, he supposed. Jas had to be somewhere, and Hobart was where the action was today. Briefly, Jet considered accosting him, asking after Grete. The temptation flickered and died. Water under the bridge; he'd won that last round. Grete was history, and Jet Diamond wanted a flesh-and-blood woman, not a memory, and certainly not a meeting with a poker-faced twin brother. The brother whom he'd cuckolded successfully once again.

If such a word still existed.

Jas would know. The man had a dictionary in his brain, a dictionary and a Thesaurus. And always the right word for every occasion. That was what made him so infuriating. Well – they might meet tonight at the Ruby, but the confrontation need not be yet, and if (and when) it did come, he'd be ready with a brand new lady on his arm. Preferably one who would appeal to Jasper too.

Jet walked smartly away from the *Lou Galah*, in search of female company.

14

CHAPTER 2

Aberdeen clasped her broad-brimmed hat against the harbour breeze as the yachts came in. Her eyes were dim and she blinked through tears, envying life's winners. She wanted to go back to the cottage.

She searched for her mother, but Kate had wandered off. Aberdeen shrugged philosophically. 'I am not my mother's keeper,' she said. 'I am *not* my mother's keeper. Thank you, Lord.'

Yes, Kate was just as wayward as ever but Aberdeen, with no need to rush back to Sydney, had found balm for her soul in Tasmania. Temporary balm, as she knew too well. The place was quaint and beautiful, but could she settle there forever as Kate had done? Not very likely.

And where was Kate? Somewhere in the crush. Squirted with champagne or strewn with streamers, propositioned by balding sailors . . . and what would Kate do then? Would she, *could* she snuggle up to a salty-tasting yachtie? Kate was sixty-seven but she still had a lively eye for a man. Aberdeen shivered, feeling like a voyeur, as gales of laughter competed with the breeze. Champagne corks popped and children yelled.

Constitution Dock on its day of days. She might as well enjoy it.

Two hours later, she had given up on Kate and was letting the spirit carry her where it willed. More yachts were in, corks were popping and the bubbly was flowing like lemonade. She was wearing a blue and white striped dress, Kate's Christmas gift, and a hat she had found to match. The hat had a life of its own, and now it suddenly whipped from her head and cartwheeled through the air.

'Zounds!' Aberdeen blinked furiously in the sudden brilliance of the setting sun on the water. Her curly hair whipped about, the gold of a wheatfield in summer, and her full skirts belled around her. She set off in pursuit of the hat, but a touch on her elbow made her pause.

'*There* you are, Kate,' she said. 'I thought you'd gone.'

'*Guten tag*, Lorelei!' A man's voice, not her mother's. It was masculine and amused, and the hand on her arm was firm. 'I've been looking for you all over.'

Aberdeen turned and looked up at the man who had accosted her. He had a laughing reckless aspect, with dark red hair like polished mahogany. He had somehow been spared a freckled complexion, and his eyes were a warm deep brown, fringed with spiky lashes. He needed a shave.

'No,' she said, and smiled in response to his laughter. 'My name isn't Lorelei.'

'Lorelei, golden *Göttin* of the Rhine. I'd know you anywhere. And this is your hat, *nicht wahr*?'

'Thank you.' She reached for the hat. 'It blew away just now.'

'I know. I caught it. Catching a leaf gives you a

16

happy day. What about catching a hat? A happy year?'

'Not *my* hat,' said Aberdeen. 'I haven't any luck to spare.'

'Then I'm claiming a forfeit for its return.'

'You're a yachtie,' said Aberdeen, identifying the euphoria, the unshaven, strung-out expression. Exhausted, but hyped up on adrenalin.

'From *Lou Galah*, *pro tem*.' His smile widened, revealing excellent teeth. 'We're all *zufrieden*, high as kites, and in an hour or so we'll hit the town to celebrate. I'm off; there's someone I don't want to see. Care for a drink?'

'No, thank you. Just my hat.'

'*Bitte?*' he urged. 'Please? I'm all alone.'

'No, thank you.'

His hand slid down to her hand, and he raised it to his lips, his mouth brushing her ringless fingers. 'Come,' he said, 'what harm could it do? Why not have a fun evening, no strings?' He paused. 'Call it local hospitality for a lonely Sydney-sider.'

'I'm not Tasmanian,' said Aberdeen tartly. 'I'm from Sydney too.'

'Then we're kissing cousins!'

She smiled unwillingly.

'Please, Lorelei? *Darf ich Sie heute abend zum Essen einladen?*'

'Why are you speaking German? You don't look German.'

'I have lately spent much time in the company of a fair *Fräulein* . . . now, alas, returned to Bonn via Britain. You haven't answered my question.'

'I don't *sprechen Sie Deutsch*.'

He laughed. 'I was asking you out to dinner, *Fräulein* Lorelei. My name's Jet Diamond.'

17

She wavered. Her five-year plan, so recently aborted, had left little time for romance or even fun. 'Dinner? Where?'

'I have a suite at the Ruby.'

Aberdeen recoiled, but he laughed aloud. 'The dining room is below. Humour me, Lorelei. I need protection.'

She laughed a little. 'My name is Aberdeen Shawcross.'

Twenty minutes later, Aberdeen was sitting at a beautiful repro table, whose gloss owed little to polish but much to the sealant that protected it from spills and heat. The chandeliers sparkled and the carpet was lush and velvety, and yet – it was a little too opulent. The crimson drapes were too rich, the ruby crystal pitchers too shining. Her blue striped dress was out of place, and so was she.

Jet had gone to change so she drank her squash and poked at the lemon slice with her straw. This was ridiculous. She didn't belong in this place; she was unemployed! And who did he think he was? She asked for her bill, but was told indulgently that it was to go on Mr Diamond's account. They knew him, then. People without identification didn't run accounts. She went to a phone and asked for an outside line.

'Hello, Aberdeen,' said Kate calmly. 'I was wondering where you were.'

'I'm at the Ruby Motel,' said Aberdeen. 'It's exquisitely tacky. Someone asked me for a drink. We might have dinner later.'

'I'll leave the key in the usual place,' said Kate, and hung up.

Aberdeen stared at the dead receiver. 'He says his name's Jet Diamond,' she said, clamping it back to her ear. 'He's an eighteen-carat wolf and he picked me up. He oozes charm and speaks German for effect. And oh, yes, Kate, I will be careful. No, Kate, I won't be late. Goodbye.' She hung up the telephone, and returned to the table. It couldn't be spring fever, for summer was well under way.

Jet Diamond was waiting, dressed in casual pants and a shirt which breathed expense without ostentation. 'I thought you'd deserted me, Lorelei,' he said with a lift of one fox-coloured brow. 'What are you drinking?'

'Lemon squash,' she said.

'You can do better than that.' Jet held up a finger and a waiter materialized beside them. 'Dry white, Henk,' said Jet.

He took his glass, and raised it to Aberdeen. 'To lovely *Lou Galah*, without whom we would never have met.'

Aberdeen laughed. 'You mean the boat. Does it belong to you?'

'Oh no, I have a yacht called *Aphrodite*. A lovely lady, nearly as lovely as you.'

'Do you do much sailing?'

'As much as I can.' He grinned. 'I'm off on a voyage very soon. I should have left next week.'

'Oh?'

'But now it'll be the end of March. My crewman is in plaster.' He smiled. 'For every cloud . . .'

'I beg your pardon?'

'You're the silver lining,' he said and winked. 'And maybe I can be yours. For a drink and dinner, and whatever else you fancy.'

Aberdeen smiled back and sipped her drink. It was exhilarating to see that light in a man's eye, to feel the

19

unspoken sizzle of his interest. It made a change from Brian and Hugh and others who pitied her now. Why not enjoy it?

Why not? Because, well – *because*. Because Jet Diamond was financially, socially and sexually out of her league. Especially sexually.

'What are you thinking, Lorelei?'

'Of a polite way to turn you down.'

His eyebrows climbed. 'Whatever for?'

'Habit. Caution. A dislike for starting things that can't be finished.'

'Stomach flu? A jealous husband?'

'I'm not sick and I'm not married.'

'*Wunderbar!*'

'Neither,' she said deliberately, 'am I involved with anyone.'

'Neither am I,' he said. 'Not since Grete said a last *auf Wiedersehen*.'

'Grete?'

'A German au pair. Are you always this up-front?'

'It saves time and trouble later.'

'Are you a corporate executive, Lorelei?'

'Do I look like one?'

'Not exactly. From the wary and militant gleam in your eye I'd hazard that you've encountered the glass ceiling.'

'No ceiling,' she said tartly. 'Just a constipated committee. I'm a conservator at Pitt Gallery. At least, I was. There's not a lot you can do with a degree in art history in the current climate. What about you?'

'Oh, I'm all sorts of things. I deal in stocks and shares, and I'm sometimes a financier. I have an interest in property.'

'A *Wunderkind*.' That accounted for the confidence and the ease of manner.

'I get by,' he said. 'But what about you? You said you *were* a conservator.'

'I failed to be reappointed.' Bitterness touched the back of her throat. 'I was *too* damned good at my job, so – goodbye, job, goodbye European study tour, goodbye my museum.'

'You need another drink.' He filled her glass with dry sparkling wine. 'Now, where shall we have dinner?'

'Not here,' said Aberdeen. 'It's far too ostentatious. Whoops!'

'Oh?' His brown eyes gleamed wickedly.

'I'm treading on your toes,' she apologized. 'You must like the place, since you pay top dollar to stay here.'

'I don't, though.'

Aberdeen sighed. 'I'm sorry, but I'm not playing games. Don't what? Don't like the place, don't pay top dollar, or don't stay here?'

He reached for her hand. 'I don't have to pay at all. My family owns the property.'

'So now you're offended.'

'Of course I'm not. The Hidden Treasure chain isn't my taste either, but my uncle keeps a *pied à terre* for us here.'

Aberdeen looked around at the opulence. 'Who's this person you didn't want to meet? Is it your German au pair?'

'Not at all! It's just my cranky brother who isn't very pleased with me. Now, let's go and find some other place to eat.'

She allowed him to help her out of her chair.

21

Immediately the waiter was beside them. 'Everything all right, sir?'

'Fine, Henk,' said Jet with his warm smile. 'Tell my uncle I'll see him later.'

Henk Vandenberg watched wryly as Jet Diamond and his golden lady left the bar. Henk had been at the Ruby for years, and he knew the Diamond clan. Godfrey Diamond ran the place, and members of the family used it as a base whenever they hit Tasmania.

Henk respected Godfrey, but some of the others were hard to swallow. Tam Spellman, for example, musician and some-time television presenter. Jet Diamond, playboy and speculator, and his sisters Sabrina and Gentian, the terrifying twins. Then there was indolent Krista, Godfrey's sister, who ran the Emerald Motel in Adelaide.

Finally, there was Jasper Diamond, who seldom stayed at the Ruby. A pity, that, thought Henk, for Jasper was the pick of the lot.

Jasper missed seeing the first yachts come in, but it really didn't matter. The incident at the cliff face might be worth ten times the film of a yacht winning a race, no matter how prestigious. The *Lou Galah*'s victory would be as stale as last week's buns when *Tasmania – In the Rough* was shown, as topical as a Christmas special shown in June. The only reason for the visit to Constitution Dock was to get a few shots of Tasmanians and tourists at play. Now they had their shots, and it was time to break.

The team got on pretty well as a rule, but Rod was tense and his mood affected the others.

'Break, everyone,' said Jasper. 'Get some space.

You all know where we're staying?'

'Yes, Papa,' said Rod.

Stew and Steve went off together with Dottie in their wake, neatly avoiding a dark young man who came up and gave Jasper a friendly punch. 'Coming down to the tavern, mate?'

'Do I know you?' asked Jasper.

'You ought to, since your yacht just beat mine in a race.'

'Not me,' said Jasper.

'Sure you did. I'm from the *C.J. Corella*, and I saw you yesterday aboard the *Lou Galah*. Remember? I chucked you a banana.'

'Jet,' said Rod softly. 'What do you bet?'

'I wouldn't bet,' said Jasper acidly.

The yachtie shrugged. 'If it wasn't you, it must have been your double, but come on down to the tavern anyway. That's where the action is tonight.' He grinned at Ellie.

She glanced hopefully at Jasper, and he sighed. The beer would be flowing and he felt responsible for his team – especially for little Ellie, his sisters' friend.

'OK, let's go,' he said. 'But remember we've an early start in the morning.'

Aberdeen and Jet had dinner at the Van Diemen Restaurant, then moved next door to the tavern, a cheerful place that brimmed with roistering yachties and their courts. Every so often more came in, tired but exultant at having finished the race. The *Lou Galah* crewmen were well away, drunk on achievement. Aberdeen accepted a shandy, feeling the warmth of acceptance as the yachties greeted her. Jet was with them, they felt he was one of them, and Jet was her

23

ticket to share their celebrations. After a while, she excused herself to go to the loo, where she and some of the other women tidied their hair and toned down their flushed faces.

'I must have been laughing too much,' said Aberdeen, looking at her pink cheeks with disfavour. The fluorescent lights made her narrow her eyes.

'Mine's windburn,' said Marie, a friendly girl whose husband had skippered *Lou Galah*. 'There's nothing quite like the combination of salt, wind and sun – not to mention tearing along at so many knots – to tangle your hair and muck up your skin. So. How do you know our Jetsetter, then?'

'He picked me up on the docks,' said Aberdeen.

Marie laughed. 'That's Jet all right! What happened to his German girlfriend, or shouldn't I ask?'

'I think she's out of the picture.'

After Marie had gone out, Aberdeen winked at her reflection. 'Nothing like a sexy man to bring the roses into your cheeks,' she said aloud. 'Balm to the soul and a Band-Aid on hurt feelings.'

'If you rip off a Band-Aid, it hurts,' said another yachting wife.

'That sounds like a warning.'

'It is,' said the girl. 'You're with Jet Diamond, right?'

'Yes.'

'He's cute but they're all the same,' said the girl. 'They buy a yacht to sail at weekends, they say. Exercise, an interest, networking. After a while it turns into a sort of mistress. It skims the cream and leaves you nothing much.' She dried her hands savagely, her gaze meeting Aberdeen's in the mirror. 'You'll know it's taking over,' she said, 'the first time

24

he calls you "the old woman". Or the first time he forgets you're supposed to be with him. After that, you've just three choices. Leave him, share him or find some consolation.'

'I met Jet today,' said Aberdeen mildly. 'It's our first date.'

'I wish someone had warned *me* years ago. Preferably on *my* first date. Goodness, I'm sorry. I've had too much to drink.' She left abruptly.

Aberdeen let her get clear, then followed. She was a little troubled, and her eyes widened as she saw Jet heading for the door, arm in arm with a girl she hadn't met. Leaving in full view of everyone who had seen them come in together. Passing her by as if she didn't exist.

'. . . *the first time he forgets you're supposed to be with him*,' said the yachtsman's wife in her memory.

'We've got to be in Stanley by eleven,' Jet was saying, 'and that's a good five-hour drive. An early night's in order.'

The girl laughed, and Aberdeen felt an icy tide roll over her; a tide of pique and offended dignity. He was sneaking off with another woman! So much for wanting her company.

'Thanks for the dinner, Diamond Jim,' she said loudly. 'Don't worry; I can make my own way home.'

The man swung to face her, and she had a dizzy impression of mahogany hair and dark red eyebrows, brown eyes and a pronounced chin. She blinked. It was and yet it wasn't Jet Diamond.

'I'm sorry,' she faltered. 'I'm so sorry.'

'That's all right,' said the man resignedly, and now she caught an unfamiliar timbre in his voice, a tone that marked him apart from the man she knew. He glanced

25

at his companion. 'You go on with Rod, Ellie; I'll be with you shortly.'

'Sure, Jasper.' The girl winked impudently and went out, leaving Aberdeen to confront Jet's double.

'I thought you were my date.' She felt herself beginning to perspire. She hadn't had that much to drink – just wine at dinner and one shandy since. She peered at him, and *still* his face was Jet's. Poor lighting or not, she couldn't be so badly mistaken. It wasn't a common-issue face, it was strongly moulded, and the colouring was unusual enough to merit a second look. Jet's colouring, but perhaps the face was a touch broader. And perhaps the hair had a rougher, less sculptured cut.

He was looking at her directly now, with dark brown eyes, the pupils a little widened by the dimness. She was struck by the stillness of his face. 'You thought I was Jet Diamond.'

'Of course I did.'

'Of course you did,' he said sardonically. 'You're a very beautiful blonde.'

His tone made it clear that this wasn't a compliment, and she shivered, and took an unconsidered backward pace. 'I beg your pardon? Who exactly are you?'

'The only people who *don't* think I'm Jet when we first meet simply think Jet's me. Very few people know both of us; we mix in different circles and inhabit different levels.' He didn't raise his voice, nor did he smile. The face was Jet's, all right, but the person who lived behind it was very different. Not to speak of slightly crazy.

A mob of hilarity-struck yachties trooped past, and the man took her arm to guide her out of their path.

Reflexively, she recoiled, his fingers seemed to leave a brand on her skin, and the smell of him was alien, a mixture of leather and green and growing things. 'I suppose you're his brother,' she said lamely. 'He's got one, I know, and you have to be *some* relation, looking like that.'

Unless he was an android and she'd fallen into a science fiction novel?

'I'm Jasper Diamond. Jet and I are identical twins.' His eyes were scanning her face. 'It isn't all that uncommon. One in eighty pregnancies results in twins.'

But not identical, surely.

'Do you sail yachts as well?' she asked.

'I have done, but I prefer my motorboat.'

'Do you like blondes?'

'I have done.'

'German au pairs, perhaps?'

'I have done.'

She gave him a saccharine smile. 'Two of a kind, how nice! I suppose you're looking for Jet, Mr Diamond?'

'I wasn't.'

'He's over there if you want to talk to him. Maybe you could compare notes on blondes.'

'Thank you,' he said. 'I don't play kiss and tell.'

'And neither do I. Less is more, even when it comes to Diamonds.'

She was pleased with that riposte, but he was still staring at her, still touching her arm, and she moved uneasily. 'Is he giving you the run-around?' he shot at her.

'We've only just met.'

'You thought he was walking out on you,' he pointed

27

out with justice. 'You sounded remarkably hostile for a casual acquaintance.'

'We've only just met,' she said again, through her teeth.

'Tonight? You met him *tonight*?'

'He picked me up on the docks today.' She wanted to shock him, wanted to see him change expression. 'He asked me to dinner, and when I saw you I thought he'd decided to walk out on me. I found that very offensive. Satisfied?'

'No, but I bet he is. You're exactly the type he *would* pick up.'

'Blonde. So you said. Thank *you*.' She glowered at him. 'You may be his brother, but you're not much like him really. Jet has much better manners.'

'Jet eats blondes for breakfast. He sucks them dry and spits out the husks.'

'I'm sure he'd find me indigestible, and we won't be having breakfast,' she said sweetly. 'Goodbye, Mr Diamond. Isn't – er – Ellie – waiting for you?'

'Take care,' he said, and the meaningless farewell had the quality of a warning. He took his hand from her arm at last, leaving a phantom coolness. 'What's your name?'

'Aberdeen,' she said, repressing a desire to lick her dry lips. 'Aberdeen Shawcross.'

'Take care, Aberdeen Shawcross.'

'How cruel of you to spoil my night out,' she said facetiously.

'I'm cruel to be kind. Jet can be kind to be cruel.'

'Why do you say that?' she challenged him. 'What's it to you if your brother eats blondes?'

He blinked, and she jumped. 'Nothing to me, and maybe he won't eat you. You're not as soft as you look.'

28

'Thank you.'

'You're welcome,' he said with irony. There was a faint flicker in his eyes, as if he'd almost smiled at her, but then he sobered and the undertone of menace returned. 'Don't tell him you've met me,' he said. 'Don't tell him about this conversation.'

'Why ever not?'

'Because he'll see that as a challenge.' A crooked smile did flicker then, but it did nothing to make her more comfortable. 'He doesn't mean any harm,' he said. 'That's what makes him so dangerous. And here's a piece of free advice, Aberdeen Shawcross. If you play with Jet, make sure you know the rules.'

He left her then, and she stood staring after him uneasily. Then she licked her lips at last, and returned to the table, where, after all, Jet was waiting for her. Her knees were shaking, and she felt as if she'd passed through a cloud of some indefinable substance, as if it might have coated her skin. Nothing sticky or soiling, but something, nevertheless. Something glittering and bitter, like grains of sand, like diamond dust, like the needle-spray of a shower.

'You look as if you'd seen a ghost, Lorelei!' said Jet.

'I have,' she said. 'I saw your double. I saw your *doppelgänger*.'

'Damn, you've spotted Jas,' he said. 'So now you know I'm not unique.' He smiled so ruefully that she warmed to him.

'I was only taken in for a moment,' she said. 'He's nothing like you, underneath. He told me not to tell you I'd seen him, and he said you'd give me the run-around. He said a lot of things, and it all boiled down to some kind of warning.' She smiled uneasily. 'It was just like something from one of those *film noir* classics.

Only of course he should have been shot immediately afterwards, then turned up alive in the final reel. I think he must have been a little bit pissed.'

He grinned. 'I believe *you're* a little bit pissed!' he said. 'I'd better take you home.' He tossed off his drink, and caught her apprehensive glance. 'We'll take a cab. Where are you staying?'

He took her arm, and she relaxed into his warm grasp. 'In Battery Point. And I'm not pissed at all. I'm angry.'

'Of course you are. By the way – you're busy tomorrow, if anyone asks.'

'Not especially.'

'Yes, you are. You're busy with me. I want to see you again.'

Aberdeen *did* find herself busy, not only the next day, but for several days thereafter, and when the *Lou Galah* left for Sydney on New Year's Day, she sailed without Jet Diamond.

'Shouldn't you be somewhere else?' asked Aberdeen.

He grinned. 'I should have been sailing the Pacific soon if Nick had stayed intact. Since he didn't, I'm not, but keeping you company makes a very pleasant substitute.'

Aberdeen smiled at his nonsense. The odd meeting with Jet's twin had bothered her for a while, but she had thought it through and concluded that Jasper Diamond must have been drunk. Drunk or touched in the head. Or maybe both.

'He says you eat blondes for breakfast,' she told Jet on New Year's Day.

'So I do.' Jet nibbled her fingers gently.

'I'm trying to understand his motivation.'

30

'Don't,' he said. 'It's a game we play. I'm winning on points just now.'

'Oh?'

'The last round pissed him off, but he'll get over it. I'll introduce you one day, just for a laugh.'

There had been lots of laughs with Jet already and these continued well into New Year. His company was a blessing and a balm, especially since Kate had gone away for a week.

'It was arranged before you came,' Kate reminded her.

'That's all right. You warned me on the phone. I could go home, if you like.' Hollowly, she wondered what she would do if she *did* go home. 'Home' was a dingy flat in Blaxland. A place to sleep, a place to keep her things. 'Home' offered no job, no money and no Jet Diamond.

'Stay on a while,' said Kate. 'I get lonely sometimes.'

'You never said.'

'You have you own life,' said Kate. 'Your own road to travel. I didn't want to stand in your way.'

So Aberdeen stayed, and thanked God for her mother's welcome, and for Jet Diamond, whose attention was slowly rebuilding her confidence in her worth. Foolish to measure worth in other people's terms, but probably inescapable. Brian Cooper and the committee had found her wanting.

Jet Diamond seemed to find her satisfactory. She was serious herself, and often she found herself playing straight man to his nonsense.

'My family,' he said one day as they drove back from an outing, 'wears a chain of motels like a chain of office.'

'A *chain* of motels?' she queried. 'I thought it was just the Ruby?'

31

'The Hidden Treasure chain. Apart from the Ruby, there's the Emerald, the Sapphire, the Topaz and, of course, the Diamond of Bondi. All overblown, but hey! They please the plebs.'

'Five!' she said.

'Five. Aunt Krista manages the Emerald, but it's Uncle Godfrey's dream to see every Diamond immovably set in a three-storey pseudo-colonial gem.'

'That sounds positively dynastic, but I can't imagine your brother Jasper acting mine host.'

'Neither can I and neither can he.' Jet grinned. 'Hope springs eternal in Uncle Godfrey. Whenever he gets a twinge of rheumatism he starts talking retirement. Then it's brandy all round and *"Come, m'boy, don't you think the time is come?"* He really does talk like that.'

'Dynastic,' repeated Aberdeen. 'Are you your uncle's heir?'

'No,' said Jet, 'but you might say I was my grandfather's, after a fashion; me and all the others.' He sighed. 'Let's go to my suite at the Ruby and enjoy the family ambience.'

'I don't think so, thank you.'

'I'll think of a better lure, then,' he said. He took her, not to his suite, but down to Constitution Dock, where the lights were shining over the harbour in long bright streaks. 'Warm enough?' he asked as he opened the door of his rental car.

She looked up at him uncertainly. 'That depends on where we're going.'

'Aboard the *Aphrodite*. There she is.' He indicated a yacht moored to a nearby stanchion. 'She came in today,' he said. 'I had Charlie and the boys sail her down as soon as I knew I'd be staying on in Hobart.'

'And when was that?'

'Five minutes after meeting you.' He was holding both her hands, looking down at her in the moonlight. 'Are you game?'

Aberdeen allowed him to draw her down the wharf to the yacht. 'How do you get aboard?' she asked, eyeing it doubtfully.

'Step over on to the gangplank. Easy as boarding the Manly Ferry.'

'I always travel by bus or train.'

'Boats are so much more romantic.'

She looked him in the eye. 'But I can't swim.'

'I'll soon teach you how. Come on – Charlie's waiting on board.' Jet swung her up into his arms, kissing her soundly before stepping aboard the yacht.

'Put me down!' she cried in protest.

'Hush,' he said, and kissed her again then set her to stand on the deck before him. His eyes gleamed down at her. 'It's nice to see you flustered, Lorelei. I was beginning to wonder. You go on below, I need a word with Charlie.'

Slowly, gripping the polished rail, she let herself down the narrow staircase that led like a throat into the bowels of the yacht. Maybe she was making the biggest mistake in history. He could be (probably was) bent on seduction. Or worse.

'*Jet eats blondes for breakfast. He sucks them dry,*' said Jasper Diamond's voice in her memory.

Oh, yes. So Jet was a vampire. Or maybe he was a white slaver and she'd end up wearing crotchless harem trousers in some unspecified place in the Far East . . . She could just see Jet in a burnoose, making like a Sheikh.

The cabin was small, but beautifully appointed. Aberdeen stepped across the floor to inspect the kitchen

33

– no, the galley. The *Aphrodite* seemed to move a little, uneasily, shrugging like a sidling horse. Aberdeen sat down abruptly. Jet would soon be with her and, despite her amusement a moment earlier, she was a little apprehensive. Maybe she should go back up on deck.

Before she could move to do so, Jet's feet came down the companionway with none of the caution hers had shown. He was looking a little preoccupied, but his eyes glowed as he saw her. 'Lovely Lorelei, golden *Göttin* of the Rhine,' he said. He leaned down to brush his lips against her cheek in a casual but intimate caress.

Aberdeen tried to shrug off her uneasiness and smiled back, forcing herself to relax as his arm came around her in a hug.

'*My* lovely Lorelei.' Still casual, but the kiss he gave her next had an underlying seriousness about it, a question. His mouth was warm and practised, and she found herself answering the question with a hesitant reply.

Jet drew back a little and laughed softly. 'Was that a "yes", Lorelei? Are you *my* Lorelei?'

'It was a "maybe",' she said. 'That's all.'

'Maybe "maybe" isn't enough for me.'

'It will have to be, for now. Tell me the story of your life. Begin at Chapter One, The Birth of the Twins.'

His lips touched hers again, with expert pleasure. 'I'd rather begin at Chapter Ten, The Big Seduction Scene. *God*, Lorelei, let me make you mine . . . let me take your rosy rosebuds in my lecherous lips . . .'

For a moment her heart thumped unpleasantly, then she spluttered with laughter. 'What the heck have you been reading, Jet? Barbara Cartland?'

'Maybe,' he said, gleaming again. 'Have you?'

CHAPTER 3

Tasmania – In the Rough was not going well. That was serious, for although he had a market and the funding was secure, Jasper felt his professional reputation was at stake. He was missing Tam. That was part of his discontent. He missed her slow smile and generous, Junoesque presence. He also missed her certainty.

'Don't blame me,' said Rod morosely. 'I'd have stayed behind if she'd agreed to come.'

'I need you both,' said Jasper.

'But you need her more. Hey! I'm just the roadie and bit-part player, Mr Nobody. She's part of the show.'

'We can manage,' said Jasper, but there was some truth in what Rod said. Australian viewers had enjoyed three servings of *In the Rough*, so it wasn't good idea to depart too much from the pattern.

What pattern? mocked the imp that lived in the back of his mind. Haven't you always prided yourself on the fact that there *is* no pattern? Yes, he had, but there were certain constants in all his documentaries. A certain rough-cut feeling, an air of warts-and-all. Jasper liked to show all faces of his chosen destinations; he didn't deal in selected facts or truths.

It wasn't only Tam he was missing. There was

something in himself, some extra dimension that had kicked in that day on the clifftop when he had first seen Rod's bleak misery. It had driven home the essential poverty of his feeling for Grete Fischer. He had been piqued and offended when she had chosen Jet, but not bereft. And yet that day had touched him with the final bitterness that had made him lash out at an innocent – the new blonde girl in Jet's life. He had not been proud of that and, ever since, the feeling of mild self-disgust had coloured his view of Tasmania and had coloured his work. Something vital was missing, so he made an effort to find interesting locals, who would add their expertise and personal views to the film.

The team had been in Tasmania for a month now. They had covered a great many locations, had seen Tasmanian life through the eyes of a great variety of people. Subjects ranged from those whose ancestors had settled the island close to two centuries ago to those who had just arrived. Some of the island's more unusual industries and occupations had been covered, and there had been apparently ad lib shots of the crew; the making of the show had been documented along with the subject. Rod's clifftop mishap had been just one slice of real-life action.

Usually, Jasper was happy to leave intact any film of mild disagreements that might occur, feeling that odd moments of disharmony added flavour to the show. This time, though, the balance of the team was flawed. And balance was important, for, unlike in many personality-driven programmes, there had never been any pretence that Jasper Diamond's and Tam Spellman's travels were undertaken alone.

Today, they had been filming a segment out at the convict ruins of Maria Island and Dr Michaela

Smith, an amateur historian, was detailing the suffering of the one-time occupants for the camera. Rod was contradicting her, matching her fact for fact. It might have been funny, but there was a chilling edge to his banter.

'They were so hungry,' said Dr Smith. 'And so many had committed no crime at all, but simply misdemeanours.'

'The free settlers were hungry too,' said Rod. 'So were the guards. And besides the misdemeanours, there were any number of convictions for murder, robbery with violence and GBH.'

'Eliza Blackwell was transported for stealing three petticoats in 1845,' Dr Smith countered, whipping out a historical society leaflet. 'Her children all died in infancy, and she was forced to endure all kinds of degradation at the hands of the guards and her "employers". She died in 1855, of untreated pneumonia. She was only about thirty.'

'Mary Cameron was transported for attempted murder,' said Rod with a sardonic grin. 'She spent a few months in the female factory and then a landowner offered to marry her. Mary was freed, and spent the next sixty years establishing herself as the founding mother of a dynasty. She terrorized her descendants, and finally passed on, full of salt and brandy, at the age of ninety-one.'

'Eliza's fate is fully documented in the records from the old prison,' said Dr Smith.

'Mary's fate is documented in the Bowen family bible,' said Rod smugly. 'The evil old bitch was an ancestor of mine.'

It might have been no more than verbal sparring for Rod, but Dr Smith was deadly serious. She glowered at Rod, tight-lipped, and flounced away from the camera.

'I agreed to help you out,' she said reproachfully to Jasper. 'I didn't agree to let you make a fool of me.'

Jasper signalled to Stew to stop filming. 'Can it, Rod,' he said coldly.

'Why? It's an academic discussion.'

'Because I said so.'

'*Heil Hitler*,' said Rod unforgivably.

Jasper pushed his hand through his hair. 'Look, Dr Smith,' he said, 'a bit of chiacking is part of the deal with *In the Rough*.'

'Well, I find it very distasteful.'

'I agree that Rod went much too far. I don't know what's got into him.'

'It had better get out,' said the woman coldly. 'And I trust you won't be using this segment?'

'No, we won't. I'm very sorry you've been inconvenienced. Is there anything I can do to make it up to you?'

Mollified, she shook her head. 'No need.' She touched his arm. 'I respect your personal integrity, Mr Diamond, but I'm not so sure about the rest of your team.'

'Neither am I,' said Jasper. 'Come and have lunch with me tomorrow.'

'I don't think so.'

'Please? I hate to make enemies.'

'All right,' she said. 'If you insist.' She smiled and licked her lips. 'I know a charming little restaurant in Triabunna.'

Jet's proposal of marriage came as a shock. Not because it came so soon, but because it had come at all. 'You're not the marrying kind,' protested Aberdeen. 'I've heard you say so.'

' "Sir, this is so sudden," you *should* have said . . .' prompted Jet with a gleam in his eye.

'Sir, this is so sudden,' she said obediently. 'But *why*?'

'I love you. You'll make the perfect wife for me.' He clasped his heart and she had to smile at his clowning. 'Lost for words, Lorelei?' He pulled her close and lazily traced her lips with his fingers.

'I'm not perfect. Not only that, but we have different aims. I want to open my museum and get on with conserving the past before it all moulders away. If only I weren't so darned short of funds . . .' She saw his amusement. 'I do go on, don't I?'

'Marry me,' said Jet. 'You won't be short of funds.'

'I wouldn't marry for money!'

'Of course not, Lorelei. You want my body too. And you like my yacht.'

'Sex and money . . .' she said uncomfortably. 'That sounds very tacky.'

'Where would the world be without sex and money? And what's *your* ideal grounds for marriage anyway?'

'I want someone of my own, I suppose,' she said slowly. 'I never properly realized until now. I thought I was a career woman; now I find I'm just a nest-builder at the bottom. I want a settled base, someone to come home to. And you know you're not the settled kind.'

'I like nests,' said Jet. 'Love-nests. *Aphrodite* is a nest.'

'But you're all set to sail away! A year or more, you said.' The ground seemed to be moving under her feet, but the earthquake feeling was almost pleasant. Jet's smile, Jet's warmth, Jet's certainty made her long to be persuaded.

'Ah, but there's the rub.' He took her hand. 'I was talking to Charlie again last night. Young Nick's still laid up. They've had to break and reset his leg, poor kid.'

'You won't be going, then?' She was sorry for young Nick Green, of course, but joyful for herself.

'I didn't say that.' He was grinning now, teasing her but she didn't mind.

'I suppose you'll find another crew.'

'I have.' His eyes danced. 'Come on, Lorelei – how about it? You crew for me on *Aphrodite* for a year or so, then we come back and you can play museums?'

'I can't sail a boat! I wouldn't know how to start!'

'I'll soon teach you. *Aphrodite*'s a lady. She never does anything without due consideration. Unlike her master.'

'This voyage isn't *me*. I enjoy routine. I like my work and I want to get back to it, as I said. Lotus-eating is a holiday, but for you it's the way you live.'

'I enjoy the challenge just as much as you, only for me, it's the sea. The one thing – apart from weather and space and women – that's still beyond the control of mere men. This summer is a holiday for me as well, but I'm still set for my voyage. The only difference is, I'll have a gorgeous wife instead of another bloke who knows it all for crew. Better for my health and temper, and *much* better for my reputation.'

'Why am I even listening to you? We'll get engaged if you like, but find someone else for your crew.'

'Like who? Nick was only able to come because he's taking a year off before university. Most of the people I

40

like are tied up with wives and kids or husbands and jobs.'

'And I'm not,' she said slowly. 'I've lost my job, and I'm too poor to do what I really want.'

'This way we both win,' he said. 'You wanted to see the world. I remember you saying you'd missed out on your trip.'

'I was going to see the museums in Europe, not the oceans.'

'So? We'll go to Europe! We're free as the wind, free as the waves.'

'You're offering me the world in a bucket. What do you get?'

'I get you.'

'Some bargain for you!'

'I think it's a good one. I was locked into this year with Nick, but with you aboard we can take as long as we like. A year or so, or four or five . . . depending on the ports of call and the time we choose to spend in each. Think of it, Lorelei!'

'Four or five years . . .' She couldn't take it in.

'Put it this way . . . we'd leave at the end of March and be back before our kids start high school.'

'But it's February now!'

'Exactly!' Jet's smile widened. 'It'll be a honeymoon to remember!'

'*Come back, Tam, or all will* not *be forgiven*,' wrote Jasper from his East Coast base. He hit the software button that would send the message directly to Tam's computer at the Diamond/Spellman Studio in Sydney. He didn't bother to sign his name; she'd know immediately who it was from. And he knew it would do no good. The filming was almost finished. There were still the links to shoot and the atmosphere was thick as mushroom soup and lunch was going to be sticky.

Dr Smith was early, and her manner had certainly softened. It became positively cosy when Jasper apologized once again.

'I expect I over-reacted,' she said. 'He's only the roadie.' She mused for a few moments, then smiled, her pupils widening in a manner he observed with weary apprehension. 'I don't like to teach you your business, Jasper, but don't you think you carry this democratic ideal of yours just a little too far?'

Jasper blinked. He hadn't been aware of any democratic ideal.

'I expect Rod Bowen speaks for the person on the street,' she said, 'but don't you agree that the time has come for your work to appeal to a slightly more academic class of viewer? I've made a study of the . . .'

By five o'clock, Jasper felt his eyes beginning to glaze, but he was confident that a potential enemy had been neutralized. He only hoped he hadn't gone too far. Her eyes, so cold the day before, were positively dewy.

'I'm very glad we've had a chance to clear the air,' he said truthfully over coffee, 'but I really should be going. I have an appointment in Hobart this evening.'

'You must come to dinner with me before you leave,' said Dr Smith. 'I'm having a small dinner party next week . . . some colleagues from the Uni. I'm sure they would enjoy your company.' She touched his hand. 'And so shall I.'

As he drove down the highway towards Hobart, Jasper permitted himself to sigh. He hated dinner parties, but he'd had to accept. He only hoped she didn't want more than his company. The exercise today had minimized the damage done to Diamond/ Spellman's reputation, but he didn't fool himself into thinking he had handled the original matter well. He should have had a word with Rod – told him to heave the chip off his shoulder or stay away from the camera.

He thought about Dr Smith and mentally shied. Since Grete's defection he'd been very wary of involvement with women, except for Tam. If he couldn't offer more than he'd had to offer Grete, he probably shouldn't make an approach at all. Tam had been sympathetic at the time, but she had problems of her own with Rod.

'I should never have let him get under my skin,' she'd said furiously. 'It was bad enough when we were together and couldn't keep our hands off one another. Now we've split up we – God! Never mix business with sex, that's all I can say.'

'I never do,' he'd said, surprised.

'No. I'd say you're careful to a fault.'

'It probably isn't fair to start what will only finish. I'd rather not have a relationship at all than one that's based on nothing but my own convenience.'

'Don't be so self-defeatist!' said Tam. 'There are lots of women out there who would love to spend time with you on any terms at all. Take what's offered, and let people know there's a lovely man behind that wooden face. Otherwise you'll end up lonely.'

'Jet has the same face,' he'd reminded her.

'Jet's always laughing. He'll never be lonely. Lord, Jasper, life's not fair, is it?'

She was right on all counts, and he knew he should work on his personal presentation, away from Tam. The chemistry when he was with her was easy, for their relationship was close enough to be construed as

43

familial if they chose, but not so close as to suggest incest if they had ever ended up in bed. Not that they had, but he'd never ruled it out entirely. If all else failed, he and Tam might make it yet. Jet would gloat, for he'd always thought – or pretended to think – that Jasper lusted for Tam.

Jet. His brother's image rose and laughed at him. He hadn't been thinking of Jet the last few days, but Jet had come to mind and that meant Jet was operating on high-octane fuel somewhere close by. Maybe at the Ruby?

Jet. As he pulled into the parking lot he wondered if Jet still had his gorgeous blonde in tow. Aberdeen Shawcross, with her curling honeysuckle hair and stormy eyes.

Jet had cast lures to Grete, but Jasper had done something worse to Aberdeen. Warning her off had seemed a fair enough tit-for-tat at the time, but now he'd had a few weeks to mellow, and he regretted the way he'd used the girl to get at Jet that night in the Van Diemen Tavern. Unfair, unkind and uncool, and he hadn't been angry with her, but with his brother. It was about time they grew up, he thought, as he stepped into the Ruby foyer. About time they buried the hatchet for good and all.

He approached the desk, identified without difficulty the pretty receptionist's dilemma, and put her out of her misery. 'I'm Jasper Diamond,' he said, with the slightest emphasis on the Christian name. 'Is my uncle here?'

She smiled with relief, a dimple coming and going in one cheek. 'Of course, Mr Diamond. He's with your brother and his guests.'

So Jet *was* here. He wasn't a bit surprised.

44

'Go along up to the suite,' said the girl. 'You know the way.'

He nodded, remembered Tam's advice, and smiled deliberately. 'Would you like a drink with me when your shift has finished? Perhaps you'd come up and join my brother's party?'

'I'd have liked that very much,' she said, 'but I have a husband and I'm meeting him at nine.'

'*Touché*,' said Jasper wryly. 'Bring him if you like. Jet won't mind.'

The receptionist laughed. 'Thanks, but we're going out.'

'A virtuous woman is priced above rubies, so you must be worth more than this whole motel,' said Jasper.

'I am,' she said, and turned slightly away, breaking the tenuous thread of attraction before it could take hold.

Philosophically, Jasper headed for the lift. If he'd known she was married, he wouldn't have offered her a drink. He shouldn't have done it anyway, he supposed. He'd wanted moral support for when he met his brother, but whatever Tam and popular psychology said, there *was* more to read into the act of offering a drink to a woman than in offering one to another man. *Viz* the invitation to Dr Smith.

Jet turned expectantly as Jasper came through the door. 'Jas,' he said.

He didn't sound surprised, so Jasper knew the receptionist must have buzzed the suite with the news of his arrival. His occasional awareness of his brother's mood or location was a one-way street, an uncomfortable and useless talent that Jet didn't share. He shook hands with Jet; a ridiculously formal greeting, but he

45

was unable to come up with a substitute. They hadn't met for a couple of months, but Australian men seldom hugged the way the continentals or the Americans did, and they never bowed like the Japanese. A friendly punch on the upper arm might do, but despite his wish to bury the hatchet he wasn't feeling friendly.

He turned with relief to another, much warmer handclasp from his uncle. Godfrey Diamond had the thin, grey face of the aesthete he was not, and a peculiar manner which he seemed to have copied from ancient British films.

'Jasper, m'boy!' he said with genuine pleasure, clasping his nephew's hand in both his own. 'So lucky you could join us on this happy occasion.'

Jasper glanced warily at Jet, but his brother was smiling, enjoying the situation.

A slight pressure from his uncle's hand turned Jasper to face two women who stood a little to the side. One was a generous figure swathed in loose printed cottons, the other was the lovely blonde he had warned away from Jet. He froze, feeling the cold stab of premonition.

'Kate, this is my nephew Jasper Diamond,' Godfrey was saying. 'Jasper, Mrs Kate Shawcross.'

The older woman offered her hand and smiled at him vaguely, then her gaze sharpened and she turned back to look at Jet. A small frown appeared between her eyes.

'Aberdeen, my dear, this is Jasper, Jet's twin brother,' continued Godfrey. 'Jasper, Miss Shawcross, Kate's daughter and Jet's intended.'

In other circumstances, Jasper could have laughed at his uncle's punctilious introduction, proof that Godfrey had had order of precedence drilled into

46

him from an early age. Introduce the elder to the younger, the woman to the man. Oh, and let the lady offer her hand if she chooses.

Any faint trace of amusement died as the girl – Aberdeen Shawcross – offered her hand. She was half-reluctant, it seemed, and Jasper was aware of an equal reluctance to meet her eyes. He knew what he would see reflected in their depths. She probably thought him mad as well as bad and it was all his own fault.

The pink-shaded light cast a deceptively rosy warmth over the scene; her hair appeared the burnished gold of a sunset, and her eyes were so wide he could scarcely see their colour. Blondes usually had pale blue eyes, but Aberdeen Shawcross's gaze was nearer to navy than to sky. A very stormy navy at the moment.

Their fingers brushed as if in slow motion, and he made himself grasp her hand. 'Good evening, Aberdeen,' he said.

'We've met before,' she said. 'I thought you were Jet.'

'No, darling,' put in the older woman, Kate. 'Jasper produces and presents *In the Rough*. Remember I asked you once if you'd been watching it?'

Some small corner of Jasper's mind acknowledged that Kate Shawcross had put it correctly – so many people called him 'the star of the show'. The rest of him was only too aware of Aberdeen Shawcross's apparent displeasure at meeting him again; and of being reminded of their other, earlier meeting. He couldn't honestly blame her.

'I thought you were Jet,' she said, 'until I had a good look at you. Then I realized you couldn't possibly be.'

Her tone was almost – but not quite – insulting.

'I'm not surprised you were confused,' said Kate. 'The likeness is remarkable.' She smiled from Jasper to Jet and back again with no sign of discomfort at her daughter's pointed comment. 'I expect you boys get tired of being told how much alike you are.'

Definitely, thought Jasper.

'We don't mind, Kate,' said Jet indulgently. 'It's an old joke, but a good one. Two for the price of one.' He struck a pose. 'Jas and I are both mature enough not to feel threatened by the existence of a virtual double.' His eyes met Jasper's in a laughing challenge. 'It offers some interesting possibilities.'

'No,' said Jasper, more harshly than he intended.

'I think it does,' said Jet. He put out a hand to draw Aberdeen away from Jasper. 'Let's say Jas and I make a deal, Lorelei! Both of us come to pick you up tomorrow, and you spend the day with the one you think is me. Better yet, choose the one you like better!'

'*No,*' said Jasper, appalled.

'M'boy, that is extremely distasteful,' put in Godfrey.

'Only joking,' said Jet. 'I'm sure she could tell us apart. Tam could always do it. So could Grete – most of the time.' He beamed at Kate and Aberdeen, and glanced at Jasper as if to draw him into reminiscing about some shared boyhood mischief. 'Tam is Uncle Godfrey's daughter, Kate, and Grete is a German au pair Jas and I were both pursuing at one time. I was the victor, *pro tem*, but Jas got his own back, didn't you, bro?'

'How did he do that?' asked Aberdeen. 'Did he try to steal a girl from you?'

'No, but he accosted a girl I wanted and told her

some rigmarole about my being a cannibal . . . or a vampire, maybe – I've never been quite sure.'

'And did she believe it?' Aberdeen's eyes were wide with pretended suspense.

'No,' said Jet, and bent to kiss her hand. 'The darling had too much sense. She spiked his guns by coming straight to me and telling me what he'd said.'

Godfrey's obvious distress made Jasper come to his own senses. Jet was out to see him squirm, and so was his beautiful blonde. Perhaps he deserved it, but not right here and now. 'Cut it out, Jet,' he said. 'Kate and – Aberdeen, is it? – don't want to hear our grubby ancient history. And it *is* ancient, isn't it, since you've just got engaged?'

Jet grinned. 'So I have – and don't you wish you'd seen her first! But perhaps it's just as well you didn't, since I'd have gone for her anyway.' He glanced at the women again. 'Jas and I are always attracted to the same . . .'

'Jet, that's really going too far,' interrupted Godfrey. His normally sallow cheeks were a dull red.

'It's all right, Mr Diamond, Jet's just teasing.' Aberdeen Shawcross smiled at Jet, tucking her hand around his arm, making Jasper's own arm tingle with vicarious pleasure. 'Jasper teases too, or so I understand. It's a little game they play.' Her glance flicked over Jasper and he almost thought he felt the heat of her scorn and shrivelled a little in his soul. 'You may be sure I'll never be fooled about which is which of them,' she said coolly. 'Not for more than a couple of seconds. They might look alike on the surface, but underneath they're cheese and chalk – or champagne and vinegar.'

Her voice was light, but Jasper felt very uncomfortable. Aberdeen Shawcross didn't like him, and hadn't forgiven him for speaking out of turn.

Her scorn stung like salt in a cut, and he winced.

He accepted a drink from Godfrey, and turned to exchange innocuous conversation with Kate, but all the while the analytical imp in his mind was busy pondering both problem and possible solution. He had offended this girl and, more, he had done so needlessly. Jet *hadn't* eaten her up, he *hadn't* sucked her dry. Instead, he had asked her to marry him. Jasper had got his brother wrong, and he had distressed Aberdeen Shawcross. He would have to apologize, but not in front of the company here. And not in front of Jet.

He supposed he could write her a letter, plead current tension and past provocation. That might help if she had a forgiving nature, but now he came to consider it, he rather thought she had disliked him from the start. Instant, instinctive aversion was every bit as common as love at first sight, and sometimes a dashed sight more enduring.

That was a pity, for his strong reaction to her presence tonight had nothing to do with aversion, instant or otherwise.

Kate's voice, placid and soothing as her daughter's was acerbic, jolted him from his abstraction.

'I'm sorry?' he said, a little more curtly than he had intended. 'I was thinking of something else.'

'Don't be sorry, Mr Diamond,' she said. 'I can see you're a bit preoccupied. I was asking about your work.'

'Perhaps you'd care to repeat the question,' he said. 'I promise to give it my full attention this time.'

He tried to do so, but though he was looking at the

mother, the daughter's face seemed to hover before his eyes. He blinked. It was much too hot in the suite. He was very aware of the girl's dislike, boring into the back of his head. 'You've seen the view from the top of the Ruby?' he said abruptly.

If Kate found such a question surprising in the middle of a discussion on his film, she didn't show it. Instead, she smiled at him. 'Actually, I haven't.'

'I'll show you now,' he said with relief. 'If you'd like to step out on the balcony.'

Kate Shawcross smiled with apparently genuine pleasure. 'If you knew how many years it was since a man made *that* suggestion to me!'

Jasper offered his arm and she took it, but although his film-maker's eye was, as usual, enchanted by the panoramic sweep of harbour and mountain and city lights, it was Aberdeen's image that hovered in his mind. Blue-eyed and forthright. Golden and unattainable. Infinitely desirable.

Jet had seen her worth and was going to snap her up.

Oh, my God, thought Jasper, dazed with genuine horror. Oh, my *God*.

CHAPTER 4

Three days after the party at the Ruby, Aberdeen had almost come to believe in her wonderful future. It wasn't what she had chosen a year ago, but how much better than the one she'd had to face on Christmas Eve!

Love and marriage, adventure, travel and ambition – most women would give their eye-teeth to stand in her shoes. How had she got so lucky, anyway?

She lay back on the grass in her mother's garden, watching the cloud shadows drift. 'Someone up there likes me now,' she observed.

'That's the way I felt when I found this gem of a cottage,' said Kate.

The cottage *was* a gem, and its surroundings were as close to a colonial replica as Kate could make them. 'I love the Australian native flowers,' she said now, 'but I want a cottage garden. And cottage gardens, wherever they're planted, *should* be essentially English. Take this knot garden – it's laid out to a traditional pattern. Culpepper or Gerard would have recognized it instantly, but neither of them would have known a waratah from a flannel flower from a Sturt pea.'

'A lot of these flowers and herbs are actually Mediterranean,' said Aberdeen slyly.

'They're become British by adoption. And how do you know?'

'I've been reading your books. They make a change from databases of costume.'

'I think I hear someone,' said Kate. She was grubbing in the clumps of alyssum, extracting bulbous clover roots but leaving the hawkbit behind.

'I'll go. It might be Jet, come early.' Aberdeen's mouth was curling with pleasure at the thought.

'He can come to you, then,' said Kate. She raised her voice. 'We're in the back garden!'

'So am I,' he said.

He must have been on his way even when Kate had called, for now he was standing on the crazy paving between the annuals and the knot garden. His hands were in his pockets, his burnished hair was shining in the sun. He could have been a statue, thought Aberdeen, a bronze or terracotta. The colouring was almost right, even to the casual fox-brown T-shirt. His eyes were fixed on her face and for a moment she seemed to see herself reflected in their depths.

Her smile died aborning and she scowled at him, unable to look away.

'Hello, Jet,' said Kate, blinking up from beneath the brim of her hat. 'Just in time for a cup of tea.'

'That isn't Jet,' said Aberdeen.

'Hello, Jasper,' said Kate. 'You're still in time for a cup of tea and equally welcome.'

'I came to invite you two to lunch,' he said.

'I'm tempted,' said Kate, 'but I'm expecting some garden club friends.'

'Aberdeen?'

'No, thank you,' said Aberdeen. 'I'm expecting Jet.'

53

'I know,' said Jasper. 'He's taking you sailing at two-thirty. We could be back by then.'

'How did you know what we'd arranged?'

'He told me.' He was looking at her intently. 'You thought I'd gone behind his back. You thought I was poaching, didn't you? Paying him back for Grete. Planning some devious revenge.'

She felt mean and shabby, because that *was* what she'd thought.

'In my day a man who was going poaching didn't invite old ladies,' said Kate drily.

'These days, the old lady is probably the one that gets poached,' said Aberdeen. 'I'm sorry you've had a wasted drive. You should have telephoned.'

'I did,' said Jasper. 'I presume you didn't hear.' He came forward to the flowerbed and crouched on his haunches. '*Limnanthus douglasii*,' he said, touching the ferny leaves. 'Pretty thing. I haven't seen that for years.'

'Poached egg plant,' corrected Kate. 'So it says on the packet.'

He made a gesture of apology. 'Of course. And this one is kiss-me-quick, and there's love-in-a-mist.'

'*Valerian* and *Nigellus*,' said Kate evilly.

'And this must be – let's see – love-lies-bleeding?'

'Bleeding hearts, actually. It's a very old variety . . .'

'If you two want to show off,' said Aberdeen waspishly, 'maybe you'll let me pass.'

'How do you take your tea, Jasper?' asked Kate, as he shuffled obligingly aside.

'Strong white, no sugar.' His long, hard fingers were gentle as they tipped up a red and white daisy. 'Ah – *Bellis perennis*? What's that doing in a bed of annuals?'

'I hadn't the heart to dig it up,' said Kate.

Aberdeen flounced into the kitchen. She wanted to go out of the door and keep on walking, but that was childish. It would accord Jasper Diamond an importance he didn't deserve. Warnings for her and a buttering-up for Kate. Perhaps he had a thing for older women.

The kettle boiled, and Aberdeen dropped a single tea bag in the pot. The tag dangled accusingly and she sighed and took it out. Teabags were acceptable among friends. An enemy at the gate, inside the gate, demanded sterner stuff. And *stronger* stuff perhaps.

Viciously, she spooned in loose tea, then filled the pot.

The resulting brew was so strong her palate cringed at the smell of it. She poured half-cups for herself and Kate, adding hot water with a generous hand. She filled Jasper's cup to the top. Milk, no sugar, a teaspoon, and Lord, what an evil brew! It gleamed like poison.

She carried the tray to the garden where Kate and Jasper were discussing the exact floral status of speedwell. 'A weed,' said Kate, pontificating, 'is a plant growing in the wrong place.'

'Tea,' said Aberdeen.

'Tea's a member of the camellia family.' Kate reached for her cup, and Jasper nodded his thanks before doing likewise. He sipped, and looked a little surprised.

'I hope it isn't too strong,' said Aberdeen insincerely.

'I like it strong,' he said, and actually smiled at her. This exercise should have increased his likeness to Jet, but instead it destroyed it utterly. Jet's smile was a gleeful affair of sparkling eyes and a dimple. Jasper's was lopsided, belying the normal symmetry of his features. He saw Aberdeen staring and returned his face to normal. 'I must have drunk a thousand mugs of stewed billy tea on location,' he said. 'It makes the normal seem insipid.'

He drank the tea in one long draught, leaving Aberdeen with the pained feeling that he knew exactly what she had tried to do.

'Another one?' she asked.

'Biscuits,' said Kate, who had been watching their interplay with a bemused expression.

'I didn't see any,' said Aberdeen.

'I *need* some biscuits for this afternoon. It's too late to make any now, but if you'll excuse me, Jasper, I'll drop round to the corner shop.'

'I'll go,' said Aberdeen.

'I don't know what I want until I see them.' Kate vanished into the house.

'I must get changed,' said Aberdeen.

She hoped he'd leave, but he remained where he was, apparently watching the scurry of sugar-ants on the path. Then he looked up, and his intent gaze brought a flush to her cheeks.

'Are honours even now?' he asked.

She stared, her flush growing deeper, and he ticked off points on his fingers, seeming to conjure an invisible lecture hall. Or perhaps an invisible court-room.

'The Red King stands accused of one crass attempt to warn the Queen away from the Black King, whose record is distinguished only by the brevity of each relationship,' he pronounced. 'That's his only crime?'

Speechlessly, she nodded.

'The Queen has delivered one public blistering in

the Black King's presence, allowing him to add gratuitous shots of his own.'

Aberdeen swallowed and Jasper tapped another finger.

'The Queen has attempted poisoning by tannin, and has scorched an olive branch.'

'The Red King made the first attack,' she snapped.

'It was his reaction to a series of feints and pinpricks.' He looked at her steadily. 'The Red King's mistake was just that: a mistake. He believed, at that time, that the Black King could never change. He admits his fault and will take his medicine. *Has* taken it in the shape of a truly disgusting cup of tea.'

'And that makes it right!' she said. 'You slandered Jet and you implied I was a good-time bimbo!'

'Nothing will make it right. I offered a reason for behaving as I did. A reason, not an excuse. I was so far out of line I was practically a line on my own.'

'Mr Diamond . . .'

'Jasper, please.'

'*Jasper.*' It was an odd name, harsh and soft together. 'I suppose I'll have to accept your explanation, since you're to be my brother-in-law.'

He inclined his head, but she thought his jaw clenched as if in denial.

'Jasper. What makes *you* the Red King and Jet the Black?'

'Guess.'

'I don't like guessing games.'

'Then I'll make you a gift of the answer. Jasper is a kind of red-coloured quartz, while jet is shiny black coal. Jasper was used for carvings, and jet for mourning jewellery. And no, I *don't* know what our respected parents were thinking of, but at least they didn't

57

burden us with garnet or carnelian. Are honours even now?'

'I suppose so,' she said grudgingly. 'The Black Queen shouldn't hold a grudge.'

He put out his hand and, very reluctantly, she placed her own in it.

'You're not the Black Queen,' he said, and lifted his free hand to touch her hair. 'I rather think you're *La Belle Dame sans Merci*.'

He was standing very close to her, and now he lowered his head.

He's going to kiss me! she thought in horror, but Jasper didn't kiss her. He simply rested his forehead against hers for a moment, and tangled his fingers in her curls. She heard him draw in a long, trembling breath, then he released her gently, turned and went away.

She was still shaking when Kate came back.

'Has Jasper gone?' She sounded disappointed.

'You can see he has,' said Aberdeen.

'I was going to show him the primrose sports.' Kate sighed. 'There aren't many men who'd understand what they are.'

'He was leading you on,' said Aberdeen harshly. 'He's not interested in flowers. He's only *schleimig*.'

'*Really*?' Kate sounded thrilled.

'Creeping under your guard, I can't imagine why. Unless he wants to be your toy-boy.'

'Bliss,' said Kate. 'A gorgeous young man who finds me attractive enough to pretend an interest in my hobbies!' She gave Aberdeen a cat-like smile. 'He must have spent *hours* learning all those Latin names, just to impress me. Just in *case* I happened to be a gardener.'

58

'It didn't impress *me*.' Aberdeen felt prickly, as if from heat rash.

'Nice day for sailing,' said Kate. 'There's a good breeze blowing.'

'Is that good?' Aberdeen rubbed her arms. 'I suppose it must be. Lord, Kate, I feel so pig-ignorant. I don't know the first thing about sailing, and I've got to become an expert!'

'Read some Bernard Cornwall books,' advised Kate.

'Maybe. Or maybe I'll just ask Jet. I'll go and get our picnic packed; do you want some sandwiches for your garden friends?'

Putting together a picnic was soothing, and it helped to focus her mind where it belonged: on Jet and sailing.

It was going to take a while to adapt, she knew. She had never consulted others very much, and her years at college and work had left her little time for hobbies or romance. She didn't swim, she didn't surf or sail or ride . . . marriage would open a whole fresh vista of exercise for her body and her mind. She closed her eyes and saw herself, poised on a deck, gripping a tiller, or splicing the main-brace or whatever one did on yachts. Wearing a bikini, perhaps, her hair flying sideways in a following wind.

Unlikely, since her hair was short and a following wind would probably blow it forward over her eyes in a tangle.

Sailing the Pacific, gypsying through the islands, Fiji and Atonement, on to Europe to leave the yacht in port while they toured the museums. There were garments hundreds of years old that still existed there. If she could talk to the conservators of *them* – how much she would learn for her own museum!

Once, she put her head out the door. Kate's garden

club friends were arriving, so she slipped out to smile and shake hands with them. 'Kate,' she said, under cover of offering tea, 'who was La Belle Dame sans Merci? Was she some old legend?'

Kate seemed not to find the question disconcerting. 'I think she was in a poem by Keats,' she said. 'A sexy faerie lady who held a knight or two in thrall.'

Aberdeen felt her face go cold, and went smartly back to the kitchen. So Jasper thought she was holding Jet in some kind of thrall! He really was completely crazy. He probably sacrificed black cocks in the moonlight.

Food, she thought firmly, and put together biscuits and pâté and fruit.

Jet arrived at two-thirty. 'Is your mother about?' he asked with a grin. 'I saw her broomstick parked outside.'

Aberdeen smiled at his nonsense. 'She's out the back with some garden club friends, discussing primrose sports.'

'How athletic. Should I pay my respects?'

'They're probably up to their eyebrows in the compost heap and jack-in-the-green,' she said, leaving the possibility open.

'I don't like compost and *Aphrodite* awaits.' He kissed her, then led her out and helped her into the car. 'Are you going to sell your flat when we go back to Sydney?' he asked, as he pulled out of the narrow parking spot.

'I'm only renting,' said Aberdeen. 'I'll let it go.'

'I might let mine go too, then we can get a new place when we come home. A house with room for your museum, if you like.'

'I have a place picked out,' she said eagerly. 'A

terrace in Glebe. It might be still available.'

'You live in Glebe?' His eyebrows climbed.

'No, no. I live in a boring flat in Blaxland. This was the place I meant to have for my costume centre – before I lost my job. I paid for an option, but the agent wouldn't hold it any longer.'

'We won't acquire any property yet,' said Jet. 'We'll wait until we come back from overseas.' He patted her thigh. 'Lorelei, we might meet some storms at sea, but we're going to be remarkably free of problems.'

'I hope so,' she said.

'I *know* so. Problems come from money, sex, children and in-laws, none of which is likely to trouble us.'

'Oh?'

'Your mother's a great old girl,' he said cheerfully, 'and you've sure charmed Uncle Godfrey. We'll come down south and see them now and again, but we needn't live in their pockets, *nicht wahr*? Your mother's self-sufficient, she's lived down here without you. Which disposes of the in-law bogeyman.'

It doesn't dispose of Jasper, she thought. And wondered what it would take, exactly, to dispose of Jasper Diamond. Ground glass? A silver bullet? Or maybe a big wax doll and a fist-full of pins?

A nasty *frisson* pattered down her spine at the thought, a shivering of flesh and nerve and sinew. What kind of a person *was* she, to harbour such savage thoughts about Jet's brother?

And what kind of a person was *he* – to engender them? The answer came pat: the sort of person who thought *she* was a Venus fly-trap.

'. . . the money's safe as gold shares,' Jet was saying, 'and that's without the family trust. And as for sex and children – one needn't lead to the other.'

'Not for a few years, anyway,' said Aberdeen. 'What about the family business, Jet? The Hidden Treasure chain? Does your uncle really need help?'

'One of us will take it on, eventually, but it needn't be me. There's Jas at Windhill, and our sisters are at Sydney University. They're always in the throes of some drama, but they might turn into hoteliers one fine day. And of course, there's always Tam.'

'Your cousin,' said Aberdeen, getting it straight.

'And maybe my sister-in-law soon, if I read the stars correctly. Which would get her two votes in the stakes. As Uncle Godfrey's daughter *and* his niece by marriage, how could she lose?'

'I see.' Aberdeen felt as if she'd bitten a quince. 'It would put your brother in a good position, too.'

'Dynastic marriages happen in our family,' said Jet. 'My grandparents were cousins. And that gives me another reason for marrying you, Lorelei. I'm not a bit dynastic, and I doubt if even Great-aunt Jane, the family historian, could find shared blood between you and me.'

'Where does she fit?' asked Aberdeen.

'Neatly in the Diamond family plot,' said Jet. 'Between Great-uncle Edward and his wife and Great-aunt Jewel and her two husbands. Under a clump of heirloom roses. Every time I visit I expect to find she's sprouted a family tree.'

Aberdeen laughed. 'About the wedding . . .' she said.

'My sisters will carry bouquets of mauve lilac and fight over who *doesn't* catch the bouquet, and Jas, as my elder brother, will try to insist on a spot of *droit du seigneur.*' Her horrified expression made him laugh delightedly. 'You look just like an appalled corn goddess now. Demeter, maybe, after she heard about Persephone's dirty weekend with Pluto.'

'The wedding,' she said, gulping. 'You can't just pop into church. You need arrangements.'

Jet stopped near the wharf and smiled at her. 'We'll make a proper splash.'

'That might be difficult too,' she said. 'There's only Kate on my side. I've been so tied up this last couple of years I've lost touch with a lot of friends.'

'You'll have to share my friends, won't you?'

'What about your brother? Will he come?'

'Of course he'll come. He'll have to be Best Man.' He raised his brows. 'Have you a double cousin to console old Jas? I think he was hot for you. And now you're appalled again. Don't worry – I'll wear a carnation so you'll know which one to marry.'

The wind whipped Aberdeen's hair around, numbing her face despite the warmth of the day. The thought of marrying the wrong twin had made her stomach lurch sickly. Real nightmare stuff, she thought as they walked towards the wharf.

'The others are here already,' said Jet.

'The others?'

'Charlie Green and two of his kids. *Aphrodite* isn't a one-man yacht, and we need more hands while you learn the ropes.'

'Of course,' she said. 'Wasn't it Charlie's son who broke his leg?'

'That's right,' said Jet. 'You're taking his place, but Charlie won't hold it against you. There's only one disadvantage in taking a beautiful woman as crew.'

'What's that?'

Jet put his arms round her. 'My usual jig with the Greens is to take night-watch in turns,' he said, 'but

63

once I go off watch I shall want you with me, and we will be occupied. We'll have to tie the tiller and hope for the best.' He laughed. 'Only joking, Lorelei. She has an auto-pilot.'

Aberdeen felt a jolt of apprehension. So little time to arrange a wedding and master a demanding skill. Positive thinking, she told herself. If she wanted to do it, she could, and if she could do it, she would. And if she couldn't, the departure date could be postponed until she had.

'Come aboard,' said Jet. 'Charlie's all ready to cast off.'

'Right.' Charlie was a man of few words, but his kids had a lot to say.

They stared at her, then grinned in unison. 'You're crewing for Jet instead of poor old Nick,' said one. 'By the way, I'm Todd. He's Tiger.'

Aberdeen smiled back. 'I'm sorry about your brother, but glad for me. That's if I can learn to sail.'

'There's a lot to learn,' said Todd.

'How come you don't know how?' asked the younger boy, Tiger.

'I never learned. I suppose your dad taught you.'

Tiger shrugged. 'Dad and Mum and Rusty and Nick all sail as well. Todd and me have got our own Half Tonner, *Website*. And Rusty runs *Greensleeves* as a charter yacht out of Manatee.'

'Mum crews for us, sometimes,' said Todd.

'Mum says if we spent as much time on homework as we do on sailing, we'd be bloody geniuses,' said Tiger.

'As it is, we're just bloody ignoramuses, Mum says,' said Todd.

'Only she says she's one too, so it doesn't matter that much,' concluded Tiger cheerfully.

Aberdeen laughed. These two were a proper double act. She wondered if Jet and his abrasive brother had ever been like this, freckled kids with good humour and steady hands. Probably not. It was obvious that Jet and Jasper didn't get along.

'Mum will be glad you're marrying Jet,' said Tiger.

Aberdeen could just imagine their mum; she'd be wiry and windblown and freckled, the breezy mother of at least four boys, resigned to a masculine household of pasta and meat pies, beer and Coca-Cola. 'Are there any more of you at home?' she asked.

'Just us and Will and Matty. Nick's in hospital and Rusty's up north at Manatee.'

'Nick was supposed to be in the race last month,' said Tiger, 'only he went and broke his leg. Lucky for you though,' he added with an evil grin. 'This way you get to marry Jet.'

'*I'm* the lucky one,' said Jet, coming up behind. 'You and Todd get forward and help your dad. I'm going to stay with Aberdeen.'

The boys departed, and Jet put his arms round Aberdeen. 'They'd talk the hind leg off an octopus,' he said. 'But at least they've got good taste. Their eyes did pop when they spotted you.'

'Rubbish,' she said. 'They're kids. They seem to know you pretty well.'

'God, yes, the Greens are my second family. Carol – their mum – and I have known one another for twenty-five years. But why the frown? Are you jealous?'

'No,' said Aberdeen.

'Good! There's no need to be. Carol was our nanny when Jas and I were small. That's why she's got so many kids, she says. After us rough Diamonds, bringing up her lot is child's play. I remember her dumping

65

Rusty on my lap, then later it was Nick and Will. Kid after kid after kid, all brown and freckled, just like Tiger and Todd.'

He zipped her into a life jacket and kissed her nose. 'Now,' he said, 'for your first taste of the best fun you can have standing up. Hold on.'

She clung to the rail as Charlie started the engine, breathing deeply, enjoying the salt in the air. It seemed extraordinary that this great dancing gull should obey the dictates of humans, but *Aphrodite* did.

Beautiful, graceful and obedient – no wonder the disaffected wives of yachtsmen sometimes thought of the yachts themselves as courtesans. The secret, Aberdeen thought dreamily, was to put aside jealousy and love the yachts as well.

The sun glittered on the wavelets, and the horizon swung, reassuringly close to hand. And then the *Aphrodite* left the mouth of the Derwent and inhaled the wind. She heeled and sprang forward as her sails filled and drew her out across the waves like a swan. The engine died, but there was no unearthly silence such as Aberdeen had envisaged. Instead, there was a humming, thrumming of wind in ropes and sails and the hard slap of waves against the hull. The obedient courtesan was developing notions of her own.

'I'll leave you to get your sea legs,' said Jet, and removed his arm from her shoulders.

Aberdeen's answer was swallowed by the other sounds, and she found herself swallowing again and again. It must be the taste of salt that was flooding her mouth with saliva, salt and cold wind that blurred her eyes. The cooked-spaghetti feeling in her legs was due to the unaccustomed movement of the deck. She had to get her sea legs; a quaintly old-fashioned term.

She needed her concentration, but now that Jet had gone, the boys returned. They pointed out parts of the yacht and released a flood of information about techniques and the excellencies of *Aphrodite*.

'You have to keep her headed right,' said Tiger seriously. 'Here, put your hand on this sheet, and you'll get the feel of her. She's alive. That's what Rusty always says about *Greensleeves*.'

Aberdeen supposed the 'sheet' must be the rope he was indicating, but when she tried to obey his instructions, she found herself quite unable to let go of the railing. The wind was in her face, the spray was stinging her eyes. The deck was heaving and though she could appreciate the beauty of the sky-blue sails, her head was beginning to pound.

She found her legs shaking and, now she had noticed the intensity of her grip on the rail, her knuckles ached fiercely. The boys were staring as if, she thought dazedly, she had grown an extra head.

'You seasick or something?' asked Tiger.

'No,' she said. Her lips could scarcely shape the word.

The horizon seemed to be acting oddly, heaving and switching about. There was a dazzle about her vision and it had darkened one-sidedly. She would have raised a hand to the affected eye if she had been able to spare one from the railing. She blinked instead. Distantly, she could hear the boys' voices, then Jet was there, his hand on her bare arm.

'You OK, Lorelei?'

She could feel his fingers, she could hear his voice, but she couldn't respond. Her jaw was clenching and she was convinced she would throw up or scream if she opened her mouth.

'Aberdeen? What's wrong?'

'Don't – know,' she jerked out, then her sight seemed to close down in a maze of jagged streaks and swarming black dots. She retched suddenly, and threw up over the railing. She was beyond humiliation, and then she was beyond anything but increasing pain and disorientation as the deck and the railing became the only solid places in the universe. And then the railing was gone.

She woke in the car, half-opened her eyes, moaned and closed them again. Jet's hand was hard on her shoulder, shaking her. 'Aberdeen – Aberdeen! Listen!'

'Yes?' she said faintly.

'Do you need to see a doctor?'

'No.'

'For God's sake!' He sounded exasperated. 'What's wrong?'

'Headache,' she said, although the word was inadequate.

'Is that all?'

Tears spurted from her eyes. 'Just get me home.'

Kate's placid face was a comfort, Kate's cool hands were capable as she stripped off Aberdeen's clothing and tipped her gently into bed.

'What the hell's wrong with her?' demanded Jet.

'She's got a headache,' said Kate.

'Oh.'

'It isn't a brain tumour and I doubt if it's catching.'

'I suppose you'd know.' Jet realized he sounded ungracious, but he didn't much like Kate's tone.

'Not from personal experience,' said Kate, 'but my

68

father used to get the occasional attack. I think they were called cluster headaches.'

'What about Aberdeen? Does she get them often?'

'Not to my knowledge. Don't worry, Jet. I'm sure she'll be better in the morning.' Kate touched Aberdeen's cheek. 'If she starts to run a fever we'll think again. Do you want to stay with her?'

'I ought to be getting back to Charlie.'

'Of course,' said Kate politely. 'Come back later, if you like. Don't worry about disturbing me. Just let yourself in and slip into bed next to Aberdeen. That way you can help her if she's sick again.'

'Thank you so much,' said Jet. His sense of humour was beginning to reassert itself and his gaze followed Kate's stately retreat with something that was almost admiration.

Slip into bed next to Aberdeen.

He wondered if she would have said that if they hadn't been engaged. Then he wondered if she would have said it if he hadn't been Jet Diamond, part-heir to the Hidden Treasure chain. His fiancée seemed to think her mother was wholly detached from the world; for his money, Kate Shawcross had her eyes fixed firmly on the main chance, and he couldn't really fault her for that.

CHAPTER 5

Aberdeen woke slowly the second time, resisting the return to consciousness for as long as she could.

Any hope that the nightmare experience had *been* a nightmare departed when she licked her lips and tasted the salt on her skin. 'Kate?' Her voice was a dry croak. 'Kate, are you there?'

Kate came in with a steaming mug in her hand. 'I was having a cup of tea,' she said, and handed it to Aberdeen, leaving her daughter confused about whether the drink was Kate's own or whether it had been made especially for her. She heaved herself up and sipped the tea gratefully.

'Jet didn't come back, then,' observed Kate.

'Didn't Jet bring me home?'

'Yes, then he went back to someone called Charlie.'

'A yachtie,' said Aberdeen. 'I suppose Jet had to go and swab the decks. Ugh. I hope I didn't throw up on the deck.'

'What happened?'

'I suppose I was seasick,' said Aberdeen gloomily. 'I thought seasick was just – sick. You know. Throw up and you're better.' She put down the mug. 'Lord, Kate, I wish I'd learned how to swim and sail when

I was a kid. Those boys of Charlie's – they couldn't *believe* I'd never been out on a yacht. Frankly, neither can I.'

'You did go sailing once,' said Kate abruptly.

'*Did* I?'

'You fell overboard. You weren't harmed, but after that you used to scream whenever we tried to get you near water, so we gave up. You wouldn't learn to swim.'

'And you've only just thought to tell me?'

'It's so long ago,' said Kate blandly. 'I thought you remembered, but if not, why give you a phobia?'

'It's a hidden memory. I could have paid a shrink mega dollars to dig that up.'

'Hidden memories are hidden for a good reason,' said Kate. 'And it's never been any drama.'

'It's a drama now,' said Aberdeen, 'since I'm marrying a yachtie.' Then she brightened. 'I'll be fine now,' she said. 'That's the way it works, isn't it? You look at the memory in daylight and then you're not afraid any more. I'll even learn to swim. You could teach me, Kate.'

'Not me,' said Kate. 'I had enough of that when you were smaller. Ask Jasper. I should think he'd be a good teacher.'

Aberdeen's mouth tightened. 'I'll ask Jet,' she said.

Jasper tossed restlessly in the narrow bed. He should never have gone to the Shawcross cottage. Jet had given permission in his amused and superior way, but he shouldn't have gone. It did no good to harrow up his feelings, but the thought of Aberdeen Shawcross was like a bruise; he knew it would hurt but he couldn't keep from touching it. As he couldn't have helped touching her hair. *La Belle Dame sans Merci*, he had called her, but that had been unfair. As she had pointed out so stringently, *he* had begun the hostilities.

Added to the pain was dismay that he was behaving just as badly over Aberdeen as Jet had done over Grete. No, he was behaving worse than Jet had done, for he had never wanted a permanent relationship with Grete, whereas Jet was planning to marry Aberdeen at Easter. Marry her and take her off on a romantic cruise. Long tropical nights, the glassy waters of the fjords, bustling ports in Asia and brilliant distant isles in the Pacific. Raging storms and mountainous waves, broken masts and jellyfish.

Jet would show her the world all right, from the deck of the *Aphrodite*. And in between, they'd be wrapped up in one another as lovers always were. Cut off from the world in their own private floating Eden, Jet and Aberdeen.

If he'd thought he had a chance, he'd have tried to win her away from Jet.

'You're sick, Diamond,' he said to himself aloud in the night. 'You've met her, what – three times? She hated you on sight and nothing you've done is likely to change her mind. Three times and you'd have her if you could! Have her away from your brother and into your bed. You are sick.'

He remembered the smell of beer and salt in the Van Diemen Tavern, he remembered the opulence of his family's suite in the Ruby. Most clearly of all, he remembered the summer scents in Kate's cottage garden, the tang of fresh-turned earth, the bitter fragrance of that tea, the scent of sun and blossoms on Aberdeen's skin and hair. It was the garden that had done for him. Those other times he had been in company. In the garden Kate had left them alone. Was Kate his fairy godmother or an evil genius? He wasn't sure, but he feared it was the latter.

He was sick, but what, precisely, was his illness? Was it envy, jealousy, obsession or just plain lust that afflicted him, distracting him from his duty by day and his sleep by night? And was it the same malaise that had afflicted his work since the night they had met in the tavern?

After several miserable hours spent pondering his iniquity, he got up and dressed, and was almost grateful to be distracted by a new sickness, this time afflicting somebody else.

'It's my gran,' said Ellie. 'She got the flu, her neighbour says, and they'll have to put her in hospital if there's no one to nurse her.'

'You'd better get going, then,' said Jasper.

'Can you manage without me? The continuity, I mean?'

'Rod will have to do it . . .' He saw her anxiety and divined its cause. 'He won't do half the job you do, but we're close to the finish here, so you might as well go home early. We'll be in contact when we get back to see how you're placed.' He touched her shoulder. 'Go on, Ellie – if we're short-handed it will get me out of this dinner-party affair.'

Her tense face relaxed a little. 'Thanks, Jasper. I appreciate it.'

'See if you can get a flight today,' he said. 'I'll run you to the airport.'

She nodded, and went off to sort things out, and he wondered, briefly, if Dr Smith would think him foolishly democratic. Ellie was a good continuity girl, but there were plenty of others to be hired.

73

Yes, and you might have hired trouble, he thought. One young woman travelling with four men, that could have been a recipe for disaster if Ellie hadn't been Ellie.

He cried off the dinner party and loaded Ellie and her case into the van. At the last minute he invited Rod along as well; he needed a serious word with Rod, and the drive back would supply him with a ready-made opportunity. From Rod's ironic glance it was obvious he knew what was in store, but he climbed in beside Ellie.

The two men waited to see the plane take off, and Jasper sighed. 'I can just see Gen and Sabby flying off to nurse an elderly relative,' he said.

'Yeah,' said Rod. 'So can I. So, let's have it.'

'Have what?' asked Jasper automatically.

'What you've been screwing yourself up to tell me about you and Tam.'

'Me and *Tam*? There's nothing to tell,' said Jasper. Rod was staring at him, so he said it again, more emphatically. 'There's nothing to tell.'

'Then what's been up with you?'

'Maybe you should tell me,' said Jasper wryly.

'*Something's* wrong,' said Rod, looking at him hard. 'If you don't believe me, look at the rushes of *In the Rough*. Compare the Tasmania footage with the stuff you did in Arnhem Land. You look like death warmed up.'

Jasper glanced at his own face in the rear-view mirror. 'You're imagining things,' he said impatiently. 'I look the same as I always do.'

'I'm imagining nothing,' said Rod with unwonted seriousness. 'It's something in the eyes. A sort of

74

dumb, suffering animal look. Look, mate, I know the symptoms of woman trouble. I've got it myself with Tam as you know damned well. So it seemed logical that you were in the same boat with the same woman.'

'I promise you I'm not involved with Tam.'

'Maybe you'd both like to be,' said Rod sourly. 'You match up to her a damned sight better than I ever could. And, being the good bloke you are, you might have wanted to warn me.'

'It's amazing logic,' said Jasper. 'But you couldn't be more mistaken.' He squeezed Rod's shoulder briefly. 'Thanks for the concern – although I'm not too clear about its exact object.'

'You're *not* cut up because of Tam, then?' said Rod, getting it clear.

'I just said so.'

'Grete Fischer gave you a hell of a serve, swinging over to Jet.'

'That's behind me, and let's face it, I didn't offer her any great incentives to stay with me.'

'Then who the heck is it now? Not *Ellie*?'

'Give me a break. And don't start guessing, Rod. I'm fine. More to the point, you'd better pull yourself together, at least in front of the camera . . .'

'Yes, boss,' said Rod, but he didn't sound unfriendly.

Rod's perception of his misery worried Jasper. Of course Rod was in a unique position, being personal friend as well as employee and some-time lover of Jasper's cousin, but the last thing Jasper wanted was a rumour floating off and reaching Jet. Therefore, he made every effort to appear as his normal pre-Aberd-

75

een Shawcross self while filming the final links for *Tasmania – In the Rough.*

These links could have been done in the Sydney studio, but Jasper liked to use as much location filming as he could, and there was always the chance of picking up the odd gem of a scene along the way. And this programme, as he told Tam unhappily when he telephoned her from Hobart, could do with all the gems it could gather.

'It's your fault for defecting,' he said.

'Balls,' said Tam. 'How's that bugger Rod?'

'Bruised. The way you left him!' snapped Jasper. 'What went wrong? Really?'

'Let's just say we had different destinations?' said Tam. 'How much devil footage did you get?'

'Devil's Gate Dam, Devil's Kitchen.'

'Tasmanian devils, Jasper. Little black critters.'

'None,' said Jasper.

'Get some. Look, Jasper, I know how you feel about exploiting cutesy-pie, but those creatures are unique. Trust me on that.'

Thus, at Tam's insistence, the final link was filmed at a wildlife park where the nocturnal devils could be seen during the day. The devils were carnivorous marsupials which had once roamed much of Australia but which were now confined to Tasmania. They had neither the charm of the kangaroo, the sentimental appeal of the koala nor even the weirdness of the platypus but, from a film-maker's point of view, they had something better.

'Attitude!' said Jasper to Stew's camera lens. 'Tassie devils are animated attitude, snapping, snarling, scrapping little bundles of the stuff – and they could teach a few anarchists a thing or two about aggression! Death to the chooks – get off my leg, you little bugger.'

'It's feeding time,' said the park keeper lugu-briously, and Jasper could have blessed Tam for here, undoubtedly, was a gem: an unconsidered char-acter who would be magic on film.

'I take it I'm the main course?' he said quickly, playing along.

'They don't eat people,' said the keeper. 'They like their rabbit legs and bits of chicken. That doesn't mean you ought to stick your finger in his mouth.'

'Get him off me, then,' said Jasper, although the devil, in fact, was doing no more than sit on his shoe.

The sequence was interrupted by the slightly breathless arrival of a very young reporter from a local paper. She was accompanied by an equally young photographer.

'I'm sorry – we're late . . . What are you doing?' This last, slightly indignant question was put to Stew.

'Making a documentary,' said Jasper. He saw that Stew had widened the shot to include both the original tableau and the new arrivals. 'Don't worry about Stew. We're only filming links to be cut in at post-produc-tion.'

'I know about the documentary, Mr Diamond. Your publicist said we could run a feature for *Summer Daze*. It's an insert distributed once a week inside one of the big dailies.'

'I've seen *Summer Daze*,' said Jasper, 'I was reading one this morning.' He rubbed his chin. 'So – our publicist said you'd catch us down among the devils.'

'That's right.'

'We haven't got a publicist,' said Jasper to the camera, 'so I presume my cousin Tam has been talking out of school. She couldn't come to Tassie, but she's still directing operations from afar.'

The young reporter bit her lip. Green as grass, thought Jasper, and had mercy on her. 'We'll be happy to do an interview in a minute,' he said. At that moment he felt a tug at his trouser leg, and an ominous sagging as his belt dug into his flesh. He glanced down and saw, without pleasure, that the young devil, tired of being ignored, was clinging to the loose cloth of his trousers by its teeth.

'Do you *mind*?' said Jasper to the devil.

Kate was chuckling gently over her Tuesday paper, and Aberdeen, strung up but determined, was preparing for another outing on the *Aphrodite*.

'It's dead calm today,' she said.

Kate chuckled again.

'I'm glad you think it's funny.' Aberdeen complained. 'This is my future you're cackling at.'

'Look,' said Kate, and pushed the summer supplement across the table.

Jet! Aberdeen felt a stab of pleasure, then she realized the man in the picture wasn't her fiancé but his twin. Her face went cold, literally, as if all the blood had drained away. When she had regained her equilibrium, she peered at the supplement again. And after all he was a man, not a demon, not an evil *doppelgänger*.

'Are honours even?' he'd enquired with painful directness in the garden, and she had allowed that they were. And so they would have remained, if he hadn't come any closer. But that touch of face to face, his hand in her hair! Homage or subjugation? At the thought, her chest constricted with painful claustrophobia.

He's just a genetic mistake, she told herself savagely.

The flip-side, the down-side of Jet. No wonder he makes you shiver. Look at him and get over it.

The photograph was no better than most newspaper shots, but the pictured face held a human quality that had been missing in her encounters with the real thing. The suggestion of a crooked smile hovered around the firm lips. She couldn't see the expression in the eyes, for the face was tilted downwards, as if Jasper Diamond had been caught off-guard, contemplating something pleasing but faintly ridiculous.

'What's *he* smiling at?' She was startled at her petulance.

'Read the caption,' said Kate who had been watching with fascination.

She focused on the line of print. '*Jasper has a devil of a time.*'

Kate reached out to reclaim the paper and Aberdeen made an instinctive motion to keep it. 'Sorry,' she said shortly, taking her hands away. 'I suppose you want to keep this since you're Jasper Diamond's number one fan.'

Kate put on her spectacles and began to read aloud. ' "*Jasper Diamond, producer/presenter of the* In the Rough *documentaries . . .*" etc., etc. . . . ah! "*He and his crew visited the Devils' Inn Wildlife Park and Restaurant. As may be seen in the photograph above, Mr Diamond was soon standing knee-deep in devils!* '*I'd recommend a visit to anyone,' he says, 'but I'd also recommend a good stout pair of boots.*' " ' She beamed at Aberdeen. 'I suppose that accounts for the rather apprehensive expression! I always liked his documentaries, but I find him even more attractive in the flesh.'

'I'm glad someone does,' said Aberdeen sourly.

'I like him,' mused Kate. 'I like him a lot.'

79

'I don't. He's sarcastic and cold-blooded – and he'd make trouble if he could.' Aberdeen broke off, aware that she was sounding melodramatic. 'Trouble between Jet and me, I mean,' she added, when Kate didn't respond.

Kate turned a page.

'He practically said so. He even told me not to tell Jet I'd seen him.'

Kate raised her eyes with a sigh. 'Nonsense. It was Jet who introduced you.'

'We'd met before that. I thought he was Jet, until I had a good look at him.'

'You do sound hostile. Not to say paranoid. Do I really need to know all this?'

'He'll make trouble.'

'He certainly will if you go on like that!' said Kate with sudden severity.

Aberdeen gaped at her mother. She was so used to Kate's detachment that it was as if a church pew had bounced up and given advice.

'If you love Jet and trust him, nothing and no one can make trouble between you,' said Kate. 'The very idea is ridiculous.'

'What? How?'

'You must put a very low value on yourself if you believe you could be seduced away from Jet by flattery or attention or lying words. It makes me so *angry*,' said Kate vigorously, 'when I hear of so-and-so *stealing* so-and-so's husband or wife. You cannot steal love. It can be freely granted or given unwillingly, but it *cannot* be stolen. The idea's absurd, and that's that.'

'My goodness,' said Aberdeen, 'that was enough. So you really believe . . .'

'Aberdeen,' said Kate calmly, 'I have given you

advice, which I almost never do. Take it or leave it.'

'You think I've got your precious Jasper wrong? He implied I'd set out to trap Jet somehow.'

'You heard what I said,' said Kate.

Aberdeen wasn't sure whether she should be offended or amused by her mother's outburst, but she did deduce that criticism of Jasper Diamond wasn't allowed.

'I ought to watch one of these documentaries,' she said aloud. 'But I suppose by the time there's one on TV I'll be overseas.'

'I have videos,' said Kate. 'They're in the top drawer of the cabinet.'

She retreated into her reading and Aberdeen, after washing the breakfast dishes very crossly, investigated the cabinet.

She expected a home-recorded videotape, and was startled to find that Kate had several commercially produced cassettes, complete with boxes showing stills from the programmes. Not only Jasper Diamond was represented. Also in her collection were samples of David Attenborough and Major Les Hiddins, the Bush Tucker Man, both very popular figures on Australian television. They were engaging characters, so how would Mr *Doppelgänger* Diamond compare? She inserted the cassette and watched as the title came up, superimposed against a background of burning blue sky.

BREONA BELT – IN THE ROUGH
A Diamond/Spellman Production

The title shimmered and broke up into a mass of jagged fragments which sped across the screen and vanished.

'*There are two ways of getting to most destinations, and*

81

the Breona Station Belt obeys the rules,' began the voice-over. *'One way is by small plane as far as Rosella, and the other by road through Burumburra Junction. A couple of hours, or a couple of days? Being impatient, our crew took the plane.'*

Aberdeen's scalp seemed to prickle as she recognized the deep tones of Jasper Diamond. The words came clearly, and the voice remained enough like Jet's to make her shiver, yet whereas Jet had a cosmopolitan accent, Jasper could never have been anything but an Australian. His origin came through in the intonation, in the vocal edge, which was even more pronounced on tape than it had been in Kate's back garden.

The sky shot fuzzed and the focus zoomed in on a landscape growing steadily closer as a plane came in to land.

'That's Rosella down there,' said a woman's voice. It was deep and merry, as if the speaker were about to smile. *'The shops are pretty basic, but it's unique in other ways. The Breona Belt is unusual in that the range attracts much more rain than you'd expect. The Belt supports livestock throughout the year, but the rain can be a mixed blessing, as you can see from that brown stuff there. It looks a bit like a petrified lake, but actually it's a stretch of mud called . . .'* The voice broke off, and there was the amplified sound of clicking fingers. *'What the dickens is it called, Jasper?'*

'It's called the Sludgery, Tam,' said Jasper's voice. *'And you should know, since you wrote the script.'*

'What script?' said Tam's voice. *'That's my shopping list.'*

Aberdeen realized she was still crouched by the video cabinet, as if about to partake in some exotic primitive ritual. After a while, she rose wincingly to her feet and backed up until she could sit in Kate's armchair, never taking her gaze from the screen. The documentary continued, with the two presenters passing the conversational ball effortlessly back and forth. Sometimes other voices chimed in. There were brief interviews with the inhabitants of the area, and then the crew went out on horseback to explore the hills. Aberdeen saw Jasper looking relaxed and casual in the saddle of a lively bay, and had her first good look at his cousin and co-presenter, Tam Spellman, a statuesque brunette whose face was as animated as Jasper's was calm. The chemistry between them was evident, but they knew when to step back and let the unique outback setting speak for itself.

When the cassette finished, Aberdeen sat staring at the credits for a while. She was thoroughly unnerved. The Jasper Diamond *she* had encountered had been harsh and abrasive and very eccentric. The personality reaching out from the television screen had been completely sane and likeable.

'Well?' said Kate as Aberdeen returned to the kitchen.

'The bugger can act, all right,' said Aberdeen.

'There's another one . . .' began Kate, but Aberdeen shook her head.

'No, thanks, Kate. I've already seen more than enough of Jasper Diamond. I'm sorry. I know you like him, but there's something very off-centre about that man.' She sighed. 'I suppose there's just one bright spot. He and Jet don't get on so well, so I doubt if we'll see much of him once we're married.'

'Probably not,' said Kate.

'And there's another bright spot too,' said Aberdeen. 'With any luck he might decide to do a piece on

83

crocodiles – an inside story. The sort that Jonah might have done on the whale.'

Kate wouldn't be drawn, so Aberdeen was able to enjoy that thought for a while before her satisfaction faded. The chances of anything unpleasant happening to Jasper Diamond were remote, and she couldn't really wish harm to Jet's twin brother. The best she could hope for was a distance kept between them, a no-fly zone. She might even suggest it to him, next time they met. Lord, what was she thinking of? Better to tell *Jet* she'd rather keep clear of his brother.

She collected her scrambled thoughts and directed them to her second sailing lesson. 'Have you got any headache pills?' she asked Kate.

'Somewhere. I don't get headaches much.'

Aberdeen found some crumbling pills and put them in her pocket as insurance. If she had them, she probably wouldn't need them.

When Jet arrived, she did her best to seem entirely confident. Migraine headaches, she had learned from Kate's ancient medical book, had several possible causes. They could be influenced by hormones, diet, heredity and tension. Aberdeen's hormones had never given her the least trouble and she couldn't see why they should start to do so now. Of course, Jet's love-making stirred her senses to quite a degree, but she had herself well in hand. They had agreed that she should begin taking the contraceptive pill, but she had not yet been for a prescription, so there was no use blaming that. Tension was the obvious culprit. Tension over her need to please Jet and over the hidden memory of that boating accident. Now she had identified and faced that tension, there was no need for it to cause another migraine.

Aberdeen was pleased with her reasoning, and expounded it to Jet on the way to the wharf.

'Fine,' he said with a sideways grin. 'You're *not* one of the Admiral Nelson brigade!'

'The what?'

'Seasick, sweetie, on every voyage.'

'This time, everything will be fine. I'm going to redeem myself in front of Tiger and Todd!'

'They're in Sydney,' said Jet. 'School's gone back.'

'Of course. But who's crewing for you today?'

'I've found someone marginally competent.' His eyes danced. 'You've met before, and it's time you got to know one another properly.'

'Your uncle?' she hazarded, but she knew, from the dullness in the pit of her stomach, whom it would be.

'It's Jas,' confirmed Jet. 'He's finished playing movies for now, so he's moving into the Ruby suite for a few days before he goes home.'

'I see.'

'Jas isn't so bad,' said Jet, amused. 'I know you didn't exactly hit it off but you'll get used to him. People do.'

'Of course,' she said. 'I hope he won't mind my company on the yacht today.'

Jet laughed. 'Not much good if he does, since it's my yacht and your education is the object of the exercise!' He pulled into the parking space and got out to open the door. 'Give me a kiss, Lorelei,' he said. 'I've hardly seen you lately.'

'Three days,' she said.

'It's seemed forever.'

'I thought you were cross because I spoilt your day.'

'I had things to do, that's all.' He kissed her lightly, then gathered her against him. The sunlight fell on her

85

closed eyelids, making a rosy dazzle, and she relaxed into his embrace. Jet's hands were stroking her hair, his lips playing over her face, lightly and sensuously, and she began to feel the familiar stirring of passion, deep within her, like the stirring of fish in a clear blue lake. Her apprehensions were far, far down in the ooze at the bottom of her consciousness, where something shifted, monstrous but invisible.

She pressed against Jet's body, fighting to regain the purity of pleasure. Jet reacted to her passion with his own, and soon they were clinging together, the kisses deepening. Jet was the first to break away, and he did it gradually, turning his face so his lips brushed her cheeks and nose and forehead, then simply holding her against him while the urgency faded from his hands and body. 'We're supposed to be going sailing, Lorelei,' he said lightly.

She opened her eyes, seeing the brilliance of the February sky above her. For a moment she thought of a paintbox sky over the Breona Belt.

'*There are two ways of getting to most destinations . . .*' said Jasper Diamond's voice in her memory.

She shook herself, swaying a little on her feet. Jet's hands came down to steady her, and for a moment his touch felt like an intrusion. She stepped away, smiling to soften the rejection. The smile drained as she realized, with a jolt, that Jasper was standing a metre away, hands thrust in pockets, staring at them. For a frozen moment, she stared back. How long had he been there? Had he witnessed her embrace with Jet? Or had she somehow summoned him like an evil demon when she had remembered his voice? Had *he* been the monster in the depths?

Defensively, she stepped back against the curve of

Jet's shoulder. His arms curled around her, one hand brushing the underside of her breast while his chin came down on the top of her head. 'Ready, sweet-heart?'

She swallowed, and nodded, and Jet let her go and turned to Jasper. 'There you are, Jas – I've just been telling Aberdeen you've finished dancing with the devils.' He reached out to punch his brother's shoulder lightly. 'What's the confusion-count since that piece in the local rag? I've had three people offer me advice on treating devil bites so far today . . . I bet no one's mentioned *Lou Galah* to you at all?'

'Not lately,' said Jasper, speaking at last.

A deep shiver ran through Aberdeen and she reached up to rub the back of her neck. That face, so like and so unlike Jet's. That voice – Jet's voice roughened and deepened. The touch of forehead to forehead, the scent of a Tasmanian summer garden mixed with that of healthy male.

'How quickly the public forgets,' said Jet. 'Yester-day's heroes, we are.'

'You seem to have found a new audience,' said Jasper, and his dark brown eyes were fixed on Aberd-een.

'So I have,' said Jet. 'We're getting married in Sydney towards the end of March. Easter Saturday, probably, since we leave on the 31st. Better get your suit out of mothballs.'

'It's only a few weeks since you dumped Grete,' said Jasper.

'It seems a lifetime.'

'She left in mid-November,' said Jasper harshly. 'It's now early February. That makes eleven weeks.'

'A lifetime,' agreed Jet. 'And you sound a bit

obsessive to me. Counting weeks since our jointly much admir'd *Fraülein* departed us; that's not healthy. Are you still in touch? You might be in on a fresh chance there.'

'She sent me a postcard from Bury St Edmunds,' said Jasper.

'Snap!' said Jet. 'Only mine was from Hay-on-Wye. She obviously wasn't in that much of a hurry to get back to the Fatherland.' He laughed, and after a moment Jasper did too.

'Honours even!' said Jet.

CHAPTER 6

Mystified, Aberdeen stared from one to the other. For a moment they had seemed bent on snarling at one another like territorial dogs, but now the tension had broken. She remembered, belatedly, that she had not greeted Jasper, nor had he greeted her. It was too late now, even if she'd wanted, for they were heading down to the docks.

'Come on,' said Jet. He swung her aboard the yacht, kissed her soundly, then set her down.

'I'll take her out under power,' said Jet. 'You stay with Jas.'

He started the engine and Jasper stood by Aberdeen, explaining the procedures in layperson's terms, just as young Todd and Tiger had done before. She concentrated fiercely on his words, trying to ignore the tone, keeping her dislike to herself. His grudge against Jet seemed to have worn out – or else he was resigned.

Aphrodite began to tread across the bay, the wind and the waves were languid, a long, slow swell in place of a galloping tide.

'Kate showed me your piece in the paper,' she said to Jasper.

'*My* piece? I'm not a feature writer.'

'The piece about you, if you must be pedantic. Were you pleased?'

'Naturally,' he said. 'It was a piece of favourable publicity, which is why Tam arranged it.'

'In a little local rag?'

'Why not? Reporters and photographers can move on, and they remember. Today's trainees are next decade's aces.'

'So you make it your business to be friendly to them.'

'It costs me nothing and it could return a good rate of interest.'

'It would have cost you nothing to be friendly to me,' she said sharply, 'since today's stranger is tomorrow's sister-in-law.'

His expression never altered, but she thought his eyes darkened a fraction. 'Cost me nothing? Is that what you believe, Aberdeen?'

'I wouldn't have said it otherwise. I don't say things for show.'

'Then you're less perceptive than I thought. Less intelligent, too. Of course, that might be an asset, when dealing with Jet.'

She stared at him, unbalanced.

'It's the truth,' he added. 'If you marry Jet, you'll have to cultivate shallow thinking and superficial insight.'

'Jet's perfectly intelligent!' she snapped.

'I never said he wasn't. It's difficult to judge, but I suspect his IQ is at least as high as mine. And so it should be. But for an accident of nature, we would have been the same person. Blink, Aberdeen.'

'Why?'

'Your eyes are fixed, and it isn't healthy. Blink, and

look about. Get your focus muscles working. I hope you enjoy the ocean, since you'll be seeing such a lot of it.'

She dragged her gaze from his face and looked out over the dazzle of the water. Seagulls dipped on the waves. 'Why should I cultivate shallow thinking?'

'You'll find it more comfortable. Don't ask why and don't ask how. Just accept things. Treat life as a joke and you'll never have to wonder if it's serious.'

'Is that what you do?'

'It's what Jet does. Are you all right?'

'Of course,' she said, but her stomach had tightened ominously. She had met some astringent people in her life, but never one who affected her as sharply as Jasper Diamond.

'You look pale.' He was watching her closely.

'For crying out loud! I am not seasick. I have not been seasick. I will not be seasick. I am not in any fashion related to Admiral Nelson!'

'I believe you.'

'I had a migraine, that's all. A migraine! I was scared of disappointing Jet, but now I'm not. Sailing is wonderful – and he's going to teach me to swim.' She stopped abruptly, aware of her incoherence.

'Have you never learned? Is that why you're clinging to that rail?'

'I'm not.'

'Look at your hands,' he said quietly. 'You're scared to death.'

She looked at her hands, white-knuckled on the rail.

'I'm angry, not scared. I'm afraid I'll hit you, and that isn't civilized.'

'Prove it.'

'I've no need to prove anything to you!'

91

'You need to prove it to yourself. Let go and walk a few steps towards me. Come on. I won't let you drown.'

She gazed at him, acutely aware of the blood throbbing through her veins, and pounding her temples. Slowly, she pried her fingers away from the underside of the railing, until her palms were almost flat. She lifted her hands and took a step, and another. The deck felt insecure.

'Just another couple of steps,' said Jasper. His hands were stretched towards her, curved a little. She stretched out her own, and stumbled. Her fingertips brushed his, and a tingle of electricity seemed to pass between them. Static electricity from the fibreglass railing, she supposed. She could feel it sparkling along her arms and in her hair.

'There!' he said, and gave her fingers a friendly little squeeze. His lopsided smile came and went. 'You've proved you don't have to cling to the rail. You're safer than houses, really. The sea can be unforgiving, but it's worth knowing.'

'You're not a sailor, though,' she said stupidly.

'But I do have an island.'

'Really?'

'Allirra Island,' he said. 'My private Eden. A seabird colony on one side and the most glorious collection of surreal rocks you ever saw this side of Stonehenge.'

She opened her mouth to ask more, but *Aphrodite* lurched a little and she gasped instead.

'Kate says I fell off a boat once,' she said defensively.

'I fell off a pony once,' he said.

'You're not scared of horses, though.'

'How do you know that?'

'I saw you riding. I never saw anyone *less* afraid.'

'It must have been Jet. I haven't been on a horse in months.'

'On one of your films.'

'I thought you'd never seen them? Kate said you didn't have TV.'

'I watched the *Breona Belt* tape this morning,' she said.

'And?'

She was uneasily aware that his hands were still touching hers, and pulled away. 'I thought you were a dashed good actor,' she blurted. 'It must be a strain, broadcasting that friendly persona. Seeming so nice and normal and making people like you.'

'You liked me?'

'On the screen. In real life you're a different person.'

He stared at her. 'Didn't we call a ceasefire in the garden?'

'That was before . . .' She gulped.

'Before . . . ?'

Her mouth went dry and she resisted the urge to rub her forehead. She was still trying to formulate a reply when Jet touched her shoulder. She spun round. 'My God – who's steering the boat?'

'I've lashed the tiller.' He smiled at her. 'So you've been watching Jas on the telly, have you? Careful, you'll give him a swollen head.'

She said defensively, 'Kate bought the videos ages ago.'

'Thank her for that,' said Jasper. 'And tell her I've remembered the title of the book she wanted. *Old Cottage Garden Flowers* – by Roger Banks.'

'Tell her yourself,' said Jet. 'Tell her at the wedding. Better still, Kate can be chief bridesmaid and you can give it to her as a present. Better again, you can *marry*

Kate. Great-aunt Jane would have a ball unravelling the relationships if you did! You'd be Aberdeen's stepfather for a start, and my stepfather-in-law.'

'Jet, that's not very funny,' said Aberdeen.

'You're right,' said Jet. 'The mind boggles! Come and practise steering.' He put his arm round her. 'Oops!' he said as she stumbled. 'Take the tiller – that's right. You hold it and I'll hold you. Keep her headed as she is.'

Aberdeen leaned against him, the tiller responsive under her hands and his. The yacht was alive, and beautiful, a lady, as Jet had called her. The sea and the glinting sunlight could not have been more lovely, and the sight of their clasped hands on the tiller seemed to augur well for their life together. She smiled dreamily, seeing the play of bones and joints, the smooth, well-shaped hands that rested on her own. It seemed unfair that she had developed a faint headache from the glare. Or perhaps it had come from her earlier sparring with Jasper? She realized her eyes felt dry and stretched.

'*Blink, Aberdeen,*' said Jasper's voice in her mind.

She blinked obediently, but there was something wrong with her vision; a wavering darkness crowded around the edges.

The unfairness lacerated her. She thought of the headache pills in her pocket, but the idea of swallowing them without water made her gag. She dragged her hands from beneath Jet's light clasp, and clapped them over her mouth.

Jet caught her as she stumbled and the *Aphrodite*, unguided, began to lose way. Her graceful certainty became an aimless wallow, and Aberdeen's head spun and throbbed.

'I'm going to be sick!' she gasped.

'Hold on.' Jet's voice. 'I'll get her headed properly.'

'I'll take over.' Jasper's voice. 'You look after Abbie.'

Abbie? Who was that?

The wallowing eased, but Aberdeen's misery increased. She resisted Jet's attempts to guide her to the cabin, convinced she would suffocate.

'Right,' said Jet. 'Sit here and I'll get some Alka-Seltzer.' He pressed her down on the sun-warmed deck. Sweat prickled around her hair-line and the life-jacket was much too hot and bulky. She fumbled with the clasps.

'Leave it, Aberdeen,' said Jasper sternly, and then his hands were holding hers. 'It's only sea-sickness.'

'Headache,' she gasped. 'I've got pills.'

'Too late now.'

Too late for a lot of things. She tried everything, pressing her temples with her hands, pinching the web of skin between forefinger and thumb, breathing deeply, but by the time Jet had returned with the Alka-Seltzer fizzing in a glass she was retching painfully. She supposed it was Jasper who hauled her over to the rail. The hands were anything but lover-like.

'You'll feel better now,' said Jet cheerfully, but she didn't. She swallowed some of the liquid he offered, but it made her feel worse. His face and Jasper's; the effect of double vision made her wince.

'Take her back,' said Jasper.

'The sea's like a blasted mill-pond! Oh – all right. Home, Lorelei?'

Aberdeen could only nod and wonder that her head didn't fall right off.

★ ★ ★

'I can't understand it!' she despaired to Kate that night. 'It wasn't rough today. I was fine, then I had a little headache and then – whammo!'

'Some people are bad sailors,' said Kate.

'Maybe it was because Jasper was bugging me. That man really has a problem. Seriously.'

'You could try some sea-sickness pills,' said Kate.

'I could . . . dammit, what's sea-sickness, anyway? Some disturbance in your ears, isn't it? Surely that can be fixed?'

'There's one fool-proof method,' said Kate very drily. 'Stay off yachts.'

Aberdeen bought anti-nausea tablets. She half-expected Jet to refuse to take her out again, but he was perfectly cheerful when she asked for another chance.

'We'll go out again tomorrow, and as often as you like,' he agreed.

'We?'

'You and me and Jas.'

'Can't you get someone else?' she asked. 'Your brother must have things to do.'

'He can spare us a day or so,' said Jet.

Aberdeen took the tablets and ate a solid, non-greasy breakfast, facing the *Aphrodite* as Marie-Antoinette might have faced the tumbril.

'Did they work?' asked Kate when she returned.

Aberdeen sat down. 'They worked,' she said. 'I wasn't sick.' She blinked and leaned back, her eyes half-closed, and yawned.

'Cup of coffee?' asked Kate.

'Hmmm?'

'Would you like a cup of coffee, Aberdeen?'

'Yes. Thanks . . .' Aberdeen yawned again. 'And make it a strong one, Kate. I feel bombed out.'

'Jet didn't want to come in for coffee?'

'No – he had some work to do on the boat. He said he'd come back for one next time.'

'What about Jasper?'

'What *about* him?' asked Aberdeen.

'I hoped he might have come in,' said Kate. 'I've got those primrose sports and a few more Latin names to confound him.'

'Jasper didn't want a drink,' said Aberdeen, who hadn't asked him. 'And he doesn't want to see your primrose sports. He said they sounded athletic. No, that was Jet. Damn, I wish my head would clear.'

'It must be the pills,' said Kate.

'Perhaps,' said Aberdeen. 'I'll just have to get used to them.'

After another two sailing excursions, Jet was satisfied. Aberdeen could function on the yacht and even steer a little. She disliked the effect of the pills, but there wasn't any point in complaining. It was take them or stay ashore.

'We could manage on our own now,' she said one day. They had been sailing every day that week, and in all that time she and Jet had had little time alone. The yacht and the suite at the Ruby were shared with Jasper, and though Jet took her out to dinner he often saw people he knew and beckoned them over. Or sometimes Jasper would join them. His brother's presence didn't inhibit Jet at all. If he felt like kissing Aberdeen he would do it quite readily in front of an audience. It bothered her a lot, especially since the audience never looked away.

Often when Jet was kissing her she would be skewered with an urge to open her eyes and, sure enough, there would be Jasper, watching with shuttered eyes. Only this morning Jet had unbuttoned her shirt, tugged down the top of her swimsuit and dropped a kiss on her breast. She'd pulled away, for it had tickled her, but when she had readjusted her clothing she had looked up right into Jasper's dark gaze. Her scalp had crept and she had fought a desire to fold her arms across her chest.

'Can't we go out alone?' she asked Jet now.

'We could,' he said lazily, 'but why should we?'

'We'll have to eventually,' pointed out Aberdeen. She was leaning against him, not completely at ease. Not only was she fighting the drug-induced drowsiness, but her awareness of Jasper at the tiller. She could see his broad back, the skeleton at the feast.

No matter how often she looked away, and how hard she tried to concentrate on Jet's hands and the sensations they drew from her sun-drenched skin, her gaze kept swivelling around to Jet's twin brother. He'd finished his filming – why didn't he go away and play with it? Why didn't he go back to his gorgeous cousin Tam?

Jet had his arm around her and was idly caressing her breast inside the life-jacket. He was swaying with the *Aphrodite*'s motion, and Aberdeen couldn't seem to find the rhythm. It was a glorious summer day, but she felt jumpy and irritable; the effect of a dose of anti-nausea drugs and the human irritant, the sharp-edged pebble in her shoe of content. Jasper's shoulders flexed as he adjusted their course. The yacht swung into the breeze, and Jasper swung with it, gracefully partnering *Aphrodite* in her dance. Jet's body adjusted against hers as he, too, mirrored the movement of wind, tide and sail.

'How do you two *do* it?' she asked, following her train of thought.

'Do what?' asked Jet, not unreasonably.

'Keep your balance so well.'

'It's easy,' he said. 'Let your body do what it wants, find its own rhythm. Just as you do when you're dancing or swimming or having sex.' He squeezed her breast gently, and pressed her down towards the deck.

'Or riding a horse,' said Jasper without turning.

Aberdeen tried to sit up, 'I still can't swim,' she said. 'Will you teach me, Jet, before we go?'

He grinned. 'You didn't learn at school?'

'No. They gave up on me, but now I've got a reason to learn. If I ever fall off this boat, I want to be able to swim, not just float and wait to be rescued.'

'Want the first lesson now?' He gathered her up and carried her to the rail. 'Shall I toss you over the side and jump in after?'

She forced herself to laugh. 'I want to learn to swim, not drown.'

'You wouldn't drown. Not in a life-preserver.'

She clung to his shoulders, protesting. 'Put me down, you brute.'

'*Oh*, no! This is too good a chance to miss!'

He lifted her a little higher, and she began to struggle. His grasp slackened so she slid to land staggering on the deck, clutching at him for balance.

'Make up your mind!' Jet laughed and heaved her over his shoulder in a fireman's lift. 'A – one, and a – two . . .' He was swinging around, gathering momentum.

Aberdeen screamed, although she hardly had the breath, and squirmed frantically to free herself. The life-jacket was riding up, her bare legs felt ridiculously vulnerable.

'*Over* you go,' said Jet with relish, and swung again.

'Cut it out,' said Jasper's voice. 'Bloody well put her down.' The sound of it acted like a slap to Aberdeen. She stopped struggling and hung there helplessly, her head pounding as the blood rushed down at an unfamiliar angle.

Jet put her down, then grinned at Jasper. 'Come off it, Jas – we were only having fun.'

'That kind of *fun* can have dangerous consequences.'

Jet reached for Aberdeen again, but she backed away. 'I'll go below and . . .' She allowed her voice to trail off as she crept down to the little cabin where she crouched on the bench and tried to keep from shaking. If only she wasn't so damned sleepy . . . and so damned frustrated . . . she might have turned it aside with a joke.

Normally she enjoyed Jet's fun and games, but now he simply stirred her up and left her dangling . . . kisses and touches in plenty but never any time alone. Stirred her up – He might have been showing off to Jasper, but that was mad. He wasn't eighteen, and neither was she.

Jasper steered in silence for a while. When Aberdeen didn't reappear, he turned to Jet. 'What was that meant to prove?'

Jet's eyes danced. 'I was having fun with my girl.'

'*You* were having fun,' said Jasper roughly.

'Are you implying she wasn't?'

'Of course she wasn't. She was trying to get away.'

'So? You didn't see where I had my hand!'

'You should have put her down.'

'I did,' said Jet. He gave Jasper a muscle-numbing buffet on the arm. 'Right on her pretty little feet.'

'You're not fit to be let loose,' said Jasper, rubbing his arm. 'You know better than to mess about at sea! What if you'd lost your grip and let her fall?'

'I'd have jumped in after her, and you'd have turned back to fetch us.'

'That would have been wonderful, trying to get a hysterical non-swimmer on board.'

'Hysterical? Aberdeen?' Jet hooted. 'She's the coolest thing on two legs!'

'She's sick and she's scared and up to her eyeballs on antihistamines,' corrected Jasper. 'She's a disaster waiting to happen, and if you go on pushing her like this, it'll happen that much sooner.'

'I love it!' laughed Jet. 'My brother all self-righteous over the way I treat my fiancée! And what do you mean, sick and scared? She's not been sick since she got those pills, and what has she to be scared about? *Aphrodite* has all the safety gear. Hell, I've even had you along as an extra precaution! I don't invite you for your pretty face.'

'She's sick and she's scared,' repeated Jasper. 'She can't swim, she can't sail, she can't handle the calmest seas without swallowing half the flaming chemist's shop. She can't even handle your so-called *fun*. As for the way you were mauling her – Lord! Have a bit of respect!'

'I didn't see you turning down a peep this morning,' said Jet. 'Your tongue was fairly hanging out, you poor old sod.' He patted Jasper's shoulder. 'You can look all you like, bro, but keep your hands to yourself. I'd have

101

shared *Fraulein* Grete with you – hell, she was all for it – but Aberdeen's all mine.'

'What do you want with her?'

'She's bright and biddable,' drawled Jet. 'And remember what old Ben Franklin said? About marrying an older woman?'

' "*She's so grateful*"? But Aberdeen isn't older.'

'No – but she's grateful, all the same. And as for safety on board – just don't forget who's the skipper here. Your sailing's about on a par with your sense of humour. Go back to your island and lord it over the seagulls.'

Jasper's hands curled into fists.

'Tell me something,' said Jet.

'What?'

'There was a weird thing you used to be able to do, years ago.'

Jasper's thumbs pricked, but he forced a noncommittal reply. 'There were several things I used to be able to do. Like eat an entire cream cake.'

'You know the thing I mean . . .' Jet let the sentence trail off while Jasper's mind slid back. 'We used to practise that mind-reading act,' said Jet. 'We thought we'd make millions on the stage: out-Copperfield David, out-Geller Yuri.'

'We couldn't get it to work,' said Jasper.

'There was something you *could* do, though,' said Jet. 'You couldn't read minds, but you *could* pick up something from me – or so you said.'

'Oh, that.'

'Oh, that,' mocked Jet. 'I used to leave the room and suck one of those fruit jellies. You'd know the flavour as soon as I got it in my mouth.'

'So?' said Jasper.

'You said you could taste it somehow. Can you still do that?'

'I don't know,' said Jasper. 'Probably I never could. Maybe I got to recognize the smells or something.'

'Through closed doors? I doubt it. But if you could still tune in on that, you might tune in on other things.' He beamed. 'She's got soft hair, hasn't she? And that spot I kissed this morning is softer still.'

Jasper looked wonderingly at his brother. 'Sometimes I suspect you're seriously warped,' he said. 'Sometimes I bloody well know it.'

'Can you?' Jet persisted. 'Can you tune in on things like that?'

'I have no idea. I haven't tried. I wouldn't try.' Jasper glanced at the head of companionway. 'Aberdeen's been down there a long time,' he observed. 'You should see if she's OK, instead of pulling my chain. One of these days . . .'

'You'll knock me down?'

'One of these days you'll pull the wrong chain and someone will knock you down. Not necessarily me.'

Jet nodded, then gave his brother a gleaming, foxy smile. 'One of these days. But not today, *mein bruder*. Today I am going down, as bidden, to check on Aberdeen's health. I may be gone some time.'

Jasper gave his attention to the tiller, and blessed his poker face.

The *Aphrodite* danced with the waves and the keen sea breeze blew into his face. He was not the seaman Jet was, but still he loved the freedom and the beauty of it all. Loved it as an occasional experience. Could he settle for loving a woman in the same fashion? Perhaps – but he'd be better off out of it, for anything he said to Jet would simply make things worse.

He forced his mind away and began to think of his island. Allirra Island, gleaming in the sun. He should go there soon and let its peace wash over him, and hope he might be healed.

Aberdeen was immeasurably relieved when Jet told her Jasper was returning to Sydney. Kate was out shopping, but she had asked Aberdeen to take delivery of a package she was expecting.

Aberdeen had waited for the courier, then given up and washed her hair. 'He's bound to show as soon as I get a lather up,' she muttered, but she was able to shampoo and rinse in relative peace. The sun and salt of sailing had dried her skin and hair, so she smoothed on lip-balm and used a conditioning mousse. Rather than subject the result to the hair-drier, she went out into the garden so her hair could dry in the breeze. Jet found her there and told her the welcome news.

It was a glorious day and, after his arrival, the sun seemed warmer and the sky more sweetly blue. Bees worked among the blossoms in Kate's garden, too drunk with nectar and flowery scents to bother with Aberdeen and Jet.

'I suppose he's got work to do on that film.' Aberdeen tried to hide her relief.

'And you're a fully fledged crewperson now.' Jet gave her a curls a tweak. 'Next step – the ocean highway!'

'Next step, the wedding,' corrected Aberdeen. 'We have to give notice of intention at least a month beforehand, and send out invitations and do something about the flats . . .'

'A mate's been caretaking mine, he might stay on.'

'Then we'll have to have passports and inoculations,

and check-ups and buy stores and I've *still* got to learn to swim! Oh, and I suppose we should have wills. We have less than six weeks and we'll never be ready in time!'

'I've got a passport,' said Jet. 'Haven't you?'

Of course he had a passport. Many Australians never had either the cause or the chance to leave their own country, but Jet Diamond must have travelled extensively from childhood. The ocean was his highway, the seas his country lanes. She felt her smile becoming fixed. 'I never actually applied,' she said. 'I was going to Europe in June, but of course, it all fell through.' She scanned his face for pity, for the slight derision she had sometimes seen in other much-travelled acquaintances. 'I must seem very parochial.'

Jet put his arms around her, then nibbled her lips gently. 'Mmm,' he murmured, 'what is that stuff?'

'Lip-balm,' she said.

Jet's tongue touched her bottom lip. 'It tastes just like strawberry jelly.'

'Stay for lunch?' suggested Aberdeen. 'Kate's out, and I'll make us an omelette and salad.'

'Let's go out instead. What about the Van Diemen? Or maybe I'll just eat you.'

'I'm waiting for a package. We could go out afterwards, but wouldn't it be nice to have some time to ourselves? We need to sort out the wedding and a date to go back to Sydney. Shall I fly up or do you want me to crew the *Aphrodite*?'

'Of course I want you to crew,' said Jet. 'I have a few things to do this morning, so I'll get cracking and pick you up later this afternoon. We'll talk it over then.'

'Fine,' she said. 'I wish I could come now, but this package is from a nursery . . .'

'My *God*,' said Jet. 'You don't mean – you're not . . .?'

'Oh, yes, I'm having triplets, due tomorrow! A plant nursery, darling! That's why someone has to be here, to put it in the shade.'

Jet went away, and Aberdeen sat down. She wished he could have stayed, for the cottage garden was private and sheltered. It would have been nice to make a meal for Jet, nice and ironic too, for hadn't women had to struggle to free themselves from the image of cooks and home-makers? Yet here was she wanting no more than to make a cosy nest . . .

The thought dismayed her, so she reached into her mind and captured her ambitions. The terrace in Glebe – or another one like it. With the rooms set out according to her aborted plans. The best equipment and the time to conserve things properly. Replica costumes. *That* was the answer to the revenue-versus-conservation dilemma that had plagued her department at Pitt Gallery. She would make modern replicas of all the important garments, two of each; one for display alongside the original and another, with more robust seams and a slightly more generous cut, for hiring out. It would mean a large initial outlay, but would bring in more money in the end. She would do it *right*.

The desire to make it all happen was still very much within her, so this other nesting instinct must exist concurrently. she wanted to have it all and she *could* have it all, thanks to Jet.

She lay down in the shade of Kate's apple tree and tucked her hands under her head. The ground was cool and blessedly still, and her head was clear. In a couple of days it would start, the hustle and hassle that

106

accompanied the quietest wedding, but for now she could rest until Kate's package came. Rest and dream of an optimistic future.

'Someone up there still likes me,' she murmured.

Footsteps made her open her eyes, to look up the length of legs to battered cut-offs and a shirt that had once been brown, but had faded to a kind of coppery cream. Even with the face in shadow she knew it wasn't Jet.

'What the heck are you doing here?' She sat up with a jerk. 'Jet said you'd gone to Sydney.'

'I leave tonight. May I sit down?'

'I suppose you want Kate,' she said.

'I had morning tea with Kate at the Cat and Fiddle Arcade.'

'If you're looking for Jet, you've missed him.'

'I've been with Jet every day this week and spent every night worrying my guts out in that dashed suite of my uncle's. I came to see you, Aberdeen.'

Damn, she thought. 'I can't imagine what for,' she said aloud.

He looked into her eyes and she flinched. She was as familiar with Jet's laughing eyes as with her own in the mirror; meeting Jasper's gaze made a nonsense of familiarity.

'You mean that, don't you?' he said with evident surprise. 'You really can't imagine why I came to visit you. May I sit down?'

'If you must,' she said ungraciously.

He folded economically to sit with his arms around his bent knees, quite unlike Jet's expansive sprawl.

'Does Jet know you're here?' she asked.

'Not this time, but you'll tell him, since you tell him everything else. Or at least, you think you do.'

'So?' She licked her lips, tasting the strawberry lip-balm, reapplied. 'What do you want, Jasper?'

'I want to talk to you. It's no use talking to Jet. His main ambition is to wind me up, as always. But what do *you* want, Aberdeen?'

'I want you to go away.'

'That's letting me have it straight from the hip!' he said after a moment.

She shivered, and concealed it with a shrug. 'I'm sorry if you're offended, but you asked.'

'I exposed my jugular,' he corrected, 'and you went straight for it. Why, exactly?'

'Why?' She was nonplussed.

'It's a simple question, Aberdeen, or rather, it's two simple questions. *Why* do you want to marry Jet? And *why* do you want me to go away? If looks could kill, I'd have been six feet under the night we met. You dislike me thoroughly, but I don't know *why*. Surely you're too much of a gentleman to hold that first unfortunate impression against me?'

'Let's put it this way,' she said. 'If someone gave me a genie lamp, and I could rub it and have a wish, I'd ask it to send you to Timbuktu on a very slow yak.'

'Ouch,' he said. 'But *why*?'

He put his hand on her arm and Aberdeen stood up abruptly. 'Please go now,' she said.

'You won't answer my questions?'

'I'll answer one of them! I want you to go away because I think you mean to make trouble for us. For Jet and me.'

'Of course I do,' he said.

CHAPTER 7

Aberdeen gaped at him. 'You admit it?'

'I've never denied it.' He reached up a hand. 'Won't you sit down again, Abbie? I'm going to get a crick in my neck. I'll keep my hands to myself.'

'You bet you will. Why not just stand up?'

'That would imply that I'm leaving the field,' he said grimly. 'And since I have no such intention, I'm sitting put.'

'You're a pig.'

'That's too much. If I'm a pig, so is Jet. It stands to reason, since we're twins.'

'You're a changeling, then,' said Aberdeen flatly. 'If I tossed you on the fire you'd fly up the chimney.' She turned away.

'Where are you off to?'

'I'm going into the house. I can't make you leave, but I can go myself. I don't want to see you. I don't want to talk to you any more.'

'What are you afraid of, Aberdeen?'

'I'm afraid of what you might do,' she said. 'You're trouble; you admit it. And besides, you bother me. You look too much like Jet.'

'And you find that threatening. Odd. I never had you tagged for a coward.'

'You had me tagged for a fool, a snare and an easy pick-up.' She rounded on him. 'You simply don't want me to marry Jet.' It wasn't a question, she was quite sure of her ground.

'Got it in one,' he said.

'You're unbelievable!' She sat down again. 'What is it with you, Jasper Diamond – jealousy? Snobbery? Or just plain evil?'

'I've been asking myself that,' he said soberly. 'Have you asked yourself the same question?'

'Zounds!' said Aberdeen. 'You're the sort who'd expect a convicted criminal to build her own gibbet! I suppose you want me to give you a good excuse for trying to get rid of me.'

'Just tell me the way you see it,' he said. 'Why wouldn't I want you to marry Jet? This is important to me.'

'Then you're a blasted egotist,' she said. 'Me, me, me. What you think or want doesn't really matter to me. It's not as if you and Jet live in one another's pockets! You move in different circles, so you say. You hang round studios and islands; he sails yachts and goes to restaurants.'

'Egotists don't question their motives,' Jasper pointed out.

'Don't be so damned reasonable! An egotist might ask questions, if it were the only way he could keep the world revolving on his axis,' muttered Aberdeen. 'I suppose you're jealous of anyone Jet might love. As you said – you're twins, so you must have been closer than most brothers once. Either you can't bear to share his attention with anyone, or else you lean the other way and can't bear it when someone gives him more attention than they give you. You're a nasty little boy who never grew up, in fact.' She paused, but he didn't respond. 'Lord, this is a surreal conversation!' she added. 'I can't believe I'm sitting here talking to you. It's like a psych tutorial.'

'Interesting conclusions, but wrong,' he said quietly. 'Jet has always had plenty of friends, and I'm not very fond of attention.'

'Then *I'm* your objection. You think I'm not good enough for your precious family! I can see your point, if you're interested. I'm not a wonderful bargain for a family that goes in for dynastic marriages. I'm out of work, and there's not much going in my field. But I've pointed all that out to Jet already, and he claims to be satisfied with what he's getting.'

'So he bloody well ought to be satisfied,' he said coolly. 'Good enough? I think you're much *too* good for Jet.'

Aberdeen felt rage, scalding, clarifying rage, building up in her. 'Bullshit!' she screamed at him, suddenly. 'Don't forget – I've heard this sort of rubbish before!'

Jasper stared at her.

'You're just bloody Cooper all over again! Brian Cooper from the Pitt Gallery!' she hissed. ' "*You're too good at your job, Ms Shawcross*".' Savagely, she imitated Cooper's voice and phrasing, then boiled over into her own. 'Too competent! Too honest! Over-dashed-conscientious!' She broke off short, her chest heaving as she fought for air. 'I was too good at my job, so they took it away from me, and not only my job, but my chance of learning more! They let me make plans, arrange my tickets for the trip, pay a deposit on a venue, then they jerked the rug right out from under me. Jet gave my future back to me, and now you come sneaking behind Jet's back, trying to pull the same filthy trick again!'

'I don't know what you mean,' he said. 'What's this about the Pitt Gallery?'

'Never you mind. Just get out of my sight, Jasper Diamond! If Jet thinks I'm good enough, if Jet wants me around him, then what the heck does it have to do with you?'

'Aberdeen, Abbie – listen a minute. You're over-wrought.'

'Get out!' she screamed at him. 'I've seen the way you stare when Jet and I are together! You try to put me off, try to embarrass me. You won't give it up, will you? You'd do anything to push a wedge between us! Anything at all!'

He was still staring at her, his eyes seeming to probe hers.

'Not quite anything,' he said, and gave her his crooked unexpected grin. 'I'd draw the line at murdering Jet. Fratricide's a crime.'

'This isn't funny!'

'No, and you're right about one thing, Aberdeen. I won't give up. I thought I should, but I've thought again. I'll leave you now, since you really don't want me to stay, but I won't give up on convincing you.' He held out his hand, palm upwards. 'Goodbye, Aberdeen. I'll be seeing you in Sydney.'

He expected her to shake hands with him now?

'Of course, it's up to the woman to offer her hand,' he said, as if he had read her mind.

'*If* she chooses. And I don't choose to offer.'

'Then I'll choose for you.' He took two rapid steps

112

towards her and caught her right hand, holding it firmly when she would have pulled away. 'I'll be seeing you very soon, Aberdeen,' he said, and to her sensitized ears it sounded like a threat. He bent and kissed her fingers then let her go and backed away.

A red mist seemed to be rising in front of her and she spun round and ran up the path and into the cottage, locking the back door behind her. Her chest heaved with uneven breaths and her heartbeats were pounding in her ears. Just let him try to follow her now! She'd call the police, she'd scream for Neighbourhood Watch.

But Jasper didn't follow her. Instead, he walked back the way he had come.

Aberdeen flung herself on her bed and cried with rage and hurt. By the time she had finished, she had a thumping headache and aching, watery eyes. Her freshly washed hair was clinging to her cheeks.

'Whoever said crying made you feel better had rocks in his head,' she muttered as she splashed water over her face.

A knock brought her belligerently into the kitchen, but when she flung open the door, she found herself facing a middle-aged delivery man. 'Kate Shawcross?'

'I'm her daughter.'

He fetched a long black-swathed package which he dumped in Aberdeen's arms. 'Sign here please,' he said.

Aberdeen juggled the package into her left arm and signed the delivery docket. She hadn't a hand free for a handkerchief, so she sniffed, hard. Her eyes felt hot and puffy.

'Lot of flu about,' said the man.

'Is that what you call it?' she said. 'I call it a lot of Jasper.'

113

The man gave her a funny look and retreated to his van. Aberdeen stared malevolently at the package. 'If it hadn't been for *you*, I wouldn't have had a close encounter of the worst kind.'

Kate came back eventually, her hair cut short and styled. Typically, she made no comment on Aberdeen's flushed, damp face, but she did ask after her package.

'It's in the shed,' said Aberdeen morosely.

'Jet not here?'

'He's coming this afternoon.' Aberdeen sniffed. 'Bloody Jasper was here.'

'I suppose he called to say goodbye.'

'He came to make trouble, as usual.'

Kate switched on the kettle.

'He came right out and said so! Kate, the man's incredible! No ifs and buts or veiled hints for Jasper Diamond. He doesn't want me to marry Jet, he says.'

'I knew that already,' said Kate.

'He *told* you?'

'No. It's obvious.'

'I told *him* where to get off, and he had the cheek to say I was overwrought!'

'So you are,' said Kate calmly. 'Look what you're doing to that skirt.'

Aberdeen glanced down and found her fingers clenched in the soft blue fabric. 'Damn!' she said. 'If I am, it's his fault. I was enjoying the peace and quiet before he came.'

'It's understandable,' said Kate. 'You've lost your job and trip, and got engaged and planned a voyage, all in a very brief time. Your life's spun round on its axis. If you switch from one track to another you're bound to feel the jolt.'

114

'I can handle that,' said Aberdeen. 'I can't handle Jasper. He's going to ruin everything if he can, and I simply don't know why. None of the ordinary reasons seem to apply. He even tried the old chestnut about my being too good for Jet – I mean, that's so *likely*, isn't it?'

'At least you've been forewarned,' said Kate. She looked closely at Aberdeen. 'You *have* considered that he's in love with you himself?'

'Naturally!' said Aberdeen crossly. 'I'm neither stupid nor naïve. But he isn't in love with me, no matter what he pretends. Or if he is, it's only part of this idiotic game they play. There's a sort of rivalry – they even seem to score game points. Jet stole Jasper's girlfriend Grete . . .' She caught Kate's ironic gaze and broke off with a laugh. 'OK, I'll retract that statement in the light of your known feelings. Girlfriends can't be stolen. Check! What I mean is that this girl Grete was going out with Jasper and then she decided she liked Jet better. They went out for a while, then things went sour. Jasper was really wild when she left him for Jet.'

'Who told you that?' asked Kate.

'Jet did. He never makes any secret about things like that. It's not very admirable, but at least he's honest.' She sighed. 'He admits he set out to charm this Grete, partly to score over Jasper, so Jasper wants to get back at him over that. Why are men so darned childish?'

'Man loves to be the hunter,' said Kate. 'We understood it in my day.'

'*Your* day! Anyone'd think you were out of the Ark!'

'You won't be seeing much of Jasper once you're off on your trip,' observed Kate.

'No, thank God. With luck he'll find someone else to hassle while we're gone.'

'In *my* day,' said Kate with a sidelong smile, 'it was considered something of a coup to have two men on a string. It gave some girls a feeling of power; perhaps the only taste of power they'd ever have.'

'I don't want power. I don't want to grab and get. I just want to accept what I'm offered, keep what I have.' She turned to Kate. 'Do you think I'm mercenary? I didn't ask Jet to marry me. I didn't ask him to take me to Europe, or to finance my museum. It's all his own idea.'

Kate touched her cheek in a rare gesture of affection. 'What I think doesn't matter,' she said. 'It's what you think and what Jet thinks. What *does* Jet think, by the way?'

'Jet thinks he's getting a pretty good bargain.'

'Then *I* think Jet's got better sense than I thought.'

'Oh, Kate,' said Aberdeen. 'Things have moved so fast; I don't know where I'd have been if it hadn't been for you.'

'I haven't done anything to help you,' said Kate.

'No, but you've given me moral support and helped me to help myself. I won't forget it.'

'That's what mothers are for, or so I always understood,' said Kate.

Aberdeen relaxed once Jasper had gone, but she hardly had time to enjoy his absence. She and Jet went out sailing twice more, then Jet announced it was time to take *Aphrodite* back to New South Wales. 'It will make a good practice run for us,' he said cheerfully.

Aberdeen was far more nervous than she liked, especially when she thought about Bass Strait's reputation. Luckily, all went well. The weather held, the trip took four days, and Aberdeen was kept too busy to

116

worry about her next meeting with Jasper. The anti-nausea pills kept her upright and functioning, but they also made her feel a little distant and depressed. Since they slept aboard *Aphrodite*, she had to take them heel and toe, and after a time she could scarcely remember whether she had taken the doses or not. Jet was cheerful and would have been romantic, but for all her longing to spend time alone with him, Aberdeen couldn't relax.

'It's those darned pills,' she said, when Jet's kisses failed to move her to enthusiasm. 'They keep me damped right down.'

'Anti-aphrodisiac,' he said. 'You'll have to learn to do without them.'

She was aching with tension by the time they docked at Gipsy Quay, but Jet seemed pleased with her crewing performance. 'You can learn to sail in a weekend, but you keep on perfecting the art for the rest of your life,' he said.

Aberdeen smiled, but she was more interested in getting a good night's sleep before beginning preparations for the wedding.

'You can't organize a big wedding in just a few weeks,' she said to Jet as they settled the *Aphrodite* in her berth. 'Not to speak of the cost! We'll have to keep it very small.'

'Don't worry about the cost,' said Jet, 'I'll take care of that. And what's to organize, really? A dress, a celebrant and a cake, and party, party, party!'

She was touched by his generosity, but she thought he was understating the organization. It would be so much less daunting, she decided, if they could simply sail away and get married somewhere later.

'Not so simple really,' said Jet. 'It mightn't be legal

117

once we got back to Australia and then we'd have to do it all over again!' He laughed at her expression. 'Now don't fuss! One of the things I like most about you is that you don't go on and on about things. Now, there's still a fair bit left of the day, so why don't we hit the . . .?'

Whatever he would have said was cut off in a shout of welcome as a group of three young men hailed him from the deck of another yacht. 'Jet – Jet Diamond! What's all this about you looking for a new crew?'

'No idea!' he called back, his arm round Aberdeen.

'Nick's still crook – ' said one. 'You're never sailing alone.'

'I have a replacement here. Aberdeen, these are three of the worst yachties this side of Bass Strait . . . Drew, Scott and Chick. Don't say you haven't been warned. Guys, this is Aberdeen.'

'Hello,' said Aberdeen, but it seemed the conversation wasn't over yet. The three came swarming over to the *Aphrodite* and began dissecting the Sydney-Hobart race with Jet, casting sidelong glances at her but making no real effort to include her in the conversation until they had extracted all the crumbs from Jet.

'Help!' she mouthed, but Jet just pulled a comical face of apology and winked at her.

He led two of the men off to see something he had done to the mast, but the third one lingered. 'Done much sailing, Abigail?'

'Not a lot,' said Aberdeen.

'You must have other talents, then. You know the old Jetman well?'

'We're getting married at Easter.'

The man – she thought it was Scott – did a stagey double-take. 'Whew! You *must* have pulled a swift one!'

118

'Have you got a wife?' asked Aberdeen.

'Who, me?'

'Then you've made some woman very lucky.'

She was still watching him work that out when Jet came back from the bows. 'What's this I hear about a new keel design you want backing, Chick? Shades of the old America's Cup!'

'It's all perfectly legal,' said Chick earnestly. 'According to Des Lake . . .'

'Who's a fine bloody authority . . .'

'Come and have a look at the specs,' urged Drew. 'It'll be a top investment, I promise you.'

Jet laughed. 'I've got things to do, and people to see,' he said. 'Catch you later.'

'Down at the pub,' suggested Chick. 'Bring your old lady – might get Binnie off my back if there's another woman along.'

'Not today,' said Jet.

'Who on earth were they?' asked Aberdeen, when the three had finally left the *Aphrodite*.

'Just some blokes with big ideas and big egos, little brains and little business sense.'

'I thought they were your friends.'

'So do they. What would you like to do this afternoon?'

Sleep, thought Aberdeen. 'I suppose I ought to go to my flat,' she said. 'See about cancelling the lease and so on.'

She hoped he might suggest something more romantic, but he nodded agreeably. 'You do that, then we'll meet up at the Mizzen Mast at nine. That suit you, Lorelei?'

'Hold on,' she said, a little bemused. 'Where and what is the Mizzen Mast?'

'A place near Darling Harbour where all the yachties go – I'll see you there, OK?'

'OK,' she said.

Perhaps Jet detected a lack of enthusiasm in her voice, for he squeezed her hand and gave her a kiss and special smile. 'Not long now, and we'll be away on our own, just you and me and the Lady *Aphrodite*.'

'Are your friends going to be at the Mizzen Mast?'

'That lot? Doubt it. Bound to see some others, though.' Jet grinned at her. 'I want to show you off! Now, I'm going to sort things out with my mate who's been looking after my flat. Why don't you take a taxi back to your place?'

Aberdeen opened her mouth to protest against the expense, but Jet had already flagged down a Blue Cab and pressed a twenty-dollar note into her hand. 'See you soon, Lorelei,' he said, and pressed his forefinger to his lips and then to hers. 'Nine o'clock.'

Aberdeen got into the taxi, acutely conscious of her salt-stiff hair and rather grubby shirt. She had a small bag with her; the rest of her belongings had been sent by air and were, she trusted, waiting at her flat.

'Wentworth Street in Blaxland,' she said to the taxi driver. 'Number 44a.'

Sydney washed over her as the taxi made its way through the streets. The weather was both hotter and more humid than it had been in Tasmania, and the street crowds of Sydney were subtly different. The dress was a little more casual, the ethnic composition much more varied; Aberdeen was perspiring when the taxi drew up, and after she had paid the driver and let herself in to the foyer of 44a she fanned herself as she climbed the stairs to her flat.

It was stale and musty, so she dragged up the

windows and chocked them with bits of wood. Number 44a wasn't historic, it was just plain old. There wasn't much in the pantry, but she made herself some tea before showering and changing into light-weight summer pants and a pale amber shirt that picked up the glints in her newly conditioned hair. Clothes that Jet had never seen.

How odd! He knew only her Tasmanian wardrobe, her staying-with-Kate persona. He knew none of her friends, none of her former workmates, had never known how she had conducted her life while working at Pitt Gallery. He featured in the gossip columns, which she never read, and she went to plays and galleries which he would never frequent. He was wealthy and self-assured, she was poor and had little but her tenacious spirit to her name. And yet – they had come together. Just like Cinderella, thought Aberdeen. And Kate, with her invitation to stay in Hobart, was the fairy godmother.

Aberdeen sat down to make some notes, beginning with arrangements for her flat, and continuing with preparations for the wedding and the trip. Reception venue. Invitations. Passport. Inoculations . . . the list went on. Within half an hour, it covered three whole pages, and Aberdeen simply stared at it, then dropped her head in her hands, laughing until the tears started from her eyes.

'This is utterly impossible,' she said aloud. 'All this in a matter of weeks? Just what in heck do you think you're doing, Shawcross?'

Panicking, came the answer. She was panicking. And for what?

She picked up the paper and went through it meticulously, dividing the entries into order of urgency. As she worked, her panic subsided. She was efficient. She was good at organizing. So! She'd organize this wedding and Jet could deal with the trip. Why should she try to do a job he would do by second nature?

The timeframe still seemed too tight, but they could easily postpone their departure. It would work out much better all around. Jet had planned originally to sail just after New Year. Nick Green had had his accident, and Jet had added twelve weeks to allow for the broken leg to mend. That schedule no longer stood, so what had been postponed once could be postponed again.

Now to sort out her lease. Her landlord lived on the ground floor, and seldom bothered his tenants at all except to collect his rent. One thing he *did* keep track of was the visitors who came and went. Unless they possessed a pass-key, no one entered Number 44a without Ed Peters' knowledge. That could be irritating, but it did help with security.

Aberdeen knocked on his door to give her notice. He insisted on a month, neither more nor less, which left her with an awkward five-day hiatus between the end of the lease and the date they had picked for the wedding. 'End of March is a bad time for getting new tenants,' he stated. 'I ought to insist on three months, really. It's only a month as a favour to them that gets transferred in a hurry and don't want to forfeit their bond.'

They eyed one another without friendship, each weighing the worth of continuing the argument. Aberdeen disliked being manipulated, but she supposed he had the law on his side. 'All right,' she said. 'But I want the bond back now. I could use the money.'

He jerked his head for her to enter, and began the paperwork. 'You got a transfer, then?' he asked.

'I'm going to be married.'

'That accountant chap?' He sounded surprised, as if she had risen in his estimation.

'I'm marrying Jet Diamond.'

'Diamond. Not the one on the telly? The chap who does *In the Rough*?'

She frowned. 'That's Jasper Diamond. I'm engaged to *Jet*. His brother.'

Now his face came up in real astonishment, and she added impishly, 'He's a wealthy playboy. Heir to the Hidden Treasure motel chain. He's taking me overseas on a cruising honeymoon.'

His pale eyes narrowed, and he half-reached out to reclaim the contract.

'It's quite true,' she said. 'The engagement notice will be in the newspaper.'

She left him staring as if he'd seen a ghost, or a Cinderella, and escaped to her soon-to-be-former flat. Hers for a month, and then she was out. Five days short of the wedding. She would simply have to move in with Jet or, if he had decided to dispose of *his* flat, they would find something else. Jet would organize that, and for him, money wouldn't be a problem. Yet even Jet had chosen to put up free at the Ruby suite rather than pay out for a place that would have had a more comfortable ambience.

She pondered that for a moment. Inherited wealth was an odd concept to the average Australian, and one with which Aberdeen still wasn't entirely comfortable. Jet never appeared to want for anything, but neither did he ever waste money.

Taking up the pad and pen again, Aberdeen began to

123

survey her belongings. A clean sweep would be best, she concluded, and felt the stirring of positive excitement. After years of walking a predictable path, Aberdeen Shawcross had taken a step away from the trodden route. And soon, she would be making a complete right-angled turn into the life of Aberdeen Diamond. Perhaps it was fitting that she should dispose of all this baggage and begin her new life without encumbrance.

She was still in this uplifted mood when she heard a tap on the door. This was unusual, for Ed Peters invariably intercepted any guest and often buzzed to make sure she was at home. Not for her sake, either, but for the sake of his insurance and reputation. It must be one of her friends, someone he knew.

She opened the door and stared with outrage at Jasper Diamond. 'What the hell are you doing here? How did you get in past Mr Peters?'

'He recognized me,' said Jasper. 'He watches *In the Rough*.'

'Go away,' said Aberdeen.

'I said I'd be seeing you in Sydney, Aberdeen.'

'So you've seen me. I haven't changed. Go away.'

'I've brought you a letter,' he said. 'Our cousin Tam wants to say hello.'

He made no move to give her the letter, so she put out her hand. That was a mistake, for he took it in his and stepped over the threshold. He closed the door and looked down at her intently.

'You look tired,' he said.

She pulled free of his grasp as if he'd burnt her. 'I am tired. I've been stuck on a yacht for four days! Go away, Jasper. I didn't invite you in.'

'You'll be stuck on a yacht, as you so illuminatingly

124

put it, for a lot more than four days if you marry Jet. This is only the first trip, for you, but I'd better warn you, he'll be off and away on *Aphrodite* every chance he gets. He's footloose, and his major problem is mustering a suitable crew. Or it has been until now.'

'Now he has me,' she said. 'I'm looking forward to it.'

He shook his head. 'Abbie, I believe that's the first deliberate lie you've ever told me.'

'I *am* looking forward to the trip. To parts of it, anyway. Who wouldn't be? And please don't call me Abbie.'

'I'm damned if I'll call you "Lorelei".'

'I wouldn't want you to! That's Jet's name for me. You can call me Aberdeen – if you insist on calling me anything at all.'

'The original Lorelei was a German water witch,' he said. 'She sang sailors to their doom, like the sirens that nearly did for Odysseus.'

'I'm not singing anyone to his doom, if that's what you're implying! I'm not trapping anybody, either.'

'Not intentionally, I'm sure. *Do* you sing?'

'Only in the shower.'

'As for who wouldn't look forward to months on end spent on a yacht in the ocean – I can tell you that. Anyone who gets seasick on a dead calm day.'

'I don't get sick any more.'

'So long as you take those pills, perhaps, but that's no way to live. I've seen what they do to you.'

'Oh, yes?'

'They quench your light and muffle your reactions. They iron out your personality. You're so low when you've taken them you can scarcely even snap at me, let alone go for the jugular in your usual way.'

'It's worth it,' she said. 'It'll be worth it to be with Jet. And don't you think I want to see the world? I was all set to head out to Europe before I lost my job at the gallery, so this is the chance of a lifetime!'

'Unless you're a mad-keen yachtie, it's a darned uncomfortable way of seeing the world,' he said.

'So. Maybe I'll become a mad-keen yachtie.'

'I think it has to be in-born. Jet and I started sailing together; he got addicted, I didn't. You didn't either.'

'How the heck do you know?'

'You don't light up when you think of it, that's how.' He shook his head. 'You'll see tropical rainstorms like you wouldn't believe. You'll spend days and nights on end being soaked to the bone, and your beautiful face will end up like sharkskin. Think again, Aberdeen. If you want to see the world, ask Jet to take you on a nice package cruise.'

'He'd hate that,' she said unguardedly.

'You'll hate this even more by the third week out. I guarantee it.'

'Listen,' she said. 'I'm going to see the great museums, to learn more about their methods than I could ever get from books. I've been in touch with so many conservators, and they've all been welcoming.'

'You're going to see teeming harbours and more salt water than you'll ever want to see again.'

'I was planning to go to Europe anyway.'

'By plane,' he cut in. 'The most direct flight you could get. Weren't you?'

'That was because I could only get a month off from my job. It made sense to maximise the time I could spend rather than have it taken up in –'

'Travelling,' he said. 'You simply haven't thought this through, have you, Aberdeen?'

'I have.'

'Get this straight. You're not going to have the trip you planned, not ever. Not with Jet along.'

'Of course I'm not!' she exploded. 'I never thought I was! This is something entirely different, entirely new and better! I get to see the people and things I wanted and I also see a whole lot more as a bonus. Plus, I see it all with Jet for company. Jet makes everything fun.'

'You're really set on this, then.'

'You can bet your doublet and hose I am.'

Jasper thrust his hand through his hair. 'What you really want is to see museums and other things connected with your own line of work. Right? So what if I offer to make you a present of the trip you really want? A month in Europe, doing the rounds of the museums with some friendly costumier or curator as your guide?'

Aberdeen's brows drew together. 'Why the heck would you want to do that?'

'What would you say if I did?'

She smiled and held out her hand. After a moment, he took it, gazing down at her. 'What would I say?' she asked lightly, suppressing a shiver. 'I'd say thank you very much, sir.' She dropped a little curtsy. 'And *then* I'd tell you where to stick it.'

'You would, wouldn't you?' he said with a gleam of appreciation.

'I surely would. This girl is not for sale.'

'I wasn't trying to *buy* you.'

'Just trying to buy me off?' she said sweetly. She realized she was still holding his hand and let it go abruptly, rubbing her palms against her thighs. 'What about this letter?'

Jasper took it out of his pocket and straightened the

creases before handing it over. The envelope was warm from his body heat. 'Tam wants to say hello,' he said as she untucked the flap.

'So you said before. Don't let me keep you.'

He knuckled his forehead. 'Sorry, Miss, but I gotta wait for an answer.'

She gave him an exasperated look. 'Tam's your cousin? Your Uncle Godfrey's daughter? Why didn't she telephone me instead of writing?'

Jasper shrugged, reverting to his own persona. 'She didn't have your number. I delivered the letter by hand.'

'How did you know where to find me? Did Jet tell you? Or did Kate?'

'I got your address out of the telephone directory.'

'You *what*?'

'It was easy,' he said. 'In the National Phone Directory there are fifty-six entries for "Shawcross". Twelve are in New South Wales. There are four entries with the initial A, two of which are in New South Wales. You had to be one of those two, and since the other one is in Newcastle, it came down to A Shawcross, 44a Wentworth Street, Blaxland.'

'My word!' she said. 'It was that easy? Who needs the notorious Australia Card or the Secret Police if they, too, can have access to Detective Jasper Diamond's machiavellian methods?'

'People looking for someone whose surname is "Smith" or "Anderson" would find it impossible. Since your name is uncommon, it took me five minutes on my computer and a little elementary deduction.'

'Then why didn't you give the number to your cousin?'

'I wanted to talk to you myself.'

'Why didn't you phone?'

'You would have hung up when you heard my voice.'

She stared at him. 'You're unhinged. I mean that. You're barking mad. You've got an answer for everything.'

'Of course,' he said. 'Now read your letter.'

The letter was a short, friendly greeting, and an invitation to Aberdeen to meet the writer for lunch.

'*I don't know how you're fixed,*' it ran, '*but on Tuesday I'm having lunch at the Diamond Motel in Bondi. I'll be there around twelve if you'd care to join me.*'

'The *Diamond*?' said Aberdeen.

Jasper shrugged. 'Why not?'

'If it's anything like the Ruby . . .'

'Practically its double.'

'Tell her I'll be there,' said Aberdeen, giving in abruptly. 'And now, since you've got your answer, you can leave. I have things to do and things to organize and not much time for any of it.'

'Fools rush in, Abbie Shawcross.'

'Go away, Jasper!' she said. 'And don't come back.'

He reached behind him and opened the door, departing abruptly. She banged it shut behind him and hooked up the chain. Next time he called, he'd have to conduct his business through the gap. *Next time*. She'd told him to stay away, but there *would* be a next time. The man was a human gadfly.

Slowly, she drew her notes towards her. She ticked off the cancellation of the flat, and added a note about meeting Tam Spellman. *The Diamond Motel, 12 o'clock on Tuesday*.

CHAPTER 8

Jasper caught a bus at the foot of Wentworth Street. He sat hunched in the seat, contemplating his own iniquity, then rang to indicate his Windhill stop. He was halfway to his own house when he sighed in exasperation, turned about and headed for the station where he took a train one stop on to the studio.

Tam was in her office, pencilling notes on a musical score. She didn't look up as he entered, but gestured with her pencil at the second chair. 'What's the matter, Jasper? You haven't come to hassle me, I hope?'

'Would I do that?'

'Of course you would,' she said. 'And of course you will. You're like a dog with a bone. You always have been, and I don't know why I put up with you.'

'Because I'm your kid cousin?' he suggested, and added insinuatingly, 'The one you bail out of trouble?'

Tam looked up, her mobile face creasing into a grin. 'What kind of trouble are you in now, Jasper? Is someone suing you?'

'Not that I've heard,' he said, surprised. 'Unless *you* sue me, of course.' He picked up a pencil and twirled it, then began to draw faces on the nearest envelope.

Tam reached out and took the pencil away. 'Stop fidgeting, Jasper, and let me look at you.'

He met her gaze, and did some looking of his own. He hadn't seen her for weeks, and thought she seemed a little worn. The bust-up with Rod had affected her badly.

'Hmm,' said Tam.

'What's that supposed to mean?'

'Just that. Hmm. You look awful. Confession time, I think.'

'I've been deceitful and borderline dishonest.'

'That's a first. I hope you haven't involved me?'

'It's nothing to do with Diamond/Spellman. Not directly.'

'Good.'

'You are involved, though, on a personal level. I've invited a girl to lunch at the Diamond in your name.'

'Run that past me again?'

Jasper flushed, and Tam stared in fascination, removing her glasses to view the phenomenon more clearly.

'Stop staring,' he said. 'I said, I've invited a girl to lunch at the Diamond, and I allowed her to believe the invitation came from you.'

'That's a blush,' she said. 'A veritable blush! I didn't know you still could.' She peered at him for a little longer. 'Curiouser and yet more curious. Does she know me? Do I know her?'

'No and no.'

'Then I don't see,' said Tam. 'What do you expect me to do? Go to lunch with her or not? And why?'

'I was hoping you'd join both of us for lunch on Tuesday. That's tomorrow.'

'Lord, this is like pulling teeth,' complained Tam.

131

'Stop being coy, Jasper, and tell me what this is all about. You said you'd been deceitful, but as far as I can see you're simply being obscure.'

'I want to have lunch with a girl,' said Jasper patiently.

'Check. You're taking my advice. Why issue the invitation in my name?'

'Simply so she'd accept.'

'You're mad.'

'That's what she says. If she sees me waiting at a table, she'll leave, but if she sees *you*, alone, she'll think it's safe. When lunch is served, I'll join you.'

'And that's my cue to slip off to the powder room, I suppose.'

'You'll have to stay at the table,' said Jasper. 'If you rush off, so will she. Before or after dumping her soup plate over my head.'

'Why?'

'Because she thinks she hates me.'

'And you're willing to stage this complicated scenario just to have lunch with a girl who hates you.'

He nodded.

'Then you're either out of your tree or madly in love, neither of which is exactly *you*.'

'Both,' said Jasper. 'Will you do it?'

Tam laughed. 'I will not! I've never heard of anything so juvenile!'

'Neither have I,' said Jasper, depressed. 'Forget I asked.' He reached for the pencil again. Tam took it away. She sat regarding him for fully thirty seconds, watching with fascination as the dull colour came and went in Jasper's impassive face.

'Tell me about it,' she said at last. 'I've never seen such a Technicolor display. Who is this girl, anyway, and what have you done to her? Most women find you a touch formidable, but I've never known one to hate you before.'

'I met her in Tasmania,' said Jasper. 'I did something very crass. I've made several attempts to put things right, but she isn't having any. She riles me, and I rile her and we have a slanging match and then she throws me out. Chapter and verse. It's driving me mad.'

'Oh, dear. When you toss your cap over the windmill you don't do it by quarters, do you?'

He shook his head.

'And this is what you want me to lunch with? The pair of you having a slanging match? No way! I had enough of that with bloody Rod.'

'She might listen if there was someone else,' he said. 'Someone who isn't either her mother or her fiancé. The mother likes me; but the fiancé . . .' He smiled very faintly. 'Let's just say the fiancé would do anything in his power to queer my pitch.'

Tam frowned. 'I'm not a bit surprised, and if this girl is engaged you ought to leave her alone!'

'You don't know the half of it.'

'No. And if you don't mind me saying so, this is very peculiar, Jasper, even by Diamond standards. Can't you get a girl who isn't entangled with someone else? It was bad enough when you and Jet were both chasing Grete Fischer.'

'Correction,' said Jasper. 'I was going out with Grete Fischer in the first place. *Jet* was chasing her.'

Tam waggled her hand in apology. 'Who is this mystery girl, anyway? What's her name?'

Jasper reached for the pencil, and this time Tam let him take it. 'Her name,' said Jasper unhappily, 'is Aberdeen Shawcross.'

133

Tam gasped, choked and began to cough. 'Tell me this is a wind-up, Jasper,' she begged. 'Tell me you haven't been stupid enough to go after this girl of Jet's. For God's sake . . .' She gulped for breath, and mopped at her streaming eyes. 'For God's sake, Jasper, my father says they're getting married at Easter!'

'Not if I can help it,' said Jasper.

'It's bad enough having Jet spring this wedding on me, without you getting your fingers in his pie. Or anything else in his pie. You haven't have you?'

'No, I haven't!'

'Let's be thankful for minute mercies! You cannot go around poaching Jet's fiancée just because he yanked your chain over Grete. Jet deserves anything you want to dish out, but you might think of the unfortunate girl.'

'This is nothing to do with what Jet did to me.'

'Come on, Jasper! At least be honest about it.'

'It's true,' he said. 'I admit it started out like that – I warned her off him the day we met – but after that they got engaged and I tried to put things right. Unfortunately, the more I tried the deeper I dug myself in. Won't you help me sort it out?'

'No,' said Tam. 'You're deceiving yourself. You want to get at Jet – that's understandable, if amazingly immature – so you're using this girl as a pawn.' She looked directly at Jasper. 'There's no free lunch to be had from me, Jasper. You leave Jet's girl alone. As for this ridiculous invitation idea – !'

'I'll go, you won't, she'll come and then she'll run away,' said Jasper. 'You're right. I'm out of my tree to even suggest it.'

'I won't play it your way,' said Tam, 'but I don't

want to look bad. How's this? *I'll* go to the Diamond, *you* won't, *she* might and if she does she and I'll have lunch together *à deux*. I'll welcome her to our family and keep stumm about your nasty deceitful ways and you'll spend the entire day at the studio with a sandwich to keep you out of mischief. Deal?'

It was more than he had any right to expect. 'Thanks, Tam. I owe you.'

'I'm not doing this for you,' she said sharply. 'I'm doing it for Aberdeen Shawcross, and for my own reputation. If I didn't show up she'd be hurt and feel as if she'd been used. This way, *I'm* the only one who's being used. Is she a nice girl?'

'Not exactly. She shoots straight and always hits the bullseye. Put in a good word for me?' asked Jasper wryly.

'I won't mention you at all unless she does first. How am I supposed to have invited her, anyway?'

'By letter.'

'I hope you didn't sign my name.'

'I signed a scribble. I told her you didn't have her address.'

'Thank the Lord for a piece of truth!'

Jasper got up and tossed the pencil on her desk. 'I didn't actually lie, you know. I simply allowed her to draw erroneous conclusions.'

'Allowed?'

'Encouraged, then. Believe me, I'm not proud of myself.'

'I should hope you weren't,' said Tam.

'I can't *imagine* how I came to get in this mess.'

Tam looked at him drily. 'Poor Jasper. Thirty-one's a hell of an age to discover you're only human.'

★ ★ ★

135

Aberdeen caught the bus to Darling Harbour and found her way to the Mizzen Mast. When she walked in, she saw Jet, deep in conversation with two young men and a woman. Jet gave her a flashing grin of welcome and put out a hand to draw her to his side. 'Here's Aberdeen,' he said to his companions. 'Are we ready to eat?'

'I've been ready for the past hour,' said the woman. She smiled at Aberdeen. 'We met in Tasmania . . .' she prompted.

Aberdeen's face cleared. 'Of course! Marie. You're Macka *Lou Galah*'s wife, but I don't think I ever heard your other name.'

'You wouldn't,' said Marie amiably. 'It's McKenzie. You know my husband Macka here, and the other one's my brother Dave.' She stuck her elbow in the second man's ribs. 'Say hello to Aberdeen, Dave.'

'Hello to Aberdeen,' said Dave.

Marie smiled. 'I'm glad you're going off on the *Aphrodite* with Jet, Aberdeen. Since poor Nick Green's out of it, I've been dead scared Jet would ask Macka or Dave to go along as crew. They'd just about ditch their jobs and do it, too.'

'What about you?'

'I teach at Lawson Primary School, and I'm not about to ditch *my* job.' She reached over and tugged at Macka's arm. 'We're all here now, let's eat!'

They went through to the dining room, but the men scarcely paused in their conversation. Marie ignored this, but tapped the menu pointedly as she thrust it under Macka's nose. 'So – what do you do, Aberdeen, that you can drag yourself away from for a year?'

'I'm between positions,' said Aberdeen. She saw the narrowing of Marie's eyes and continued hastily, 'I

136

was a conservator at the Pitt Gallery, but my appointment ended in December.'

'That was well-timed,' said Marie. 'An interesting place, the Pitt Gallery. I took my Year Sixes there when they had that exhibition of underclothing . . . I suppose you saw it?'

'I planned that,' said Aberdeen.

Marie laughed and tapped Macka on the arm. 'You hear that, Macka? Aberdeen here got that underclothing exhibition together . . . remember?'

Macka clearly didn't remember, but he nodded anyway.

Aberdeen waited for Marie to comment on her skills as an organizer, but all Marie said was, 'Glad I didn't live in those days. Control-top tights are about as much as I can stomach.'

After dinner, the conversation rolled on over coffee, but at eleven o'clock Marie got up. 'Macka, it's time we went. I've got school in the morning.' She glanced at Aberdeen. 'How are you fixed for transport? We could run you home if you like.'

Jet looked up from the chart he was studying with Dave. 'I'm taking Aberdeen home, Marie.'

Marie and Macka left, but it took the arrival of a politely insistent waiter and another fifteen minutes before Dave rolled up the chart and departed.

'Got rocks in his head,' said Jet. 'He's trying to tell me a short-cut past Atonement Island.' He put his arm round Aberdeen and guided her out of the restaurant. 'Coming back to my place for a nightcap before I run you back to your flat?'

'I might as well sleep at your place,' she said.

'Great, if you don't mind Dave snoring next door.'

'What do you mean?'

'Dave's the bloke who's looking after my flat,' said Jet. 'His wife chucked him out and Marie won't have him at her place.'

'I'll go home, then,' said Aberdeen, a bit numbly. 'I live in Wentworth Street, remember? 44a.'

Jet leaned over and opened the back door as Dave loomed out of the night. 'Get in; we're just dropping Aberdeen off at her flat.'

He drove slowly back to Blaxland, flipping a two-dollar coin into the tollgate on the Sydney Harbour Bridge. Number 44a looked very shabby to Aberdeen as she saw it for the first time through Jet's eyes, but he didn't seem to notice. He parked the car and got out. 'I'll see you in, make sure the bogey-man doesn't catch you,' he said.

Dave guffawed. 'See you next year,' he quipped.

'Don't mind him,' said Jet. 'He's a Neanderthal.'

'I don't.' Aberdeen let herself into the foyer and led the way upstairs. 'This is my place – *pro tem*,' she said. 'I handed in my notice this afternoon.' She unlocked her own door, trying not to mind, trying not to explain that her preferred address would have been a terraced house in Glebe. 'You're a bit late to protect me from bogey-men,' she said. 'I had one on the doorstep practically as soon as I got home.'

'The landlord?' guessed Jet. 'After the rent arrears?'

'Rent's paid up, thank you.' She switched on the light and closed the windows. 'The bogey-man was Jasper.'

'What did he want?'

'Tam – your cousin – has invited me to lunch on Tuesday. I don't know quite why Jasper did the asking.'

'He works with Tam,' remined Jet. 'I guess she

138

asked him to play postman since he knows you.'

'I wish she hadn't. Somehow he gives me the shivery-shakes. Would you like a coffee?'

Jet held out his arms. 'What I'd like is you, Lorelei.'

Aberdeen went into his embrace and stood there relaxed and happy. It crossed her mind that this was the most notice he'd taken of her all night, but she pushed the thought away. She would have felt awkward if he'd kept kissing her in front of his yachtie friends and, as he had pointed out that morning, they'd be alone together soon enough. Alone on the ocean.

'I'll be round in the morning,' said Jet at last.

'I'll give you the pass key so you don't have to rouse Mr Peters. Or you could stay the night with me . . . except there's Dave out in the car . . .'

'Bugger Dave!'

'. . . and I've only got a single bed.'

'In that case,' said Jet, flicking her nose gently, 'I think I'll pass.'

He left soon after, and Aberdeen closed the door and hooked up the chain. She was thinking of Jet, but her mind slid around to Jasper who had come through her door like an invader.

'Get out of my head!' she muttered, but she supposed it was only natural. If there were a redback spider on the ceiling or a European wasp around the picnic table it paid to keep your eye on it in case it moved in for the kill. So – better to think of Jasper now and then. Remember what he was like, and then he wouldn't take her unawares if and when he appeared again.

Jasper had been gone two hours when Tam Spellman reached for the telephone. It was the third time she'd done so, and this time she got as far as keying in Rod Bowen's number before jamming down the rest.

'Damn,' she said.

She considered Jasper's manner and his request and groaned aloud. Disaster was probably – no certainly – approaching. Rivalry between her twin cousins was nothing new, but the potential for mayhem in this case was immense. It would have been better if Jasper *had* been trying to get at Jet. She could have reasoned with him then, and talked him round.

Jasper wasn't playing games this time; he seemed totally obsessed by this fiancée of his brother's. The only good thing about the whole affair was that Jet was planning to marry and go off on one of his ocean jaunts. He'd be away for a year, he had told Godfrey Diamond, and maybe more. Tam hoped it would be a year at least. Surely that would be enough for Jasper to sort himself out?

It just wasn't *like* Jasper to behave underhandedly, nor to toss his cap over any windmills. It was like Jet, though, and Tam couldn't help wondering if Jet had somehow engineered this situation. She would be meeting Aberdeen Shawcross tomorrow if all went according to the script, but she could scarcely ask the bride-to-be if the Diamond twins had been fighting over her in Tasmania!

Rod Bowen could answer that question. He had known Jet and Jasper for as long as he'd known Tam, and he understood all about the trouble over the other girl. Nothing she could say about the twins would be news to Rod, and he wouldn't pass it along.

Tam took her finger off the rest and hit re-dial.

'G'day.' Rod's usual greeting, and of course he had

140

answered the telephone after the third ring. Living in an on-site van meant he was never far from the phone.

'Hello, Rod. It's Tam here.' As if he wouldn't recognize her voice.

'What do you want?'

'If you're going to be bloody-minded, I'll hang up!' she snapped.

'You already have,' he observed. 'Pointedly and often. What's up, Tam? And don't say nothing is, because if it wasn't you wouldn't have rung me.'

'I need to see you.'

'I see.' His voice gave nothing away. 'Shall I come round to the office?'

'Come to my place tonight.'

'Of course,' he said. 'Seven o'clock?'

'Make it nine,' said Tam, 'and don't stop off and have a beer with Jasper on the way. I want you sober.'

She hung up then dropped her face abruptly in her hands. 'It's the first drink,' she said aloud, and she wasn't referring to a beer with Jasper.

Promptly at nine, Rod arrived at Tam's house in Major Mitchell Close with a bottle of cider in one hand and a packet of photographs under his arm. He had let his hair grow while he was in Tasmania, and it flopped over his forehead, making him look even younger than usual. Rod was actually thirty, but even in a good light he could have passed for twenty-five. Tam was thirty-three, and she knew she looked every year of her age tonight.

'*Must* you?' she said, taking in his sky-blue polo shirt, grey trousers and slip-on shoes.

'Must I what?'

141

'Must you look like something out of a Summer-lands catalogue?'

'I can't help that,' he said, 'because that's where I get my gear. Whereas *you*, Ms Spellman, do your shopping at Opal Road and it shows.'

They stared at one another for a few seconds and Rod didn't smile. 'Is there any point in my coming in?'

Tam stood back and Rod walked past her into the bright sitting room. He glanced around, not, she thought, to see if anything had changed since their break-up, but merely to accustom himself to the feeling of space. She enjoyed space, and her sitting room took up the whole of the top floor, the polished boards relieved here and there with Persian rugs and a large sheepskin. She saw Rod glance at the sheepskin now, and wished she had put it away. They had chosen it together.

'Sit down,' she said, and motioned him towards an armchair.

'Thank you.' He put the cider on the window ledge and settled into the chair, leaning back and crossing his legs. 'What do you want?'

'I need to talk about Jasper.'

'*Jasper*?' Rod sounded amazed. 'You've dragged me over here to talk about *Jasper*? God, Tam – you're something else!'

'Just because we can't agree on personal matters, it doesn't mean we can't discuss other things,' she said with difficulty.

She thought he might storm out, but he sighed and made a gesture of surrender. 'You want to know what's bugging Jasper, I suppose,' he said.

'I know what's bugging him, I just want to know how it came about.'

Rod's eyebrows climbed. 'Then you know more than I do, but I suppose you charmed it out of him.'

'No charm needed. He came to ask me a favour.' Briefly, Tam explained. She didn't tell Rod the whole story, merely that Jasper had wanted her to meet Jet's fiancée for lunch. 'Have you ever met her, by the way?' she added casually.

Rod was not misled by her light tone. 'I've seen her once or twice,' he said.

'What's she like?'

'Blonde, but not Jet's usual type,' said Rod. 'When I first saw her she was flaming mad, ripping a real strip off Jasper down at the Van Diemen Tavern.'

'What for?'

'Dunno. I had the impression she thought he was Jet.' Rod thought about it. 'Jet had just come in on the winning yacht and he'd taken the Shawcross girl to the tavern. She saw Jasper and me leaving with Ellie and hopped into Jasper to some order. She thought he was Jet walking out on her.'

'She didn't know Jasper then?' said Tam, getting it clear.

'Jas had never laid eyes on her, didn't know she existed until she made that scene.'

'What happened then?' asked Tam.

Rod shrugged. 'I don't know. I went on with Ellie and Jasper stayed to sort out Ms Shawcross. He must have done it, because the next thing we heard was that she and Jet were engaged.'

'Then she already knew Jet when she first met Jasper,' said Tam.

'I just said so.' Rod twisted the onyx ring he wore on his finger then looked straight at her. 'What's all this about, Tam? Haven't you got better things to do than gossip?'

'Yes, well, it doesn't look as if you can help since you don't know any more than I do.' She half-rose to her feet.

Rod looked up at her sardonically. 'You're not throwing me out just yet, I hope,' he said. 'Not after inviting me over. Ordering my presence, in fact.'

'I thought you might have plans for the rest of the evening. So, how did you enjoy Tasmania?'

'Not a lot,' said Rod. 'Got some good shots of a swamp hawk and some yellow-tailed blacks here, if you're interested in seeing them.' He balanced the packet of photographs on the arm of the chair, steadying it with one hand.

'Tough shoot for *In the Rough*?'

'Jasper and I between us loused things up,' said Rod. 'There was a guest called Dr Smith – she didn't like me at all, but she was hot for Jasper.' He caught Tam's eye and gave a sudden grin. 'Don't say it. She was showing nice discrimination there. What *is* it with old Jasper, though? He doesn't smile, he looks like Tojo the wooden Indian, he's got keep-off signs all over him since that balls-up with Jet and Grete Fischer, but this woman would have had him if he'd dropped his guard, and I'm not sure he even noticed. I mean, it can't be his dress sense that slays them.'

Tam made a slight movement of distaste. 'Not everyone goes for the window-dressing.'

'No,' said Rod.

'Some people look for the quality of the goods underneath the wrapping.'

'Yes,' said Rod. 'Jasper was really down about something, but he wouldn't tell me what.'

144

'You came home before him,' said Tam.

'S'right. I came with Stewie and Steve. Ellie had already flown back to nurse her gran and Jasper stopped over with Jet for a few more days.'

'So he could have met this Aberdeen Shawcross again.'

'I suppose he would have done.' Rod looked at her hard. 'Why do I get the feeling I'm being pumped?'

'Because you are. Look, I care about Jasper, but this isn't entirely personal. He's family, but he's also my business partner. I saw him today and he seemed pretty down, so I thought the filming must have gone badly. If *Tasmania – In the Rough* isn't up to scratch, it will reflect on Diamond/Spellman as a whole.'

'It's not going to win us any awards, let's face it,' said Rod acidly. 'But that's your fault as much as Jasper's. You should have been there, Tam.'

'I had my reasons for staying here.'

'Which all boil down to me. I could have stayed here and you could have gone. I did make the offer.'

'I couldn't let you make a sacrifice.'

'No sacrifice. I'm the roadie – remember? I get paid, just the same.'

'You'd have spent the time at the solarium and watching telly.'

'I'd have house-sat for Jasper and looked after his precious birds,' corrected Rod. 'Do you want to see these prints?'

Tam began to spread out the prints Rod had taken in Tasmania. Typical, she thought. There were all those mountains and rivers and historic buildings, stunning world heritage scenery, but Rod's entire collection consisted of birds. Young wild birds, not the aviary-bred antiques that belonged to Jasper.

Rod got up and wandered over to the small bar, helping himself to a handful of rice bits on the way. He poured two glasses of cider then came back and set one down on the coffee table in front of her. 'I took that with a filter,' he said, tapping one of the prints.

His bare arm brushed Tam's. For a moment it was nothing more than a fleeting warmth, then the rush of familiarity drowned her. She closed her eyes, moving abruptly aside while he continued to explain the technical details of producing the print. 'What do you think?' he demanded.

'What?'

'About enhancing the colour with filters,' he said impatiently, settling back into his chair.

'I suppose it depends whether you're using the camera as a recording device or an art-form.'

'I'm not an artist,' he said. 'You know that.'

'No,' she said. She felt sweat starting out on her upper lip and reached for the cider, trying not to inhale the familiar mix of soap and aftershave. 'It's hot tonight,' she said.

'Hey, I'm the one who's just come up from the frigid south!' He reached over and swept the prints together, bundling them back in their folder.

'I haven't finished looking yet,' she protested.

'You're not interested anyway.' Rod drained his own glass and got up. 'I'd better be going.'

She got up as well. 'It was nice of you to come round.'

'Yes, wasn't it? Why did I come round, anyway?'

'Because I asked you to, I suppose.'

'Whistle and I'll come to you, my lass,' he said.

'You could have said no.'

'Maybe I should have,' he said morosely. He looked

146

at her directly. 'Would it help if I dressed like Jasper? And got rid of the ring?'

'I beg your pardon?' said Tam.

'You know what I'm saying, Tam. All those pointed little comments about flashy exteriors were aimed at me, right?'

'We were talking about Jasper.'

'Jasper's your ideal,' said Rod. 'You like him better than Jet.'

'So do you.'

'Jet's never had any use for me. I don't fit into his mould. You know what, Tam, you're a lot like Jet in some ways.'

'What's that supposed to mean?'

'When we first knew one another in the good old days,' said Rod. 'Jasper and me were mates, but Jet thought I wasn't quite up to his standard. You feel the same way, Tam. So. Would it help if I dressed like Jasper and got rid of the ring?'

'Would you do that?'

Rod looked down at his onyx, at the gold eagle set in relief against the black. 'Do you know where I got this?' he asked.

'Out of a catalogue?'

'Yes,' said Rod. 'Paid in four easy, no-interest instalments of three hundred and fifty each, plus postage and handling. A hand-cut onyx embellished with genuine 18-carat gold.' He spread his hand and the ring swallowed the light. 'It wasn't cheap and nasty, but Jasper would never wear anything like it.'

'No,' said Tam. 'It isn't his sort of thing.'

'And Jet might wear it as a joke. Now me,' said Rod, 'I like this. I know you think it's kitsch, but I really like it. So, even if I stopped wearing it, even if I got rid of my Barrier Reef T-shirt, it wouldn't make any difference to you. You'd still see the real me, and you still wouldn't be able to lower yourself. You never would have let me near you in the first place if I hadn't taken you home that time you were pissed.'

Tam bit her lip, unable to meet his gaze. He had it all so *wrong*.

'I couldn't believe my luck when you made a pass at me.'

'I was drunk,' she said. 'I was lonely.'

'*In vino veritas*, Tam. But your face when you woke up and found me beside you! I suppose I should be glad you kept me around so long.' He touched her cheek and she shivered, despite the heat. 'I could probably get you into bed tonight if I really put my mind to it,' continued Rod. 'We were always good together. You might give me another few weeks or days, but eventually I'd start to grate on you again and we'd have another bust-up. So, I'm not going down that road again. My clothes might have come out of a catalogue, but my feelings didn't.'

'Oh, Rod!' She put her hand on his arm, but he moved away.

'It's OK,' he said. 'I'm not laying a guilt thing on you and I'm not going to kill myself. Hey! We had some good times together and we're bound to see one another now and again. So next time you feel like ringing me up and asking me to come over . . .' He broke off and headed for the door.

'What?' asked Tam.

'Don't,' said Rod. 'Just don't, all right? Just *don't*.'

He went out then, leaving Tam very much shaken. She closed her door abruptly, not wanting to stand there in case he was looking back. Then she sat down in the armchair and drank the rest of the cider, trying to dull her humiliation and her guilt.

'And you had the cheek to tell Jasper he was being adolescent!' she said aloud.

CHAPTER 9

Aberdeen was astonished when Jet refused to postpone the sailing date he had chosen.

'I can't see why,' she argued. 'You've already postponed it once.'

'I don't like putting things off, Lorelei,' said Jet. 'It's unlucky. Once is bad enough, but if you do it twice, ten-to-one your window of opportunity closes.'

'There's so much to do!' she protested.

'Don't fuss. I've made all the arrangements for *Aphrodite*. You've applied for your passport – as soon as that comes through, we just up and go.'

'How long until we get to Europe?'

'It's far too soon to tell,' said Jet, patiently, for him. 'I have some business up in Queensland first – a consortium's setting up a marina not far from Manatee. After that, we'll be free to head north, but the time it takes will depend on the sea and the weather and a thousand other variables.'

'I can't drop in on curators without warning.'

'Fax them from on board when we get a better idea of our time scheme.'

'Of course,' she said. 'I'd forgotten faxes.'

'We're going to be sea-gypsies, but we won't be cut

off from the world,' said Jet. '*Aphrodite* has state-of-the-art communications and navigational equipment.'

'I know,' she said. 'It's just such a rush.'

'I've already arranged to go and there's nothing to keep you here,' he said logically. 'You don't have to get leave of absence from a job, for example, or arrange for someone to sit with your ageing parents – or even mind the dog. Not like Jas, who has to get a sitter for his bloody parrots.'

He was beginning to sound less patient, so she smiled and changed the subject. 'Are you coming to lunch at the Diamond today?'

'I expect Tam wants to talk girl-talk.' He winked. 'She'll probably give you all kinds of solemn warnings about me! Why not ask Marie if you need moral support?'

'She's a teacher, remember? She'll be at work.'

'Just you and Tam, then. Shall I drop you off?'

Aberdeen nodded gratefully. It would ease the situation considerably if Jet made the introductions. And if she could find the right clothes to wear for the meeting. What *had* Tam been wearing on that video? Jeans? Tropical-weight pants and a printed shirt?

She could remember Jasper's clothes, all right. Moleskin trousers and a casual shirt of an odd shade of bottle green. Dark for television, she recalled, but a perfect shade for someone of Jasper's colouring. It would have suited Jet too, but Jet went for prints and patterns, or sleek executive wear. Jasper had been wearing a hat in some shots, too, she recalled, a broad-brimmed affair in soft, grainy leather. Very Indiana Jones, but it had suited him. Most things did; even frayed old cut-offs and a faded shirt.

She dragged her mind back to Tam, whom she was scheduled to meet in an hour. 'Could you run me up to my flat to change?' she asked Jet.

'You look fine the way you are.' Jet surveyed her lazily, apparently approving her wheat-coloured sundress overprinted with rioting blossoms. 'Don't fuss, Lorelei. You can give Tam a good ten years – not to speak of ten kilograms.'

'I'm not dressed for the Diamond, though. Not if it's like the Ruby.'

'You're dressed for *this* Diamond,' he said firmly, and ran his fingers down the low neckline, lingering in the hollow between her breasts. 'We'd better not go to your flat, or you're likely to be very late for your lunch.'

'If you think I'll do, I'll go as I am.'

'Of course you'll *do*,' said Jet. 'Haven't I just said so? Don't keep putting yourself down, Lorelei, you're perfect as you are.'

'Jasper doesn't think so.' It was out before she realized.

'Oh?' Usually, Jet laughed off any mention of his brother, but today his tone was different.

'He thinks I'm out for what I can get,' she said. 'For this trip to Europe and because you offered to help get the museum up and running.'

Jet laughed. 'Jas is a suspicious sod, always was, always will be, so don't let him get to you! Seriously, Lorelei, he's got rocks in his head. So what if you get a bit of financial backing for your hobby? *I* get a gorgeous wife. What the hell does it matter what Jas thinks? He's only my brother.'

'You must care what he thinks.'

'Don't run away with the idea there's any special

152

bond between Jas and me,' said Jet. 'He disapproves of me and all my works on principle. Do you want me to get him off your case? I can, you know.'

'I'll handle it,' said Aberdeen. 'Just as long as he doesn't get up when the celebrant says that bit about the "just impediment" . . . he wouldn't, would he?'

'If he did,' said Jet, 'I'd kill him.'

Jet drove Aberdeen to the Diamond. It didn't resemble the Ruby from the outside, but the interior was very similar.

'People find it comforting, or so I'm informed,' said Jet. 'If you've been in one, you know where to find the bar and the bathroom in the others.' He took her arm and approached the receptionist, a beautiful Filipino. 'Hello, Mimi. Is Tam here yet?'

The girl smiled and looked at her list. 'Table ten, Jasper.'

'Jet,' he corrected.

'Sorry,' she said in her faint, singing accent.

'You must get really tired of that,' said Aberdeen as they went to look for Tam.

Jet shrugged. 'It has its moments, but Mimi has an excuse; Jasper's far more likely to be having lunch with Tam than I am. There she is.'

Tam Spellman was reading the menu, but she looked up and smiled as they approached. Jet performed the introductions faultlessly, bending to kiss Tam's cheek and offering to fetch them drinks.

'Are you lunching too, Jet?' asked Tam.

'I just came along to make sure you were in a sweetheart mood. Jas has been giving Aberdeen a hard time and she's afraid the feeling's general among the Diamonds.'

'Don't worry, Aberdeen, I'm not about to give you a

153

hard time,' said Tam. 'Quite the contrary – I've been hearing about you from my father. He thoroughly approves of you, and of your mother too.'

Jet glanced at his watch. 'I'll see you girls later. Do you need me to pick you up, Lorelei?'

'I'll get the train,' said Aberdeen.

Jet kissed her cheek and left the restaurant with his usual buoyant step. Aberdeen and Tam gazed after him and Tam sighed. 'He's always in such a hurry. I can never think why.'

'There's a lot to do before we leave,' said Aberdeen. She need not have bothered about her clothes, for Tam was wearing jeans and a T-shirt. Her dark hair was tied back and she had large gold hoops in her ears and shadows under her eyes.

'It's good to meet you, Aberdeen,' said Tam. 'Are you always called that?'

'Mostly – except by Jet.'

'Nobody calls you Abbie?'

She hesitated and shook her head.

'Quite right,' said Tam. 'If you have a distinctive name, use it. That's my motto anyway! I'm a Tasmyn, by rights, but Tasmyn Spellman is a bit much, don't you think?' She shrugged. 'I could have reverted to "Diamond" after my husband died, but what the heck, I was used to it by then.'

Aberdeen nodded. She had the feeling Tam was talking for the sake of it and wondered why. She didn't look nervous. 'I saw you on a documentary,' said Aberdeen when the waitress had taken their order. 'It was about the Breona Station Belt.'

'Interesting place. So. Jasper's been giving you a hard time, has he?'

'Well . . .'

'You're scared of telling tales out of school,' said Tam. 'Don't be.'

'He's your partner.'

'In business, yes, but we don't always work together. I didn't come down to Tasmania, as you know. Or at least I assume you do.' Tam smiled at her. 'And, contrary to what Jet probably told you, there isn't the slightest possibility that Jasper and I will ever be more than friends. Jet likes to pretend to think there is, but he's only trying get Jasper's goat. And mine. Am I offending you?'

'Not at all,' said Aberdeen. 'I know Jet's a stirrer. So you and Jasper get along, that's great.'

'We're friends, though I'm a good bit older. There's no spark between us – never has been. In fact, we have a good cry on one another's shoulders when our sex lives go off-course.'

'What about Jet?'

'Jet never feels the need to cry.'

Aberdeen relaxed. 'I've been a bit on edge,' she said. 'Jet seems to think you can organize a wedding at the drop of a hat. I wanted to put it off a while, but we're locked into this end-of-March date for some reason. I think there's something he wants to do in Queensland.'

'Second thoughts?' asked Tam.

'Not at all! It's just I feel I need a bit of time to get used to the idea, to get to know the *Aphrodite* – and Jet. It's all happened rather suddenly.'

'The thing about Jet,' said Tam, 'is that he's quite brilliant at playing hunches. Right from when he was a kid, Jet's been able to look something over, play the probabilities, make a snap decision and stick to it.'

'And he's always right?'

'Usually,' said Tam. 'And when he isn't, he doesn't

155

waste time fretting over it. He just slaps on a Band-Aid and goes on to the next thing. He'd have made a good general, I always think, because he never gives a monkey's about what anyone thinks of him. He's nothing like Jasper, which is why they always rub one another up the wrong way.'

'I see,' said Aberdeen.

'What do you see?'

'I see why Jet doesn't want to postpone our trip, quite apart from this deal in Queensland he wants to see. He's decided to leave at the end of March, and that's that.'

'That's Jet all right,' said Tam lightly. 'So, when I heard he was engaged to a girl he'd only just met, I wasn't surprised, because I knew it was Jet being Jet. He saw what he wanted and he went out after it. Snap!'

Aberdeen laughed. 'It was like that. He picked me up on the docks and tucked me under his arm and we've been together ever since.'

'You're very lucky, you know?' said Tam.

'To be collected by Jet Diamond?'

'No, to be able to leap in the dark. You say he collected you, but you had the guts to go along with him, the courage to say yes when he went snap and proposed.'

'I am lucky,' said Aberdeen. 'And I suppose there's really no point in trying to get him to postpone this trip, is there?'

'None, I should think,' said Tam frankly. 'And if you want my advice – which you probably don't – you won't waste your breath trying. There are no hidden corners in Jet, my dear. He's a stirrer, and he likes scoring off people, but most of them forgive him and he doesn't give a toss if they don't.'

156

'Not like Jasper,' said Aberdeen. 'He's not the forgiving type.'

'Oh, dear, he *has* got across you!'

'He has indeed,' said Aberdeen shortly. 'I wish he'd go to Mars on a one-way trip.'

'Exactly what did he do to upset you so much?'

'He's trying to make trouble between Jet and me. He offered me a bribe to break off our engagement.'

'That doesn't sound like Jasper!'

'Maybe that isn't quite fair. What he actually did was ask what I would say if he *did* offer me a bribe.'

Tam nodded to show she appreciated the distinction. 'You're dead sure it was Jasper you were talking to at the time?'

Aberdeen put down her fork. 'Now I'm really confused. Who else could it have been?'

'Jet, perhaps? It's just the sort of thing Jet might do. Impersonate Jasper, I mean. He'd think that was very funny.'

Aberdeen achieved a wintry smile. 'I see what you mean, but this was definitely Jasper. He was right there in my flat!'

'They look an awful lot alike,' said Tam.

'They sound different,' said Aberdeen. 'And Jasper gives me the shivers somehow. Whenever he touches me . . . brrr.'

'You'd better keep him at arm's length, then!' suggested Tam.

'I would if I could, but he won't stay away.' She shook herself. 'What about you, Tam? You're a widow?'

'For years. I made an early mistake, but poor Chris didn't live long enough for us to decide to do anything about un-making it.'

'You haven't remarried.'

'No. To get back to the purpose of this lunch . . .'

'It was kind of you to invite me,' said Aberdeen, feeling snubbed.

'*De nada*! What I'd like to say is, if there's anything I can help you with, any help you need, just ask. Your mother doesn't live here, does she?'

'She rang this morning to say she's coming up on the twenty-first,' said Aberdeen. 'And that's just one more complication. I've surrendered my flat and the lease runs out a few days before the wedding. Jet's got a friend staying on in *his* flat, so . . .'

'Your mother is very welcome to stay with me if she'd like to,' said Tam. 'I have a house in Windhill. Would that be a help?'

'It's putting you to a lot of trouble.'

'Not at all. I live alone, and I have plenty of spare room. What sort of reception had you planned, by the way? You could have the Diamond staff cater for you, or if you can't stand the decor I could suggest a few other places. Shut me up if I'm being pushy.'

'I'll have to talk to Jet about what he wants,' said Aberdeen. 'Just one thing more – Jet's sisters. I haven't met them yet and I don't know how they're going to react.'

'It doesn't matter how they react,' said Tam. 'They're so busy with their own lives they'll hardly notice you. Now don't you *worry*, Aberdeen. Everything will be fine.'

Jasper was waiting when Tam got back to the studio. 'Well?' he said.

Tam poured herself a drink and swallowed it. 'Not a word, Jasper.'

'Did you sort her out?'

'I'm tempted to sort you out. You've really upset the poor kid, haven't you? She's stressed clear up to the hairline.'

'She'll be more stressed if she marries Jet.'

'Will you stop obsessing about Jet! As far as I can see she has a perfectly sound picture of Jet. She sees his faults and she's willing to give as well as take. She's a nice little girl, and Jet's on to a good thing. Why can't you just try and be happy for them?'

'Did she tell you she gets seasick?'

'Why should she tell me that?'

'I saw her! I was standing right there and she was practically laid out for the count. Bloody Jet didn't want to take her back.'

'She'll be all right, Jasper,' said Tam. 'I can see why you've come over all protective – those gold curls and that valiant chin – but she'll be all right with Jet, if you'll keep your fingers out of the pie.'

'They've got virtually nothing in common.'

'They will have once they've been on that blessed yacht for a few months. People grow together, Jasper. That's what marriage is all about.'

'Why don't you marry Rod, then?'

'That, my friend, is none of your damned business.'

'It is if it ruins *our* business,' said Jasper. 'That experience in Tasmania is one I never want to repeat. What is it with you two, anyway? You said it yourself – you could hardly keep your hands off one another.'

'We're just too different,' began Tam. She caught Jasper's eye. 'All right! So my problems with Rod may impinge on your business a little bit. If he's along on a shoot I won't be willing to go. But as for Jet and

Aberdeen – their marriage and how they choose to arrange it has absolutely nothing to do with you. If you want to help Aberdeen Shawcross, Jasper, stay away from her. Get yourself laid or have a cold shower, but stay out of her hair. She's had a lot of bad luck and she deserves a break.'

She saw a stubborn look harden his always impassive face and was suddenly tired of the whole business. 'Face it, Jasper,' she said cruelly, 'even if you managed to get her away from Jet you wouldn't have a hope in hell of getting her for yourself – always supposing that's what you think you want.'

'Why?'

'To put it in the crudest possible terms, Jasper, she says you give her the creeps.'

After that cold little lecture from Tam, Jasper tried to put Aberdeen Shawcross out of his mind. He knew he'd made a fool of himself when he'd pulled the stunt with the invitation, but it was Tam's final words that chilled him. Never, in his most paranoid nightmares, had he seen himself as a man who would give a woman 'the creeps'. The notion, with its suggestion of clammy hands and nudging smiles, made him feel almost physically ill.

Hating his own insecurity, he looked back across his encounters with Aberdeen. She had been angry with him most of the time, he thought. Always on her guard, hackles up the moment he came near. Hostile, yes, but *cringing*? At least twice – in her mother's garden where they had called the truce, on the deck of the *Aphrodite* before she was overcome with sickness – she had seemed to look at him with something approaching friendship. Both times he had spoiled things, by being tactless, by snatching for something she hadn't offered him.

She had glowered at him often enough, she had told him to get lost; at least once she had seemed about to hit him, but so far as he could remember she had never cringed away from him. Which probably went to show him how selective memory could be.

'You give her the creeps', Tam had said, and he supposed he would have to accept it. Tam was his friend as well as his cousin, and they had never been less than honest with one another.

Maybe, whispered the imp in his mind, maybe Tam is mistaken. Maybe Aberdeen said something else, meant something else. Idiomatic language was full of pitfalls, and men and women often used the same words to mean different things. 'I love you,' from a woman, might mean, approximately, 'I am offering my soul. I want to belong to you.' 'I love you,' from a man, was just as likely to mean, 'I think you're sexy and I'm ready and willing if you are.'

This wasn't always the case, naturally. Sometimes the meanings could be reversed, and sometimes they didn't apply at all. 'So – let's hear it from the masters,' said Jasper aloud, and dredged his memory for ancient wisdom. ' "Love is a sickness full of woes, all remedies refusing . . ." Lord, that's a comfort! "Love is not love which alters where it alteration finds . . ." All right, let's *not* hear it from the masters!'

As he sat down at his desk, the thought intruded that he'd like to hear Jet's definition of love; always supposing his brother had one. And Tam's. And – of intense interest, this one – Aberdeen's.

Before he began editing the rough cut of any *In the Rough* documentary, it was Jasper's habit to view all

161

the rushes in sequence. That took time, for there were many hours of footage which had to be edited down to a two-hour feature. Since much of *In the Rough* was filmed ad-lib, it was more a case of choosing which segments rather than which versions should be used. The team might film something two or three times if it was important and if something went badly askew with the first attempt, but it didn't necessarily work like that.

If a semi-trailer thundered past while Tam was expounding the peace and quiet of a particular stretch of forest road that scene might need to be cut – or it might be left in as an ironic comment on the incongruous ways of the world. It all depended on Jasper's mood at the time, and how the remaining segments slotted in. He followed his gut feeling rather than any particular rules, but he knew he must achieve a balance between the abrasive, immediate flavour the viewers expected and an overly harsh or careless effect.

Because each segment was so personal, it was a difficult task to delegate. Often one of the others would look in to comment or advise, but they all – even Tam – accepted that Jasper must have the final say. The balancing act must bisect not only the extremes of sugar and vinegar, but also the line between artistic honesty and the necessity for each programme to turn a profit.

Mix and match, that was the secret, and Jasper did it with all the natural flair of a highly-qualified chef. At least – he had until now.

After that uncomfortable Tuesday chat with Tam, Jasper spent three days closeted in the viewing suite while he watched the rushes. At first he simply viewed the mass of material and marked the obviously flawed scenes, then re-ran the entire sequence and made detailed notes, discarding the unusable footage. When he had a list of functional scenes, he would progress to plotting out a mix of long and short, sweet and wry, juxtaposing quirky character studies with the grandeur of scenery, a certain amount of necessary exposition and odd little snippets that showcased the team. After *that*, he would be ready to begin the rough-cut proper.

It was a three-day marathon, and from it he emerged exhausted, unshaven and hollow-eyed, hyped up on caffeine from endless cups of black coffee and queasy from too many order-in meals.

It was eight o'clock on Friday when he finally left the suite, startling Tam as she passed through the corridor. 'God, Jasper, you scared me out of a week's growth!' she exclaimed. 'I thought you'd gone home long ago!'

'I thought you had,' he said morosely, rasping his thumb down his chin.

'Have you been home at all?' asked Tam. 'You look like something the cat dragged in.'

Jasper shrugged. 'I went home Wednesday night. Since then Ellie's been seeing to Doc and Dottie and Co. off and on between nursing her granny.'

'Which explains why Doc's been squawking the street down, since today is Friday. The rushes must be riveting to keep you immured so long.'

Jasper looked down at her. 'You don't look so hot yourself, Tasmyn.'

'It's muggy, and I've been sweating like a pig,' said Tam, taking his arm and urging him along the corridor. 'Want a pick-me-up in my office before you hit the road?'

'So long as it isn't coffee,' said Jasper.

163

'So that's it,' said Tam. 'You've been overdosing on that damned stuff. No wonder you look as if you'd been soaked in caffeine and hung out to dry.'

Jasper winced. 'You're so good for my ego.'

'If you want an ego trip, baby, you'd best find yourself a girlfriend. Sorry.'

'Don't be,' said Jasper. He shied as he encountered his reflection in the smoked-glass door. 'Be sorry about something that matters. Tam, will you do me a favour?'

'I might,' she said, opening her door and heading for her small bar. 'Though I did swear last time was going to *be* the last time.'

'I want you to look at the rushes.'

Tam handed him a can of beer and made herself a gin and tonic. 'Anaesthesia,' she said as he glanced at the proportions.

'I didn't say anything.'

'You didn't have to. I drink too much. So, what do you want me to look for? Anything in particular, or just a general impression?'

Jasper peered at the moisture beading his can. 'You haven't seen any of this lot?' he said.

'I thought I'd wait to be asked.'

'Shit, Tam, you know you never have to wait!'

'I don't *know* anything,' she said. 'Sorry. I'm lousy company these days.'

'You'll look in on Monday, then? Just to get a general impression?'

'Why not tonight?'

'I can't ask you to work any more tonight.'

'Cut it out, Jasper,' said Tam. 'This solicitude routine doesn't come off. You wouldn't ask, but you hoped I'd offer, didn't you?'

He turned out his hands. 'We'd better eat first. I

164

need something to sop up the coffee and beer. Then, if you're game, you might just watch a couple of hours.'

'Have a shower,' said Tam. 'I'll phone for a pizza.'

Jasper groaned. 'Not pizza. Please. Nor pasta. I've had enough cheese sauce and pastry to kill a lesser stomach.'

'I'll have them send something from the Diamond.' She smiled slightly. 'That'd please my father, if he knew.'

Jasper left her to it while he showered. The bathroom behind Tam's office was on the primitive side, but Tam found it useful when she had a date directly after work. In the humidity of a Sydney summer a cool shower could do more to freshen her than a mere change of clothes.

There was a razor in the cupboard. He supposed it was Tam's – or maybe Rod had left it behind. Jasper used it, wincing equally at its bluntness, and at his own ghastly appearance. No one of his colouring could ever look wan, but the all-over brown effect could and did make his skin look like week-old wholemeal bread. He splashed his face with cold water then went out to wait for Tam.

'We struck it lucky,' she said. 'They had a dinner ready to deliver then some cretin called and cancelled. I said we'd take it off their hands.'

They ate silently while Tam watched the rushes and Jasper watched Tam. To save time, he showed her the cut version, with the obviously impossible scenes left out. Other than that, he simply let it flow.

Tam watched for two hours, then she switched off the machine. 'Is it all like that?'

'Mostly,' said Jasper. 'You missed the scene where Rod got stranded on the cliff . . .'

'I didn't hear about that one.'

'Let it roll a few more minutes,' he said. 'It's one of the best.'

Tam set the tape running and thumbed the fast-forward.

'There's input from Stew's master camera and from my camcorder,' said Jasper. 'It's cut together, but not edited. Stop it there.'

Tam nodded. Jasper was familiar with the material, so again he watched her reactions instead of the screen. At first she was impassive, then he saw a reluctant smile twitch her lips. The output of Stew's camera cut to Jasper's own, focusing on Rod where he crouched on the lip of the cliff. The dialogue was a little thin, with cliff-top wind behind it, but it was easy enough to hear and understand.

'What kept you, Diamond?' asked Rod.

And here came his response, clear enough although he was out of shot. . . . *'Do you want to be rescued?'*

'I'm thinking, I'm thinking.'

'I'm going to chuck you the rope,' said Jasper's voice. *'Pull me in so I can pull you out. And don't fall off, or Tam will sue me.'*

'Tam would thank you,' corrected Rod's voice.

Tam hit the button and Rod's image froze in place on the screen, wavering a little. 'Was that crack about me really necessary?' she asked. Her face was in shadow.

'It wasn't a crack,' said Jasper. 'We were just ad-libbing as usual.'

'Of course.' Tam pulled herself together and re-started the tape. Another hour went past as she fast-forwarded through the mass of material, pausing now and again to watch a scene in part or in entirety.

166

'What's your impression?' asked Jasper at last, trying to keep his voice impersonal.

'It's pile of shit,' said Tam.

'That's giving it to me straight.'

'You wanted it. It isn't news to you, either.'

'I've lost my touch.'

'It isn't all shit,' said Tam, relenting.

'No. It's OK in parts – like the curate's egg. That sequence with Rod, the snowstorm that blew up across the highlands, the chairlift and the Tasmanian devil park – all those are quite acceptable.'

'You could edit round them,' said Tam.

Jasper spread his hands. 'No cohesion. Damn.'

'Why did you ask me if you already knew?'

'I'm so tired and so preoccupied I couldn't trust my judgement. So, Tasmyn Spellman, what do we do? Cobble it together into a short feature? Schedule a reshoot? Chuck the lot and take up finger-painting?'

Tam rubbed her temples. 'If I were you I'd go ahead with the rough cut and then think again. Sorry I can't give you any better advice.'

'The chemistry is wrong without you.'

'Maybe,' said Tam. 'It wasn't only that, though. I don't like to say this, but you just didn't come across. Your face . . .'

'What about my face?'

'It's never the most expressive dial in the world,' said Tam, 'but you *can* smile. Not often, but the viewers look forward to that damned crooked grin, especially the women.'

'I had a lot on my mind,' said Jasper. 'Rod was cranky with me for reasons you really don't want to know. And then there was Aberdeen.'

'Ah,' said Tam.

'Ah nothing! I ran across her badly that first day, and spent the next few weeks wishing I hadn't.'

He got up and Tam reached to put a hand on his arm. 'You're as tense as a wet rope. Go home and get some sleep, Jasper – it's gone midnight. Leave this lot until Monday.'

'Sleep!' He pulled Tam to her feet and put his arms around her. 'I'm so strung up I've forgotten how to sleep,' he said. 'And you're not in very good shape either. Rod, isn't it?' He felt her recoil and gave her a little shake. 'You know all about my guilty secret, so let's have a bit of *quid pro quo*.'

Tam leaned against him. 'All right,' she said against his shoulder. 'It's Rod. I miss him like hell.'

'Then tell him! There's nothing stopping you going after him – nothing but a bit of stiff-necked pride.'

'You don't know what it's like.'

'I wish I didn't.'

'You *don't*,' persisted Tam. 'I lived with Rod, slept with him. I know what I'm missing. You've just got this fantasy idea in your mind, that's all. Having met Jet's Aberdeen, I can't see her allowing you anything more.'

'She didn't. So. Live with him again.'

'It wouldn't be fair, not now. He's not a toy to be picked up and put down – even if he is a bit of a toy-boy. He said so himself.'

'He *did*? When?'

'He came up to my place a few nights back. I invited him.' She shivered in his arms and Jasper felt his exhausted body reacting to her nearness. 'Oh, Jas – I've made such a dog's breakfast of all my relationships! You're the only one I seem to get along with.' She tilted her face up and grinned half-heatedly. 'I suppose that's because there's no sexual component involved.'

'Isn't there, now?' said Jasper.

He freed one hand and slid it gently around to her breast. Tam gasped – with incredulity rather than passion, he thought – and stepped away. 'Jas – ' Her cheeks were crimson. 'I wasn't trying it on!'

'No,' he said. 'I was.' She was staring at him still, as if, he thought irritably, he had grown an extra head. 'Why not?' he said. 'I've always wondered if we might get together some time.'

'You're out of your tree!' said Tam. 'All these years – why now?'

'Why *not* now? You're hung up on Rod but you can't or won't go back to him. I'm hung up on Aberdeen, who hates me and is going to marry Jet. We're both strung up as tight as watch-springs. So why not? It's better than a one-night stand with a stranger. I assured Rod there was nothing between us, but I didn't say there never would be.'

'You're *mad*,' she said with conviction.

Jasper stood back, his hands in his pockets.

'Don't look like that,' said Tam after a while.

'I'm not looking like anything. I'm the original wooden Indian, remember.'

'You're feeling very rejected, I can tell.'

'I *am* rejected. Often. Usually in favour of Jet. Now, in favour of nothing at all.'

Tam sighed. 'That's a low blow. All right, then. You're un-rejected. We both know where we stand – and at least I'm not pissed this time.'

'What?'

'Last time I started out on an unlikely relationship I was pissed. And don't look like that either. I'm talking

169

about Rod, not some rough trade from a pub!' She held out her arms and Jasper closed the distance between them. They held one another for a while, then Jasper tilted her face up for a kiss. They had kissed before, countless times, in greeting, in farewell, on birthdays and at Christmas. At first the very familiarity of it was warming, and Jasper felt her response with a quiver of gratitude. He sighed, and she broke the kiss and tucked her face against his shoulder.

'At least I don't give you the creeps,' he said.

'Oh, dear,' she said ruefully. 'That did rankle, didn't it?'

'Of course it did.' He touched her breast again; it was warm and full in his hand, nice to hold, and she was rewarding to kiss, but it came to him that he'd felt more stirred by the mere touch of Aberdeen Shawcross's hand in very reluctant greeting. He cupped Tam's head in his hand, tangling his fingers in her springy dark hair. It was pleasant, but nothing like the pang of painful joy he had known after his fingers had made brief contact with Aberdeen's wheat-gold curls. Tam deserved better than this.

Tam tipped back her head, letting it rest in his palm, then leaned forward to brush a kiss on his jaw. 'I really love you, Jasper,' she said. 'And if I thought it would help I'd ask you to come home with me.'

'It wouldn't, though, would it?' he said resignedly. 'It wouldn't help either of us.'

'No,' she said. 'It wouldn't.'

CHAPTER 10

Aberdeen's list became disfigured with ticks, question marks and amendments. It never got shorter, for as fast as one item was crossed off, another would force itself upon her notice.

Jet was busy too, but apart from one morning spent at a jeweller's choosing an engagement ring and matching wedding bands, his activities centred on making final contacts with friends and business colleagues. Aberdeen called some of her friends, but there didn't seem to be time to arrange meetings. Besides, she didn't think they'd blend with the people Jet knew. She was learning that Jet's friends belonged to two distinct types. On the one side was the financial set, the whizz-kids and yuppies with their Gucci shoes and mobiles joined to their hips. Some were younger than Aberdeen, but she felt they had glanced at her and discounted her as a pretty accessory.

On the other side were the yachties, ranging from the ones Jet cheerfully called 'no-hopers' like Chick and Drew and Scott, to the dedicated weekend and racing sailors like the McKenzies and the Greens. She and Jet had been to visit Nick Green in hospital; he was

171

a nice youngster, very frustrated at his current help-lessness.

Aberdeen met Tiger and Todd again, along with their parents. Aberdeen liked Charlie and Carol, but she knew they couldn't quite place her. It seemed they regarded her in the same light as their own children, as a generation apart from themselves, whereas Jet was admitted as their equal.

'And that's weird,' she said to Kate on the telephone. 'Carol used to be Jet's nanny, so she's quite a lot older.'

'Jet has the knack of being all things to all people,' said Kate. 'How do these assorted friends of his get along?'

'Fine, oddly enough,' said Aberdeen. 'Most of the stockmarket brigade are weekend sailors, and the yachties tend to be fairly well-off. The ones that aren't expect to be some day, and they hope the stockmarket brigade will show them how.'

'Have you found a dress yet?'

'I was hoping you'd help me to choose.'

'That's cutting it fine,' warned Kate.

'Come earlier, then. Fly up, and I'll fetch you from the airport.'

'I could always take the bus,' said Kate.

'I'll be there.'

'I'll look forward to seeing you,' said Kate. 'And Jasper.'

'You mean Jet.'

'I know I'll be seeing Jet, but I did mean Jasper. He said he had a book for me. He was going to send it; tell him not to bother, I'll get it when I see him.'

'I won't be seeing him,' protested Aberdeen. 'Not if I can help it.'

'Never mind, I'm bound to see him if I'm staying with his cousin.'

172

Kate hung up, and Aberdeen was left feeling, as usual after a conversation with Kate, a little like Alice-through-the-looking-glass. Talking to Kate in the flesh wasn't much trouble; body language and Kate's expressive face helped to join up the dots of her conversations. It was only when dealing with her over the telephone that the trouble cut in. And there was a point. Kate had wondered how Jet's assortment of friends might get along, but how was vague, middle-aged Kate going to handle a week with the formidable Tam Spellman? For she *was* formidable, no matter how pleasant she had been to Aberdeen.

On Saturday morning, halfway through March, Jet went sailing with Tiger and Todd. Aberdeen found their small yacht *Website* uncomfortably frail, so she decided to visit Tam. Since Kate was coming earlier, adjustments would have to be made in her plans. Tam had offered to put Kate up for five days, not fourteen.

Aberdeen rarely went to Windhill, but trains heading north came along at regular intervals. She was standing on the platform watching a southbound train dispensing passengers when a hand touched her shoulder. She drew in a startled breath, and, beyond the usual station odour of oil and steam, she caught a faint whiff of something that made her pulses race with apprehension.

'Jasper,' she said.

He must have stepped out of the carriage, and his hand was merely resting on her shoulder, so she was able to dip and turn to get free of him. Her instincts told her to hurry away down the platform, but the train would be along in moments, and she was darned if she'd let him put her out, even to the extent of catching

173

a later train. He was watching her, his face impassive, but something about him made her bite back the waspish remark she had been about to make. 'Have you got the flu?' she asked.

'Would you care if I had, Aberdeen?'

'You wouldn't see me for dust,' she said frankly. 'I have enough to do without catching flu.'

'I don't have flu.'

'I suppose you're hung-over, then,' she said. 'Your eyes look glassy.' Her train was approaching and she was poised to board it quickly, to get away from Jasper before he said something impossible. The carriages were rolling alongside the platform now, slowing down, and would-be passengers were hurrying along like lemmings, afraid there would be no room for them. The doors slid open and the usual crush developed with people trying to get on and off at the same time.

Aberdeen stepped into the crush and went up the steps to the upper deck, reaching a seat at the top just as the warning came. The doors sighed closed and the train began to move. She settled herself, trying to toss off the disagreeable feeling of awareness that Jasper always engendered in her. Not awareness of himself, exactly, but of her body and its surroundings. Now she could feel the dinginess of the upholstery under her legs, the faint clamminess of the back of her knees, the very throbbing of her pulses, the slub of her raw silk dress.

She resisted the impulse to rub her shoulder, but she was hardly surprised at all when he settled beside her, effectively blocking her into the corner between the front of the carriage and the window. He made no move to touch her, but he was so close that she could feel the warmth emanating from his thigh and upper arm. If she'd had a bag or a package, or even a coat, she could have wedged it between them. As she had none of these, she moved over until she was jammed against the side of the carriage. She stared stubbornly at the map of the city rail system for as long as she could, her eyes following its multi-coloured loops and curves.

'It always reminds me of a board game, like Snakes and Ladders,' he said.

Startled, she glanced at him.

'You might put your counter on Central Station, then throw a one to land on Town Hall, a two for Circular Quay and so on,' he continued. 'And if you land on a station where the train doesn't stop, you have to go back to somewhere impossible like Rooty Hill or Black Town.'

'Ashfield,' she said. 'Trains never seem to stop at Ashfield.'

'At least you're talking to me,' he said, and gave her his lopsided smile. It sat strangely on his drawn face and she stared at him.

Not hung-over either, she decided. There was no smell of alcohol, nor of anything that might have masked it. His eyes were strange, but neither yellowed nor bloodshot. Drugs, perhaps? But if he were an addict, he wouldn't have reacted so against her taking of anti-nausea drugs.

'What are you doing here, Jasper?'

'Going north by train,' he said.

'Obviously. But didn't you just get off a train that was going south?'

'How do you know I wasn't on the platform already?'

'I'd have known.' She was sure of that.

' "*By the pricking of my thumbs, something wicked this*

175

way comes. Open locks, whoever knocks . . ."' he quoted.

'If you like, and I bet you could, at that. But I'd have seen you if you'd been on the platform. You do stand out in a crowd.'

'So do you, Abbie.' He smiled again, a little more easily this time. 'That dress you're wearing matches your hair.'

'Oh, certainly, if my hair happened to be green and white.'

'The background colour,' he said patiently. He touched a fold of her dress as it lay between them and she stiffened. 'Silk has the same sheen as your curls. Synthetics can't compare. You look tired,' he added.

'I'm busy arranging a wedding, if you recall?'

'I haven't forgotten,' he said. 'You're not taking those seasickness pills at the moment, are you?'

'No.' She turned to stare at the city rail plan again. 'You did get off that train, didn't you?'

'I did.' His hand touched hers and again she almost jumped up. 'Nice ring,' he said. 'Did Jet choose it?'

'We both did,' she said firmly, taking her hand away. The size of the diamond troubled her a little, for she seldom wore jewellery, having found it got caught up in the fragile threads of costumes.

'Very nice,' he said again.

'Stop being snide, Jasper. I'd have been happy with a cubic zirconia. I'm equally happy with a diamond – or nothing.'

'I'm not being snide!' He sounded surprised. 'I mean it. I like the ring, and I suppose a diamond was unavoidable, considering the name.'

'If you got off that train, going south,' she said, 'why did you get on this train, going north?'

'If I tell you I suddenly realized I was going the wrong way and decided I'd like to go north, you'd think I was out of my tree again,' he said.

'You are.'

'Tam agrees with you wholeheartedly and so, if it's any comfort to you, do I. In this case, though, I'm telling the exact truth.'

She was uneasy now, hot and shivery from the effect of his proximity, so she said nothing at all, hoping he'd take the hint and keep quiet or, better yet, leave the train. It drew into a station, and paused, but he made no move to leave his seat.

'I was on my way to visit you,' he said in her ear as the train sighed and rolled onward. 'That's why I got on this train. I could see you weren't home, so I would have been wasting my time by going along to Blaxland.'

'You still are wasting your time,' she pointed out, 'riding back and forth.'

'If you're headed for Bondi you've missed the connection.'

'I'm going to visit someone,' she said.

'Me?'

'Not you, Jasper. I don't know where you live and I don't want to know. I can't imagine myself visiting you under any circumstances. And, since you happened to mention you were on your way to my flat, I might as well tell you I wouldn't have let you in.'

'Not even with a letter from Tam?'

'Have you got a letter from Tam?'

'I haven't.'

'If you'd had one, you could have pushed it under

the door or passed it through past the chain. I won't let you into my flat again.'

'Why not?'

'Because I don't want to. Last time you came in without asking, and I couldn't get you out. Just the same thing happened in Kate's garden. You sat down and wouldn't get up.'

'You're sitting here talking to me now,' he said. 'You haven't caught leprosy or plague or even the flu.'

'This is a public place,' she said as evenly as she could. 'I can get away from you here whenever I choose.'

'But you haven't,' he said. 'You haven't made a move to get past me or to change carriages.'

'You'd follow if I changed.'

'So I could. You could leave the train, though.'

'So could you. So *would* you.'

'So, talking to me is marginally less trouble than getting off the train and waiting for another one.'

'No. I'd do that in a flash if I thought it would work, but, as I said, you'd simply follow. Wouldn't you?'

'I might, I suppose. Unless you screamed for Security.'

'That would be close to harassment,' she said sternly. 'I could probably report you for stalking. It wouldn't stick, but you can't deny you followed me on to this train.'

'I've already told you that,' he said. 'However, it *is* the train I take to get me home. Are you going to report me, by the way?'

'Not unless you force my hand. I'm more likely to report you to Jet.'

'Jet knows what's happening.'

'For pity's sake!' she said helplessly. 'I give up!'

'Do you, Aberdeen? I wish you would. Give up on

Jet, back off and give yourself breathing space. Later, you can start again.'

'No,' she said. 'I'm going to Tam's, and she's expecting me, so you can push off right now. I can't keep you from going to your own cousin's place, but I told her you'd been bugging me. She believed me, oddly enough, so she won't ask you in for coffee. I take it you haven't seen her yet this morning?'

'We spent a fair chunk of the night together.' He looked down at her sardonically. 'We were watching rushes for the documentary, in case you were wondering, and she was there by choice.'

'I wasn't wondering,' she said. 'But if I had been I'd never have thought you were doing anything else. Jet said you and Tam were very close, but Tam told me it was strictly platonic and always would be.'

'Did she, now?' He sounded amused. 'She's right, but I never actually knew it until last night. Shall I tell you what happened, Aberdeen?'

'It's got nothing to do with me,' she said, and shivered.

'But it has.'

She put out her hand to stop him, then drew it back. 'Jasper, Tam seems to think you're a good bloke. Even Jet thinks you're OK, and as for Kate – she thinks you're a cross between the wizard Michael Scot and the herbalist Gerard.'

'I like Kate,' he said. 'She's a witch.'

'Kate likes you, but I –'

'You can't be doing with me at all.'

She shrugged, and winced away as it brought her shoulder in contact with his. 'Put it that way if you like. So will you please act like the nice guy they all assure me you are really and go away?'

179

'All right,' he said. 'I won't get off the train before my stop, but I'll go on up the carriage and I won't come to Tam's until you're well away. That's unless you'd like a lift from the station?'

'No!'

'I'll pretend I don't see you, then, even if I pass you toiling uphill. That do?'

'Great,' she said in relief. 'That'll do.'

She smiled at him in thanks, but he looked away and continued to do so until the next stop when he got up and walked along the carriage. The back of her neck prickled with the effort of not looking behind her, but she became so absorbed in the timetable that she narrowly missed being carried past her stop.

Windhill was a pretty suburb, not far from Gordon and Pymble. The sun baked down, the sky was the hazy blue of Australian summer cities everywhere. Aberdeen climbed the steps and traversed the overpass, descending to street level. Away up the street she saw the large, warehouse-like building that housed Diamond/Spellman Productions. She supposed she'd noticed it before, in passing, but it had never had any meaning to her then. Now that she had seen one of their films, now that she knew Jasper Diamond and Tam Spellman, now that Kate had identified herself as an enthusiastic fan, she supposed for ever after Windhill would bring their faces to mind.

Not so difficult, since Jasper's face was a copy of Jet's.

She looked up and down the street, wondered exactly which way she should go. Tam lived in Major Mitchell Close. That was somewhere west of the station, she supposed, up in the leafy, lofty residential area. She had arranged no particular time for her visit,

180

so she turned off the street at random, passed a bookshop and arcade, and asked for directions.

'It's a fair way,' warned the girl. 'You go over that way –' she waved her hand ' – and then up the hill. You could call a cab, but it's changeover time so you could be waiting a while. Otherwise, get on a train going south and get off after one stop. It might be a little shorter walk. Maybe.'

'Thank you,' said Aberdeen. She set off along streets that became more and more tree-lined. The bush came down the hills and encroached a little on the city, she could smell gum blossom and hear the occasional call of birds. A kookaburra swooped past and laughed at her from the top of a flowering eucalyptus. On the face of it, it was a beautiful day for a walk, but by the time she reached Major Mitchell Close she was aching and breathless; far more so than the exercise seemed to warrant. Her dress was sticking to her like a second skin, and she was prickling and bathed in cold sweat.

Major Mitchell Close was another steep pitch, so like true bush that it came as a shock to hear the traffic thundering on the highway just a few hundred metres out of sight beyond the trees. The houses here were gracious and quite large, built into the side of the hill in a riot of split levels, balconies and sculptured yards. Halfway up was a particularly gorgeous garden; despite her spinning head, Aberdeen recognized a vivid confusion of flowers. There was a gigantic aviary housing cockatoos, one of which screeched at her as she passed. The lucky owner had a creek running through the garden, she saw, dripping over mossy stones and pooling in a fountain. Her feet were swelling in her shoes, and she longed to dabble them in the creek, but she looked resolutely away and climbed the rest of the way to the top.

Tam Spellman's place was the last in the Close. It would be, thought Aberdeen. There was no number visible, but the letterbox proclaimed the inhabitant in neat black letters. Aberdeen waited until her breathing returned to normal, and then knocked at the door.

'Aberdeen!' Tam was welcoming, shaking her head over the heat and humidity. 'You didn't walk up from the station . . . why didn't you give me a call?'

'I didn't know it was so far,' said Aberdeen with a wry smile.

'It isn't, when you've got wheels.'

Aberdeen lifted her hair from the back of her neck, wincing as her curls caught in the raised setting of her ring. 'I'm out of condition,' she said. 'Or else I've got acclimatized to Tasmanian weather!'

'We'll have a cold drink,' decided Tam. 'And I'll put the fan on – if the draught won't bother you?'

'Not at all.'

'Aren't we polite, though,' said Tam, 'considering we'll be cousins soon?' She stepped back, ushering Aberdeen into a huge airy room. 'This is the sitting room. You have to go downstairs to the rest of the house.'

'It's lovely,' said Aberdeen. She thought she'd never dare invite Tam to her flat after this; Jet's place was a typical bachelor roost, but Tam's house underlined the enormous gap between Aberdeen's former life and her future as part of the Diamond clan. It would take time to get used to wealth and privilege, and she wasn't sure how she would handle it. Fortunately the burden sat very lightly on Jet, and she had a year or more before she needed to try to live up to it in Sydney.

Tam went to fetch the drink and Aberdeen relaxed in the squashy leather chair. A photograph lay face-down on the floor and she bent to retrieve it. She didn't know what she expected; a family snapshot, perhaps, but the print was of a black swan preening itself at the edge of a wide bay.

'That's Hobart – isn't it?' she said as Tam handed her the glass.

'What?' Tam was startled, but she put out her hand and took the print. 'I suppose so.'

'I recognized the bay. I'm sorry, I thought it was one of yours.'

'I'm no photographer,' said Tam. 'It must be Rod's – the guy I lived with for a while.' She took a long swallow of her drink. 'He cleared out his stuff, but it's odd the way things keep turning up. You know – his shampoo at the back of the bathroom cupboard, his damned monogrammed pens by the telephone. It's like peeling potatoes, trying to get him out of my life. I think I've done it, but there are those nasty little eyes left behind. Watching me.' She flicked the print on to the coffee table. 'How are things going, Aberdeen? I hope Jet's helping you with all the wedding arrangements?'

'Oh, yes.'

'Remember,' said Tam, 'if there's anything at all I can do to help . . .'

'You offered to put up Kate – my mother.'

'That won't strain me. Jasper says I'll like her a lot, and he's usually a very good judge of who will mix and who will match. What day is she coming, do you know?'

'On the sixteenth, we think, but of course she'll be staying at my flat for the first week.' Aberdeen couldn't meet Tam's eyes, so she looked down at her drink instead. It was a sharp, lemon-flavoured concoction, clinking with ice, but she glanced up again, a little offended, as Tam laughed. 'I beg your pardon? Did I say something funny?'

'I wasn't really laughing at you. It was just that you reminded me of what Jasper did to me last night.'

Aberdeen froze.

'I won't say too much, because it's Jasper's business, but he had a favour to ask, and he wouldn't do it outright. Which is odd, because he's not so tactful as a rule.'

'Was it something about the film?'

'How did you guess?'

Aberdeen shrugged, wishing she'd held her tongue.

'It was,' said Tam, 'but that's immaterial. At a guess, I'd say it would help you out a lot if your mum stayed here the whole time – right?'

'She'd certainly like Windhill better than where I live,' said Aberdeen, 'but there's no way I'm going to expect you to invite her early. Five days is quite long enough to put up a stranger.'

'If I took her early, it would give you and Jet somewhere to be alone,' went on Tam, 'since I understand he has a very adhesive lodger at present.'

'Dave's not exactly a lodger; he'll be subletting from Jet while we're away.'

'Oh, but –' Tam stopped, and took another swallow. 'Yes?'

'It's nothing. I was just going to say he couldn't be subletting because Jet doesn't lease his flat; he owns it.'

'Of course,' said Aberdeen.

'You'll be looking for a house when you get back,' said Tam, and again Aberdeen had the feeling she was

184

talking at random, filling in an awkwardness with words. 'Are you planning to have a family?'

'Not for a while,' said Aberdeen. 'There's my costume museum to get up and running first.'

She told Tam about her plans, but it seemed a long way off. She doubted if the property in Glebe would still be available when she returned, so she would have all that to do again. She tried to let her enthusiasm for the project colour her voice, but she was mainly conscious of feeling tired. She shivered, aware that the heat generated by her long walk had given way to a goose-flesh chill. 'I ought to be going soon,' she said. 'I'm meeting Jet down at the quay.'

'Come and see my spare room first,' said Tam. 'I do hope your mum's reasonably fit? This place is all steep stairs.'

'Oh, yes,' said Aberdeen. 'Kate's probably fitter than I am. She walks a lot and she's always in her garden.'

'Great. Jasper really took to her, you know. He suggested she might see over the studio while she's here, and have a look at the editing process – that's if it ever gets under way.'

'Oh?'

Tam shrugged. 'There are a few problems this time, but I dare say he'll sort himself out.' She looked directly at Aberdeen. 'We all have to sort ourselves out, don't we? It's no use depending on anyone else. Nor can you force feelings that don't exist.'

'Are you talking about Jet and me?' asked Aberdeen. 'I thought you were in favour of us!'

'I wasn't talking about you and I *am* in favour,' said Tam emphatically. 'I was talking about Jasper. And a little about myself.' She smiled, and Aberdeen saw that under her welcoming manner she looked tired and dispirited. 'I can't tell you how pleasant it will be to have a normal, happy couple in the family, Aberdeen. Krista is divorced, my father is a widower, Jasper and I seem to have had nothing but disasters, and the girls look as if they might be heading the same way, the way they hop merrily from man to man.'

'It doesn't take much to make me happy,' said Aberdeen.

'Then you're a lucky girl as well as a beautiful one. Jet's happy too, most of the time, so I think you'll have a lovely time.' Tam smiled again, then bent to kiss Aberdeen's cheek. 'Just get yourself past the hassle of the next few weeks and you'll be off on the big adventure. Now, I'm going to drive you home, unless you'd rather go straight down to the quay? Independence is all very well, but I expect Jet's got something lively planned so you won't want to be tired out when you meet him.'

Aberdeen allowed Tam to drive her back to her flat, where she showered and changed. Usually she didn't wear much make-up in summer, but this evening she looked a bit pale, so she smoothed on blusher and lipstick before going out to meet Jet at the quay for dinner at a pub.

Once there, Aberdeen picked at a salad she didn't want, and was about to suggest he might take her back to her flat when some of Jet's stockbroker friends stopped by at their table. One of them, Shane Tyrone, knew something about her line of work. She mentioned her museum plans, and he told her that he, like Marie McKenzie, had seen the 'Colonials Undercover' exhibition.

'I hear you had something to do with that?'

'I organized it while I was working at the Pitt Gallery,' said Aberdeen. She glanced at Jet, but he just grinned at her and gave her knee a friendly squeeze under the table.

'It's incredible, the things women used to wear, just to impress men,' said Tyrone.

She pulled a face. 'That's the popular view, but it's not exactly accurate,' she said. 'Surveys show that most women dress to please themselves – or other women – and I can't see why that shouldn't have been true in colonial times as well as today.'

'If that's what you want to believe.'

'It's quite true,' she said sharply. There was a nasty little headache nagging behind her eyes, and she was in no mood for wanton stupidity. 'You can't tell me *men* had a lot of time for the crinoline, for example. At its most extreme it meant ladies' escorts had to stand a good two metres away.'

'I'm sure you didn't choose that dress you're wearing now to please yourself,' said Tyrone.

Aberdeen glanced down at herself. She was wearing a printed cotton skirt and matching top. 'I did,' she said.

'Those corsets,' said Shane Tyrone, reverting to a subject that evidently fascinated him. 'Have you ever tried them on?'

'One, that was too badly damaged to display.' Aberdeen's ribs ached at the memory.

'Must have been interesting, having charge of all that stuff. I bet you did a few turns as a singing telegram.' His knee nudged hers. 'I know I wouldn't leave you standing on *my* doorstep.'

'You wouldn't find me on your doorstep in the

187

first place,' said Aberdeen crisply.

'Maybe you do private viewings?'

She was beginning to feel most uncomfortable, so she turned her shoulder on Tyrone. 'It's nearly ten,' she said to Jet.

'Bedtime?' suggested one of the other men playfully.

'Just about,' said Aberdeen. 'We have a lot to do.'

Tyrone sniggered, and Aberdeen gave him a cold look. 'And when do you leave school, little Mr Tyrone?'

There was much merriment at Tyrone's expense, and Aberdeen felt she had handled him pretty well, especially when he left the table and headed for the bar. Unfortunately, Jet wasn't yet ready to leave. He laughed with the others at her riposte, and put his arm round her, but she was forced to wait another half-hour, growing more and more prickly and uncomfortable. Even then goodbyes were protracted.

'What's the hurry?' he asked as they left the lounge.

'I'm tired and there's a lot to do.'

'You worry too much,' said Jet. He laughed suddenly. 'You certainly put the old Shane in his place!'

'He was making me uncomfortable.'

'He's a bit of a sleaze,' agreed Jet, 'but he's all talk. Put him in bed with a naked woman and he wouldn't know where to put himself. Speaking of which, Dave's gone over to see his old lady tonight, see if he can sort something out.'

Aberdeen put her arm up to his shoulder. 'Do you think he will?'

'He'd better, otherwise he's up for a big pay-out.' Jet kissed her lightly. 'He signed one of those pre-nuptial agreements, and now his old lady gets half his earnings for the next fifty years – unless she remarries.'

188

'We should have one of those,' she said.

'Don't you trust me, Lorelei?'

'I trust you, but maybe you shouldn't trust me. I mean – ' she stumbled ' – if something happened, you – I – wouldn't want anyone to think I thought I was entitled to half *your* earnings. I'm not putting much equity into this partnership, so it's only fair that I don't . . . don't . . .' She had lost the thread of her speech, and Jet was hustling her along now with his hand on her hip.

Now they reached the car, and he took hold of her hands and looked down at her. It should have been moonlight, but the brilliance of Sydney made it difficult to tell. 'Lorelei, we've been through this before,' he said. 'You're bringing me everything I need. If you insist, we can get someone to draw up a paper, but we could just as well do it ourselves.' He considered. 'Potential earnings are a blasted pain, because nobody knows which way they'll go. How would it be if we sort out a lump sum now, and I settle it on you when we get back? That way, you can be financially independent. You can invest it however you like, use it to finance your costume place, or any trips you might want, and you'll be OK if I'm away any time. How's that?'

Aberdeen dropped her gaze so he wouldn't see the sudden tears in her eyes. 'You're so kind to me, Jet,' she said helplessly.

'Why wouldn't I be?' He gave her a teasing pat on the bottom. 'Now, as I was saying, Dave's away, so the mice can play, *nicht wahr*?'

Aberdeen had been to Jet's flat before, of course, but always Dave had been in residence. She liked Marie McKenzie, but she was hard put to like Marie's

189

brother. Probably because he was always *there*. She looked about with puzzled eyes as Jet unlocked the door. She had thought it a rented flat like her own, and now she came to see it as Jet's currently owned home, it seemed curiously impersonal. 'Where are your books and things?' she asked.

Jet indicated a small shelf. 'I don't go in for a lot of stuff like that, Lorelei, too much dusting. As for bric-a-brac, every time one of my mates gets smashed, so does the Royal Doulton. How did you get along with Tam, by the way? Is she going to put your mother up the whole time, or will she need to stay at a motel?'

'Tam offered the whole time, but I don't know.'

'I should let her, if she wants to,' said Jet. 'You'll be busy enough without running round after your mother.'

'Tam says Jasper will show Kate round the studio,' said Aberdeen.

'There you are, then! Jas likes old ladies. Problem solved.' Jet put his arms round her and kissed her.

'Kate isn't a problem,' said Aberdeen.

'Of course not.' Jet kissed her again, and drew her over to an armchair where she relaxed into his embrace, her body aching with something she assumed was tiredness and tension. 'Steady on, don't go to sleep on me!' he teased.

'I'm not.'

'You're doing a pretty good imitation of it.' Jet was laughing, she could feel his body shaking against her, and after a moment she managed to smile. So many men would have taken offence at her lack of ardour.

'Tam says we're going to be very happy,' she said.

'Tam says? Tam says? What's all this?' His hands

slipped around her ribs, under her shirt. She drew in a deep breath and, unexpectedly, coughed as it tickled her throat.

'Sorry. It's been a busy couple of months.'

'It's going to be a busy couple of hours,' he said.

She tried to smile again, but she was tired, so tired, and there was a catch in her chest and a nasty dull headache up behind her eyes.

The intercom squawked suddenly, and Jet raised his head. 'Who the devil is that?'

'Probably Dave,' said Aberdeen resignedly. 'It figures.'

The intercom squawked again, this time more urgently, and Jet got up, spilled her off his lap and tucked in his shirt before depressing the button. 'Bloody hell, Dave – *Jas*? No, I did not know! How the hell did that happen?' He turned to Aberdeen, and she saw, for the first time ever, anger in his eyes. 'Some bloody idiot's rammed the *Aphrodite*,' he said furiously. 'I'll have to get down there right now!'

'Would there be anything I could do?'

'Not really – look, you stay here. I'll go with Jas and we'll pick up Charlie. Be back as soon as I can.'

'All right,' she said, but she could sense his mind wasn't on her at all.

Jet rushed out, and Aberdeen, having switched the television on and off twice, sat down drearily. All she wanted was to go to sleep. She should have been worried for Jet's precious yacht, but she couldn't summon the energy. Jet and Jasper would deal with *Aphrodite*, and perhaps, if there was a lot of a damage, Jet might postpone the looming voyage.

She looked longingly through the door to Jet's bedroom. There was no reason why she shouldn't use it, but she knew Dave might come back and she wasn't anxious to be found in bed asleep by Jet's quasi-tenant. Finally, she compromised by taking the quilt and stretching out on the sofa, trusting that she'd wake as soon as Jet – or anyone else – came back.

CHAPTER 11

Jasper was both tired and frustrated. The evening with Tam had depressed him on two counts, for not only had she reinforced his own opinion of the rushes, but his attempt at making love to her had cruelly underlined his dilemma: if he couldn't find peace with Tam, whom he had known and loved for years, what hope was there for him? Besides – Tam still wanted Rod.

He thought fleetingly of Dr Smith, who might have wanted *him*, but to whom he had not been drawn at all. Merry-go-round, he thought, but it wasn't so merry.

It was too quiet at home, and he couldn't go to Tam for company. Rod was a possibility, but he was feeling mildly guilty about Rod. It was a hellish mess, and the only company he wanted was Aberdeen's. He knew she was no longer with Tam, for he had seen Tam's car go past in the late afternoon, probably heading for Aberdeen's flat. He would have volunteered himself as chauffeur if he'd had the slightest hope that she'd accept.

'*If you want to help Aberdeen Shawcross, Jasper,*' said Tam's voice in his mind, '*stay away from her. Get yourself laid or have a cold shower . . . To put it in the crudest possible terms, she says you give her the creeps.'*

Tam had said it, and Aberdeen herself had seemed to confirm it. Sitting in the train she had begged him to stay away, had agreed she couldn't be doing with him at all. The only smile he'd got had been just to acknowledge his leaving.

Restlessly, Jasper left Windhill and drove down to the quay. He hadn't eaten since breakfast time, so he stepped into a pub to order a bar meal. With the perversity of fate, one of Jet's friends, a man named Shane Tyrone, was approaching the bar. Jasper turned away, not wanting conversation or bad jokes about his identity, but Tyrone caught him by the arm.

'Jetman! What have you done with the singing telegram?' He thumped Jasper in the ribs. 'Have you ever seen her in her corset outfit, eh? Eh? You might have stuck up for me, Jetman, when she turned on me like that.'

Jasper moved aside. 'I'm Jasper, Shane,' he said impatiently.

The man grinned at him. He wasn't drunk, thought Jasper, but he must have had a bit. 'Jasper, old son!' Another thump in the ribs, making him itch to thump Tyrone back. Instead, he edged along again, until he was braced against the wall. He had a sudden flash of Aberdeen moving away from him in the train.

'So, how's the telly business?' asked Tyrone.

'Fine,' said Jasper shortly. 'What's all this about singing telegrams, Shane?'

'Abigail. That girlfriend of Jet's. And I was joking about the telegram. Don't reckon she'd know a bit of fun if it grabbed her on the bum.'

'You mean Aberdeen Shawcross,' said Jasper evenly.

'That's right. And she *shaw* is *cross*.' He chortled at the pun. 'Can't see her and the Jetman making a go of it.'

'Neither can I,' said Jasper.

'I bet she doesn't give him any change, if you know what I mean.' Tyrone gave him a final buffet in the ribs. 'What are you drinking, Jasper?'

'Nothing,' said Jasper. 'Where are they?'

'In the lounge,' said Tyrone.

Jasper got up and headed for the lounge. He didn't like Shane Tyrone, but he, too, had been insulted by Aberdeen. Maybe he had read her all wrong and she was nothing but a gold-digger bent on landing the golden fish she had hooked. And how ironic if Jet, the great stirrer, should be snared by a pretty face. It occurred to him that he should see them together, see them when Jet didn't know he was being observed. During the sailing expeditions Jet had been deliberately provocative; how did he treat Aberdeen when he had no need to tease his brother? And how did she react?

The lounge was no better lit than most places of its kind, so he was able to slide unobserved into a corner seat. He studied the menu, then glanced about as if searching for a waiter. His eyes found Jet's party immediately; his brother was sitting with his back to Jasper, but it was clear from his body language that he was enjoying himself. The other two men with him were laughing, but Aberdeen, although she sat in the circle of Jet's arm, seemed curiously apart. As he watched, she glanced at the clock over the piano and then fell to studying the menu as he had done. After a moment she tossed it aside, not petulantly, but as if already over-familiar with its contents.

195

She was unhappy about something, and he couldn't fool himself that it was Jet's casually affectionate arm. Perhaps, he thought superstitiously, she could sense his presence . . . *by the pricking of my thumbs* . . . If not, she was a twitchy person, something he hadn't noticed about her before. She wasn't sparkling, was making no effort to fascinate.

During the twenty or so minutes he watched them, she spoke to Jet several times. Jet acknowledged her the first couple of times, but gradually he began to turn away from her. She seemed increasingly ill at ease, and when at last Jet rose to go, she got to her feet with what seemed to be an effort. His arm went around her in a casual hug, and after a moment Aberdeen responded.

Shame at having spied on his own brother rushed over Jasper, and he stayed resolutely where he was as the pair left the lounge. A waiter, clearing the tables of the late diners, approached Jasper apologetically. 'We don't serve meals after ten o'clock, sir,' he said. 'The menu makes that clear.'

'That's all right,' said Jasper, 'I came to see someone.'

The waiter looked at him closely for the first time, opened his mouth then clearly changed his mind. 'We'll be closing in ten minutes, sir.'

'I'll be gone by then,' said Jasper. 'It looks as if I'm wasting my time.'

He sat on until closing time, then left the lounge. He felt grubby and disgusted with himself, but it was an addiction. Just as Tam could not break her desire for Rod, nor his for her, so Jasper couldn't keep away from his brother's fiancée.

Sex, he thought darkly, had a lot to answer for. Sex, or the lack of it, was making Tam and Rod miserable, was keeping Aberdeen Shawcross firmly welded to Jet, and was driving Jasper slowly out of his tree. Sexual jealousy over Grete Fischer had led him to yank Aberdeen's chain the day they had met. If he hadn't been so bloody-minded, she might have liked him, and he could have made a move before Jet had consolidated his position. As it was, he'd allowed events to lead him by the nose. The whole darned sexual brew had already blighted the documentary he was supposed to be making, so he couldn't even immerse himself in work.

Bloody sex. He wished it had never been invented.

Get yourself laid or have a cold shower, he thought. He could manage the cold shower, or even a cold bath if he jumped in the harbour, but as for getting laid, that no longer seemed a viable idea. He might visit an obliging woman friend, but the memory of the way he had felt with Tam would probably intrude. He'd been straight with Tam; another woman would be offended if he laid the facts on the line.

Jet and Aberdeen would be well away by now, probably heading for a mutual bed. If he opened his mind he might be able to sense something, taste some pleasure of Jet's.

'*She's got soft hair, hasn't she?*' remarked Jet's voice in his memory. '*And that spot I kissed this morning is softer still . . .*'

Jasper flung away from the pub and the thought together. He knew she had soft hair. He had touched it himself. He had touched her face and her hand, and so he knew her skin as well. They were his own memories, he thought fiercely, owing nothing to any fancied transference from Jet.

Down by the quay, a group of yachties conversed

197

urgently. He passed them by, but one of them flung out a hand to intercept him. 'Hey, Jetman – you better get down to the *Aphrodite*. Someone's tried to stave her in!'

Twice in one night! he thought resignedly. Sometimes weeks went by without anyone mistaking him for Jet. On the heels of that thought came realization of what had been said. He might have turned back towards the quay, but his resolve hardened. He didn't owe Jet any favours. It was up to Jet to look after his own backyard, and if it spoiled his idyll with Aberdeen, that was reality. He wasn't far from Jet's flat, so he stopped off there and buzzed him from the door.

There was a pause, during which Jasper refused to visualize what Jet might be doing, then his brother's voice, distorted by the squawk of the intercom, answered.

'It's me,' said Jasper baldly. 'You'd better get down to the quay, Jet. Someone's bounced a boat off *Aphrodite*.'

He waited impatiently, then Jet emerged, shocked for once out of his usual good cheer. 'Bloody hell, Jas – how bad is it?'

'I don't know,' said Jasper. 'I don't know anything other than what I heard. Do you want me to come with you?'

'Of course, and we'd better grab Charlie on the way. There might be trouble, and he'll want to check in on *Website* and *Christmas Carol*.'

'If there's trouble the harbour police will look after it,' said Jasper, but Jet was rushing past him, and was already heading for Jasper's van which was parked behind his own BMW.

The news when they reached *Aphrodite*'s berth

wasn't encouraging. 'Not much damage done,' reported Jet, 'but she's not the only one – some bloody vandal's cut loose in a motor-boat. Slipped straight through the water rats. Looks like I'd better sleep on board – you staying too, Charlie?'

'Might as well,' said Charlie.

'You can go, Jas,' said Jet. 'Not much you can do.'

'What about Aberdeen?'

'What about her?'

'Hadn't you better let her know you won't be back tonight? She is at your flat, isn't she?'

'She'll be cool,' said Jet. 'I'll give her a ring in the morning. Or, of course, you could drop by and let her know.'

Jasper gave his brother an incredulous look, but Jet's attention was back on the damaged hull. There was no arguing the issue with Charlie Green standing by, so Jasper got in his van and sat behind the wheel, fighting temptation. He didn't think there was any danger of the vandals coming back; more than likely it was kids who'd gone joy-riding and lost control of their boat. They'd probably run her aground somewhere and taken off and that would be the end of the incident.

He knew he should drive straight home to Windhill, but instead, he went round to Jet's flat and let himself in. If she was awake, he'd do as Jet said, tell her what was going on, assure her Jet was all right, then go on home.

Oh, yeah, sneered the imp in his mind, but Jasper was in no mood to take any notice of the imp.

His eyes adjusted to the dim light that entered through Jet's high windows, and he saw that Aberdeen was asleep on the couch. He was almost unbearably tempted to kneel and kiss her awake.

199

The sleeping beauty, he thought derisively, had welcomed a prince, but might not have been so pleased with the attentions of a frog. And, if he remembered his myths properly, it hadn't really been a kiss that the prince used to waken the princess. That refinement had been made in the repressed Victorian age; in the original versions of the robust old tale the prince had employed a method far more direct and basic.

So, no sleeping princess for Jasper Diamond, for it would be no light and playful kiss if he embraced temptation along with Aberdeen Shawcross.

Any decent man might be tempted, but no decent man would have given in. He stretched out a hand to wake her, then touched her hair instead. The curls were soft and natural, and his fingers caught a little in their spirals. Jasper closed his eyes, breathing in the stillness and the faint scent that came from her skin and hair. He wondered if Jet understood what he was risking, using him as a messenger to Aberdeen, and concluded that Jet probably did. Jet knew him inside out, and knew just which buttons to press. Oh, Jet understood him all right, and he would know his Aberdeen was not in the slightest danger. It was *Jasper* who was in danger, of tearing himself apart with his own integrity.

He reached out again to wake Aberdeen, then realized how he would frighten her if she opened her eyes right now. Abruptly, he straightened and backed away to the door. He would have left without waking her, but as he touched the handle she stirred and stretched, thrusting back the quilt.

'Jet?'

Jasper gave up any idea of leaving quietly. If she had

seen him, if she thought he was Jet and hadn't answered her, it could lead to too many complications.

'It's me, Abbie,' he said harshly. 'Jasper.'

'*Jasper?*' She sat up, still dazed with sleep but rapidly coming into focus. 'What is it? What's the time? Oh, dear – is Jet all right?'

'Jet's fine,' said Jasper. 'It's just after two.'

'Where is he? What are you doing here?'

He heard the reserve in her voice, and it cut at him. 'Jet asked me to drop by and say he was spending the night on the *Aphrodite*,' he said. 'There isn't much damage, but he stayed on in case there's more trouble.'

'Oh.' She thrust her fingers through her hair and he saw her wince.

'Is anything wrong?'

'I got my ring caught in my hair. It's the claw setting.'

'Of course.'

'I suppose I should go home,' she said uncertainly. 'Did Jet say what he wanted me to do?'

'You might as well stay on here and go to bed.'

'Who else is likely to come walking in? I was half-expecting Dave to turn up, since he lives here, but I never thought of *you*. How many others might wander in without knocking?'

'Jet told me to come,' he said again.

'He could have rung me instead. He's got his mobile phone.'

'Of course he could,' said Jasper irritably.

Her face was closed and she was staring at him with rising suspicion in the dimness. 'Turn on the light,' she said abruptly, and he did so, narrowing his eyes against the glare and seeing her pupils contract. 'So, why didn't he?' she challenged.

That stung, so instead of staying where he was, he strolled over to her and watched cynically as she tensed. 'At a guess,' he said, 'I'd say he did it to save himself the trouble of explaining, or maybe to torment me. I doubt if he knows himself.'

'Tam says Jet's straightforward.'

Jasper laughed, shortly. 'Tam says a lot of things, but she doesn't know it all. Especially when Jet's concerned. She'd never want to be Jet-fodder herself, but I notice she has no compunction about recommending him to you.'

'That's horrible!' she said. 'How can you be so cruel?'

He looked at her narrowly. 'You're starting to realize it now, are you? That you've made a mistake?'

'Rubbish.'

'He's going to go on doing it,' he said. 'He's going to go on putting his own needs and wants before yours – even his mates' wants, sometimes.'

'Jet is generous and considerate. He's bent over backwards to make me comfortable.'

'If it doesn't interfere with something he wants to do. Aberdeen, I've been beating round the bush for far too long. I know you think I want to split up you and Jet for some twisted reason of my own –'

'Twisted is right!' she flashed.

'But I do have your welfare in mind.' He knew he sounded pompous, and he wouldn't be surprised if she laughed at him.

'You're hurting me for my own good, I suppose,' she said resentfully. 'I don't want to be hurt for my own good. I want you to –'

' "Go away, Jasper",' he cut in. 'Yes. I know the drill by now and I will go away, but you're going to listen to me first. I saw you tonight, you know. At the pub. I was watching you with Jet.'

'I didn't see you!'

'I didn't want you to see me. I was there to see, not to be seen.'

'You're disgusting!' she said in a high voice.

'Damned right,' he agreed. 'So I told myself, several times. I saw you sitting with Jet. He was being the spirit of the party, as usual. You looked tired to death.'

'So? I was tired. I told him so and we came back here.'

'I watched until you left,' he said remorselessly. 'You were tired and fed up, and you wanted to go home. And what did Jet do? Kept right on having a splendid time with his mates!'

'I could have left alone if I'd wanted,' she said. 'I could have caught a bus or a taxi.'

'Tonight, yes, but have you thought about what it will be like when you're off on that damned boat together?'

'We won't be sitting with boring people all night!' she said tartly. 'I'll turn in when I feel like it – and so will Jet.'

'It will all fall back on you to keep Jet entertained. He has to play to an audience, always. He loves a challenge and he loves to see admiration in people's eyes. He has to impress and if he can't do that, he moves on. Why do you think he always chooses younger crewmen and friends who are less intelligent than he is himself?'

'Looks like I fit his bill very nicely. I don't know about intelligence, but I am younger.'

'I don't think you impress easily.'

'I don't.'

'You're too straightforward and in-your-face to be impressed. And one day you're going to show that side of you to Jet and he's not going to like it. One day, you'll ask for something he won't be able to give, won't *want* to give. Do you think it's an accident that he chose to marry you? You, out of all the playmates he's had?'

She stared at him, and for the first time he saw fear in her eyes. 'Tell me,' she said. 'You're dying to give me the bad news.'

'He's offering you what *you* want, and he thinks you can give him what *he* wants,' said Jasper. 'You're young and beautiful, you offer admiration, sex and a kind of dependency.'

'I don't have to listen to this!' she said, and he saw her face was flaming. 'I'm neither a bimbo nor a doormat!'

'He doesn't want a doormat, but he *does* want someone who will be grateful for whatever he chooses to spare.' Jasper waited for another explosion from Aberdeen, but for a few seconds all he heard was her heaving breath. 'It's like something out of colonial times! A young, compliant wife . . . You're too young to settle for that, Aberdeen, too young and too intelligent. In the long term, it won't be enough.'

'Jet *loves* me,' she said.

'Jet loves you in his fashion, but you –'

'What about me?' she asked dangerously. 'It keeps on coming back to *me*, doesn't it? All this about Jet is simply a smoke-screen.'

'You think you love Jet,' he said, 'but how do you know at your age?'

'I'm twenty-three! In colonial times, I'd be married with two or three children. Or practically on the shelf.'

'This isn't colonial times. This is our time, today.

204

Aberdeen, you were in a very vulnerable state when you met Jet, weren't you? Not by colonial standards, but by our own. You'd had a responsible job and lost it, you'd had your independence, and then you were back with your mother, making tea and weeding the garden!'

'I didn't run home to Kate. I simply went down for a holiday, for some breathing space!'

'You went to lick your wounds,' he said. 'It's understandable; you'd lost one game-plan, you were ripe to fall into the one Jet offered. Even though it involves a voyage that you'll hate.'

'Sure, I was down, but I could have pulled myself up again!' she said stubbornly. 'I chose to marry him, but I could have managed without. I could have got the money together, got my museum under way.'

'How?'

'As for the other, I can manage.'

'How?'

He saw her lips move as she repeated his question silently, then she pushed her fingers through her hair again.

'You can't answer, can you?' he said softly.

Her fingers tensed, and his own scalp twinged in sympathy. 'It's not that I *can't* answer,' she said harshly. 'It's that I *won't*. You have no right to ask me that question, Jasper. What I choose to do, how Jet and I feel about one another, and how we arrange our lives together is for us to know, not you.'

'Postpone the wedding!' he said intensely. 'Don't rush into it; there isn't any need.'

'Jet's set on leaving at the end of this month, and he says it mightn't be legal if we marry overseas.' He could hear the doubt in her voice, could see it in her eyes, but she wasn't going to give way. She was at least as stubborn as he could ever be, but she was also unhappy. Unhappy enough to plead with him again. 'Jasper, can't you see this is stressful enough without you stirring things up?'

'I'm trying to ease the stress. To get you to give yourself time, to think again!'

'But why must you interfere? What do you *want*?'

If she hadn't moved then, he might have faced the impossibility of telling her, but she flung out her hands in exasperation and Jasper snatched them in his own. Her reaction was immediate and unmistakable. She tried to jerk away, but the contact was enough to ignite his smouldering desires. He closed the gap between them with a swift stride. For a moment they stood breast to breast, barely touching, then he slipped his hands under her arms, drawing her hard against him before she could back away.

'*Want*! What the heck do you *think* I want?' he cried, then bent to kiss her with a starving intensity that shocked him as much as it apparently shocked her.

Their lips met, and through the roaring in his ears he heard her hoarse cry. For a moment she went still, then she pulled her face away with a gasp, floundering for balance. His hands were still on her back, he was looking down at her, wincing away from the expression in her eyes. They were dark, wide and shocked, drowning with helpless tears.

His hands tightened reflexively, and he watched the tears spill over. 'I'm sorry, I'm sorry!' he whispered, and leaned her forehead briefly against hers before drawing away.

Her lips opened and he braced himself for a stream of invective, a shriek . . . instead, she stared at him in

206

silence, a tide of crimson rushing into her face. She was shaking, her full lips quivering. 'You want *me*,' she said. Her voice was low, hardly more than a breath, and it struck him like a blow.

'I thought you knew,' he said. 'You told Tam I gave you the creeps.'

'I never did, I *never* said that!'

'What, then?'

'I said . . . I think I said . . .' She swallowed, and licked her lips, and he waited an endless aching moment while she fought for memory and control. 'I said you gave me the shivers – I think. The shivery-shakes. And you do.'

'That isn't the same thing at all, is it?'

'No.' Her voice was almost lost now, and the quivering of her body gave substance to her words. 'It isn't the same thing, but it doesn't make any difference. I'm just – sorry – that you feel that way, that you make me feel this way.'

They stared at one another, the tears sliding unregarded down her cheeks.

'Jasper,' she said at last, 'could you please let go? You're hurting me.'

He cursed and let go of her, sliding his hands down her arms and on down to link lightly behind her. 'You're sorry . . .' he said, and bent to kiss her again. His fingers clenched themselves in the cloth at her waist, and touched bare skin. It was hot – surely hotter than it should have been – and she continued to tremble. She was kissing him back, pressing against him, and he felt her breasts heaving with what he suspected were suppressed sobs. He wrapped his arms around her, stroking the bare skin of her waist, up towards her shoulder blades.

He was lost, he knew that. He was lost and so was she, they were lost in their blazing response where the only reality was the heat of skin, the pressure of curves and planes and angles, the mingling of mouths and breath as they gasped and strained together. And then the shrilling of the telephone.

'Jet!' cried Aberdeen, and was shaken by a fresh flood of tears.

CHAPTER 12

Aberdeen sat hunched on the couch with both fists pressed to her mouth to still its trembling.

'Of course it's me,' said Jasper's voice, falling harshly on her ears. 'I'm just about to drive Aberdeen back to her flat . . . I know that, but she's a bit nervous in case Dave comes back . . . Well, you should have thought of that!'

He held out the telephone, his face as harsh as granite. 'Jet wants to talk to you.'

Aberdeen shook her head frantically, but he continued to hold out the phone. 'Don't be such a coward,' he snapped, which was so unfair that she drew a shuddering breath and took it in her hand.

'Lorelei?' Jet's voice sounded just as usual, lighter and more sophisticated than Jasper's. 'Sorry I got held up, but I take it Jas has explained what happened.'

'That's OK,' she managed.

'You'll be quite safe at the flat, you know. Old Dave's not about to attack you!'

'I know, but I'd rather go home.'

'If you like. *Aphrodite*'s fine, by the way. Only a bit of a scratch in the bows. I'm just staying on as insurance in case they come back again.'

'Mmm.' She looked frantically at Jasper, who made a throat-cutting gesture which she vaguely recognized as a director's 'wrap' signal. She yawned. 'I'm really tired, Jet, so I'll get home now and talk to you in the morning, OK?'

'OK, Lorelei, *Gute Nacht* . . . and tell Jas I said *Gute Nacht* to him too. Likewise *auf Wiedersehen*.'

Aberdeen put the telephone back on its rest. Something in her face must have alerted Jasper, for he said harshly, 'What did he say about me?'

'He said goodnight.' But there was more to it than that, and again he read her hesitation.

'How, exactly?'

She shrugged. 'He said it in German . . . that's odd. He used to do that a lot, but not so much lately.'

Jasper nodded. 'I'll drive you back to your flat now.'

'No.'

'Stay here, then.'

His voice was cold and indifferent, and the fevered moments clasped in one another's arms might never have happened.

'I'll take a train.'

'That isn't safe so late at night.'

'It isn't safe in flats, either,' she said tonelessly. '*You* might turn up anywhere.'

He went to the door. 'Are you coming?'

She had told Jet she'd go, so she supposed she should. Silently, she put on her light jacket and slipped on her shoes, then followed Jasper out of the flat. She was shivering violently as she got into his van, but she did up her seatbelt and leaned back so as not to obstruct his view of the street. He knew the way, so it was a silent drive. Only when they had reached Number 44a and she was about to get out of the van

210

did he speak. 'Why didn't you tell Jet I'd been harassing you?'

'*Harassing* me? Is that what you call it?' Her voice sounded both husky and shrill, and she was still shaking.

'That's what you called it. Why didn't you tell him?'

'Oh, yes – I'm really going to tell him you came in and picked a fight then made a grab for me!'

'You tell him everything else I do, every approach I make.'

'I'm not telling him this, Jasper. Not ever. It's too humiliating.'

'*I'm* the one who's humiliated,' he said grimly. 'I don't make a habit of cultivating obsessions. Or of losing control.'

'You don't, do you?' she said bleakly. 'All those other times you've tried to warn me off, you've never once lost control of yourself. It makes me wonder if it was genuine this time.'

'You know it was.'

'Really? Or was it just another ploy to get at Jet through me?' She looked at him in the harsh illumination of the street light. Her throat was so tight she could scarcely manage the words.

He shrugged angrily, and flung out his hands in exasperation. 'Will you be all right, Aberdeen?'

She nodded, and her head pounded. Another tension headache, she supposed, since she couldn't be seasick here on land.

'Goodnight,' he said, and slowly lifted his hand. She flinched away, but he was merely reaching across to open the door. She released the catch on the seatbelt and floundered out ungracefully on to the footpath. Her hand was shaking and she could scarcely unlock the outer door of Number 44a, but she didn't look back.

Aberdeen spent a restless, unhappy night, waking at intervals to a vision of Jasper's still face just before he kissed her the second time. If she hadn't had the suspicion that he had been play-acting all along, she would have blamed herself for that second kiss. She couldn't see how she could have avoided the first scuffle, but she should have seen the second one coming. She supposed it had been the shock that had made her react so slowly to the situation; or rather, the double shock. First his declaration, and then the heat of her response. If the telephone hadn't rung just then, she would have gone on kissing Jasper, would have let him touch her wherever and however he wanted, would have let him make love to her in Jet's own flat. *Let* him? She would have been just as eager herself, and where would it have ended?

Her head ached and her body burned as she fought to make sense of it all. He looked so like Jet that perhaps her senses had been confused into mistaking one for the other. Sex was such an unlikely activity that there had to be a degree of animal instinct to make it work. So, maybe Jet and Jasper, being identical twins, shared the same level of pheromones.

That was a comforting theory, but she couldn't believe it was true. They were so unlike in so many ways and besides, Jet had been kissing and caressing her for some time before Jasper's arrival with the news of *Aphrodite's* danger, and she had certainly not reacted like *that*. She writhed at the memory, with humiliation, shame and a degree of physical longing that shocked her to her soul. She didn't know what to

212

do. Her wedding to Jet was less than three weeks away, Kate was arriving in a few days' time . . .

She moaned, pressing her hands to her aching temples, tossing about until her sheets were damp with perspiration. At last, at five in the morning, she gave up trying to sleep and went to the bathroom to shower. Her legs felt like noodles and her hands were shaking. She stood under the shower spray and almost wept with frustration as she tried to adjust the water. Hot and cold, and she was shivering. She got out of the shower and wrapped herself in a towel, peering at her image in the mirror with something like horror. Flushed and glassy-eyed, her face peered back. She swallowed, and her throat hurt as well as her head. It was only after she tried and failed to recall the arrangements she had made with Jet the night before that the truth finally hit her.

She wasn't just humiliated, she was ill.

Aberdeen went back to bed. She couldn't find any aspirin, and she didn't really believe it would make her feel better. This illness was no ordinary virus, she was convinced of that. It was her punishment for losing control with Jasper. Unless – and she grasped hopefully at the straw of possibility – it was the other way round, and she had lost control because she was already ill. She shivered and burned by turns, and finally rolled out of bed and crept across the floor to telephone the doctor. She was feeling too wretched to say very much, but she stammered that she was getting married in just a little while.

'Better come in to the surgery,' said the receptionist. 'Two o'clock?'

Jet rang as Aberdeen hung up the phone. When he heard she wasn't well he offered to come over, but

213

Aberdeen was too ashamed to face him. 'I'll be fine,' she assured him. 'It's just a bit of a bug. I'm going to the doctor to get some pills.'

'You look after yourself,' said Jet. 'Stay in bed and have plenty to drink. Whiskey's best. It doesn't cure colds, but after a while you don't care if you have a cold or not.'

Aberdeen laughed feebly. If this was a cold, her name was Rudolph the Rednosed Reindeer.

Two o'clock seemed a long way off, so she dozed fitfully, then woke in a panic because it was already after one. She felt so bad it seemed physically impossible that she would be able to get across town to the doctor's surgery. She waited for her head to stop spinning then slowly swung her legs out of bed. Her feet felt hot and swollen as if they wouldn't bear her weight, but she knew she had to get up.

The doorbell buzzed while she was still sitting there, giving her the impetus to creep across the floor. 'Jet,' she croaked, fumbling with the chain, but then, with a horrible sense of *déjà vu* she realized it was Jasper. He stared at her and for once there was no lack of expression on his face.

'My *God*!' he said, and reached out for her. 'You poor little thing!'

She was in his arms, leaning against the blissful coolness of his shirt, feeling the firm planes and muscles beneath it.

'I've got some kind of bug,' she muttered.

'Flu,' said Jasper. 'It's going round.' His hand curved protectively round her head, pressing it against his shoulder, and the coldness with which they had parted the night before might never have been. Even through the general misery of her illness

214

she could feel an awareness of his body against hers, and she pushed herself away.

'What are you doing here?'

'I was worried about you.' His voice seemed to be coming from a long way off.

'How stupid . . .'

'Back to bed.'

'I have to go to the doctor.'

He frowned. 'Didn't you ask for a house call?'

'It costs – fifty-five dollars.'

That was nothing to him, perhaps, but he nodded. 'I suppose they wouldn't come for hours anyway. I'll drive you. Unless you've already arranged it with Jet?'

'He rang,' she said with difficulty, 'but I said I had a bug.'

'And not being blessed with ESP or distance vision, he couldn't see how ill you were,' said Jasper very drily. 'Shall I call him for you?'

'Later.'

'You'd better get some clothes on.'

Aberdeen contemplated the long trek to her bedroom and shook her head, so Jasper went through the door she had indicated and fetched a wrap skirt and a cotton pullover. After that, he waited outside until she was dressed and then picked her up and carried her out of the flat.

Aberdeen protested feebly, but Ed Peters was peering out of his lair at the foot of the stairs. 'Getting in some practice for the threshold?' he said, jovially for him.

'That's right,' said Jasper.

'You let him think you were Jet,' she said as he set her down beside the van.

'Sometimes it's easier,' he said. 'Which surgery?'

Visiting the doctor was exhausting, and Aberdeen felt so weak she could have cried. The flu would run its course, she was informed, but since she was getting married so soon it might pay to take the new anti-viral capsules – and perhaps an antibiotic if a secondary infection developed. Pain-killers, bed-rest and plenty of fluid and she should soon be on her feet again.

'I'll have to be,' she said, and accepted a prescription for a cocktail of pills.

With Jasper's help, she tottered up to her flat again, and slept fitfully through the afternoon. Twice, she woke, to find someone standing by the bed. 'Jet?' she asked the first time, for there seemed to be a double image.

'I'm Jasper,' he said. 'You must be slipping. You've never made that mistake before.'

'Only once . . .' She drank the lemonade he offered, then groaned and closed her eyes again.

The second time she simply blinked up at him. Her eyes refused to focus, and there were black dots dancing in her vision. 'Smile,' she murmured. It seemed to make perfect sense. He smiled, his mouth quirking up at one corner. 'You're Jasper,' she concluded.

'Yes, and I'm going to have to push off after you've had another drink,' he said. 'I'll get Jet to come.'

Her hands shook so much he had to hold the glass for her. 'I must look awful,' she said.

'Most people do when they've got the flu.'

'I don't want Jet to see me like this.'

'He won't care, but he's not much for nursing. Is there anyone who can come and look after you, Abbie?'

She thought of her friends, but they seemed insubstantial. 'Not really.' She wanted him to stay, but she tried not to let it show. Apparently she was unsuccessful, for he smiled, this time without her asking, and shook his head.

'Not me, Aberdeen. You're not yourself, remember. If you were, you'd be kicking me out the door for my real or imagined sins. As it is you're probably going to hate me more than you do already if you remember this at all.'

She closed her eyes, and he stood there uncertainly. 'Tam won't do,' he murmured. 'She's a lousy nurse, and the first to admit it; besides, she's busy.' He clicked his fingers suddenly. 'Got it! I'm going to use your phone.'

Aberdeen lay weakly in bed while he made a call, and little more than half an hour later Ed Peters rang to say a Miss Campbell was waiting to come up. 'We're expecting her,' said Jasper.

'This is Ellie,' he said, ushering in the visitor. 'Ellie works for Tam and me at Diamond/Spellman. Her official title is Continuity and Property Manager.'

'I'm the dogsbody,' said the girl.

'She's also a very good nurse,' said Jasper. 'She's just finished looking after her grandmother, who had the same bug you have. She has also, at odd times, looked after my neurotic dog and a very temperamental cockatoo. After Doc, you should be chicken feed! Now, I'm off. If you need anything else . . . call Jet.'

'Of course,' said Aberdeen.

Jasper went out, and Aberdeen sighed. 'Who's Doc?' she asked.

'A devil in feathers,' said the girl, which didn't make any sense. Aberdeen sighed again and let herself slide into an uneasy doze.

Jet arrived later that evening. Aberdeen wondered

vaguely what he would say about Ellie Campbell, but to her relief he seemed to know her quite well, accepting her presence as a matter of course.

He sat with Aberdeen for a while, but she felt too ill to talk. To her dismay, she felt nothing much when she saw him. His smile and good-humoured assurance that she'd be fine seemed a little too easy. So far as she could see, she'd never be fine again.

The next day he came back, bringing flowers, then stayed on talking to Ellie before going back to his flat. 'Get well soon, Lorelei,' he murmured as he kissed her cheek. '*Aphrodite* awaits and I'm all at sea without you!'

For two days the symptoms were so bad that putting up with them and facing the round of medication, drinks and cold compresses was about all she could handle. On the third day, she began to wonder about Ellie. 'You're not a relative, are you? Of Jet's and Jasper's, I mean?'

'No,' said Ellie. 'I know their sisters, though – Sabby and Gen. We were at Uni together.' She sighed. 'I was doing nursing, but I had to leave after my second year. Jasper and Tam were looking for a dogsbody, Gen suggested me. I didn't think I had a hope, but Jasper took me on. End of story.'

'That doesn't explain why you're helping me,' said Aberdeen.

'I *am* getting paid, you know,' said Ellie with a grin.

'Oh!' Aberdeen felt as if her already hot cheeks were about to crack. 'Of course. Only . . .'

'Not by you,' said Ellie briskly. 'It's a sort of second string to my bow. I can't work as a proper nurse, but if I ever leave Diamond/Spellman and can't get back into Uni, I thought I might do a sort

218

of Girl-for-Hire thing. Reasonable rates, respectable jobs only.'

'I should think you'd be good at it,' said Aberdeen.

'I would,' said Ellie. 'Anyone who can handle Jasper's cockatoo Doc in a temper can handle anything.'

'But doesn't Jas . . . I mean, haven't you got work to do at the studio?'

'Not at present,' said Ellie. 'Jasper's still messing about with *Tassie – In the Rough*.' She hesitated. 'How well do you know Jasper, Aberdeen?'

'Not very well,' said Aberdeen cautiously. 'He came sailing with Jet and me a few times in Tasmania; since then I've met him now and then.'

'You don't know his work at all?'

'I saw one of his documentaries at my mother's place. It was – ' She paused, and tried to think of the right words. 'It was very effective,' she said. 'Jasper and Tam – Ms Spellman – make a very good team.'

'Don't they just?' sighed Ellie. 'The trouble is, Tam didn't come to Tasmania. She and Rod had had some kind of fight and so Rod was in the dumps. My Gran got sick, so I had to leave early, and all round it wasn't a happy situation. I'm betting the rushes aren't up to scratch this time.'

Aberdeen closed her eyes. Ellie's soft voice lilted on, soothingly. She supposed the tale of the Diamond/ Spellman woes was meant to explain why Ellie had time to nurse a stranger, but she didn't really take it in.

'What are you going to do?' asked Tam.

'About which particular problem?' asked Jasper sardonically. 'At the moment I have so many I don't know which one to stress about first.'

'No wonder you're not answering your phone.'

'And I'm not happy with you either,' said Jasper. 'You did me a bad turn with Aberdeen Shawcross, didn't you?'

'I saved your hide over that lunch date,' said Tam indignantly, 'and I'm having her mother to stay! How's that a bad turn?'

'You've been encouraging her to marry Jet.'

Tam looked stubborn. 'It was their idea, and why not?'

'He's rushing her into it.'

'There's not much point in hanging about. She'll be happy with Jet, and the sooner they're married the sooner *you* can start getting over this fixation.' She narrowed her eyes at him. 'Actually, you must be getting over it now. You don't look as tortured as you did.'

'I'm not.' Jasper gave a half-smile. 'I have made a little discovery about Aberdeen Shawcross.'

'She's the illegitimate half-sister of the man we have always called your twin brother Jet, but who is actually a career criminal who has had plastic surgery?'

'You ought to be writing for the soaps. No. About the way she feels about me. *You* told me she said I gave her the creeps.'

'I suppose it was cruel of me,' said Tam, 'but I wanted to get you off her case. And she did say it.'

'She said I gave her the shivers,' corrected Jasper. 'Quite different.'

'Is it?'

'Think about it. A creep is a creep but a shiver can mean all sorts of things. I've seen *you* shiver when Rod's around.'

Tam blushed. 'Don't you start anything,' she warned.

'It's already started.'

'Jasper, you've got enough problems with *In the Rough*.'

'I know.' He turned on Tam. 'I was going to leave her alone, I swear. I would never force myself on anyone who didn't want me. You should know that.'

'She wants Jet.'

'Not really,' said Jasper. 'Don't look like that, Tam! I'm not setting out to get at Jet, but I think they're making a mistake and I hope I can persuade them of that before it's too late. And I do have an ace up my sleeve.'

'What ace?' asked Tam suspiciously.

'Not telling.' Jasper heard himself descending to childhood vernacular and cleared his throat. 'I suppose you heard what happened to Jet's yacht?'

'Someone ran into it, didn't they? Not too badly damaged?'

'I wish it had been written off,' said Jasper. 'That way it would have delayed this darned voyage which might have also delayed the wedding.'

'And what about *In the Rough*?'

'I don't think it's worth proceeding with, do you? Honestly, now?'

'Well . . .'

'I've done a very rough-cut edit of an hour of scenes,' said Jasper. 'I'm having Rod come in and view it later. Will you come too?'

'Not with Rod.'

'Now who's being childish?'

'You don't understand,' said Tam. 'It's the first drink and I'd better not take it. Not if I know what's good for me. I'll come in later with everyone else.'

221

Ellie stayed at the flat for a week, by which time Aberdeen felt better. Not well, but better.

Kate arrived in Sydney while her daughter was still ill, and was on the point of hailing a cab to take her to Blaxland when she saw Jasper waiting at the short-term parking area by the curb.

'Jasper!' she said, and ran to hug him warmly. 'How sweet of you to come and pick me up!'

'I'm not being sweet,' he said, looking down at her. 'I'm crawling.'

'To me?' Kate beamed.

'To your daughter.'

'I see.'

'I believe you do, bless you,' said Jasper. 'How did you know I wasn't Jet?'

'You weren't smiling,' said Kate without hesitation. 'Jet would have been smiling. He doesn't like me much, but he has charming manners.' She stood back to let him take her bags. 'Is Aberdeen really going to marry him, Jasper?'

'I'd love to say *no chance*, but on balance, I'd say she will,' said Jasper. He sounded calm, but there was a tell-tale strain in his eyes.

'I think so too,' said Kate. 'Aberdeen shoots straight from the shoulder. She's given a promise and so she'll most probably keep it.' She sighed a little wistfully. 'All her life she's played fair. She's taking a long time to learn that the world doesn't always reciprocate.'

'Do you play fair, Kate?'

'Mostly.' She smiled, and Jasper caught a sudden fugitive resemblance to her daughter in her softly faded features. 'I won't interfere with Aberdeen and Jet, if that's what you're asking. If he were a bad lot, if I thought he'd be cruel to her I might try, but I think

222

they'll be all right, and she has the right to make her own choices in life. It's completely immaterial that it's *you* I've grown to love.'

'What would you say if I proposed to you?' he said, opening the van door for her.

'Marriage or . . . ?'

'Marriage, of course! You don't propose "or" to a gracious lady.'

'I'd say yes,' said Kate.

'You *would*?'

Kate chuckled. 'Now you're worried! I'd probably say yes if any nice man proposed to me. I manage well alone but I liked being married. Aberdeen's dad was a very nice man.'

'Uncle Godfrey is a nice man,' said Jasper. 'And he's coming up to give Aberdeen away.'

Kate laughed. 'I'll have to bear that in mind.'

Once they reached Wentworth Street, Jasper introduced Kate to Aberdeen's landlord, then escorted her up the steps to the flat. It was the first time he had seen Aberdeen since Ellie's arrival, and he was surprised to see how fragile she still looked. She was sitting in a chair, and struggled up to greet Kate, giving him a mistrustful glance. 'What are you doing here?' she asked over Kate's shoulder.

'I brought Kate from the airport.'

He wondered just how much she remembered of their last encounter, since he was sure she had been partly delirious at the time. He waited until she had released her mother, then moved in smoothly, bending to kiss her cheek, drawing her into a gentle embrace. She had lost weight, and her skin felt like parchment. He wanted to go on holding her, but she struggled free.

'You didn't need to,' she said. 'She was going to

223

catch a cab since I couldn't get there to pick her up.'

'I remembered she was coming in today and thought I'd win some Brownie points,' he said lightly.

'Are you *schleimig*?'

'Undoubtedly,' he said. There was a bunch of florists' roses in the vase, and he surveyed them without pleasure. 'Jet?'

'Of course.'

'Of course.'

'Now Kate's come,' she said deliberately, 'I'm going to start some serious shopping for a wedding dress.'

She was speaking to him alone, and Jasper felt numb, knowing exactly what she was saying. He also understood why she had chosen to say it to him now, with Kate and Ellie present. She was begging him to accept it, not to make a fuss.

'That's it, then,' he said, then turned to include the others. 'I must be getting back to the studio. Tam will pick you up in a couple of hours, Kate, if that's all right?'

'Lovely,' said Kate. Perhaps her eyes were compassionate, but Jasper wasn't looking at Kate. He was looking at his memories, and seeing navy blue eyes, glazing with fever and brimming with tears.

Once Aberdeen was out of bed and dressed, Jet took it for granted she was completely well. He went right back to organizing dinners out, meetings with his friends and sailing parties; every day, it seemed there was something to do. They didn't spend all day together, so Aberdeen was able to go shopping with Kate and, occasionally, with Tam and Ellie.

'Girl talk', Jet called it, and she had to admit that was what it was. Because their wedding seemed set to be an

224

extended party rather than a religious ceremony, Aberdeen was a bit puzzled about the choice of a wedding dress. Since her illness, the traditional satin and tulle simply swamped her, draining her already colourless face.

'I'll have to wear a ton of make-up to get away with white,' she said gloomily.

'Try oyster,' recommended Kate, but oyster was even worse.

Jet wasn't much help. He told her to spend whatever she liked on whatever she liked, but said he was wearing a dress suit he had bought the year before. He obligingly tried it on for her, and looked so ridiculously attractive that she could only stare at him in wonderment. He grinned back, and kissed her hard, but on the whole it was a depressing experience. No way could she choose something simple if he were turned out in splendour, yet her own attempts at splendour looked pathetic.

'I don't know,' said Tam in exasperation. 'You should look gorgeous in white or cream, Aberdeen, but those dresses simply quench you.'

'I suppose it's because of the flu. What would *you* wear, if it were your wedding?' asked Aberdeen.

'We're different types,' said Tam briefly. She took Aberdeen's arm. 'I'd take the cream silk if I were you, and get a professional makeover. You'll be feeling much better in a few days, and then you'll look better too – oh, sorry, I didn't mean it that way!'

Aberdeen laughed a little shakily. 'I know.'

'You need a coffee,' said Tam.

'Or a good stiff drink,' said Kate.

'Coffee will do.' Her continuing weakness troubled her. She was still taking the capsules prescribed by the

225

doctor, but she seemed to have struck a plateau. The days were tiring, and the nights were worse. She had packed a lot of her belongings, and the flat was beginning to seem very temporary.

Aberdeen thought Dave might have the delicacy to arrange somewhere else for himself to stay for that final week before the wedding, but it seemed that Dave was impervious to hints. She might have come right out and asked Jet to eject him, but there didn't seem much point in ruffling the water since Jet was spending most nights on *Aphrodite* anyway. She arranged to move in with Tam and Kate instead.

At first they had thought the vandalism at the quay had been an accident or isolated occurrence, but the petty annoyances had continued spasmodically ever since, and all the yachties were nervous. Many of them, including Jet, had moved their moorings out to Jacaranda Bay. It was less convenient for the city, but secluded and difficult to navigate at speed, which in turn made it less attractive to troublemakers.

'It isn't much,' said Aberdeen, 'mostly scratches to paintwork and the odd can of paint splashed over the decks. No real structural damage, and no arson, but they still can't seem to catch whoever it is.'

'I suppose it isn't serious enough for much police attention,' said Kate wisely.

'If they *did* pay too much attention there'd be plenty of people who'd start muttering about wealth and privilege and favouritism,' said Aberdeen.

'Maybe there's something in that,' said Kate. 'At least the people who own these yachts can probably afford to pay for a bit of extra security.'

'So could Jet,' said Aberdeen, 'but he likes to keep watch himself. He thinks evidence of someone living

aboard is enough to put them off – whoever they are.'
She thought perhaps she should spend the nights on
board herself, but she didn't offer. She would be living
on the *Aphrodite* soon enough.

Since their return to Sydney, she had become
resigned to seeing Jet in snatches, and almost always
in the company of other people, so she was startled
when he came to her flat one morning and told her he
had organized a day's outing for the two of them alone.

'Oh, Jet . . .' she said, and let her shining expression
tell him all the rest.

'You look as if you need cheering up a bit, Lorelei,'
said Jet. 'What is it – girl-talk getting you down?'

'Not at all,' she said. 'I'm a bit tired after the flu.'

'Never mind,' said Jet. 'We'll have a good day out
and you won't have to worry about a thing. I've had the
Diamond Motel's kitchen staff pack us a picnic so
there's nothing to do. Just pop into a jacket and we'll
be off.'

Aberdeen put on her jacket as requested. 'I'll let
Kate know I won't be meeting her today,' she said.
'She won't mind, she was going to look around the
studio anyway.'

She made the call, and allowed Jet to escort her to his
car. 'I have to be out of here in another two days,' she
said, gesturing behind her up the stairs.

'Won't old Peters give you an extension?'

'I asked when I gave my notice. He said no.'

'I'll ask for you.'

And Ed Peters would probably say yes to Jet, but
then, she wouldn't be seeing Kate again for a long time,
so she shook her head. 'I'll stay with Tam. She doesn't
mind. So – where are we going?'

'Over to Sturt's Cove,' said Jet. 'Do you know it?'

227

'No,' said Aberdeen. 'Are we sailing there?'

'What else would we do on a wonderful day like this?'

'What else indeed . . . ?'

'Do I detect a touch of irony there, Lorelei?'

'Not really,' she said. 'It's too nice a day to spend in the city, but remind me when I get back I have to ring your sisters.'

'Better if you forget,' said Jet. 'They're an exhausting pair . . . party, party, party. Don't know how they ever get any work done.'

'Neither do I,' said Aberdeen with feeling. Gentian and Sabrina Diamond were only two years younger than she was herself, but they seemed a different generation.

'With luck they'll be off exhausting people in Africa or the USA or somewhere by the time we get back,' said Jet.

CHAPTER 13

The traffic was slow on the Harbour Bridge, and it took a while to reach Jacaranda Bay, but when Jet cut the motor Aberdeen looked around with delight. The bay was smooth and blue as a quilt, and the curve was traced by a walking path and waist-high wall with thick, springy grass bordering the road. There were at least fifty yachts moored to buoys and tied up to stanchions. Many of them were one-person sailing dinghies, but there were a few ocean-going or racing yachts the size of *Aphrodite*.

'Isn't she a honey?' murmured Jet.

'I can't see any sign of damage,' said Aberdeen, peering at the dazzling hull.

'I had that ironed out the day after it happened,' said Jet. 'I did tell you.'

Aberdeen supposed she had been too ill to take much notice at that time. She leaned against the wall while Jet fetched the picnic things out of the car and locked it up, then delved in her bag for anti-nausea pills. She put one in her mouth, grimacing at the taste. They were supposed to be chewable, but since the flu her tastebuds were all out of whack.

On board, she discovered changes to the yacht. Jet

had fetched in more bedding, a stock of freeze-dried foods, a first-aid kit and more electronic equipment. She examined it with some foreboding.

'Soon be ready,' said Jet cheerfully. 'You've got your passport and everything fixed? Great, we'll take her out on manual under power. You can steer.'

Aberdeen looked apprehensively at the city of yachts. 'I'd rather not,' she said. 'What if I rammed someone by mistake?'

'I'll do it, then,' said Jet. 'Come and keep me company.' He put his arms around her waist and walked her towards the tiller.

At first the ride was so smooth the *Aphrodite* might have been on wheels, but as they slid past the confines of the bay, a light breeze sprang up, whisking the waves like egg-white. Jet put her under sail as soon as he could, the engine was silenced and the *Aphrodite* danced out across the ocean.

'This is it, Lorelei,' said Jet. His voice held quiet satisfaction and a peace which Aberdeen didn't share, but which she thought she could understand. The wind, the waves and a graceful craft under sail; men had loved that combination for centuries. That mix of chance and determination was a heady brew for those who had fallen under the spell of sails and sea; and generations of women had agonized over their inability to compete. The salt spray and the hiss of the waves, the faint thrum of wind in the shrouds – the sail curved and belled like the bust of an Edwardian beauty. The tension and supple strength of Jet's body touched hers, his arms came around her and she gave herself to the moment.

The wonder lasted for an enchanted half-hour, but by degrees Aberdeen became aware that her arms and legs were aching and trembling with tiredness, that a band was tightening across her forehead, that a heavy, viscous substance seemed to be pouring into her brain. She shook her head and breathed deeply, and Jet's arms around her were interfering with her need for air. 'I'll go and rest a while,' she said, and ducked away to lean against the rail.

She fell into a kind of daze, but every time she struggled out of the mire and looked across at Jet, he was standing at the tiller, gazing out across the water like a lover or a god.

They had cut across a wide bight and were now heading for a small, secluded bay named Sturt's Cove. Aberdeen had no idea of the time, for her leaden perceptions were entirely focused on staying awake, staying upright. She *wasn't* seasick, and the pills had never made her feel so strange before. It must *be* the pills, she supposed, and perhaps they didn't mix too well with the prescription capsules.

'Would you like to take her in?' called Jet. He had slackened the sail, and the yacht was moving slowly towards the mouth of the bay.

She shook her head and smiled at him, and it felt like a grimace.

The cove was small and crystal, with a half-moon of white sand beach and shingle bank. The trees with their tangle of lianas came down close to the water, and with the *Aphrodite* now riding at anchor, it was very quiet.

'Eat first or swim?' asked Jet, coming back to lean beside her.

'I haven't brought my things,' she managed.

'Ah,' said Jet with a gleeful grin. 'I haf made my arrangements!' He produced a vast blue towel and a

231

slink of black lycra. 'For you,' he said, his eyes dancing. 'No more excuses, *Fraülein* Lorelei, ve haf vays of making you svim!'

'I don't think . . .' Aberdeen realized she was being a wet blanket, but there was a clench of apprehension in her chest. Jet had once threatened, more or less playfully, to throw her overboard and jump in after her. Jasper had stopped him then, but Jasper wasn't with them now. Where was Jasper when she needed him?

She pushed him out of her mind, as she had been pushing him every time he appeared. He had been kind when she was ill, but his kindness had come with a price tag. The fact that she hadn't struck any bargains meant nothing. He would have made another move if she hadn't cut him short. She smiled at Jet with an effort. 'I'll just pop down and get changed.'

'You can strip off here,' said Jet. 'There's no one around but me.'

Again she acquiesced, removing the bulky life-jacket and then her cotton skirt and top. She stepped quickly out of her panties and into the bathing suit, then drew it up around her hips before reaching back to unfasten her bra.

'No fair!' said Jet, and reached round to remove it himself. 'You've lost some weight,' he said, and brought his hands up to cover her breasts. 'Have you been dieting?'

Aberdeen swallowed. His hands were cool from the spray and her head seemed stuffed with dough. 'It was the flu,' she said.

'You'll have to put it back on,' said Jet. He bent to kiss the tops of her breasts above his hands, then pulled the straps of the swim-suit over her shoulders. 'There!'

He stripped to his own swim briefs and turned to lower the ladder over the edge of the *Aphrodite*. 'The water's quite shallow,' he said.

'Wh-what about sharks? And jellyfish?'

'Unlikely. I'll go down first, then you climb down to meet me.'

She was grateful that he didn't intend to toss her over the side, but she felt very much alone when Jet dived neatly off the deck. He surfaced like a seal, smiled up at her, and held out his hands. Aberdeen swallowed again, shivering, and then, with a feeling of doom, climbed down the ladder.

The water closed around her ankles, and she forced herself to step down. Calf-deep, knee-deep, and then it was up around her thighs. She could feel the cold saltiness lapping the tops of her legs and there she stuck. She peered down, past the clear sliding water. It lapped Jet's ribs, and if she were standing with him she would be breast-deep.

'Come on.' Jet's hands came around her thighs to guide her down another step. She reached down with one foot, but she was standing on the bottom of the ladder.

'I've changed my mind,' she said.

'I haven't!' Jet tugged, and she lost her balance and flailed wildly before falling towards him. Jet stumbled and went under, laughing so a great stream of bubbles boiled up. Aberdeen screamed, hitting the water face-first. Her foot was caught in the bottom rung of the ladder, and all she could do was flounder and gulp frantically for air.

Jet surfaced and stared. Aberdeen had caught her foot, but why didn't she simply twist it free? He went to support her, but in the end he had to unhook the rope himself. She was gulping and gasping. 'Sorry, Lorelei,' he said, but he couldn't quite keep the amusement out of his voice. 'I'll teach you underwater swimming, but you'd better learn to float on the top of it first!'

The water was cooler than he had expected, but refreshing, and he wanted a proper swim. Today was Aberdeen's, however, so he towed her into slightly shallower water. 'Now, all you have to do is lean forward and let the water take your weight,' he said.

She shook her head.

'Just lean forward and push yourself off with your feet. I won't let you go under.'

Her sweet mouth clamped shut and he laughed. He loved it when she looked stubborn.

'Come on,' he said. 'Or if you like, we can try another way.' He turned her so she was lying in his arms. 'There!' he said. 'You're floating. Just relax.' She wouldn't relax, though, lying stiff as a wooden figurehead. She was shivering, too, so he began to pilot her towards the beach. 'There,' he said, depositing her on the warm dry sand. 'I'll fetch the picnic things.' He collected the picnic things and the towels, then, holding them above his head, waded back to Aberdeen.

He enfolded her in one big towel, then spread the other towel on the sand and laid her gently down, peeling down the wet swimsuit and kissing her breasts. She tasted of salt and the sea, and he had a sudden mental picture of his brother Jasper. Had Jasper ever had a girl on the beach? Perhaps on his precious Allirra Island, up the coast? He ran his hands down Aberdeen's body, feeling her concave stomach and prominent ribs. She *had* lost weight; he supposed it was all the running around she had been doing after her mother and Tam. The sun was warming him, and he was feeling incredibly randy, but uncomfortable memories of seaside sex made him reconsider.

He sat up again, knees apart to ease his discomfort. 'Better wait until we can have a shower,' he said, giving her a friendly pat on the hip. 'Unless you'd like to give me a hand?' He gestured at the evidence of his arousal, but she shook her head and sat up, pulling the towel around her.

'My hands are cold,' she said.

'And sandy.' He bent to kiss her fingertips, feeling the faint grittiness. 'Better not. Are you ready to eat?'

She nodded, but when he pushed the basket in her direction she seemed clumsy and he had to help unpack it.

'What's wrong, Lorelei?' he asked.

'Hmmm?' She sounded vague.

'You've been giving me the cold shoulder all day. If you're not enjoying yourself, we might as well pack it in and go home.'

'I'm sorry,' she said, and smiled with what appeared to be an effort. 'I've got a bit of a headache, that's all.'

'Another one? You're not trying to tell me something, are you?'

'No.'

'I hope you're not going to have too many headaches once we're married. Did you get that prescription for the Pill?'

'Yes.' There was a pause, then she blurted, 'Mightn't it be better if you used something?'

He stared at her, seeing her face turning slowly crimson. 'I thought we agreed on the Pill?'

235

'I only thought – you've had a few girlfriends, haven't you.'

'Of course,' he said, and laughed. 'Lorelei, are you trying to ask if I've been practising safe sex?'

'I suppose so.'

He touched the tip of her nose. 'I have. Always. Do you think I'd put you at risk? Or myself?'

She looked so relieved that he almost laughed, but at the back of his mind was a niggling question. 'Did your mother put you up to this?'

'Kate?' Her cheeks were pale again. 'Of course not.'

'Was it Tam, then? Or Jas?'

'I haven't discussed it with anyone!'

'No need to make a drama out of it.' He leaned over and took a bunch of grapes from the picnic basket and silenced her by popping one into her mouth. He bent to kiss her, tasting salt and sweet fruit juice. Jasper was in his mind, and he wondered for a moment if he should have invited his brother along. He might have helped with the swimming lesson and it would have been amusing to see him trying not to look at Aberdeen's breasts, so temptingly outlined by the clinging nylon.

Aberdeen was uncomfortable, damp and gritty, sticky with salt and sand. She was still feeling decidedly odd, cold to the bone despite the warmth of the sun. The cold was guilt, she supposed, as well as the aftermath of the flu and the shock of her sudden submersion. Jet's kisses and caresses should have warmed her, and he had a right to expect a response, but the virus seemed to have put her feelings into the deep freeze. His light kisses were pleasant enough, but when he touched his tongue with hers and slipped his hands around her breasts, all she could feel was a jittery sensation and

236

wish he'd either get it over with or leave her alone. Presumably he had brought her to this deserted little beach with leisurely lovemaking in mind, but he didn't persist and neither did she want him to.

She would have wanted him to persist if it had been Jasper.

The thought came uninvited, unwelcome, and filled her with another chill of guilt. She remembered the events of the night at Jet's flat as if through a veil, for she now knew she had been sickening for the flu even when she travelled on the train to visit Tam. The encroaching virus accounted for the clammy heat and exhaustion she had suffered, as well as her malaise when out to dinner with Jet. She had picked at her food, had scarcely been able to keep awake. Her feelings had been out of joint, and so that sudden rush of desire for Jasper must have been another manifestation of the disease. It had not need to bother her now.

She smiled at Jet and swallowed her midday flu capsule, washing it down with a sip of Perrier water.

Kate was spending the day at the studio with Jasper.

'What do you want to see?' he asked.

'Everything,' said Kate blissfully. She was basking in the novelty of Sydney. 'Not that I won't be happy to go home to my peace and quiet,' she said, 'but it's so exciting. I've never been here for more than a day or so before.'

'Everything it shall be,' said Jasper. 'First, the grand tour, such as it is.'

Diamond/Spellman was a dinosaur of a place. Sometimes Jasper and Tam leased space to other companies, and the building had hosted more than one convention as well as exhibitions of everything from Irish dancing to body painting.

'We've got a sort of a museum here,' said Jasper, shepherding Kate through a maze of corridors. 'Old film-making equipment – did you know the first feature film ever was made in Australia? Then there's Tam's area, which is involved more in light-shows and fashion shows . . . This is Ellie's room, and the common kitchen.'

The day culminated in an informal meeting of the *In the Rough* team including, despite her protests, Tam Spellman. Kate had planned to disappear for the duration, but Jasper told her with some irony that she'd better attend as a sample representative of the viewing public, so long as she agreed to represent the interests of her peers.

She supposed it was unusual, but why not? It was bound to be interesting.

At four, everyone collected in the viewing room, and Jasper ran what he said was a rough-cut tape of the documentary he had been filming in Tasmania. Kate found the experience interesting from more than one angle; she was very fond of Jasper, she knew many of the places showcased, and she found it intriguing to see a television show in embryo.

Quite apart from the material, she was interested in the various people present. Ellie and Tam she knew quite well, but there were three men she hadn't met. Stewart and Steve had tow-coloured hair and blue jeans; they lounged together and she thought they were probably gay. The third man, Rod Bowen, featured in more than one of the sequences on the film. He said he was the general assistant, roustabout and roadie, but Jasper treated him as a very good friend. Although he smiled and greeted her politely she could see he was strung up almost as badly as Jasper. Tam was unhappy too . . . she was sitting as far from Rod as she could get, but their awareness of one another was almost visible. Did she love him or hate him? Loved him probably, thought Kate. Tam's hate would have made him belligerent, not worn him to a thread.

All her life Kate had made it her rule to stay out of other people's business, but the tension affecting Jasper, Tam and now Rod Bowen was far too plain to miss. She knew and sympathized with Jasper's problem. Tam's and Rod's might be similar, but she couldn't work out what was keeping them apart. Tam was a widow, but maybe Rod was married to someone else? For the first time she was glad she was sixty-seven, and could hope she was past these wounding passions.

She tugged her mind back to the tape, which was ending in a scene with Tasmanian devils.

'So there it is, crew,' said Jasper, switching off. 'I won't insult you by pretending we haven't got a monumental problem. Comments?'

'It's too short,' said Ellie. 'And disjointed.'

'Darned right, but this represents all the decent footage I could wring out of it. And let's not be mealy-mouthed. It isn't only the length; my performance stinks.'

'We could film more material,' suggested Stew.

'That's a possibility. But what's to stop it being as bad as the stuff we have already?'

'Make it a short,' said Steve.

'There's enough good stuff for an hour's special,' agreed Rod. 'At least you're not locked into a contract length.'

239

'That's very true. I thank God daily we don't have to deal with a peeved sponsor or backer.' Jasper turned to Kate. 'Kate? You know Tasmania. Would you be satisfied if you saw a tidied-up version of the material you just watched?'

'I'd be disappointed,' said Kate. 'Not because it's bad, but because I expect the best from *In the Rough*. I've been spoilt.'

'Thank you Kate.' Jasper's crooked grin appeared. 'You've picked up on my own gut feeling. Tam?'

Tam turned out her hands and pulled a face. 'What can I say? I know you're all gunning for me because I didn't come with you, but I didn't have a lot of choice.'

'You had a choice,' said Rod Bowen coldly. 'You just didn't have the guts to make it.' He turned to survey the rest of the assembly, and Kate was struck again by the drawn look of his outrageously handsome face. 'You want to know what the reason was?' he demanded. 'The real reason Ms Spellman wouldn't join us in Tasmania?'

'Shut up, Rod!' snapped Tam, but Rod got up in one economical movement and stalked over to her sagging chair.

'I was busy!' she hissed, struggling upright to confront him.

'And?'

'And I didn't want to be pestered by you!'

'By "pestering",' said Rod pleasantly to the transfixed witnesses, 'she means she wanted no repetition of a proposal I dared to make. Not when she'd be forced to travel in the same vehicle with me for hours at a time.'

'I *told* you,' said Tam, 'I've been married once, and I don't want to risk it again.'

'Not with me, you mean!' said Rod. 'She feels that I lack aestheticism and taste and a few other virtues she requires in a husband,' he told the others flatly.

'I'd say you've just about proved her point about the lack of taste,' put in Jasper. 'A lack of sensible timing, anyway. Go home.'

'Don't interfere, Jasper!' flashed Tam.

'Then don't wash your dubious linen in public. You're embarrassing all of us, especially Kate.'

'I didn't start it – but he's got it wrong, anyway.' She was scarlet by now, but whether from rage, shame or incipient laughter Kate couldn't be sure.

'All right!' yelled Rod. 'How have I got it wrong?'

'If you don't know . . .'

'Cut it out, Tam! I'm not a mind-reader!'

'Go home!' bellowed Jasper. 'For God's sake, go back to Tam's and don't come back here until you've sorted yourselves out!'

The air between the combatants was practically sizzling, and when Jasper grabbed each by an arm and urged them out the door, Kate almost expected to see him recoil from the shock of touching them. He seemed to feel some discomfort, for when he closed the door behind them, he leaned against it and pulled out a handkerchief. 'Three deep breaths, everybody,' he said. 'And nobody, *nobody*, strike a match!'

'Just as well Tam didn't come to Tassie if they're going to carry on like that,' said Steve into the silence. 'Otherwise we'd have even less to work with.'

The team broke up and went to their various homes, leaving Jasper with Kate. 'What can I say?' he asked. 'Except that we usually don't play host to such unseemly displays at Diamond/Spellman?'

'You don't need to say anything,' said Kate. 'It was

obvious something was brewing from the minute we came in.'

'Lord, yes.' Jasper shook his head. 'We've been flying storm warnings for weeks. Which brings us to a further problem. What are we going to do with you for the night? You can't go back to Tam's. Not with those two. Would you like to stay at my place?'

'I'll stay with Aberdeen,' said Kate. 'She's out sailing with Jet today, but I could go round later. Even if she's not home, Mr Peters will let me in.'

Jasper's face never altered, but his fists clenched slowly. As if, thought Kate, a dentist had hit a nerve and he had braced himself for another throb to come. 'I'll drive you round to Blaxland,' he said slowly.

Kate's heart ached for Jasper, but she had to consider Aberdeen first so she said briskly, 'I'd better get a train or a cab.'

'I'll drive you,' said Jasper again. 'But first, I'll take you out to dinner by way of an apology.'

'For what? A thoroughly stimulating day?'

Jasper stared at her, then suddenly, he laughed. 'We'll still have dinner,' he said. 'You can tell me about primrose sports and I'll tell you all about my island.'

' "No man is an island",' quoted Kate, but it occurred to her that perhaps Jasper Diamond was.

Back on the *Aphrodite*, Aberdeen changed into her skirt and top, then combed her curly hair. It was stiff with salt, but she could wash it when they got home. By the time they reached Jacaranda Bay, she was so tired she could scarcely keep awake. That blend of anti-nausea and anti-flu medication ought to be marketed as a sleeping pill – and an anti-aphrodisiac, she thought.

242

'I suppose you're sleeping on board again?' she said.

Jet nodded, so she took a deep breath. 'I could stay with you tonight. There's enough food in the basket and we could go back into the city in the morning.'

'I have to see to something first,' said Jet, 'so we might as well have dinner in town.'

'I'm all sticky . . . I couldn't possibly go to a restaurant.'

'At the flat,' said Jet. He smiled at her, his eyes glinting in his tanned face.

'Lovely,' said Aberdeen, and yawned. 'Sorry.'

It was dusk by the time they drove back to the city, and Aberdeen was half asleep. She was reluctant to enter Jet's flat, knowing it would hold the memory of the charged scene with Jasper. Her legs were trembling as she followed Jet up the stairs, and she leaned against the wall as he opened the door to a sudden whiff of smoke and beer. She supposed that was what alerted her, for she had heard nothing from behind the closed door. They must have been very, very quiet, lying in wait for Jet and herself to come back.

'Come on, Lorelei!' said Jet, and put his arm round her, urging her forward.

'Wait – ' she said.

His hand on her hip was inexorable, and she heard the latch click as he closed the door. For a heartbeat she stood staring through the gloom, then the lights sprang out.

'Surprise!' yelled someone. She wasn't sure if it was meant to be ironic or not, but the flat certainly held a crowd of people.

She looked around, her face cold with shock and a high degree of outrage. A crowd of elegant strangers, and she was covered in salt, wearing an old cotton skirt

243

and top. No make-up, her face pale from the flu and her hair in piglets' tails.

'Surprise!' said Jet.

'Nothing like sand, sun, sea and sex to give a girl a glow,' remarked Shane Tyrone.

'Nothing,' agreed Jet. He kissed her heartily and she could have bitten him.

It was eleven o'clock when Jasper drove Kate to Blaxland. Aberdeen's door was locked, and a call from Kate produced no answer. She shrugged and got Ed Peters, grumbling a little, to let her in. The flat had an uninhabited air already. 'I'll be fine now, thanks, Jasper,' said Kate briskly. 'You'd better be gone before she comes back.'

Logic told him Kate would be perfectly safe in a flat Aberdeen had inhabited for a year, but still he felt a little dubious about leaving her.

Liar, said his imp. You want an excuse to hang around.

Recognizing this uncomfortable truth, Jasper left, but he didn't go right home to Windhill. Cursing himself, he pulled over, took out his mobile and keyed in Jet's number. At least he could ascertain that his brother and Aberdeen had returned from sailing. If they were spending the night on board the *Aphrodite* he would let Kate know that Aberdeen wouldn't be back.

Jet's mobile was switched off, so Jasper tapped the reset key and called the flat instead. Dave would probably be there, if no one else, and so he could leave a message for Aberdeen to call her mother in Blaxland.

The phone rang a few times, and then Aberdeen

answered. He knew it was Aberdeen, though the background noise was loud enough to make it difficult to hear what she was saying.

'It's Jasper here,' he told her curtly. 'Kate's at your flat.'

'I can't hear you.' The strain was clear in her voice.

Jasper repeated his message as loudly as he could, but her reply was still uncertain. She sounded as tense as over-stretched elastic, and he felt his own nerves twinging in sympathy; and not only his nerves. For a moment, he felt her bitter exhaustion seeping into his own muscles, and tasted the sourness of whatever she had been trying to drink. 'Abbie?' he said urgently, 'Abbie – don't worry, I'm coming.'

He knew she wouldn't have heard him, so he cut the connection and pulled out into the traffic, driving around the block then heading back towards the quay and Jet's flat. It was close to midnight when he arrived, but there were cars and motorbikes right along the street. He could feel the subdued beat of music through the soles of his feet, and the structure of the building seemed to vibrate slightly. He wondered why the neighbours hadn't complained, then concluded that Jet had probably invited them all to his party.

There was no reason why Jet shouldn't have a party, and no reason why he should have invited Jasper. Nevertheless, Jasper felt a kind of rage building up in his mind and body as he bounded up the stairs. The door was on the latch, so he let himself in, releasing a blast of sound that seemed to buffet him like a storm at sea. There had to be at least fifty people present; not a huge crowd, but a lot to jam in a bachelor flat. Most of them were men, yachting or financier friends of Jet's,

Wunderkinds and *infants terrible*. The few women present were slickly dressed, either in well-cut trousers and designer shirts, or in brief tight skirts, low-necked tops and fragile high-heeled shoes. Fingernails and lipstick glinted under the lights, and thighs in translucent stockings gleamed as the dancers swayed to the music.

Jet was laughing with a crowd of friends. From the gestures they were making, they appeared to be capping fish stories. Whether the fish were piscine or human clients was open to question. The air was wisping with smoke; just the thing for a girl recovering from the flu, thought Jasper savagely as he shoved his way through the crowds.

Aberdeen was in the kitchen. She had obviously been making coffee, but now she was sagging wearily over the sink. The skirt and top she was wearing might have been crisp and fresh that morning, but after a day of sailing they were as limp as their occupant. Her hair was curling, but the strands seemed dull as if she'd been swimming and hadn't rinsed out the salt. As he watched she wearily rubbed her neck. He closed the door behind him. It made little difference to the noise level, but gave the illusion of privacy. Presumably she noticed this, for she turned round abruptly. Her face was as defeated as her pose.

'Abbie,' he said, and strode forward to confront her.

He waited for a leap of suspicion, for the animosity with which she always greeted him, but she just looked at him dully for a while. 'Jasper?' she said at last, uncertainly.

He couldn't hear her voice, but he read her lips. He bent to speak directly in her ear. 'I've come to take you home.'

The rush of gratitude couldn't possibly be misinterpreted. 'I'm so *tired*,' she said, in explanation.

'You've been ill,' he reminded her. 'Fetch your jacket and come with me.'

CHAPTER 14

Aberdeen had no idea how Jasper had come to appear, but she knew she was pleased to see him. She would have been pleased to see anyone who had offered to take her home. She fetched her jacket and looked across uncertainly at Jet.

'Ring him tomorrow,' urged Jasper, but she couldn't leave the party just like that.

She went to Jet and he made a long arm and pulled her against him, stroking her breast without looking at her once. 'I'm going home!' she called, but the effort of speaking at such a pitch was making her cough.

Jet noticed that, and glanced down at her. Eyes watering, ribs and midriff aching, Aberdeen gestured towards the music centre. Obligingly, one of the dancers turned it down. Jet raised an acknowledging thumb then turned his attention to Aberdeen.

'I'm going home,' she wheezed.

'It's early yet!'

'Not for me . . .'

'Can't you wait a while? The Greens are dropping by later with Rusty – the charter business is in trouble and they want me to look at the books.'

'Jasper says he'll take me home,' she said.

She expected Jet to nod amiable acceptance, but his immediate companions, who included Chick, Scott, Drew and Shane Tyrone, took up a would-be witty repartee.

'Jasper will take her home!'

'Ah, but *whose* home?'

'Better watch your back, Jetman – you know how these women go for telly stars.'

It was puerile and ridiculous and she thought Jet would ignore it, unless he decided to join in.

'Can she tell you apart in the daylight?' asked one wit.

'Doesn't matter,' said Tyrone snidely, 'so long as she knows which is which in the dark . . . eh, Drew?'

Jet laughed, but there was an edge in his voice as he said, 'Tell Jas not to be so bloody officious – I'll look after you.'

'You tell her, Jetman – don't take any lip from the old woman!'

'Shut up,' said Jet. He patted Aberdeen's shoulder. 'Why don't you have a lie down if you're tired?'

She stared at him, seeing her chance for escape receding. 'All right,' she said. 'I'll do that.'

She turned her head and saw Jasper waiting across by the door. His gaze was trained on her as if there were no one else in the room. She lifted one shoulder in a shrug, giving him an apologetic and dismissive smile. He made no move to leave, so she picked her way across to him.

'Are you ready?'

'No.' She smiled again. 'I'm not coming. I've decided to lie down here instead. There's nothing wrong with me, I'm just tired, and the Greens are coming round later.'

'You can't rest with this row going on.'

'The music's not so loud now. Thank you for dropping by.' She knew she sounded like a hostess, and squirmed inside.

Hostess? That was a joke! She felt more like a sixteen-year-old who had wandered into this party by mistake. By turns sophisticated and crude, Jet's friends seemed to meld with no trouble at all, and left no room for her.

Perhaps if she'd been sixteen she would have cast herself on Jasper's broad chest and begged him to take her home. Instead, she simply offered her hand as graciously as she could. He took it, and for a moment the noise and the crowd retreated, leaving the two of them alone. 'I'll be all right,' she said, and looked up into his eyes; a mistake, for his expression was so savage that she dropped his hand and fell back a step or two.

'You're living on your nerves.' He touched her cheek and she flinched and stifled a cry. 'You see? You're living on your nerves, and soon there won't be anything left. But you'll be all right, of course. Jet has spoken.'

People were peering at them curiously, and Aberdeen flushed. 'I'm going to lie down,' she said shortly, and stumbled into Jet's bedroom and closed the door.

She kicked off her shoes and lay down, shivering. The beat of the music came dully through the door and after a few minutes she felt herself drifting . . . she woke with a jolt as the music poured forth, loud, discordant and distorted as if even Jet's splendid sound system could not cope with the decibel level. She stared wretchedly at the ceiling for a while, but the sound did not diminish. Then suddenly it cut off in the middle of a track.

It's blown a valve! she thought in confusion, although she doubted that modern systems would have a valve to blow. An IC, perhaps? Almost immediately, she became aware of an unnatural quiet. Had the police come, to warn the party-goers to keep the noise down?

She rolled off the bed, and crept across to open the door. The crowd had not diminished, but it had coalesced around the edges of the room, and everyone seemed to be staring at Jet and Jasper who were somehow facing one another in the middle of the narrow space. They're going to fight! thought Aberdeen. Shocked, she hurried over, rumpled and barefoot. It was a ridiculous situation, all the melodramatic old movies rolled into one. The Regency wench rushing between the drawn swords . . . the twins meeting with pistols at dawn . . . the lady trapped between two opposing knights. And why didn't someone stop them?

'What are you *doing*?' she gasped. Her chest was heaving with fright and apprehension, and she stared wildly from one man to the other. Jet was still wearing his sailing clothes, casually insouciant, as assured as if he had been dressed in the pinnacle of fashion. Jasper was also dressed casually, in his usual faded denims and a chambray shirt that had clearly seen several summers. He, however, looked neither relaxed nor insouciant, but rigid and extremely dangerous.

'What are you *doing*?' cried Aberdeen again, and in that instant the tableau broke. Jasper moved a fraction, turning to her. Jet's mobile face broke into a wide, delighted grin.

'What do you think we're doing, Lorelei?' he asked lazily, but with a perceptible edge on his voice. 'Pistols at dawn, or maybe fisticuffs?'

She blinked, wishing the floor would open and let her drop down to the foyer without benefit of stairs. 'Of course not – oh, I don't know!' she said dazedly.

'Well,' drawled Jet, 'Jas was just explaining exactly why he thought he had to come to fetch you. That's all.'

'But the music stopped. I thought something had gone wrong.'

'We couldn't hear ourselves speak, and though we did have a try at mind-reading in our youth, it never worked very well.' He kissed her cheek and pulled her to his side. 'Remind me to tell you about it some time. Or maybe you should ask Jas.' He held out a hand towards his brother. 'Now we have silence in the court, you might as well say your piece.' He glanced mockingly at his watch. 'You have exactly sixty seconds to make a case for stealing Aberdeen away from us. Your time starts – now!'

It was a parody of a quiz master and everyone laughed. The tension broke, and Aberdeen felt she hadn't been the only one to misinterpret the twins' behaviour.

Jet was holding her lightly, but she focused her attention on Jasper who went on saying nothing but held out his hand as if by force of will he could draw her to his side. She trembled, feeling that tug in her nerves and muscles and the pit of her stomach.

'Spoilsport,' said Jet, and his voice was soft in the continuing silence. He smiled down at Aberdeen. 'Your mother wants you, Aberdeen. Nothing's wrong, but she's spending the night at your flat and she wants you to come back and keep her company. Apparently she rang here earlier but couldn't make any sense of whoever answered the phone. Not surprising, with the music going and half those present pissed.'

That wasn't Kate who rang, thought Aberdeen stupidly. That was Jasper. She looked up at Jasper, perplexed. If only he would smile or frown or do anything other than stand there, a lodestone dressed in shabby clothes and the face of an effigy.

'So,' continued Jet, with enjoyment, 'your mother got hold of Jas and sent him to fetch you home. Are you going to go, or shall we send him back to Blaxland with a message tied to his leg like a carrier pigeon?'

'I'll ring Kate from here,' said Aberdeen. She broke away from Jet and headed for the telephone, determined to make some sense out of all this.

The phone rang half a dozen times and then Kate answered. 'Aberdeen! Are you all right?'

'Of course,' she said. 'Are you? I had a message saying you wanted me back at the flat. *Do* you?'

'That depends,' said Kate judiciously. 'Are you having a lovely time?'

'Not exactly.' Aberdeen was aware of the silence behind and tried to keep her voice light and her answers non-committal.

'Do you *want* me to want you back here?' pursued Kate.

'Definitely.' She injected more lightness into her voice. 'Some of Jet's friends threw us a surprise party! They were all waiting here when we got back from sailing. The party's set to go all night.'

'I want you to come back,' said Kate. 'I'm a selfish old biddy and after next week I won't be seeing you again for a year or more.'

'Oh, all right. Since you've sent Jasper all this way I'd better not keep him waiting.' Aberdeen hung up the telephone and tried to settle her features into a

253

suitably regretful expression. 'Kate does want me,' she said. 'It's pretty late anyway, so if you'll all excuse me, I think I'd better go home. Jet?'

'Catch you in the morning, sweetie,' he said, and gave her a lingering kiss.

There was a roar of approval, and Aberdeen's ears were still burning when she followed the silent Jasper down the stairs to his waiting van.

'Thank you,' she said evenly as he started the engine.

He didn't pretend to misunderstand her. 'You sounded at the end of your tether.'

'I was. I am.'

'Jet ought to be thumped,' he said with controlled fury.

Aberdeen leaned wearily against the sheepskin upholstery. Like most of Jasper's belongings the van was neither new nor state-of-the-art, but it was comfortable. 'It wasn't Jet's fault,' she said. 'His friends gave us a surprise party. They were waiting when we got back from sailing.'

'And Jet didn't know about it?'

'We were out all day,' she said indirectly. 'And we *did* consider sleeping aboard *Aphrodite*. Lucky we did come back, otherwise Dave would have had to cope alone.'

'And *you* might have had a good night's sleep,' said Jásper.

'What's up with Kate? She didn't sound worried, so what's she doing at my place?'

'Tam and Rod had a very melodramatic showdown,' said Jasper. 'I sent them back to Tam's to fight it out. By now they're probably tearing one another apart, which will make a change from doing it unilaterally.'

'Rod's the one she was trying to dig out of her life,'

254

said Aberdeen. 'She said he was like potato eyes.'

'She'll never do that. She'll just have to settle on whether to stop digging and let him take root or gouge him out and live with a seeping wound.'

'That's horrible,' she said, shaken by his violent imagery.

He shrugged. 'Love is horrible sometimes.'

'Not for Jet and me.'

Jasper gave her an ironic glance. 'Grow up, Aberdeen, now, before it's too late.' He drove on for a few minutes then said conversationally; 'I thought at first that Jet would hurt you. I wanted very much to keep you from being hurt. You looked so sweet and so vuliunt.'

'And now?'

'Now I'm actually more afraid that you never *will* be hurt. You'll drift through life with Jet, and his wealth and smiles will wrap you in a pink cottonwool cloud. Your life will be silicon-coated.'

'I suppose *you* know what you mean by that.'

'I do.'

'But you're not going to tell me, right?'

'I am.'

'What *are* you – an Irishman? Get to the point!'

'There's a considerable dash of Old Erin in my pedigree, indeed.'

'Then *tell* me!'

'You work it out.' He must have heard her indignant intake of breath, for he continued, 'What did you really think was about to happen when you came out of that room tonight? After I turned the music off?'

'So that was you?' It figured. 'I suppose I thought you were going to fight,' she said offhandedly. 'Stupid of me.'

'We *were* going to fight,' he said. 'I was all set to knock the grin off his face all right, but he turned it aside. You saw the way he did it. Pink cottonwool cloud time. Silicon-coated.'

'I see,' she said, wincing at his bitterness. 'What about Tam and Rod?'

'No pink clouds for them,' he said, 'but I'll bet they had mind-blowing climaxes if they ever stopped warring and got it together tonight.'

The word pattered silently in Aberdeen's mind for a moment then she realized what he meant and blushed furiously. '*Jasper!*'

He pulled up in front of her flat and leaned across her to open the door. 'They'll fight hard and love hard and we'll just have to stand back and mind the sparks. Maybe it will work for them. Go on up.'

'Aren't you coming with me?'

'I am not.'

'Kate will want to see you.'

'Not like this,' he said. 'No one wants to see me like this, least of all you.' He shifted uncomfortably. 'I'm going home.'

Aberdeen slept poorly, although she was exhausted. She could quite see Kate's reason for moving into her flat for the night, but that didn't alter the fact that she had to vacate it in two days' time. She bent her pride to ask Ed Peters for a few days' grace, but he said, with what seemed to be genuine regret, that he had a new tenant moving in immediately. That was a blow, but she supposed they could always put up at the Diamond or some other motel for a while. It wasn't a problem; merely a minor inconvenience.

Then, on the last day of Aberdeen's tenancy, Tam telephoned the flat.

'I'm so very *sorry*,' she gasped. 'Would you believe I quite forgot about Kate until we got home? I would have gone back to the studio to fetch her, but . . .' There was a slight pause and she quite obviously censored whatever she had been going to say. 'Rod said Jasper was bound to look after her.'

'It's quite all right,' said Aberdeen. 'She's with me now.'

'Tell her I'm wearing sackcloth and ashes.'

Anyone less like a penitent would have been difficult to imagine. Tam's voice sounded as if it might gush over into laughter at any moment.

'It's all right,' said Aberdeen again. She felt chilled, as if she had lost or forgotten something very precious. 'Tam – if it's inconvenient to have us come we can easily go to the Diamond.'

'Bless you!' sang Tam. 'But that isn't necessary. Rod isn't moving in with me or anything. We went that road before and now we're going to try a different way. He's coming courting, onyx ring and all.'

'I beg your pardon?'

'Never mind – never mind. I'm only babbling. Kate and you are welcome to come here any time now, or later.'

'I guess that's that!' said Aberdeen as she hung up the phone. 'We're still staying at Tam's, and I'll be getting married from there on Saturday.'

'Everything's all right with her now?'

'More than all right, I'd say. I'll have Jet come and fetch us. Tam offered, but her car wouldn't take all this stuff.'

'Get Jasper and his van,' said Kate, then caught

257

Aberdeen's eye. 'No, you're right. Get Jet.'

Jet arrived an hour later. His face creased into its usual grin as he took in the sight of Aberdeen and Kate standing outside Number 44a with several boxes and cases. 'Have you been thrown out into the snow?'

'Not much snow today.' Aberdeen reached up and kissed him. 'Who's that in the back seat?'

'A couple of the Green kids – Rusty and Tiger. They're at a loose end, so I had them come along to help.'

'That's kind of them,' said Aberdeen rather blankly. She still wasn't quite used to Jet's ability to conjure helpers out of the atmosphere. She smiled at Tiger, and at Rusty, whom she had never met. Another stocky, freckled Green – as mad about yachts as any of the others, probably. 'How's poor Nick?' she asked.

'Mad as hell,' said Jet. 'He's been trying to persuade me to wait a while so he can come sailing with us.'

'What did you say?'

'What do you think I said? The date's set and we don't want a third party along for the honeymoon!' As he spoke he was energetically stowing boxes and cases in the boot of the car. The two Greens helped, tossing Aberdeen's belongings from hand to hand. Tiger was delighted to see her, delighted she had really learned to sail. Rusty was rather dour, merely nodding a greeting to Aberdeen as the work continued.

'That's it, then,' said Jet with satisfaction, as the last of the boxes was somehow crammed into the car. 'We'll take you round to Tam's now. It won't bother you if we drop Rusty and Tiger off at home first?'

Aberdeen glanced at Kate.

'I want to pick up Aberdeen's wedding shoes before the shop shuts,' said Kate. 'The salesman was going to

258

ring the flat when the shoes were ready, but that's no use to us now. Drop me at the end of Wentworth Street, please, Jet. I'll find my own way on to Tam's from there.'

'I'll see about the shoes,' said Aberdeen, but Kate shook her head. 'You go with Jet, darling, and take those things to Tam's. I'll go on to the studio and get a lift with Jasper. Or if he's not there, I'll ring you or call a cab.'

'I'll go,' said Aberdeen, but Kate gestured to the small space left in the loaded car. She bent and said softly, 'I'd be crushed to a pulp in there, darling, what with boxes and those youngsters. And don't you think you should go along with Jet?'

Once Kate had made up her mind there wasn't much anyone could do, so Aberdeen acquiesced. Even after Kate set off on foot along the street there was very little room in the car, and, since the conversation centred entirely on the problems with Rusty's charter business, Aberdeen soon wished she'd gone with her mother to get the shoes.

'I could still make a go of it, if that new marina goes ahead,' Rusty was saying resentfully. 'Thing is, *Greensleeves* needs a thorough re-fit and the bank won't play. It's the old cashflow problem. If people would pay *me*, then I could pay the bank.'

'Are you staying down here for long, Rusty?' put in Aberdeen, trying to be friendly.

'No,' said Rusty curtly, 'I'm going back to Manatee. Might get a job on a fishing boat or something, if I can't sort things out with the bank.'

It was clear that Rusty considered this a very poor prospect. Aberdeen sympathized, but there was really nothing much to say. Life was full of disappointments, as she had cause to know. But she had been one of the lucky ones. Maybe Rusty hoped that Jet would help with a loan? He just might do it, for he was generous, but he could be very hard as well if he thought someone was taking advantage. He certainly hadn't helped out Chick and Drew and Scott.

They stayed for coffee with the Greens, and it was close to seven when they finally arrived in Major Mitchell Close. They unloaded the baggage and, while they waited for Tam to open the door, Jet drew Aberdeen into the shadows by the house and kissed her. 'Only another week,' he murmured.

'Five days,' corrected Aberdeen.

'Eight, actually. We leave on the 31st.'

'Five. We get married on the 28th.'

Jet laughed delightedly. 'Had you going there!' He released her and picked up two of the cases as Tam emerged. She looked almost incandescent with happiness and Aberdeen felt a ridiculous urge to shade her eyes.

'You haven't brought much,' said Tam, and her voice seemed to be on the edge of song. 'How many more trips will it take?'

'None. I got rid of the rest of the things,' said Aberdeen. 'They weren't worth storing and Mr Peters had already settled on a new tenant so all I have is my clothes and books and a few favourite bits and pieces.' She smiled. 'It's very liberating to be almost without possessions for a while. And of course my wedding things were already here. Did Kate manage to get my shoes before closing time?'

'Isn't Kate with you?'

'No,' said Aberdeen, 'we dropped her off near Blaxland Mall. I would have expected her to be back by now.' Her face cleared. 'She said she might call in at the studio. She's probably with Jasper.'

'Then he'll run her back here when he comes home,' said Tam.

'Won't it be out of his way?'

'A couple of hundred metres! He lives just down the hill. Didn't you know?'

'I never thought about where he lived,' said Aberdeen. He skin prickled a little at the thought of such proximity over the next few days. But then, she wouldn't have to see him. She had often gone for days without glimpsing any of her fellow tenants at 44a. 'Are there flats down the street?' she asked, following this thought.

'No. Jasper bought a house at about the same time I did.'

'Very cosy,' put in Jet sardonically. 'They tried to talk me into making it a hat-trick, but I thought two Diamonds in a street was quite enough. Three of us in the one setting might have looked ostentatious.'

Tam tried to frown at him, but her happiness kept on bubbling up again.

They carried the rest of the baggage up the stairs, then Jet kissed Aberdeen, patted Tam's head and told her to be good, and departed. 'Catch you in the morning, Lorelei? I'm running Rusty down to Central Station to catch the Brisbane train. That's unless Carol gets her way and Rusty stays on for our wedding.'

Aberdeen, who found the Greens a good deal more congenial than she found some of Jet's other friends, agreed quite happily. Jet departed, but Aberdeen and Tam hadn't had time to do more than kick off their shoes before there was a brisk tattoo on the door.

261

'Kate's back,' said Aberdeen, 'or Jet's forgotten something.' She opened the door, but it was Rod Bowen, dazzling in a sky-blue shirt and light grey pants, peering anxiously over her shoulder as if she didn't exist.

'What are you doing back here?' asked Tam. 'I told you to stay away until tomorrow.'

'That's why I came back tonight.' Rod focused on Aberdeen and smiled at her. 'Sorry if I put your mum out the other day, Ms Shawcross.'

'She didn't mind,' said Aberdeen.

'She wouldn't. I reckon she's a wonderful old chook . . . sorry, sorry, Tam.'

'So you should be!' snapped Tam, but she was shining, and Rod's gaze was following her again, caressing her with promise.

'I'll go and put some things away,' said Aberdeen, although she had decided to leave most of her belongings packed. She edged towards the door.

'It's all right, Aberdeen,' said Tam. 'You're an invited guest. He's not. Rod, is Jasper bringing Kate here, or are they going to his place first?'

'How would I know? Is he collecting her from somewhere?'

'She's at the studio, isn't she?'

'She wasn't ten minutes ago,' said Rod.

'I'm sure she said she was going to drop in at the studio,' put in Aberdeen.

'It won't be much use now anyway,' said Rod. 'Jas left when I did.'

'Maybe Kate rang him from somewhere.'

'She could have done. I wouldn't necessarily have known.' Rod was trying to be sympathetic, but his eyes kept returning to Tam, and it was clear that only

Aberdeen's presence was keeping them apart.

She cleared her throat. 'I might walk down to Jasper's and see if he's heard from her since you left, Rod. It's a nice fine night for a walk. Which house is it?'

'He lives in the big house halfway down,' said Tam. 'You can't miss it – there's a creek and a pond. His dog will bark and that noisy parrot will scream at you. I'm sure he'll give you a coffee.'

'I know the house,' said Aberdeen, but she had the eerie feeling they didn't really hear her. She replaced her shoes and left them to it, her face burning with embarrassment and some other emotion she couldn't really define. The degree of sexual awareness between Tam and her handsome lover was startling, and the thought of being exposed to it for the next five days made Aberdeen very uncomfortable.

So, the lovely house she had admired when she first visited Tam belonged to Jasper Diamond. Typical! she thought as she walked downhill through the balmy dusk. The smell of trees and other greenery was very marked, and she could see his flowerbeds gleaming. The place seemed a strange choice for a bachelor, but he might have bought it while in the throes of his affair with the German girl, Grete. She put the thought away, because Jet had spoiled that romance for Jasper, although by Kate's yardstick the relationship would have failed in any case.

She opened the gate and walked through the shadowy garden, which seemed to have distilled the sweetness from all those others. She could hear the chirp of cicadas, and the murmur of the little creek. For a moment she stood lapped in peace, then a dog barked, a cockatoo screamed and a rectangle of light

263

sprang out. Against it, she could see Jasper silhouetted, and the shock of desire that hit her made her stop dead in her tracks.

'Abbie?' His deep voice made the fine hairs stir on her arms and she rubbed them nervously.

'Jasper? I've come to see if Kate's ready to come up to Tam's – but actually I think we'd better wait a while. Rod's just arrived and you could cut the atmosphere with a blunt spoon.' She was babbling, and the cock-atoo was drowning her voice and she wasn't surprised when Jasper raised a hand to silence her.

'Shut up, Doc!' he yelled, and the bird subsided. 'Now, let's take it from the top,' he said drily to Aberdeen. 'Why should I know what Kate wants?'

'Isn't she here?'

'No one's here but me – and now you. Unless you count Dottie and the feather brigade.'

She couldn't see his expression and she was glad he couldn't see hers. She took several deep breaths then said blankly, 'She said she'd be seeing you! I think.' By now she had difficulty remembering just what Kate had or hadn't said. She could smell Jasper's own particular blend of grass, plain soap and cotton above the scents of the garden, and she was prickling all over with an awareness she didn't want. 'Jasper?' she said uncertainly, and stepped forward, drawn to him as to a lodestone.

He remained where he was, half-lifting a hand to warn her away. 'When was this?'

Aberdeen explained as well as she could. Her mouth was dry and her limbs felt liquid, and she had no idea why he made her feel that way. It was Jet she loved, Jet to whom she owed her allegiance. Her reaction to Jasper that other time had been caused by the flu;

she was well again now and moreover she was marrying Jet in five days' time. Jasper was trouble, even if he didn't mean it.

'She must have missed me at the studio,' he said harshly.

'She'll get a cab to Tam's, then, I suppose.'

'We'll go and see.' He assumed she would be coming too.

'I've probably got confused,' said Aberdeen nervously.

'Confused about what?' He was staring at her intently, although she couldn't be any more than a shadow since she had backed away from the light.

'About what Kate said. Or else she's gone somewhere else.'

'Where?'

'To Jet's, maybe, if she thought I was there.'

'Get in the van, Aberdeen.'

'I should be going . . .'

'Of course. So get in the van.'

Aberdeen got in the van. Jasper started the engine and silently handed her his mobile phone. 'Call Jet now and see if Kate's with him.'

She hesitated, unwilling to speak to Jet while her senses were all trembling with this unsuitable awareness of his twin. 'Shouldn't we see if she's at the studio? I don't want to worry him.'

Jasper's wordless response made it clear he thought Jet deserved to be worried, so she telephoned the flat. Dave answered, but though he was oddly cagey, Aberdeen soon ascertained that Jet hadn't yet come home. 'He'll have gone to the *Aphrodite*,' she said with something like relief.

'Call his mobile.'

She did so, but when Jet answered it was obvious he wasn't alone. 'Where are you?' she asked uncertainly. 'Is Kate with you?'

'*Kate?*' Jet laughed. 'No, Lorelei, I'm back at Charlie and Carol's place, sorting out about tomorrow. Carol's talking very fast and Rusty's weakening. Looks like we'll have one more guest at our party after all. Is there a problem?'

'Kate hasn't come in yet.'

'She's probably stopped off somewhere for dinner or a show.'

Aberdeen considered the impossibility of telling him people like Kate didn't go to dinner alone, and that even if Kate *had* done so she would have telephoned. 'Never mind,' she said. 'Just let Tam know if she does turn up at your place after you get home, all right?'

'Of course,' said Jet. 'I might be pretty late, though. Carol's put dinner on for me. But where are you?'

'I'm going down to the studio to see if Kate is there.' She turned off the phone.

By now Jasper was pulling up at the studio. The security lights were on, but there was no lone figure standing in their glow.

'Kate?' called Aberdeen, as she scrambled out of the van to stand in the light herself.

'Not here,' said Jasper shortly. 'Get back in.' He drove a little way farther then stopped the van and went to the taxi rank near the Windhill station. Three cabs were parked there, waiting for the northbound train, but the drivers all denied seeing Kate.

'She might have gone into one of the shops to telephone,' said Jasper, and although there were public phones at the station, Aberdeen agreed eagerly.

They asked in the few shops that were still open, but no one remembered a woman of Kate's description. Certainly she had neither requested the use of the telephone nor asked directions, and anyway, she wouldn't have walked to Tam's.

'She can't have passed us,' said Aberdeen uncertainly. 'We'd have noticed a taxi and she doesn't know anyone who'd give her a lift.'

Jasper nodded, his face harsh in the glare of the streetlight. 'Is there anyone she might have visited? Any old friends? Any shows she wanted to see?'

'Not without letting me know, and she doesn't have friends in Sydney. She's never lived here.'

'It isn't so very late,' he said. 'Only half-past eight.' He crossed to the taxis again and spoke to the drivers in turn. 'They'll probably be here – or someone will – until ten,' he said when he returned. 'There are plenty of telephones around, so if she does come off the train or bus here she won't be stranded.'

'No.' Aberdeen was shivering now, with tension, dread, and the effort of standing aloof from him.

'The next thing is to telephone the hospitals and police,' said Jasper calmly. 'That will set your mind easy. There's just a chance she had a turn or lost her bag.'

'Mmm,' she agreed, hardly trusting herself to speak. She allowed him to make the calls, feeling instinctively that an assured male voice would be more effective than a trembling female one. But how many hospitals were there in Sydney? How long till she could be sure that Kate was safe?

While he tapped in the first number, she scanned the station environs, willing her mother's comfortable figure to appear with a tale of some annoying or

267

amusing mishap to account for her delay. She's not even three hours late, she thought fiercely. Hardly more than two if she missed a train or so.

'Katherine Shawcross,' Jasper was saying. 'Sixty-seven, tall and large-framed, grey curly hair, probably wearing a floral knit-cotton skirt and top and wedge shoes. Yes, I'll wait.' He lowered the telephone briefly. 'They're just checking their records . . . yes? Thank you. If she should be brought in . . . no, we don't want to keep ringing. It's inefficient and ties up the line. If she *should* be brought in, please telephone her daughter, Aberdeen Shawcross, on this number.' He quoted his number, waited while it was confirmed, then touched the reset button.

Aberdeen relaxed a little, but Jasper was already keying another number. She listened to the same conversation again, and then, as he was about to try a third time, the telephone shrilled in his hand.

'Tam?' said Jasper, and she sagged with relief. 'Yes. Thanks. I'll tell her.'

'She's at Tam's after all,' said Aberdeen.

Jasper took her arm, and she stiffened and pulled away, but he was guiding her inexorably towards his van. He opened the door and helped her in, then went round to the driver's seat while she watched him with frozen foreboding. '*Jasper?*'

'She isn't at Tam's,' he said. 'There's no way to soften this, Abbie. It seems your erstwhile landlord has just passed on a message that the police have been trying to contact you at the flat. Peters has only just found out where he put Tam's number. Kate's in the Gordon Central Hospital. They think she was mugged.'

'No – ' whispered Aberdeen. 'Oh – no.'

Wordlessly, Jasper turned and held out his arms, and she toppled into them, lying rigidly against him until her control broke in a storm of tears.

CHAPTER 15

'It wasn't a violent attack,' said the sergeant who interviewed them in the anteroom of the hospital. 'There are no knife wounds and no evidence of more than one blow being struck. It was simply a snatch and run.'

Aberdeen could only shake her head. She thought if she opened her mouth she'd be sick.

'They left the shopping she had, some shoes tagged with a name and telephone number –'

'Mine –'

' – which led us indirectly to the identity of the victim.' The sergeant cleared his throat. 'It was probably a random attack, if that's any comfort, Ms Shawcross. Your mother just happened to be in the wrong place at the wrong time.'

'Kate was *shopping*,' snapped Aberdeen. 'In broad daylight in the Blaxland Mall. I suppose *you* were out at the time chasing parking fines.'

The sergeant said nothing, but glanced at Jasper, who was standing behind Aberdeen's chair, with his hands resting lightly on her shoulders. 'I think you should take your fiancée home, Mr Diamond. There's no point in staying on here.'

'Jet!' cried Aberdeen. 'I must ring Jet – *please*, Jasper?'

'Of course.' Jasper gave her shoulders a consoling squeeze and stepped outside. He must have made the call immediately, for he came back and stayed with Aberdeen until Jet arrived forty minutes later.

'Hey, Lorelei, what's all this about your poor old mother?'

Aberdeen clung to him. She had no more tears now, but during the interminable night ahead she was conscious of Tam's arrival with Rod, of various people taking her hand or hugging her, of endless cups of weak tea and dishwater coffee.

She thought the presence of the Diamond twins confused the medical staff, who seemed unsure which man to approach, but she hadn't the heart to tell Jasper to go. He'd supported her through that first uncertainty, had made every effort to find Kate. And all that time she'd been in the hospital – all that time Aberdeen had been standing near the station, walking to Jasper's house, talking to Tam and Rod, kissing Jet, unloading the car, drinking coffee with the Greens . . .

Lord! How far back must she go to find a break in the pattern? Kate must have had time to fetch the shoes, since she'd had them with her when she was attacked. If she'd gone to the mall herself, if Jet hadn't brought the Greens, if Kate had never come to stay at her flat . . . Aberdeen's eyes were aching and burning, and she could make no sense of the tangle.

There must have been *some* point at which she could have stepped in and prevented this whole ghastly scenario!

Her mind raced, frantic and terrified, as nurses came and went, and other grim-faced, preoccupied people

271

tramped up and down drinking the same dishwater coffee, the same weak tea.

If this were a TV drama, the surgeon would be sweeping through the swing doors soon. Green gown, swinging mask, and mob-cap still in place. Followed by acolytes, hanging on to his words. Grave or quietly satisfied, confident words or a sympathetic hand on her shoulder . . .

It was a close call, but she's going to be OK!

Or –

I'm sorry, Ms Shawcross. There was nothing we could do . . .

Aberdeen shook the vision away. An arm lay heavy and warm on her back, a hand cupped her shoulder. No shivers, so it must be Jet's. She leaned against it gratefully, and he gave her a quick squeeze.

And then someone *did* approach (but it wasn't like the television), glancing from Jet to Jasper and back again.

'Tell *me*,' she said firmly, sitting up straight, away from Jet's embrace. 'She's *my* mother.'

He told her, but she couldn't take it in. Kate had severe concussion. No bones were broken . . . That should have been a relief, but everyone still looked grave. There was something about coma and possible nerve damage and inconclusive results.

'We'll know more about your mother's condition when she wakes,' said the doctor. 'Right now she's sedated, resting comfortably.'

How could he *know* if Kate was comfortable? Why was she sedated if they wanted her to wake up? Aberdeen choked down these questions, dimly supposing that doctors must be trained to speak in clichés.

'How did it happen?' she asked dully. 'The sergeant said she was mugged.'

'Probably a single push from her assailant. Not even a blow, as such. The injuries are consistent with her head having struck the edge of the pavement. There's some bruising down one side of her body and also some minor abrasions, but all of those were probably caused by the fall itself.'

'A *push*?'

'Probably an addict after money for a hit,' said Tam. 'They're desperate enough to try anything, but they rely on a quick result – if the victim fights back or doesn't fall they often take off in a hurry.'

'There's no sign that she was struck or kicked after she fell,' said the doctor.

And that's supposed to make it better?

She supposed she thanked him. He didn't deserve her rage. Perhaps he didn't deserve her gratitude either. He was only doing his job. Kate wasn't the first woman to be mugged in daylight, and she wouldn't be the last. It could have happened anywhere, in London, in Melbourne, in Hobart, in Istanbul . . . there was *no* reason to blame the city of Sydney. No reason to blame herself, to reflect that *she* wouldn't have fallen, would have fended off the attacker somehow.

'We'll know more when she wakes,' said the doctor for the final time, and went away, perhaps to treat some other patient, perhaps to eat his dinner or watch TV.

Go home, said the director of nursing. The hospital would ring as soon as there was any news. *Go home*.

'There's no reason to blame yourself,' said Jet logically. 'You offered to get your own blessed shoes, and I

273

said I was quite happy to wait for her and take her all the way to Tam's.'

That wasn't quite the way Aberdeen remembered it, but there was no use disputing Jet's version of events. It wasn't his fault Kate had decided to walk along the mall.

If it had been Jasper driving he'd never have left her to make her own way to Tam's, whispered her mind, but Aberdeen slapped it down. Jasper was fond of Kate, but he didn't treat her like a senior citizen.

'I blame the mugger,' she said. 'It's no one else's fault.'

'Of course not.' Jet kissed her. 'Do you want to go back to the hospital now?'

'Yes, please,' said Aberdeen. She knew there was nothing she could do, but since Kate had been struck down two days before she couldn't settle to anything. Certainly not to kissing Jet in one of the rare times when Dave was away from the flat.

'Unlucky it had to happen up here in Sydney,' said Jet. 'At home she'd have had friends to look after her a bit.'

'Here she's got me!'

Jet didn't answer, but drove her to the hospital and accompanied her into the ward. He stood by, looking the high window, while Aberdeen sat in the chair beside the bed.

Kate looked better today; her eyes were still hazy but she smiled a little as she recognized Aberdeen. The bandaging and a variety of tubes made it difficult to talk, but she returned the light pressure of Aberdeen's hand. 'Darling.'

'You're feeling better?'

'Hmmm.' Kate rolled her eyes sideways. 'Better when

274

this headache . . .' Her voice slurred and drifted, then she jolted awake again. 'What was I saying?'

'You have a headache,' said Aberdeen. 'Do you hurt anywhere else?'

'Not really.' Kate seemed to consider. 'I don't hurt at all, apart from my head and hands,' she said with evident surprise.

'You'll have to be out of here in time for the wedding,' said Jet.

'Not unless the doctor says so,' said Aberdeen.

'. . . some degree of paralysis,' said Kate. She was looking almost normal now the tubes had been removed. 'They don't know how much, nor whether it will be . . . what's the word?'

Permanent. Aberdeen's face whitened. 'Paralysis . . . but *why*? It isn't as if you broke your back or neck!'

'They seem to think there might be some damage to my brain.'

'They didn't tell me.'

'Why should they?' asked Kate fretfully. 'I'm not gaga yet and it's my problem.'

'I'll look after you!'

'No, darling, you'll be with Jet, somewhere out to sea.' Kate squeezed her hand. 'I'll miss the wedding, but you must come in and visit me before you go. Did you get a wedding dress in the end? And shoes – what happened to your shoes? I was going to get some, I think.'

'*Go*! I'm not going anywhere!'

'You're going on your honeymoon,' said Kate.

Aberdeen felt her face settling into stubborn lines. 'If you think I'm going to take off on a yacht while you're in hospital!'

'You must,' said Kate quietly. 'You can't expect Jet to change his plans for me.'

'I don't!' said Aberdeen. 'We'll still get married, only we won't go away – not until you're really on the mend. Or he might go alone since he has to go to Queensland first . . .'

'No,' said Kate. She closed her eyes and presently, Aberdeen went out.

She went to find Jet who was out in the grounds, talking to some ambulatory patients. He smiled at her as she approached. 'Are they letting her out in time for the big day, then?'

'No,' said Aberdeen baldly. 'They think she might be paralysed.'

Jet had hoped Kate would be pronounced completely well. She was elderly, but as tough as boots. Unbidden, he felt the niggling thought that she might be malingering just a little, playing up vague possibilities to keep Aberdeen dancing attention. He dismissed that idea almost immediately. He had sussed out Kate Shawcross soon after they had met, and he still thought that, underneath the grandmotherly charm, there was one tough cookie with a determination to see her only daughter well established. She wouldn't jeopardize that by forcing herself upon a pair of newlyweds. There had to be an alternative to this notion of Aberdeen's, and after some thought he found one. A simple idea, and the next morning he went and presented it to Kate. She seemed vague, but then she always did, to him.

'You won't want Aberdeen to put her life on hold,' he said.

'Certainly not!' said Kate. Her words sounded

certain but her tone was slightly slurred. It was obvious that she wasn't the woman she had been before.

Afterwards, he drove Aberdeen down to Darling Harbour and parked overlooking the water. The place was really humming although autumn was well under way. He saw several acquaintances and turned his head deliberately so he wouldn't be distracted by their efforts to attract his attention. 'Lorelei,' he began, at precisely the same moment as she burst out, 'Jet! I've been thinking about Kate and our wedding . . .'

'Snap!' He bent and kissed her swiftly. 'You first.'

'No, you.' She glanced indifferently out the window then focused on his face.

'I've been thinking about your mother, too, and I've made some arrangements,' he said. That wasn't quite true, but he *would* make the arrangements, now Kate had agreed in principle. He knew plenty of people who knew people, and if there were no beds available, well; endowing a bed at a nursing home would make good press as well as good sense. His reward came in her shining face and the sudden passion of her kiss as she flung her arms around his neck.

'I *knew* you'd understand!' she mumbled into his shoulder. 'I didn't want to ask you . . .'

'Look, Lorelei,' he said seriously, 'I've told you before, I'm going to settle a lump sum on you in any case. I might as well pre-pay a bed for Kate while I'm at it. Then you needn't worry.'

'I – don't think I quite understand,' she said hesitantly, and sat up to scan his face. 'How do you mean – pre-pay a bed for Kate?'

'A bed in a really good nursing home.'

'*What*?' Her voice was not uncertain now, it

277

cracked like a pistol shot. 'You're not putting Kate in a *home*!'

He stared at her, wounded, then began to laugh. 'Not *that* sort of nursing home, Lorelei! Do you think I'd dare suggest it? A convalescent home, that's all! Somewhere she can be looked after while we're away.'

'I see,' she said, 'but I can't leave her yet. Maybe in a few weeks, when she's better.'

'You're not jilting me, I hope!'

'Of course not! It's just that I can't leave her yet. Not until things are a bit clearer.'

'Aberdeen,' he said, exasperated, 'this is exactly what your mother *doesn't* want, you playing the martyr.'

'Can't you see?' she said with a sudden break in her voice. 'Can't you see I can't *deal* with this? I have a responsibility to you, but I love Kate too. You're fit and well, so she has to be my priority just at the moment. She never hesitated when I lost my job, she took me in, and she wouldn't have been hurt at all if I hadn't asked her to come here, if she hadn't gone to collect my shoes. How could I let her down now?'

'What do you have in mind?' he asked.

'We get married and move into your flat – or somewhere else. I can keep Kate company during the day.'

'And talk about her half the night!' said Jet. 'Lorelei, this simply isn't going to work. Your mother will be fine, she'll have the best care, but we can't just wait until she's better. What if she never gets better? Do you expect me to hang about waiting forever?'

'Not forever. Just for a few weeks or so.'

'Well, it's just not on,' said Jet. 'You're not being fair to me – to us. You and your mother haven't exactly

278

been close all this time, so why are you acting the martyr now?'

'I'm not!'

'Yes, you are, and you're martyring me as well. And making me look a fool. I have an appointment in Queensland, or had you forgotten?'

She stared at him dumbly.

'That new marina development! Wake up, Lorelei! I'm committed to discussions on finance there. I also told Charlie and Carol we'd call in at Manatee on our way up north and try to sort out some of young Rusty's problems. A "few weeks or so" and it will be too late for either.'

'Can't you do all that by phone and fax?'

'No. I need to call on several people and have a look at the site. Teleconferencing simply doesn't have the immediacy I need.' And he knew his own charisma worked better in the flesh. 'I have to go,' he said, and he was fighting for more than a business venture and a favour for an old friend's child.

'Well!' she said. 'There's only one way out of it that I can see . . . we'll have to postpone the wedding. You can sort out your business and I'll sort out mine. Then we can get together and set another date.'

The discussion – it couldn't be called an argument – wound on. Jet couldn't help feeling aggrieved at her attitude. He'd offered her everything, security, financial assistance, adventure, love – and she was telling him she'd marry him later, in a month or so. As for that final offer of hers! It smacked very much of a sop to get him out from underfoot. *Go and play, dearest, until Mummy has time for you . . .*

'She actually suggested I should go on up to Queensland on my own!' he told Nick Green when he visited him that evening.

'So?' said Rusty, who was visiting too. 'Sounds fair enough to me. You don't want to hang around doing nothing, do you? And haven't you got a deal going down up there on the Island Highway?'

Nick looked ruefully at his leg, still pinned and slung in traction. 'If I hadn't bust my blasted leg I'd have come with you to crew the *Aphrodite*. I guess you'll have to fly up now.'

'If you hadn't bust your blasted leg I wouldn't be in this bind,' retorted Jet. 'We'd have left at New Year like we planned.'

'And you'd never have met her – Aberdeen,' put in Rusty.

'No.' Jet stared unseeingly at the clutter that was taking over Nick's corner of the hospital ward. He had been there so long it was starting to look like home. 'There's always that, of course.'

'Is she serious about you going up alone?' asked Nick. 'Or is it a bit of what's it – emotional blackmail?'

'She's serious, all right. She's rung the registrar already and put the wedding on hold.'

'You might as well call her bluff and go, then,' said Nick. 'Since she hasn't got much time for you just now. What do you reckon, Rusty?'

'Dunno.' Rusty shrugged. 'I hardly know her and she isn't really my type. Sorry, Jet, but I can't imagine her being much good to you on a yacht.' Nick sniggered, and Rusty punched him lightly and continued; 'Did she mean it? I mean, if you *do* go off while she's got this problem, will she throw it up at you later?'

'Not Aberdeen,' said Jet confidently.

'Most girls would.'

'Aberdeen's the original straight timber. She always means exactly what she says.' He laughed briefly. 'That's what makes her so much fun when she gets riled.'

'All that and sexy too,' mused Nick. 'Tell you what, Jetman, if you don't want to fly, why not have Rusty crew as far as Manatee, at least? Save you hiring someone else.'

'Shut up, Nick,' said Rusty. 'That's the sort of thing Tiger might dream up.'

Jet glanced at Rusty and grinned properly for the first time that afternoon. 'What you reckon, Rust? You game to take on me and *Aphrodite*?'

'Nah. Better not.'

'Come on. You're going back up anyway, and it's only as far as Manatee. Could get a bit of sailing while we're there.'

'Better not.'

'Be a devil,' said Jet. 'It's Easter, so Todd can come with us if he can wangle a few extra days off school. I'll look into the marina, and after that we'll have a good look over your accounts. I'll even come to the bank with you and act like a heavy. . .' His smile broke out. ' "You givva da kid da money or I breaka da uppa da bank!" How's that?'

'Disgusting,' said Rusty. 'You'll get arrested.'

On Easter Saturday, Jet fetched the *Aphrodite* back to the quay and began to ready her for departure. His spirits had lifted amazingly now he was on the move. It was a pity about the wedding, but sharpening his wits on the Queensland coast and sussing out opportunities would be a long way better than waiting for Aberdeen's

281

mother to get back on to her feet. And sorting out Rusty at the same time should earn him some Brownie points with Carol and Charlie. It wouldn't be difficult. Probably, he thought, it was a case of bad debts and shrewd operators taking advantage of the kid. They wouldn't try it on him.

Someone was hailing him, so he turned and saw his brother standing on the quay. 'Come aboard,' he yelled.

Jasper raised a hand in acknowledgement, but he didn't look very friendly when he arrived on the deck of the yacht. 'What are you doing, Jet?'

'Getting ready to leave,' said Jet. 'Bit unfair really. This was supposed to be my wedding day, but instead of a honeymoon all I get's a trip with a couple of scrubby kids.'

'Tiger and Todd?'

'Rusty and Todd. Tiger's got the flu. Thank God, or he'd be wanting to come too. As it is I narrowly avoided Will, Matty and Carol's company.'

'And what about Aberdeen?'

'Need you ask? She's at the hospital with her mother. And don't look at me like that. I've already been there half the morning. She doesn't want me there.'

He heard the tang of bitterness in his own voice and manufactured a flippant grin. 'Sad, eh? My life's been put on hold for an OAP.'

'So you're running off to Queensland in a snit.'

'Only for a week or so, on business. What else do you expect me to do? Sit and bite my nails?'

'What's Aberdeen going to do while you're away?'

'Hold her mother's hand. That's what she's been doing while I'm here.'

282

'Have you got Dave out of your flat so she can move in?'

'That's hardly fair,' said Jet. 'He's got nowhere else to go, and he's living in the place while we're away. Aberdeen might as well stay with Tam for now – it's nearer the hospital.'

'That might be awkward if Rod wants to move back in.'

'There's plenty of room, and anyway, this affair with Rod won't last. Tell you what, you hang about and catch her on the rebound.' He looked closely at Jasper. 'You might act like Sir Galahad, but you can't tell *me* you've never tried it on with Cousin Tam.'

Jasper looked away and Jet nodded, satisfied that his shrewd guess had struck a nerve. 'You did, didn't you? What happened? Wouldn't she put out?'

'That's my business.'

'And this is mine. But since you're determined to poke your nose in, you might offer Aberdeen's mother your spare room when she gets out of hospital. I've offered to pay for a convalescent home, but Aberdeen doesn't seem to fancy the idea. No good sending her back to Tam's – not with all those stairs. It would only be for a week or so until she's well enough to go back to Tassie, and your little dogsbody would nurse her.'

He saw Jasper considering that, and had a sudden urge to hurt. 'Maybe you'd like to add the old girl to your other lame ducks?'

Jasper didn't answer, but turned to look along the quay. Jet followed his brother's gaze, and saw Rusty, Todd and Carol Green approaching. He grinned a welcome, and sprang down to give Carol a smacking kiss. 'G'day, Nanny! You coming to make sure I'm a good boy?'

'I ought to,' said Carol, but she was smiling back. By the time the greetings were over, Jet had quite lost the thread of his conversation with Jasper, which was just as well, since his brother was already out of sight.

Jet had left for Queensland, and Aberdeen felt she had lost direction again. Kate was very angry with her for upsetting her own plans, but eventually she did concede that it was a comfort to have Aberdeen close by.

'I hoped they'd let me go home,' she said, in mid-April, 'but they seem determined to keep me flat on my back like a fillet of fish.' She frowned. 'Fillet of fish – is that right?'

'They want to make sure everything settles down, I expect,' said Aberdeen. 'How are your legs feeling?'

Kate seemed to consider, as if she were communicating with some distant planet. 'They ache, I think,' she said. 'What was that tree you said Jasper had in his garden? The purple one?'

'I didn't,' said Aberdeen patiently, and her stomach seemed to clench with fear. Kate had always been inclined to pursue conversational tangents, but this was an extreme example.

'Must have been Jasper,' said Kate. 'Has he said what's happened to Tasmania?'

'*What*?'

'*Tasmania – In the Rough*, darling. It didn't work.'

'I don't know,' said Aberdeen.

'Ask him,' said Kate. 'He didn't want you to marry Jet. He'll be glad the wedding's off.'

'The wedding isn't off. It's only been postponed. Kate, how are you feeling – really?'

'Much better, darling.'

Aberdeen was still staying with Tam, but she knew

she would soon have to arrange some other accommodation. The original invitation had been for a few days; it wasn't fair to linger on indefinitely. Rod Bowen hadn't moved in, but he was spending every evening with Tam, and the occasional night as well.

'How long have you known Rod?' asked Aberdeen when Tam returned from the studio at half-past five.

'Years,' said Tam. 'Twelve or thirteen at least.'

'Then why . . . ?'

'Why are we all over one another? Chemistry', said Tam succinctly. 'We're wildly compatible in that department.' Her face creased in its merry smile. 'It's the other things that need attention, especially a huge gulf between our goals – or lack of them – and life-views. Not to speak of the difference between love and lust. I think he thinks they're the same thing.'

'I didn't mean to pry,' said Aberdeen with difficulty. She turned Jet's ring on her finger.

'I know,' said Tam. 'And you must be missing Jet. It's acceptable to be celibate if you're used to it, but it comes pretty tough if you're not.'

'I'll have to leave here,' said Aberdeen. 'I know how awkward a third person can make things, because I never could relax when Dave was around at Jet's flat.'

'*Not* the same thing at all. What Rod and I are doing is – is – redefining the parameters of our relationship.' Tam produced the cliché in a rush. 'Lord, that sounds *so* ridiculous, but we need more than sex in common if we're going to make a go of it.'

'I'll find a place of my own,' said Aberdeen. 'You'll be able to get on with your redefining a lot better if I'm not around.'

Tam didn't deny it, but she did urge Aberdeen to wait a while. 'Jet won't be away much longer, will he?

Wasn't he just taking the Green kids up to Manatee over Easter and sitting in on some meeting?'

'Todd's been back for a week already, but Jet's decided to stay on a while,' said Aberdeen. 'He's done his business, but Rusty Green's charter service is in a bit of trouble, and Jet's just the person to sort it out.' She tried to keep her voice steady, knowing she resented Jet's absence, knowing that was unfair, since she had told him to go.

'He is, of course,' said Tam. 'In fact – he'll enjoy it. He's always had a lot of time for Carol and her kids.'

'The marina looks like a go-ahead, but Jet says there's something else that's come up and looks interesting. You know Jet! He's always looking for opportunities.'

'Isn't he, though?' said Tam. 'How long till he gets back?'

'A week or so, but it doesn't make any difference. We'll still need a permanent base in Sydney until we know how Kate's going to be.'

'Are you going to see Kate this evening?'

'Yes. I'll stay with her until ten.'

'Give her my love,' said Tam, but Aberdeen could see her face brightening at the thought of an evening spent alone with her lover. It made her even more determined to find another base. A flat near the hospital would be ideal, but might prove expensive. Perhaps a B&B? She smiled wearily. Somehow she couldn't see Jet in a B&B.

Jasper arrived at the hospital at eight o'clock. Aberdeen froze as he walked into the ward. She had managed to avoid him since the night they'd found out about Kate, and she certainly didn't feel up to facing him now. Unfortunately, having told her hostess she'd be out until ten, it wouldn't be fair to return so early. She glowered at Jasper, wishing he'd take the hint and go, but Kate's face had lit up, so all Aberdeen could do was fold in on herself and stay as far from him as possible; something he made easier by greeting her with a brief, unsmiling nod then talking exclusively to her mother.

The time had crawled to nine-thirty by the time she felt she could leave. She glanced at her watch and stretched elaborately. 'Better be off,' she said. 'There's a train at twenty-to-ten and I might just catch it.' She kissed Kate and hurried out of the ward, but Jasper must have followed immediately for he touched her arm as she left the hospital's environs.

'What the heck are you playing at?' she snapped, trying to calm her jumping pulses. 'I thought you were a mugger!'

'Kate needs her sleep, and you knew very well it was me. You always know. I want to talk to you.'

'You could have talked to me any time during the past ninety minutes. Instead, you've been ignoring me completely.'

'Kate was there, and if I'd tried to talk to you you'd either have turned your back or made a fuss and upset her.'

'I wouldn't have been so childish!'

'Good. Then perhaps you'll talk to me now. I'll give you a lift back to Tam's, too. That was my excuse for rushing after you.'

A curt refusal stuttered on Aberdeen's tongue, but the alternative was a bus or train and then either a cab or a walk through the quiet streets of Windhill, something she had disliked intensely since the attack on Kate. A cab for the entire distance would be expensive, and, with Jet away, money was a looming worry. She hadn't earned anything since before Christmas. Kate had her pension, but her cottage was rented and currently empty. There were such things as carers' allowances, but Aberdeen doubted if she'd qualify, since she wasn't caring for Kate in her own home yet. In fact, she didn't have a home, except with Jet. That thought was depressing, for Jet was far away.

She might go to the unemployment office, perhaps, but she wasn't actively seeking employment at the moment so perhaps her application wouldn't be approved. The guidelines were tight and often meant that people with unrealizable assets were denied assistance. Not that she had any assets beyond an unused wedding dress and her clothes.

That thought was depressing as well.

CHAPTER 16

'I'm offering you a lift to Tam's, not a one-way trip to Transylvania,' said Jasper. His voice was exasperated, so presumably he had said it several times already.

'Yes, please.'

'That must have taken some swallowing,' he said.

'It did,' she said frankly. 'You know how I hate to be in your debt. In anyone's debt.'

'Some debt.' His voice was rough and scornful. 'I live just down the hill from Tam – had you forgotten?'

'I was thinking of something else.' She looked up at him in the harsh lighting outside the hospital. 'Kate's changed,' she blurted. 'She's changed so much. Surely you can see it?'

'An experience like Kate's would change anyone,' he said. 'More than any accident or illness, it's a betrayal of the Golden Rule. The only thing worse would have been an attack by someone she knew and loved.'

'I suppose so, but Kate's so vague. She's different – dependent – and Kate was never that.'

'It's probably the effect of being in hospital. Kate's been used to running her own life, now she's dependent on the hospital staff for her physical needs and on a few visitors – mostly comparative strangers – for company.'

'I'm here.'

'So you are. But it's a sacrifice, and Kate knows it. You must feel life's dealt you a raw hand as well.'

'So,' she said abruptly. 'What did you want to talk to me about? And don't pretend you're not pleased I had to postpone the wedding. That's exactly what you wanted.'

Jasper opened the door of his van and stood back. Last time he had bustled her into the vehicle, he had been about to break the news about Kate and she shivered at the memory. He got in beside her and the feeling of *déjà vu* intensified. 'Have you heard from Jet lately?' he asked, starting the engine.

'Yes, of course. He rings quite often.'

'Have you told him Kate isn't improving as quickly as we all hoped?'

'Of course. I tell him everything.'

Except about that one wild moment in Jasper's arms.

'I was talking to him this morning,' said Jasper. 'He seemed to think Kate was coming along well – that you'd be getting married very soon.'

'I don't know why he would think that.'

'Don't you, Abbie?'

'I've told him everything,' she said again.

'Did he tell you he sailed out to Atonement with young Rusty Green and a Californian couple after Todd came home?'

'Probably. Yes, I'm sure he did. He said there was a storm and he's got a ship's cat now. And he said they took the same couple through the Whitsundays.'

'So he's not exactly bereft without you.'

290

'I'm glad he's not!' she said. 'I'd hate him to worry.'

'He's certainly not worrying, although he did ask if I thought you'd be ready to sail by the end of this month. If not, he has plans to go out to Atonement again.'

'I *told* him I couldn't set a date just yet! But what's all this about, Jasper? I tell you I don't *want* Jet to be worried. Are you trying to make more trouble?'

'Not this time,' said Jasper. 'Trouble's making itself.' He stopped his van, and she realized they had reached his house in Major Mitchell Close.

'I'll walk the rest of the way,' said Aberdeen.

'I said I'd give you a lift back to Tam's, and I will.' He reached out for her hand, and because she was so weary she let him take it. 'You're cold,' he said. 'You're worn out.'

She didn't deny it.

'I wanted you to postpone your wedding,' he said restlessly, 'but I never wanted it this way.'

'I know.' Despite her own distress she sensed his, and tentatively squeezed his hand, trying to ignore the insistent messages tingling from her fingertips to the nape of her neck. His fingers curled around hers in silence, and she accepted the pressure as the assurance it was meant to be. Whatever he really thought of her, she knew he was fond of Kate.

'Have you thought what will happen – to you and Jet – if Kate never recovers?' he asked presently.

There was no barb in his voice, but Aberdeen tensed at the implications. 'She must. I'll stay with her until she does and Jet will have to understand.'

He brought up his other hand to cover hers and she heard him draw a deep breath. 'Aberdeen, I have two propositions to make you. No – ' He must have felt her withdrawal through their linked hands. 'Don't say

291

anything yet, just hear me out, and think about what I have to say.'

She licked her lips. 'Go on.'

'The first is that you should set a wedding date and stick to it. Go to Jet, marry him in Queensland. Go off on this odyssey of yours. Meanwhile, I'll undertake to keep in touch with the hospital, and to let you know every development – by fax. Then, when Kate's well enough to leave, I'll either take her back to Tasmania and get her settled there again, or, if she isn't fit for that, I'll arrange for her to move into my house with a companion; quite possibly Ellie Campbell. You know Ellie, and Kate likes her a lot. Best of all, she isn't actually a nurse, so Kate won't feel like an invalid.'

Aberdeen sat for several seconds in silence, stunned by his generosity. 'And that's it?' she said. 'That's your proposition?'

'That's one proposition, yes. I think it covers most of your immediate concerns, allowing you and Jet to be together while providing a settled base for Kate.'

'You certainly know how to take the wind out of my sails,' said Aberdeen.

'What's your gut reaction, then?' Jasper was still holding her hand, his warm fingers were against her wrist and she was uneasily aware of her jumping pulses.

'My gut reaction is, what are you up to now?' she said. 'Last time you made me an offer I couldn't refuse . . .'

'You refused it with quite unnecessary vigour.'

There was a smile in his voice, but not, she thought, on his face. She tried to match his lighter tone. 'Last time, you offered me an expenses-paid holiday with the express intention of getting me away from Jet. This

292

time you're trying to send me away *with* Jet. Fishy, Jasper, very. If this were a murder mystery, you'd be trying to dispose of us both with a bomb in the shape of a tropical sucker-fish.'

'It does seem like a complete volte-face,' he said bleakly. 'But you would have married Jet by now if it hadn't been for Kate's problems. I still think you two are entirely mismatched, but I suppose that's your business.'

'My word!' she said. 'You're learning!'

'Leaving aside whatever suspicions you might harbour, what do you say?'

'I have to say no again,' she said. 'But this time, I can thank you from the bottom of my heart for the offer. I know you mean a lot to Kate, and – oh, Lord, now I sound mushy. I withdraw the remark about the sucker-fish bomb. I was being facetious and you didn't deserve it this time.'

'Why say no? I'd want to keep tabs on Kate in any case and it won't be putting me out to have her in my house. I won't even be there much for the next few months.'

'You're going away?' She tried to keep her voice calm, but the world was shifting again, the ground was shaking under her.

He moved restlessly in his seat. 'I have to go and find a new subject for the next *In the Rough*, then do the preliminary scouting. And it has to be soon, to try and wipe out the damage caused by this *Tasmania* fiasco.'

'What fiasco? Was that what Kate meant when she said "Tasmania didn't work"?'

'Maybe. I mean the fiasco caused when three members of a six-person team are lovesick and let it get in the way of their joint project.'

293

'Maybe you should have sacked some,' said Aberdeen.

'Unfortunately, I was one of them.' He cleared his throat, and shifted again. 'Believe me, Aberdeen, the result is a mess. We've all agreed we have to cut our losses and start over again, and I am not prepared to warm over cold soup and feature Tasmania a second time. But we seem to be getting off the point.'

'We do,' she agreed, bemused. 'I can't quite remember what the point was – Jasper?'

'Yes?'

'Will you let go of my hand, please?'

'I suppose I'd better,' he said, continuing to hold it.

'I don't know why we're talking like this,' she said restlessly. 'Kate isn't *your* problem. Nor am I. This is simply self-indulgence.'

'You've been my problem since I first aroused your ire in that tavern. Talk about the man who fell to Earth – I fell over my own clay feet and I still haven't swept up the mess.'

'My hand?' It was becoming a matter of urgency now.

He laid it gently in her lap. 'So the answer's no?'

'The answer is thank you, but no,' she corrected, drawing a surreptitious breath of relief. 'Kate and I will manage, and Jet will have to wait a little while.'

'He might not be willing to wait too long.'

'That,' she said evenly, 'is a risk I'll have to take. I try to play fair.'

'There's another risk you might take,' he said abruptly. 'Which brings me to the second proposition.'

'Hmm?'

'You might let Jet go his own way and marry me instead.'

294

Aberdeen gasped with the suddenness of it, gasped and found herself clutching at the seatbelt strap. 'Marry *you*?' she said incredulously. 'Whatever for?'

'It might solve your problems,' he said.

'And yours, I suppose!'

'One of them, certainly. If I had you I might be able to sleep at night and work by day without feeling as if I'm being put through an old-fashioned wringer.'

'You're mad!'

'I think the word is "obsessed", Abbie. Or perhaps "hag-ridden". And believe me, I didn't choose to get into this state.'

'Obsessed. Right. *Hag*-ridden.' She swallowed.

'If you marry me,' said Jasper, 'I can get on with my work with a clear head. You and Kate could move into my house – our house – while I'm away, and Ellie too, if you like.'

'For how long?' she asked curiously.

'You – for the rest of our lives. Kate – for as long as she wishes. Ellie – for as long as you and Kate need her and as long as she is willing to stay.'

'That's putting it plainly!' she said. 'And it sounds so simple there has to be a catch. *No one* makes that sort of offer without strings. Not unless they're totally naïve. Which you're not.'

'There is a catch,' he said. 'You'd have to put up with me. No archaic nonsense about marriages of convenience. You'd have the security you need, both for yourself and Kate, but you'd have to sleep with me, shower with me, share with me. And it would be forever.'

'That's ridiculous!'

'Why? Isn't that almost the same arrangement you had with Jet? Barring the yacht and Kate? You get

295

security; he gets you? You trade some freedom for a chance to warm and widen your world?'

'That's a low blow,' she said.

'Say yes. It would take an enormous load off my mind and off my spirit.'

'You'd be burdened with a wife who wanted to marry someone else, and a mother-in-law who might never be able to live alone. Not to say a jilted brother who would have a perfect right to resent the situation. You'd be collecting burdens, not shedding them.'

'I wouldn't see it that way. I want you, and this way I'd get you. I wouldn't have to worry about you any more.'

'You'd do this to Jet?'

'*Jet* is doing this to Jet by leaving you alone. Everything else is moonshine.'

'Then you'd better stop worrying about me right now!'

'How *can* I stop?' he asked violently. 'Riddle me that, Aberdeen. How *can* I not worry? You were in a bad situation when you first met Jet; now it's infinitely worse.'

'Rubbish!' she said, although her heart was thumping hard. 'I had nothing then. Now I have Jet – he's offered to pay for a convalescent home for Kate if necessary.'

'Which one? In Sydney or Tasmania? Has it a resident specialist in head injuries? Does it encourage dependence or independence?'

'I don't know exactly.' She stumbled. 'He was talking about it before he left – but that was when he thought I'd be going with him. We'll sort it out when he comes back – or when I join him.'

'Sounds vague,' said Jasper drily. 'My offer, on the

other hand, is perfectly plain. I'll let you have it in writing now, tonight. Just come on inside while I draw it up and sign it. Tam would be happy to witness.'

'. . . said the spider to the fly!' said Aberdeen acidly. 'No, thank you, Jasper. It's very kind of you, but I told you before, I *won't* be put in your debt. I promised to marry Jet, not you, and for all the arguments you've just put up tonight for changing my mind, there's an even stronger one against it.'

'What's that? The fact that you hate me from time to time?'

'I don't *hate* you. I just don't entirely trust you, and that's your own fault for interfering in the first place. But that isn't the argument against you.'

'Tell me.'

'The things you said to me when I got engaged to Jet. *If* you remember, you told me Jet only wanted me because I would be forever grateful to him for rescuing me from penury.'

'I didn't put it like that.'

'That's what you meant. You said Jet wants to give me everything so I'll be complaisant and always in his debt. I've thought about that quite often since you said it, and I think there's an element of truth there. I also think he made his offers in good faith. He certainly didn't bargain for Kate's problems, but he's still willing to provide for her.'

'I'm more than willing. You must know that!'

She swallowed, and raised her hand as he made a violent movement. 'No. You listen to me, Jasper Diamond! I've already done Jet one bad turn by asking him to wait for me while I sort out Kate. He's agreed to wait. How would it look if I dropped him and married *you*, just because you made me a better offer?'

'A better offer?' he said swiftly.

'You must think it's a better offer, otherwise you wouldn't have bothered to make it. You're a business-man, Jasper, but not like Jet. Jet flies by the seat of his pants; you weigh things up.'

'And what about you, Abbie? Do *you* think it's a better offer?'

'Well, of course it is, from my point of view! It would give me somewhere to live – with Kate – and offer a breathing space since you'd be away. But still, I've told you once before – I won't be mixed up in any ridicu-lous rivalry between you two. I won't change horses just because it happens to suit me. In other words, and I've said it before – *this girl is not for sale*. And . . . though I do thank you for the offer, I think it's cruel to drag Kate into it as a bribe.'

'Finished?'

'Yes. I think so.' Her voice sounded cool to her, but she was quaking inside.

He got out of the van, and stalked around to the passenger side. Something in his stance alerted her to danger, and she made a quick move to lock the door.

'No use,' said Jasper. 'It operates on central lock-ing.' He yanked it open and unclipped her seatbelt. 'Out you get,' he said.

She got out hastily, stumbling over her own feet. 'Fair enough. I'll walk the rest of the way.'

'You left something out of your masterly summing up,' he said coolly, remaining where he was. 'A vital piece of the equation.'

'I did?' She licked her dry lips and backed away, trying to make it past the van so she could bolt up the hill for safety. 'Never mind, Jasper. It's finished. It never really began.'

'You left *this* out.' His hands shot out to clamp on her arms, and he drew her against him, not violently, but in a controlled motion she was helpless to evade. Her face was pressed against his shirt and she could feel, against her cheek and hands, the frantic slam of his heart.

'*Jasper!*' she gasped.

His hands were sliding down her back, slowly down to her waist, slipping inside the band of her jeans, which were still a little loose from a combination of illness and stress. She began to tremble violently as he stroked her hips and lower back, making no attempt at any more intimate caress. She tried to shut her mind to the insistent feelings, to the sullen ache that had begun in her breasts and was heading south to the pit of her stomach and points below. Her legs were sagging, but she found herself pressing against him, her hands twisting at his shirt, searching frantically for the warmth of his skin. And then it was under her questing fingers, the softness of chambray, the living heat of his back. She felt him tense, the muscles knotting under her hands.

'You don't react to Jet like this,' he said, and his voice was rough with passion. 'I've watched you together, and you don't react to him as you do to me. Neither does he react to you as I am now. He loves you – he couldn't help it – but he could find someone else to do as well. There's no one else for me.'

She hardly heard him, for she was shaking now, her breath coming in gasps as she struggled to get closer, and closer still, the soft cloth parted with a purring sound, she was clinging to him, rubbing her cheek and lips against his bared chest and raising her face as a sunflower raises itself to the sun.

'Oh, Abbie, Abbie – ' Her name was a breath against her mouth and it seemed to be the name she had always wanted. And then his lips touched hers, opening to her invitation, his arms supporting, his body taut and eager against her. She could feel, through the textured velvet of her shirt, the strong flat planes of his chest and ribs. Her hands were splayed, nervously delighting in the quivers they could sense beneath his hide.

And then suddenly, it was over. With extreme reluctance he drew away, his hands braced now against her upper arms. The moonlight blanched colour from the world, but she could see his chest was heaving, could feel the harshness of her own breathing mirroring his. Her body was screaming, crying out for renewed contact, her breasts, under the velvet, felt pulsing and swollen. As for her loins – she was aching, throbbing, deep within her, a pain that could be assuaged only by him in the most primitive act of loving. She wanted him against her, in her, touching at every plane and curve, with a desire that was as shocking as it was painful. She felt like a plant wrenched out by the roots, like the mandrake that shrieked when torn from its bed.

Jasper was in a similar state; she could see him fighting for control, breathing raggedly, could feel the fierce pressure of his fingers, holding her away from the body which clearly longed for hers. If she had ever doubted him when he said he could lose control she didn't doubt him now. But she also saw, with painful incredulity, that his will was stronger than his body, and that he was exerting that strength now to regain what he had lost.

'No,' she said with quiet desperation, 'you can't do this. It isn't fair.'

She made a sudden move towards him, but he held her away. 'For pity's sake, Abbie,' he said harshly. 'You've just turned me down. Say you love me, say you'll marry me, or we'll both go up in flames.'

'No,' she gasped. 'I've promised to marry Jet.' She shuddered, trying to throw off the intensity of her wanting ... of her *body's* wanting, she corrected herself.

The thought was like a bucket of cold water dumped over her head, and she stepped back abruptly, finding she could stand without support. 'It's all right,' she said. 'You're safe from me now. I won't tear your clothes off.'

He let his hands drop and looked down at himself. 'Too late,' he said. 'You've already done for the shirt.'

She could feel the blush rolling up her face, could feel it shining like a beacon despite the chill of the moonlight. 'I'm sorry about that,' she said in a constricted voice.

'Don't be sorry,' he said urgently. 'Don't ever be sorry. Just to feel you coming alive like that – you look like a Botticelli goddess but you're pure flesh and spirit, and you're mine. Oh, Abbie . . .' He touched her hair and, as if unable to help himself, knelt down and leaned his cheek against her belly.

At once the turmoil rose, her knees began to give again and she wrenched herself away, leaving him there, running up the hill with a desperation she hadn't felt since the night Kate was hurt.

Tam stirred. The autumn sunrise was pooled like lazy honey across the foot of the bed. She couldn't see the clock, for she was held fast in Rod's arms, her legs between his, her body fitted snugly against him. She

301

stretched, slowly, and, as if partnering her in a ballet, Rod moved to accommodate her changed position. It was early, so she let herself relax, absently stroking his forearm where it crossed her ribcage below her breasts. If only, she thought wistfully, he could have been plainer or a little less glossy. Why not *grey* eyes, instead of blue? Why not impossible hair instead of that sculptured-looking thatch? And why on earth did he have to have a dimple? And that wretched ring . . .

And why are you picking faults? she asked herself. You stupid bitch, wake up to yourself! He can't help his blue eyes any more than you can help your brown ones. And you wear gypsy earrings. Does he complain?

She squirmed round and kissed his shoulder in mute apology. Rod woke up, gave her a grave and doubtful look, then rolled out of bed, pulling her to her feet and over to the stream of sun now entering the window where he put his arms round her again and leaned his face against her hair. The warmth of his skin and of the sun surrounded her, and in the silence Tam became aware of another source of warmth, a new source welling inside her. It rose like simmering milk, percolating through her body, making her quiver with surprise.

'Are you pregnant?' asked Rod abruptly.

'What? I mean – no, of course not.'

'Pity.

'Why did you ask?'

'I just suddenly thought you might have been.'

'But why did you ask just then?' she persisted. The flood of warmth had filled her utterly now, and it seemed he had sensed the change and drawn his own conclusions. 'Did you notice something different?'

302

'There's a photographic competition and the theme was fruitfulness. I suddenly thought of you.'

'Never mind,' she said, swallowing disappointment. 'You can photograph some eggs instead. Or maybe an orange tree.'

'Or maybe some melons.' His hands slid up to stroke her breasts. 'I love you, Tam. You know that.'

The warmth was almost painful now, constricting her chest so she had to breathe in sharply.

'What is it? Did I hurt you?'

She shook her head. 'I just – I love you. I love you too. I just realized. I – ' Her mouth was going the wrong shape somehow, and she gulped, painfully. 'It hurts!' she said in astonishment. 'Even when we're not having rows, it hurts!'

He turned her towards him, holding her firmly, cushioning her against her own sobs.

'It hurts me too,' he said in a low voice. 'It always has.'

'Then why do you stay with me?' she gasped. 'Why do you keep coming back?'

'Dunno,' said Rod. 'Maybe because it hurts a darned sight more when we're apart.'

Jasper hadn't been sleeping well, but that night he hadn't slept at all. After Aberdeen had run away up the hill, he had gone drearily into his house. It was a lovely place, light and airy with a central courtyard, and room for the various creatures which shared his life. The place seemed very empty and he wondered why he bothered to keep it up. He could live just as well in a flat, as Jet did – if only it weren't for his furred and feathered dependants.

Dottie panted up at him with a canine grin, but he

patted her absently. Not even the squawks of self-opinionated Doc the cockatoo could raise his spirits. The pair of ancient galahs woke up and whistled hopefully, then offered him a cup of tea in their creaky, old-lady voices.

'I'm not in the mood,' he told them, and mechanically did the rounds of bird seed and dog biscuits and fresh water for all. Their needs had to be serviced even if his own were ignored.

He went to bed for a while, but lay restlessly, his body clamouring about unfinished business, his mountain of regret building higher by the moment. It seemed that having started off on the wrong foot there was no way of getting himself in step with his own desires and Aberdeen.

She'd made it pretty plain after that first time in Jet's flat that she wasn't to be swayed by physical means, and tonight she had made it plain she wasn't to be swayed by practical offers. Everything he did or tried seemed to loop back to some earlier mis-step. And now he'd really scared her off.

What next? That was the question. The answer was the simplest one possible. Nothing next. Do what Tam had suggested in the first place and stay away from Aberdeen Shawcross. Just go about his business; his real business, which was extracting *In the Rough* from its current bunker. The failure of the *Tasmania* project had shaken him badly.

He couldn't sleep, so he got up and packed the things he'd need for an extended time away. He could close up the house and leave now, ring the studio from wherever he spent the next night. Stew and Steve were due for holidays, and Rod would work with Tam.

Ellie . . . Jasper sat down at his computer and typed

a quick note for Ellie, then he wrote to Tam and finally, his face rigid with resolve, to Aberdeen. The letters rolled from the printer, he enveloped and addressed them and went out on foot through the dawn.

The sun was striking from the east, blessing the thick bush and the rooftops of Major Mitchell Close. His own windows seemed to be blazing, and at the top of the hill Tam's house lay fully bathed in light. The curtains were parted, and Jasper caught the impression that someone was framed between them. Aberdeen? He shaded his eyes and peered up, aware that he made a very poor figure of a Romeo.

The figure seemed curiously still, and after a moment he realized it was two people, melded in a long embrace. Tam and Rod. And somewhere in the house, lying (he was certain) awake and anguished, was Aberdeen.

Quietly, he withdrew two letters from his pocket and slid them into Tam's letterbox, then he went back to his house, had a last look round and drove away.

Aberdeen had been lying on Tam's spare bed for hours, but soon after sunrise she fell into a fitful sleep. Her dreams were uneasy and she woke, unrefreshed, at ten o'clock. She felt flat and stale and savagely unhappy, so rather than lie staring at the ceiling she went to make coffee.

To her considerable astonishment, Tam was in the kitchen, sitting in a shaft of sunlight with her face in her hands.

Intruding on someone else's misery was no way to assuage her own, and Aberdeen had no sympathy to spare. She would have retreated, but abruptly Tam sat up and blinked at Aberdeen through pink-rimmed eyes. Visibly, she pulled herself together. 'Aberdeen, are you all right?'

'No,' said Aberdeen, 'but there's nothing you can do.'

'There's letter for you,' said Tam. 'Jasper must have delivered it some time in the night.'

Aberdeen froze. 'I don't think . . .'

Tam flipped it across. 'There was one for me as well,' she said. 'Jas has gone off on his travels a few days early.'

'Is that why you've been crying?' Aberdeen could have bitten her tongue, but she was too tired to be tactful.

'Ouch. I suppose it *is* pretty obvious. But it's Rod, not Jasper, and I'm all right now. I'm more all right than I've ever been before. It's just taking me a while to get my balance. Open your letter, Aberdeen. Really, it won't bite you.'

Aberdeen read the letter, then read it again. Then she crushed it between her hands and looked blindly at Tam. 'He wants me to house-sit while he's away.'

'I know,' said Tam happily. 'It's an ideal solution, don't you think?'

'I can't accept. I've already told him I don't want his help!'

'I think he's more or less left it in your lap,' said Tam. 'And it isn't as if he's doing you a huge favour. He always needs a house-sitter on the premises, because that darned cockatoo screams the place down if he feels neglected. If you move in, you'll have to take charge of the grounds, the dog, the aviary and any mail or callers. You'll be it if the water cylinder breaks or the microwave dies or the roses get black spot. *You* live rent free, but *he* doesn't have to pay agency prices for a house-sitter.'

306

'You think I should accept.'

'I think you *have* accepted,' corrected Tam.

'But what if Jet comes back next week? What if Kate gets better?'

Tam held up an envelope. 'You sing a glad hallelujah and I forward this letter to the agency Jasper usually employs. A house-sitter appears within a day, the dog sulks for twenty-four hours and then cheers up and the birds learn a few more words they shouldn't know. Simple.'

'Simple,' said Aberdeen hollowly.

'He's left the keys for you,' said Tam. 'Why not move in now? That's if you want to, of course.'

'I suppose so.'

Tam came round the table and hugged her. 'Don't get the idea I'm trying to toss you out, Aberdeen. It's just that you've been talking about getting a place. But wait a minute! You said you'd already refused this offer?'

'Not exactly *this* offer,' said Aberdeen. 'No.'

Tam looked curious, but Aberdeen didn't say any more. No doubt Jasper would tell Tam whatever he wanted her to know when he came back. Whenever that might be.

All around the *Aphrodite* was the hazy horizon of the north. The swell was long and gentle and the sky burned as blue as it ever did in Sydney. May was the best time of year for sailing the Island Highway, for the tropical summer was marred by rain and high humidity. Rusty Green was leaning over the rail, staring at the ocean. It was four o'clock already and they'd have to be heading back. A darned shame, thought Rusty, but Jet Diamond had things to do

307

and people to see so it was no use suggesting they stay out any longer.

A splash of cold water made Rusty flinch. 'Wake up, kiddo,' said Jet with his gleaming grin. 'If you moon about like that it's no wonder the bloody sharks take you down for every dollar.'

'I don't moon,' said Rusty.

There was a wail from overhead.

'What the heck's that?'

'That's your cat,' said Rusty sourly. 'Remember? That fuzzy little blonde bundle you got for your fuzzy little blonde fiancée. It's got itself stuck up on the mast again.'

Jet stared for a moment then burst out laughing. 'Well, meow to you too! What've you got against Aberdeen anyway? It wasn't her fault her mum got herself mugged.'

Rusty hunched a shoulder. 'She's not my type, that's all. I don't like blondes. Not even blonde cats.'

Jet laughed some more. 'Get up and fetch the cat down,' he said at last.

'Bull!' said Rusty. 'It's your cat, you fetch it down. Better go soon, too, or the sail will be ripped.'

'You're lighter. Up you go.'

'No,' said Rusty.

Jet stared at the stubborn freckled face. 'A bit of gratitude would be nice,' he said.

'What for?'

'Sorting out your finances. Getting the sharks off your case. For a bright kid you made a real dog's breakfast of a golden opportunity.'

'I'm grateful,' said Rusty. 'But not very. You enjoyed it.'

There was a further wail from aloft and Rusty

cocked an eye up at the mast. 'Better hurry if you don't want Blondie falling in the sea.'

'Well, *I* can't climb up there!'

'Try a broom,' said Rusty.

Jet looked exasperated, but went to fetch a broom. He reached up, offering the broad wooden head to the plaintively wailing cat. 'Come on, Blondie,' he muttered and gave the animal a nudge. Promptly, it gave a kamikaze leap, rebounded from Jet's shoulder and scooted down to the cabin. Jet jumped and swore as the claws lanced his shoulder, and the broom came toppling down to strike him squarely across the neck. He hit the deck with a thud, his head cracking sharply against the railing.

Rusty laughed and clapped ironically, but Jet did not get up. 'Jetman – *Jetman*? You OK?'

He was lying on the deck in a huddle. Warily, Rusty crouched down and rolled him over on to his back. 'Jet? C'mon, man, this isn't funny!'

Jet's face creased with pain. 'Bloody – hell!' he muttered without opening his eyes. 'What hit me?'

'The cat and the broom,' said Rusty. 'Hey – are you OK?'

'I don't know.' Jet started to sit up and turned pale.

'Don't move.' Planting one hand on each of his shoulders, Rusty pressed him down on the deck. 'Stay put a minute till I get the ice-pack.'

'I don't need the ice-pack,' he said irritably. 'Let me get up.'

'Stay down.'

'Look, Rusty . . .' Their eyes met and Jet's voice faded out.

'All right,' said Rusty. 'Get up if you must. Don't blame me if you've cracked your skull.'

'I think I'll stay right here,' said Jet. 'Or better still, why don't you lie down with me so I've somewhere soft to put my aching head?'

'What about Aberdeen?'

'This has got nothing to do with Aberdeen.'

Rusty frowned. 'How can you say that?'

'Quite easily. I just did.'

'You really are a bastard, Jet Diamond,' said Rusty. 'I don't know why I'm stuck on you.'

'Stuck on me?' He sounded amused.

'Yes,' said Rusty frankly. 'For years. Why do you think I came up here in the first place? I knew I didn't stand a chance.'

'Whatever gave you that idea?'

'But you only like blondes,' said Rusty wonderingly. Her breath was coming fast as she stared down at him. 'Maybe you're concussed?'

Jet reached up to ruffle her spiky chestnut crop then pulled her down into his arms. 'Whatever gave you that idea?' he said again.

CHAPTER 17

Aberdeen stood in the courtyard of Jasper's house and raised herself on tiptoe to test the soil of a hanging basket. It was faintly damp and gritty, so she decided not to water it today. Absently, she wiped her finger against her jeans and moved on. It was the middle of May, and life seemed to have reached another plateau.

Kate had been installed in Jasper's ground-floor spare bedroom for a week. She seemed much better in some ways, but she still had very little use in her legs and alarmingly blank patches in her memory. A physiotherapist was visiting every two days, and the sessions seemed to exhaust Kate, but without them, she would probably not improve.

'Will she improve *with* them?' Aberdeen had asked.

'We hope so.' The specialist had looked at her blandly, his professional face firmly to the fore. 'Head injuries such as your mother's can be very unpredictable.'

'Will she ever be able to live alone?'

The specialist had glanced down at his notes. 'The problem with people like your mother, Ms Shawcross, is that they represent borderline cases. We don't have the facilities to keep them in hospital, and very often they do better in their own homes.'

'But not living alone.'

'Paraplegics can and do live alone,' the specialist had said. 'However, with Mrs Shawcross's other problems, it probably isn't advisable at present.'

That had been that, or very nearly. The specialist's expertise was in medical cases, not social work. He had given Aberdeen a number of leaflets, which she had promptly dropped in the bin.

Aberdeen bent to touch a velvet, overblown petunia. In the dimness of the courtyard the May evening could have been summer. The courtyard was her favourite place just now. Inside the house was lovely too, but everywhere she turned she was reminded of Jasper. His taste ran to faded Persian rugs, and antique tables and chairs made of glowing timbers. Even the bedstead in the master bedroom was carved and polished. She had stood in that room on the day she moved in and stared blankly at the bed. The scent of his belongings was all about her and she'd come to with a start to find herself trembling. She'd closed the door in a hurry and hadn't been in there since.

The courtyard was the place; flowers and soil and growing things; as redolent of Kate as of Jasper, of lazy summer days and autumn flowers. The two galahs perched side by side on a dead tree limb fetched in for their convenience. According to Tam, they were well over fifty, living their retirement years in comfort at Jasper's place.

There was a tap on the outer door, accompanied by a volley of barking from Jasper's dog Dottie and a series of shrieks from the euphoniously named Dr Who, a sulphur-crest of immense self-importance.

'Shut up, Doc,' muttered Aberdeen.

It couldn't be Ellie or Tam at the door, for Dottie wouldn't have bothered to bark at them. Doc would have shrieked just the same; Doc always did. Despite the freedom of a huge aviary and the company of his meek wife Nyssa, as well as other birds, Doc was much more interested in the humans he saw about him.

Looking after Jasper's house and menagerie was no sinecure, either. Tam had been perfectly correct when she had said it needed a lot of maintenance. Certainly Doc did, for he took a wicked delight in biting through perches, drinking bottles and anything else that came within reach of his voracious beak. Only the day before he had eaten a rubber glove Aberdeen had left too close to the aviary wall.

Now she frowned as she crossed the courtyard and walked through the house to open the door. 'Who is it?' she asked through the jamb.

'Me.' The voice was bubbling over with laughter, and she thrust the door the rest of the way open and tumbled ungracefully into Jet's arms.

'Lorelei!' he exclaimed, and hugged her soundly.

'Jet! You didn't say you were coming.'

'Thought I'd surprise you.' He grinned at her as if he hadn't been away for over six weeks. 'So, are you ready to roll?'

'Roll?'

'Yes, Lorelei – roll,' he said playfully. 'As in make tracks, vamoose, and sail away. I came as soon as I heard your mum was out of hospital. How is she?'

'Well, she's improving,' said Aberdeen.

'Great!' Jet gave her another hug. 'Give me a kiss – I've missed you!'

Aberdeen raised her face for his kiss, but something

313

was definitely wrong, and she couldn't pretend she didn't know what it was. She seemed to hear Jasper's voice in her memory. '*You don't react to Jet like this . . .*' And he had been humiliatingly right. She felt Jet's lips on hers, but in place of the blinding desire she had felt for Jasper there was only a mild physical pleasure. Had there ever been anything more?

Jet must have sensed her dismay, for he held her off and looked down at her. 'What's wrong, sweetie? Aren't you pleased to see me?'

'Of course,' she said mechanically. 'It's just a surprise.'

'You look a bit stressed out. Has Jas been hassling you again?'

'He's away.'

'Well, obviously. You wouldn't be house-sitting otherwise!' Jet laughed. 'The crafty sod's been making a move on you, though, hasn't he?'

Aberdeen stared at him in consternation. She felt her guilt must be written in large letters across her forehead, branding her as faithless. 'He isn't here,' she said. 'He's been gone for weeks – nearly as long as you.'

'All right, don't ruffle up.' Jet flicked her nose gently. 'I suppose he took off when Tam went back to her toy-boy. It really gets him going, being second-best all the time.'

'I don't know what you're getting at,' said Aberdeen, 'but it's kind of Jasper to let me stay here. It's close to the hospital.'

'*And* he gets someone to keep an eye on the place. *And* he has the satisfaction of making me look bad.'

'How?'

'Come on!' said Jet. 'I left you at Tam's, and while

314

I'm away he lends you his house. I hope you thanked him nicely?'

'No,' said Aberdeen coldly. 'I didn't thank him at all. He sent me the keys in a letter.'

'Couldn't trust himself to hand them over in person,' grinned Jet. 'Bet he let you think it was all his own idea.'

'It certainly wasn't mine,' she said with spirit.

'No,' said Jet. 'It was mine actually. I thought your mum would be more comfortable here until she's right on her feet again.'

'You asked him to offer the place to me?'

'Not in so many words, but I dropped some very fat hints. You're looking very disapproving, so let's find something else to talk about. What have you been up to?'

'Not a lot,' said Aberdeen mechanically. 'Gardening a bit, visiting Kate – and since she's been here Ellie and I have been looking after her. What about you? You said the marina looked good, but have you managed to sort out Rusty Green?'

His eyes gleamed. 'Yes, that's under control. It was just as I thought – a bunch of big fish were circling round and sticking in the boot. They're not keen on small independent operators. I soon sent them packing.'

'You've been out to Atonement, too?'

'Round and about the Island Highway. I haven't been marking time, that's for sure. Now, what shall we do this evening? Go out or stay in?'

'Ellie's going out, so I have to be here. If I'd known you were coming I could have arranged something.'

'We'll have some of the crowd round,' said Jet easily. 'Macka and Marie and Charlie and Carol for starters; you like them, don't you?'

'You know I do.'

'You won't want some of the noisier sods, not while your mum's here.'

Aberdeen wasn't sure about the etiquette of entertaining in someone else's house, but Jet was Jasper's brother, so she supposed it should be all right.

Jet got on the telephone and arranged the gathering, and by six-thirty the guests had arrived. Young Nick Green, freshly out of plaster but still unable to drive, came with his parents and younger brothers.

'Thought you were still away,' he said to Jet. 'Did you bring Rusty down with you?'

'Why should I?'

'Well, you've been sailing about the islands together.'

'We took a few charters out there, that's all,' said Jet off-handedly. 'I had to do something while I was waiting for Aberdeen's mum to get out of hospital.'

'I suppose you'll be off overseas now she's better,' said Nick wistfully.

'I suppose we will!' mocked Jet. 'How do you feel about helping Rusty set up a sailing school venture on Atonement if I can get the tender?'

'Now, Jet,' said Carol Green. 'Don't you put ideas in his head. Nick's going to Uni, remember. As for Rusty – we're very grateful to you for helping her sort herself out, but she has her long-term prospects to think about. She can't spend *all* her life swanning around the islands.'

'Sorry, Nanny,' said Jet unrepentantly. 'I'll talk to you later. Now, come and meet Aberdeen's mum. She and Nick can swap horror stories about the hospital food. Better still – we'll fetch her out here.'

The evening passed in a blur to Aberdeen. She

316

forced herself to play hostess, but Kate was tired, and seemed to have problems remembering names and faces. After half an hour, she asked Aberdeen to help her back to bed. 'Your friends will be thinking I'm a gaga old woman,' she said regretfully, as Aberdeen half lifted her out of the wheelchair, 'but I can't keep up with them. They're all so *loud*.'

'These are some of the quieter ones,' said Aberdeen, swinging her into the bed. She pulled up the covers and adjusted the light and Kate's knitting. 'Will you be all right if I go back out?'

'Ask Jasper to come and sit with me.'

'Jasper isn't here,' said Aberdeen in a small, chilled voice.

Kate blinked. 'No, of course he isn't. I thought . . .' She seemed to be pursuing a fugitive memory, something she did rather often. 'Oh, never mind,' she said. 'It will come to me. Did you find the shoes?'

Aberdeen hadn't lost any shoes, but she agreed smilingly that she had found them and left her mother to rest. She knew she should go back to the others, but instead she slipped out towards the courtyard.

The telephone rang as she passed through the hallway and she stopped and scooped it up. She half-expected it to be Tam, perhaps wondering if the cars parked down the hill meant trouble, but it was Jasper.

The cold thrill that ran down her spine at the sound of his voice was extremely unpleasant. She had to gasp to regain her breath, and when she could speak her tone was sharp.

'What do you want?'

'Are you all right?' he asked. 'Are you managing?'

'Of course! What do you think I am?'

'Extremely pig-headed.'

317

'If I were,' she said angrily, 'I wouldn't be in your house.'

'You would,' he said. 'You'd be there for Kate.'

'I suppose so.'

'That's why I rang,' he said. 'The hospital said she'd been discharged. Is she comfortable?'

' "As comfortable as can be expected",' she quoted.

'How are the creatures?'

'Noisy,' she said.

'Normal, then.'

'The galahs are out in the courtyard for tonight. I moved them because Doc was keeping them awake. Is that OK?'

'Of course. Don't let Doc get you down. He's evil.'

'He certainly has an interesting vocabulary.'

There was silence, while Aberdeen wondered what to say. She had overcome her first sense of shock, but her nerves were still jangling and she gasped as Jet came silently up behind her.

'*There* you are, Lorelei,' he said in her free ear and slid his arms round her waist. 'Trouble?'

'No,' she said shortly. 'It's only Jasper. He rang to see how things are.'

Jet nodded and brought his cheek down against hers. 'Hi, bro,' he said.

'Jet?' said Jasper.

'Yes,' said Aberdeen. 'He came back today.'

'Tell him I'll be staying over tonight,' said Jet, and she could hear the enjoyment in his voice.

'He says –'

'I heard what he said,' said Jasper brusquely. 'Did you want to speak to Kate?'

'It's late. I'll talk to her next time. Goodnight.'

'Where are you? Do you want to talk to –?' Aberdeen stopped short, with Jet's soft laughter in her ear. 'He hung up!' she said, holding the receiver away from her and peering at it in disbelief.

'Typical,' said Jet. 'Does he ring you often?'

'This is the first time.' She could hear how silly that sounded, so she repeated it more certainly. 'This is the first time he's rung.'

'Must have known I was here,' said Jet.

'Did you tell him you were coming?' asked Aberdeen. Some of the tension was slipping from her muscles now Jasper was no longer on the other end of the line, but she also felt oddly bereft.

'No need,' said Jet. 'He'd know.' His hands slipped up to touch her breasts. 'I feel randy,' he murmured. 'Let's slip off to the bedroom.'

'But what about the others?'

'They won't care. They'll be expecting it.'

'Well, I'd care!' she said, flushing.

'Don't be so conventional, Lorelei.' Jet hoisted her suddenly over his shoulder and rushed back to the gathering with Aberdeen bouncing like a bag of meal. It was at that precise moment that she realized fully and completely that she couldn't marry him.

The realization brought a chill of sorrow, but a much more immediate feeling of embarrassment. How *could* she have let things go so far?

Jet set her back on her feet with a thud. 'Oops!' he said, and steadied her.

Carol Green shook her head indulgently. 'Do sit down, Jet, you make me tired to look at you. Sometimes I think you're younger than Nick and Rusty – if not Todd and Tiger.' Her gaze turned to Aberdeen. 'Is Mrs Shawcross all right, Aberdeen?'

'Fine,' said Aberdeen through numb lips. 'She gets tired easily, that's all.'

'I was shocked when I heard about her accident,' said Carol. 'It could hardly have happened at a worse time, could it?'

Was there a *good* time to be mugged and disabled? Alarmed at her own cynicism, Aberdeen sketched a smile. 'It was a big shock to us too. And especially to Kate. She's always been so independent.'

'So, when's the new wedding date?' asked Marie.

'As soon as I can pin her down.' Jet put his arm round Aberdeen and pulled her against him. 'We'll hire a nurse for Aberdeen's mum and Jas will just have to find someone else to mind his house.'

Aberdeen had to let that go unchallenged, for she couldn't discuss the matter with Jet while the Greens and McKenzies were present. It was only fair to set him straight while they were alone. Typically, though she was treading on coals all evening, the guests left just as Ellie Campbell returned from her outing.

Jet lingered over the farewells, and Ellie and Aberdeen went to settle Kate for the night. It took some time, and then Ellie announced she was going to bed.

Blessing her tact, but chilled with the thought of the coming interview, Aberdeen returned to the main room. 'Jet?'

'I'm in here,' called Jet from the bedroom.

With a feeling of doom, Aberdeen went to him. He was lying in the bed with his clothes neatly folded on the chair. He must have unpacked his single small bag, for his familiar blue dressing gown lay on the foot of the bed.

'Hop in, sweetie,' he said, and turned back the covers.

Aberdeen stayed where she was. 'Jet, I have to talk to you.'

His smile deepened. 'So come and talk.'

There was a sudden cough from the next room, and a radio burst into life. Ellie was still being tactful.

'Damn,' said Jet. He got out of bed and put his arms round Aberdeen. 'Why are you sleeping down here?'

'To be near Kate.' That was true, but there was no way she could have used Jasper's room. I've closed the rooms upstairs.'

'Let's go out in the garden,' he whispered. 'It's a warm night.'

He gathered the quilt from the bed and flung on his dressing gown. She wanted to protest, but she was inhibited by Ellie's presence and by the fear that any argument would upset Kate. She would tell him out in the garden. Out of earshot. It would lead to an uncomfortable night, but it never occurred to her to let events run their course and tell him in the morning. It would be dishonest to make love to him now that she knew she no longer wanted to marry him.

Jet tripped the security lights, and drew her out into the garden. 'This is great,' he said. 'Sneaking out with a blanket . . . makes me feel about young Nick's age!'

'Jet . . .'

'Here will do.' He flung down the quilt in the deep shadow of a weeping fig, let the dressing gown fall open and tugged her into his arms, moulding her against his warm body. 'Lorelei, I think you're overdressed,' he murmured against her ear.

'There's something I have to tell you,' she said, pushing him gently away. 'I can't sleep with you tonight.'

321

'Your mum won't mind! She actually told me to get in with you that time you were a bit seasick.'

'It isn't Kate. It's me. I can't do it now.'

'You haven't stopped taking the Pill?'

'I missed a few when Kate was hurt and after that there didn't seem much point,' she said.

'Oh, great!' He felt in his dressing gown pockets. 'I haven't got anything either. We'll have to raid Jas's supply.'

Aberdeen's face felt as if it were about to burst into flames. 'No!' she said hastily. 'I mean, I expect he took anything like that with him. I certainly haven't seen them – though I haven't been looking.'

'I should hope not!' He clicked his fingers. 'Lunch-wrap!' he said gleefully. 'I'll just go and fetch some!'

'*Jet* . . .'

She really was going to tell him the truth, but just then Doc woke up. He stretched each leg and wing in turn, and detected human presence. He opened his wings and screeched his approval, then made a few of his riper comments. The noise was ear-shattering in the silence of the night.

'Shhhh!' pleaded Aberdeen. 'Doc, shut up!'

'That bloody bird! I'll fix him,' said Jet. He walked over to the aviary. 'Shut up, you!' he said, but Doc simply cackled and clambered up to the roof where he continued to squawk and flap. Lights were springing on all up and down the Close. Security floodlights came on over the road, and Dottie began to bark.

'Bugger this for a game,' muttered Jet. He was shaking with laughter. 'No wonder Jas never bothers with extensive security systems! Sounds like a prison riot already! Let's get inside before the cops come and grab us for housebreakers.'

Aberdeen followed him with alacrity, but as they shut themselves back in the house she could stand it no more. She switched on the light, and blinked painfully. 'Jet, there's no use trying to set a new date for the wedding,' she said apologetically. 'Not with the way Kate is.'

'I see,' said Jet, and for a moment his face looked as blank as Jasper's.

'I'm sorry,' said Aberdeen. 'I've thought and thought, but I just can't see how it would work. You want to be off on *Aphrodite*, but I can't leave Kate just yet. And it isn't only that. You like parties and lots of friends around, I'm happy just to be quiet. Even if you did get a nurse for Kate I'd be distracted all the time . . . and it isn't just Kate. You're lots of fun, but fun isn't what I need. Everything seems to have moved too quickly and now it's run out of steam.'

He was staring at her with the beginnings of a mocking smile, but she persevered to the end of her speech. 'It just isn't fair to keep on putting you off. What I'm trying to say is, I think we should call it a day.'

'I guess you've had a better offer,' said Jet. 'Bloody Jasper! He's given you more than a house to live in, hasn't he?'

'He did ask me to marry him before he left,' said Aberdeen.

'Can't bear to be beaten, can he? So – what did you say to this touching proposal?'

'I said no, of course.'

'Why?'

'*Why*?' This conversation was getting more surreal by the minute. Was this how Kate felt, bewildered and overloaded by what others said and did?

'Yes, why did you turn him down?' Jet's face showed cynical amusement now.

'Of course I did!' she said blankly. 'I'm engaged to you!'

'So now you want to get disengaged so you can get re-engaged. You don't want to be a bigamist, so you're playing musical fiancés.' Jet chuckled. 'At least you're consistent, Lorelei! Same face, same surname – Lord, even the same initial! So – how does J. Diamond compare with J. Diamond?'

She stared at him.

'What does he do for you in bed that I don't?'

'I've never been to bed with Jasper!' she protested, her face flaming.

'How improvident,' said Jet lightly. 'You should try before you buy, and close the second deal before you burn your bridges with the first.'

'Wouldn't you mind?' she said incredulously.

'Of course I bloody mind!' He turned on her. 'I don't like losing out, Aberdeen – particularly not to Big Brother. I knew *he'd* stab me in the back if he could, but I thought you were straight up. So – when's the wedding to be?'

'Never,' said Aberdeen. She was shaken and close to tears. 'I told you I said no! I told him, too. I said there was no way I was going to play games with you two. And that's what it would be if I married either one of you, games. Jasper would keep stirring the pot and you'd keep scoring off him. Or the other way round. It's a farcical situation and I'm not into farce. So. I'm not going to marry either of you. The risks outweigh the advantages.'

Jet whistled. 'You don't mind laying it on the line, do you? But it's a bit rough to toss *me* in just because

324

he's been hassling you! May I ask what you *are* going to do? You're not exactly swimming in liquid assets.'

'I don't know,' said Aberdeen bleakly. 'I expect I'll get a job, if I can. I might be able to get a carer's pension.'

'What about your precious museum?'

'Pie in the sky. With my luck I'd only have messed it up, anyway.'

'You haven't played your cards very well,' said Jet. 'You might have married me and got a quickie divorce. Or run me and Jas in tandem for a while. Mix and match instead of musical chairs.'

'That's a disgusting idea!'

'Not really, sweetie. If we hadn't split off in our first few hours Jas and I would have been the same person, and where's the harm?'

'I'll have to move out of here,' she said sickly.

'What for? Hang on and act noble and he might even give you a job at Diamond/Spellman! *I* can't offer you a job; you won't act as crew and I doubt if you've got the finesse for futures and property.'

Aberdeen was tired of sparring, chilled by the malice she could sense under Jet's apparently light-hearted acceptance of her decision. 'The sooner I get away from you Diamonds, the better I'll like it,' she said savagely. 'Jet – don't you care *at all*?'

'Yes, I do care. I really wanted to marry you,' he said. 'You're gorgeous, and you amuse me. I'm not quite as obsessed with you as Jas is, but maybe that's because you haven't kept me at arm's length. I *know* what you taste like and feel like; he can only imagine and hope for some crumbs.'

She bit her lip, hard, trying to cram down her distaste.

'We could have had a lot of fun, you and I,' said Jet.

'We did,' she said tightly, 'but fun isn't enough.'

'I suppose I should have seen this coming,' he said. 'You were pretty keen to push me off with Rusty.'

'Rusty? She's only a kid!'

'Rusty's twenty-one.'

'Maybe, but she's . . .'

'She's what, Lorelei? Short and freckled? Plain? I grant you she can't hold a candle to you in looks, but she's a hell of a lot more use on a boat. *And* she wants me.'

'Maybe you'd better take *her* on your voyage then!'

'I think I probably will,' said Jet. 'Carol might cut up rough, but there's nothing she can do. Rusty's known me all her life, after all.' He let the dressing gown drop to the floor and stood facing her, unconcerned with his nakedness. Aberdeen stared at him, at his familiar face and figure. Something was hurting; she supposed it must be her pride. She was jilting *him*, but it seemed he had someone in the wings to take her place. Or perhaps Rusty had been at centre stage already.

She clasped her hands together, then slowly drew off her engagement ring and held it out.

Jet took it and held it up to the light, then favoured her with his old affectionate grin. 'Just one thing, Lorelei,' he said. 'If you could wind back time, go back to the Sydney-Hobart, would you still have dinner with me?'

'Kate – ' she began.

'Forget that part for a minute. Just tell me. Would you rather not have met me at all?'

'No,' she said stonily. 'It's taught me a lot, knowing you.'

'Ditto, ditto. I know a lot more than I did about nineteenth-century costume. I also know I'll never win 'em all.' He put his head on one side. 'I suppose you could say our window of opportunity closed.'

He went back into the bedroom and got dressed, then came out carrying his bag. 'I'm off,' he said. 'I'll catch the early train and go back up north for a while.'

'Yes,' she said. 'Goodbye.'

'*Auf Wiedersehen*. Keep in touch if you like.'

'I don't think so,' she said. 'I think I'll probably go back to Tasmania with Kate as soon as she can travel. What do we do about letting people know?'

'Nothing,' he said. 'They'll realize eventually.'

Jet walked out, making a rude gesture in Doc's direction. Just as Aberdeen was about to shut the door behind him, he turned back. 'Here!' he said, and tossed her something which she caught automatically. 'You might need some cash one day.'

He disappeared through the gate. Aberdeen looked down at her cupped hands. In them sparkled her engagement ring.

CHAPTER 18

By the end of May, Jasper had driven across Victoria and South Australia and traversed the long curve of Western Australia and the vastness of the centre. He had cut across the Territory and was now in Northern Queensland. Driving himself to exhaustion was one way of exorcising his personal demons. He had no intention of harming himself or anyone else, so whenever he began to see double he parked and slept in the van. Unfortunately, he couldn't prevent the dreams.

He had the camcorder and a still camera with him, and amassed a large amount of material. Perth was interesting and so was the city of Darwin. Alice burned with the hot dry clarity of the red centre, but there was nowhere that really sparked his imagination. Nowhere that begged to be featured *In the Rough*.

It was his own perception that was faulty. He knew he should have brought someone else along. A member of the team whose judgement he trusted. But the white-hot attraction that burned between Tam and Rod would have seared him, and Steve and Stew lacked the vision he needed. Visual artists, both, but the original concepts were not their concern. Ellie would have done, but he wasn't subjecting little Ellie to his current misery. She might have tried to comfort him and he wasn't subjecting her to that, either. Besides, she was helping Aberdeen with Kate.

Never mix business with sex . . . Tam's advice, and who was she to talk?

Mount Isa to Burketown, Normanton to Cairns, east of the Great Dividing Range. Down the coast he went as far as Manatee. Young Rusty Green was there, he remembered, plying her yacht around the Island Highway. He thought he'd call on her for half an hour. No fear of Rusty trying to comfort him, for she had always treated him coolly. She was the eldest of Carol Green's children, and he thought she probably resented the affection Carol had retained for Jet and himself as her former charges.

The brief tropical sunset was flaming as he drew up at Manatee wharf. He had never seen Rusty's *Greensleeves*, but he did recognize Jet's *Aphrodite* among the yachts and pleasure craft in the bay; recognized it with a burst of surprise, for surely Jet had returned to Sydney and Aberdeen some time before? His mocking presence had been a nearly palpable accompaniment to the conversation Jasper had had with Aberdeen.

He walked the length of the jetty to investigate, his boot heels clicking on the odd cobbled surface. Manatee was a tourist town, but its tourists were fishermen and sailors, bushwalkers and skin-divers. It hadn't gone high-rise or plastic.

Aphrodite rode at anchor a hundred metres from the end of the jetty. Her inflatable bobbed at her flank as a fat duckling might bob beside a graceful swan. Jasper frowned. He was wondering whether to try Jet's mobile number when a man in a dinghy hailed him.

'Hi, Jet you need a lift out to *Aphrodite*?'

'Thanks,' said Jasper, not bothering to correct the misidentification.

The dinghy skimmed up to the wharf and Jasper sprang aboard, settling neatly in the stern.

'Your girlfriend didn't hear you hail?' said the oarsman, tilting his head towards the yacht. 'Or is she giving you grief?'

'She doesn't know I'm here,' said Jasper hollowly. 'I didn't get round to hailing her.'

Not for the first time, he gave bitter thanks for his deadpan face. Aberdeen must have yielded to Jet's persuasions after all, and hurried north. She might have let him know she'd left his house . . . So might Tam, for that matter.

'There you are,' said the Good Samaritan. He nodded affably as Jasper climbed aboard *Aphrodite*.

There was silence on deck, except for the chirrup of a small, creamy-coloured cat.

Jasper bent to offer his hand; the cat hesitated then rubbed its whiskers against him. He straightened and went across to the companionway.

'Jet?' he called. 'Are you there?'

There was silence for a few seconds, then his brother's voice answered him. '*Jas?*'

Jasper waited, feeling a muscle flickering in his cheek.

'Come on down,' called Jet.

Jasper clenched his hands slowly, then began to descend. He sensed movement in the cabin; a flurry as if someone resented his presence. Aberdeen. A great distaste came over him as he realized they were in bed. He could see Jet's bare chest and arms in the dimness, but the girl had burrowed under the light cover; he could see her only as a lumpy outline distorting Jet's familiar shape.

'I'll wait up on deck,' he said harshly.

Jet glinted a smile at him, and he couldn't wait to get back in the open air. Almost, he thought he would dive from the gunwale and swim back to the jetty. The distance was nothing; only his heavy boots and the unknown quality of the ocean kept him on the deck. Tropical waters could harbour stinging jellyfish, sharks and other unwelcoming denizens.

He leaned on the rail, his eyes unfocused, feeling physically sick with his loathing of the situation. He heard Jet's bare feet on the steps, and Jet's hand slapped him on the shoulder. 'Jas, old mate! What are you doing up here in Manatee?'

'I saw *Aphrodite*,' he said. 'I thought you were still in Sydney.'

'Lord, no. I only stayed the one night there.'

Jet looked splendid, clad only in a pair of shorts. Jasper tried to smile at him, but he felt his lopsided attempt must look like the grimace of a harlequin. 'She gave in, then,' he said, and jerked his head towards the cabin.

'Tumbled like a ripe plum,' said Jet carelessly.

'Are you married yet?'

'No hurry. Might get round to it one day.'

'Has Aberdeen made some arrangements for Kate? Does she need a nurse?'

Jet's shoulders rose and fell in a slight shrug and Jasper's hovering suspicions crystallized. Something was very wrong. He glanced down at the companionway, then back at his brother. Jet smiled blandly.

There was a faint creaking noise from below and then the girl, her face very flushed beneath her cap, appeared. She came up steadily, a stocky figure in jeans and a striped polo shirt, and planted herself next to Jet.

'Hello, Jasper.'

'Rusty.' He nodded to her, and watched her blush mounting. The shirt wasn't done up, and the exposed swell of her upper breasts was firm, full and speckled with freckles like nutmeg. She met his gaze squarely for a moment, then her eyes flickered sideways to Jet. Slowly, Jet slid his hands into his pockets.

'You bastard,' said Jasper flatly. 'You rotten stinking bastard.'

Jet said nothing, but Rusty's chin came up. 'Come off it, Jasper. I bet you've had it off with a few girls in your time.'

'Shut up, Rusty,' he said. 'I would have thought you'd know better than to get mixed up with Jet – especially now. *Christ*! Hasn't Carol taught you anything?'

'I make my own decisions,' said Rusty.

'And you made the decision to do this to Aberdeen. You've had *years* to hop into Jet's bed if that's what you want; why wait until he's engaged to someone else?'

Now Rusty's eyes wavered. 'This has got nothing to do with Aberdeen,' she said in a hard voice. 'If she'd married Jet when she was supposed to this wouldn't have happened. As it is, well. What she doesn't know won't hurt her.'

'Peace, peace,' said Jet. He tugged Rusty's cap down over her eyes then smacked her bottom lightly. 'Go down and make us a coffee.'

'Make your own darned coffee.'

'Don't, then.' Jet turned back to Jasper. 'I suppose you're going to make a Royal Commission out of all this, Jas, so I'll take you ashore and we'll talk it over reasonably.' His smile sprang out. 'To use a cliché, *this isn't what you think*.'

332

'I'm not going to think,' said Jasper. 'I'm going to do something I ought to have done a long time ago.'

'What's that?' Jet's smile was still in place, but his eyes were wary.

Jasper hadn't punched anyone in years, not since his high school days. It brought him amazing satisfaction.

Jet went down like a felled tree, and Rusty gave a screech and flew at Jasper.

'You bastard – you bastard!' Her nails, the short, square-cut nails of a yachtswoman, scraped down his cheek, rasping against his stubble of beard. 'I hate you!'

She was sobbing now, kicking at his shins. He brought his hands down hard on her forearms and held her off, but she pressed forward, trying to inflict maximum damage.

Jasper's stomach heaved. He wasn't particularly fond of Rusty, but he supposed he had always regarded her as a sort of little sister. Now, as she pressed against him, he realized she was anything but little. 'Get off me!' he said cuttingly.

Jet had picked himself up, and now strolled over and grasped Rusty by the scruff of the neck. 'Russet Elizabeth Green, you cut that out.' He raised a brow at Jasper. 'Can't seem to keep my women away from you – or vice versa.' He rubbed his jaw with the other hand. 'You want to do something about that aggression, Jas,' he said. 'One of these days it's going to land you in trouble. Jump down in the dinghy; I'll row you back to the jetty and we'll talk on the way.'

Jasper stared at him. 'There's nothing to talk about,' he said. 'That punch was for Aberdeen, incidentally. Not for me.'

'Of course,' said Jet.

333

'*This* one is for me.'

He swung again, intending to miss, and had the satisfaction of seeing Jet duck before he sprang up on to the gunwale and, after all, dived into the sea.

It was cold, and he was crazy, but at least there weren't any jellyfish. Even if there had been, he might have preferred their stings to Jet's.

The cold salt water shocked Jasper into some kind of sanity. He swam ashore, changed his clothes and got in the van and drove. Out of Manatee and down the coast, heading back towards Sydney. As he drove he sought to rationalize his actions. There was no excuse for his lack of direction, just the fact that his life, personally and professionally, seemed to have been in shambles for the past six months. It must be reconstructed, piece by piece.

Driving himself to exhaustion wasn't going to salvage *In the Rough*. It wasn't going to help him forget Aberdeen. And now, he realized as the sun plunged suddenly from sight, he had no need to forget her. Jet had shown her no loyalty over Rusty Green, so Jasper need have no compunction about confronting Aberdeen with the hollowness of her engagement. She wouldn't have broken with Jet for her own desires or Jasper's, but now that Jet had found a new companion she should, she *must*, see reason.

Jet would be better suited with Rusty anyway, he thought with relief. The girl was in love with him but she took no nonsense; she was a dedicated sailor who had known Jet all her life. A perfect match, and Jet must know it already since he had seemed not at all abashed when caught with his fingers in the pie. A perfect match, and Aberdeen must be told.

And messengers bearing unwelcome news were rather frequently shot.

'Damn!' said Jasper. He'd had great satisfaction in knocking his brother down, but now he needed his co-operation, if not his active help. He dialled Jet's mobile telephone number.

'Jet?' he said without preamble. 'What are you going to do?'

'Sue you for assault,' said Jet. 'Rusty is my witness.'

'What are you going to tell Aberdeen about Rusty?'

'Nothing,' said Jet. 'What I do with Rusty has nothing to do with Aberdeen. It's an entirely separate thing.'

'If you don't tell her, I will.'

'Blackmail now? I'm telling her nothing,' said Jet. 'I'll leave you the pleasure of that, and wish you joy. You know what they say about the bearers of ill tidings.'

Jet cut the connection and Jasper cursed again. Jet was sharp enough to know he couldn't carry tales without doing himself as much damage as the tales would do to Jet. And he didn't want to damage anyone, not now. All he wanted was an end to this snarled-up tangle his life had become.

He telephoned Aberdeen next day, staring irritably at the lines on the map while he waited for her to answer. He remembered the map of the city rail system; they'd played a silly game with that. He could pinpoint *her* position without a map when she answered the phone. Hallway table of his own house in Major Mitchell Close, in Windhill, Sydney, New South Wales. She couldn't pinpoint his unless he told her. She wouldn't know if he was calling from Perth or Queensland or even his private island.

She answered the telephone.

'Hello, Abbie,' he said, and winced as she dropped the receiver. It swung against the leg of the hall table and bounced and he suddenly had a very clear picture of the hall, of Aberdeen herself. She would be wearing jeans and a shirt, he thought. Her hair would be shining like wheat. The very smell and taste of her skin seemed to bathe his memory and catch at his guts.

The receiver connected again, with something else. It made a more muffled sound, probably rebounding from the reference books on the shelf down under the table. And that gave him an idea. 'Aberdeen? Abbie, are you all right?'

She answered in a breathless voice and his guts seemed to lurch again. He couldn't hit her with it now, over the phone. Instead, he must establish some kind of general tie, some kind of partnership in practical matters so she wouldn't take fright and run. 'I was wondering,' he said. 'Would you do me a favour?'

Silence. But eventually she spoke again and he thought he had caught her interest. He had to build on that.

Aberdeen told no one about her broken engagement for fear of upsetting Kate, who had periods when she protested vigorously that Aberdeen had put her life on hold. To avoid questions, she slid the ring back on her finger and tried to act normally as she sought an acceptable plan for the future. She could do as she'd told Jet and take Kate home to Tasmania, but not just yet. She'd introduce the subject gradually, so it came to seem inevitable.

On the first day of June, she turned her situation

336

sides-to-middle for the tenth time. No job, no home, no lover . . . the thought of Jasper hurt her and she ached for his presence. Now she knew how Tam had felt when she and Rod were estranged. If she saw Jasper again, if he touched her again, it would be the first drink. They had no future together, so she must make sure she didn't ever see him. If she'd refused him while she was still engaged to Jet, how much more unfair would it be to accept him now? It would smack of desperation, of taking second-best, and while she would know it was nothing of the kind he'd always have to wonder.

The telephone rang, and she picked it up.

'Hello, Abbie,' said Jasper.

She'd conjured him up with her wistful thoughts! She gasped and dropped the telephone with a clatter.

'Aberdeen? Abbie – are you all right?'

He sounded sharp and she had to draw three deep breaths before she could trust herself to retrieve the phone and reply. She had put her confusion last time down to Jet's presence, but she was every bit as shaken now.

'I'm fine,' she said, and breathed in again.

'Kate?'

'Kate's not too bad. She still gets confused sometimes.'

'I was wondering,' he said. 'Would you do me a favour?'

She waited.

'I just love your enthusiasm, Abbie. You have only to say yes or no.'

'That depends,' she said.

'I want you to get the atlas from the shelf below the telephone.'

Wondering, she did as he said. 'Now what?'

'That's it.' He hung up.

Aberdeen stared at the burring telephone. 'He's *mad*,' she said aloud. 'He's out of his tree!'

She went restlessly into the garden. It was winter now, but a few flowers still lingered in sheltered corners. Jasper's creek bubbled and speckled with a light shower of rain. In the aviary, Doc flew to the highest perch and spread his wings and tail to catch every drop, squawking and curtsying in a trance of pleasure. His quiet little mate watched from the shelter of the feeding box. The galahs croodled to one another and touched beaks in a human-seeming kiss. An avian Darby and his Joan.

Aberdeen patted Dottie and made a mental note that a paling in the fence needed replacing. She wondered if there would be daffodils in the garden in the spring.

Then she remembered she'd never know and hurried back into the house.

The telephone rang again the next day at five.

'Hello, Abbie,' said Jasper.

'Hello,' she said and her heart was thudding madly. 'How's Kate?'

'The same as she was yesterday. Jasper – what do you want?'

'A favour,' he said. 'Remember that atlas I asked you to get?'

'It's staring at me. So – what is it this time? A dictionary? A ten-volume Shakespeare?'

'Open the atlas at the map of Australia.'

She wedged the telephone between ear and shoulder and did so. 'Now what?'

'That's it,' he said, and hung up.

Aberdeen glowered at the phone with frustration. He was playing some sort of game, but she didn't know what. Hearing his voice did things to her, things she preferred not to examine.

She went out to the courtyard where Kate was sitting in her wheelchair. 'I was thinking,' said Kate slowly, 'I should be going home soon.'

'Whenever you want,' said Aberdeen. 'I expect it's snowing in Tassie.'

'Frosty more likely,' said Kate. 'I ought to be seeing to the bulbs.'

'I'll do that,' said Aberdeen.

Kate looked at her. 'No, darling, you won't be there. You're going away with Jet.'

'Of course I'll be there.' She drew a deep breath. 'I've been thinking, Kate. What do you say we start a little business at the cottage? A tea-room or something?'

'This won't work, Aberdeen,' said Kate.

'A nursery, then. We could grow potted plants. Or herbs. Wouldn't you like to grow herbs and sell them at Salamanca market?'

Kate sighed. 'It won't work. It isn't enough.'

'Kate!' said Aberdeen sharply. 'I asked you a question.'

'That's right,' said Kate. 'And I answered it.' She looked up at Aberdeen. 'Did I tell you Jasper showed me the footage he'd shot for *Tasmania – In the Rough*?'

'No,' said Aberdeen.

'There was some material that was good, but not enough,' said Kate. 'He needed some more, but he said it had lost its . . .' She stopped and closed her eyes. 'It's gone,' she said crossly after a moment. 'What was I saying?'

'You were saying Jasper's footage had lost some-thing,' said Aberdeen. 'But it doesn't matter in the least. It's time you were off to bed.'

Kate's eyes sprang open and their expression was not very friendly. 'It *does* matter, Aberdeen,' she said. 'It matters a lot to Jasper. He thinks his professional credibility is on the line. It also matters to me. *My* credibility is on the line here too, isn't it?'

'What do you mean?' asked Aberdeen, stung.

'You're patronizing me, treating me the way I never treated you. Next, you'll be patting my hand and telling me it was Jet who rang you tonight and lit up your face.'

'It was Jasper, actually,' said Aberdeen. 'And I'm not lit up. I'm annoyed. He's playing games again.'

'Continuity,' said Kate with satisfaction. 'That's what Jasper said it had lost. He couldn't add anything to the Tasmania footage because it would have no continuity.'

The telephone rang again the next day. Aberdeen glanced at the clock. Five-fifteen. Resolutely, she stayed away from the phone, but it kept on ringing and its persistence wore her down. She snatched it to her ear. 'Hello?'

'You've been running,' said Jasper. 'Is anything wrong?'

'No. Where *are* you?'

'In limbo,' he said. 'On an island, as it happens. I'm sitting on a rock and staring at the sea. And you?'

'You know where I am. I suppose you want a map of Alaska this time.'

'No, I want you to fetch a pin.'

Aberdeen felt the beginnings of a very reluctant

smile. 'I've got a pin right here.'

'Liar,' said Jasper. 'You have to go out in the kitchen and get one from the mending box. That's the only source of pins in *my* house.'

'It's your phone bill,' she said tartly. 'It's your mobile battery. By the way, I'm itemizing the calls I make.'

'Don't,' said Jasper.

She put down the telephone and went out to the kitchen. The mending box was up in a high cupboard, so she had to fetch a chair.

'What are you doing?' asked Ellie.

'I'm getting a pin for Jasper,' said Aberdeen without thinking. Then blushed, because it sounded so much like one of Kate's irrelevancies.

She went back to the phone. 'I have a pin,' she said precisely. 'Ellie thinks I'm out of my tree. I hope you're satisfied.'

There was silence on the line.

'Jasper?' she said sharply. 'I said, I've got the pin. Now what?'

'That's it,' he said, and hung up.

Aberdeen picked up the atlas and raised it high. She felt like dashing it against the wall, but sanity prevailed. The fine hairs on her arms were standing up and she was tingling all over. She needed a shower.

What the heck was Jasper doing?

Jasper wasn't sure of the answer to that, but he came to think of the telephone calls as little fishing trips. He had scrambled his work and emotions altogether, and he must sort it out together, if at all. He would *not* rush in, nor would he leave it too late. He wanted her to let him into her life. Hence his fishing trips.

341

On the first day she was shocked to hear from him. On the second, he thought, she was impatient to get him to the point. On the third day her exasperation was plain in her voice, but so was a quiver of fun. On the fourth day, he told her to close her eyes and stab the pin in the map. 'Thank you,' he said when she had done it, and hung up before she could tell him where the pin had hit. Talking to Aberdeen made him feel alive. So restless that he couldn't settle, but walked for hours around his island of Allirra. If he held his breath he could feel her holding his hand. If he looked inside his longing he could see her under the trees or standing at the doorway of his cabin.

When he telephoned he often asked after Kate and Doc and Dottie. He asked about her days, but he never mentioned Jet and nor did she. Perhaps she was being tactful, but tact was not a virtue he associated with Aberdeen. How was Ellie? How were Tam and Rod? Nyssa and the OAP galahs? And where had the pin hit the map?

'Kangaroo Island,' she said. 'What's this about?'

'Try again with the pin,' he said and hung up.

'I tried again,' she said the next day, 'and it landed on Thursday Island. That's ridiculous; it's way up off Cape York. So what's this all about? And I warn you, Jasper, if you hang up, I'll dial ISD and leave this off the hook until tomorrow.'

He hesitated, then told her part of the truth. 'I'm trying to find a peg to hang another *In the Rough* on.'

'You didn't finish the Tasmania one,' she objected.

'No. Driving around didn't help at all, so I thought

342

I'd stop and catch my breath and try the good old pin trick. Subconscious association.'

'By proxy?'

'If you like. I have a map but I couldn't find a pin.'

'Well, it landed on two islands so far,' she said. 'I guess that must mean you have to do lots of islands in the rough.'

'*Islands*,' he said. 'Why didn't I think of that?'

'Because it's a silly idea.'

'But it isn't,' he said. 'It'll work.'

He hung up then, leaving Aberdeen tantalised and puzzled. She was on the point of going to bed that night when the telephone rang again.

'I was going to come straight home,' said Jasper pensively, 'but now I'm calling the rest of the team to meet me here.'

'Where's here?'

'Out of limbo, Abbie. Off the island, anyway. Would you look after the house for a little while longer?'

'We're going home to Tasmania,' said Aberdeen.

'Stay,' he said. 'Wait for spring. Stay until I come back, anyway.'

'You can't go off and start filming with a day's notice,' she said. 'That's doing it backwards. What about scripts and things? What about permits?'

'With *In the Rough* we do a lot of things backwards. How are your computer skills?'

'Reasonable,' she said, surprised.

'I need a file. It's in my computer in the upstairs office, right next door to my bedroom. Could you e-mail it to me as an attachment?'

'I suppose so.'

'The file is *Rough/Tas/draft/prop*, and the e-mail address is jasperdd@sydcen.com.'

'Not so fast,' she protested. 'Spell it out.'

He spelled it out. 'You'll need my password too,' he said. 'You know it already. It's as silly as a certain old spaniel bitch.'

She grinned, and shaped the word in silence with her lips. *Dottie*. 'A silly bitch, or maybe a Dalmatian,' she agreed. 'When do you want it?'

'Would it be too much trouble to do it tonight? On your way to bed?'

'Yes,' she said. 'It isn't on my way, because I sleep downstairs. But I'll do it – if I can.'

It took a while to get the hang of Jasper's computer, which was a different make and model from the one she had used at the Pitt Gallery. It was full of files, and she wondered why he didn't keep the information at the studio. But perhaps he kept it there as well. He struck her as being a belt-and-braces man.

She fumbled a connection, and listened as the modem sang its discordant little song. The attachment seemed to work, and she sent it on its way via the world wide web; an e-mail address was as anonymous as a post office box number, so she still had no idea where he was. Ellie could have done this, or Tam, or anyone who worked at Diamond/Spellman. She supposed he'd chosen her as a disinterested party who wouldn't have the urge to read his files.

'I doubt it,' said Tam, when Aberdeen suggested this to her. 'More likely he wants you familiar with the system for while we're all away.'

'You're going with them this time?'

'Yes,' said Tam, 'this time I'm going with Rod.

344

Jasper's even hit on a way to compensate for the fact that I'm missing from the Tasmanian footage . . . but that's beside the point. Rod and I have been living in Eden long enough. It's time we went off with the team again, to see how we function in chaos.' She smiled. 'Aberdeen, can you keep a secret?'

'Probably,' said Aberdeen.

'We've been thinking, Rod and me, about having a child. How would you feel about being a sort of aunt?'

Aberdeen smiled with an effort. 'An *aunt*?'

'Or whatever the relationship would be, once you're married to Jet. Cousin by marriage, once removed, perhaps.'

I'm not going to marry Jet. I'm going away. The words hovered unsaid, and she couldn't say them now. 'I hope you'll be very happy, whatever you decide,' she said, which seemed to sum up the situation exactly.

That was only the first request Jasper made of Aberdeen. Tam, Rod, Stew and Steve left almost immediately, heading south west to meet Jasper on Kangaroo Island. Ellie stayed behind with Kate and Aberdeen. Day after day, Jasper telephoned. It was almost as bad, thought Aberdeen, as when he had seemed to be haunting her before. Almost, but not quite. However she shivered when he spoke to her, his physical presence was far away. And his words were calm and placid and unexceptional. He seemed to have given up on his obsessions.

Aberdeen sent more files, organized tradespeople, even installed an unpromising-looking bare-rooted plant in the courtyard. She collated three hundred photographs by date and took Dottie to the vet for her annual check-up. The tasks were never too difficult, never too time-consuming, and all of them, Aberdeen supposed, might be loosely lumped with her duties as a house-sitter. No call to feel indignant about dogsbodying for him, for wasn't she living in a beautiful house rent-free? Not that he needed any rent . . . he was comfortably off. Quite how comfortably she appreciated when she paid the house insurance and the household accounts. The balance shown on the receipt was extremely healthy; she supposed, now she thought about it, that Jasper must be at least as wealthy as Jet.

'It's incredible,' she said to Kate. 'I could take him for every cent if I were so inclined. Or sell his secrets to Spielberg.'

'He trusts you,' said Kate.

'More fool him,' said Aberdeen.

She tried to remain disinterested, but sometimes she couldn't help reading pieces of text and correspondence; when files had similar names, it was necessary to be sure she had the right one. She tried to remain cool on the telephone, but he began to tell her stories, odd little incidents. He began to ask her questions, practical and philosophical, and she found he'd answer questions of her own. Away from his distracting physical presence she found herself actually liking Jasper Diamond – but that of course was his stock-in-trade, and she mustn't ever forget it.

Jasper's team finished work on temperate Kangaroo Island and headed for tropical Magnetic Island. He asked Aberdeen to forward a letter which had been sent to him months ago by someone who lived there.

'Somewhere in the letters file,' he said. 'Probably under P-for-Positive.'

'Positive what?'

'Comment,' he said.

Aberdeen retrieved the letter, and was touched by the pleasure Jasper's *Top End* programme seemed to have given one old man. One of the featured characters had been a childhood friend; now they were back in contact.

Sometimes Aberdeen realized she was missing Jet, mourning the future he had offered her. Her life would be very narrow now, but she must find employment and make a home to fit her altered circumstances. She should be working now, she fretted, for the weeks of rent-free living would come to an end as soon as Jasper's team returned.

She had still not told anyone about the breaking of her engagement, but she supposed it would dawn on them eventually, since she didn't often wear her ring. She also wondered, with wry amusement, who would ask the obvious questions about Jet's continuing absence and lack of calls. Kate was vague, and Ellie tactful. There was no one else; except, on the end of an intermittent line, there was Jasper.

She would leave, she decided, as soon as he came home. She might be serving a minor purpose now (though one that Ellie could have served as well), but soon there would be no excuse to stay and every reason to go. And go she would, before he had a chance to learn about Jet, to pity her, or to try interfering again. Otherwise he'd offer her some make-work job and that she couldn't accept. Better to be gone.

How she was going to talk Kate into moving at

short notice and without seeing Jasper again she didn't know. Kate's accusation that she had been patronized had bitten home, but *someone* had to make the decisions and distance the Shawcross women from a family with which they now had no right to keep ties at all.

CHAPTER 19

The telephone rang.

She knew it would be Jasper, not through any arcane sixth sense, but because he always called at this time.

'Hello, Jasper.'

'Hello, Abbie. How's Kate?'

The ritual continued, commonplaces given and received.

'It the filming going well?' she asked, because Kate would want to know.

'Very well,' he said. 'We've finished work on those donkeys on Magnetic now. Next stop, Thursday Island.'

A wonderfully long way off, beyond Cape York, yet as close as the nearest telephone. And things were coming into perspective now. He had lost his obsession, was treating her as a kind of friendly acquaintance. So. No more amiable wrangling conversations. Let the distancing begin.

She was silent, not asking after Tam and Rod, disengaging herself from this family, just as she had disengaged herself from Jet.

'There's another file,' said Jasper abruptly.

'Yes?'

'It's down in the studio computer.'

'Are you in a hurry?'

'I am, this time,' said Jasper. 'Get a cab and book it to Diamond/Spellman. There's a pile of cab-charge dockets in the top drawer of my desk.'

So there were, neatly clipped together.

'The keys are in the same drawer,' said Jasper. 'The one with the purple tag will get you into the studio. The green-tagged one will get you into my office. The password is a certain feathered devil and the file is called New Start.'

'Right,' said Aberdeen, in a parody of her temporary PA role. 'I'm on my way.'

As she entered the studio, she wondered about the security system. Jasper had never yet given her any instructions in writing, so she'd have a sticky time explaining her presence if the alarm sounded at the police station.

Jasper would sort it out.

She locked the door behind her.

The place was a bewildering mass of corridors and wide, bare spaces, and she tried to remember what Kate and Tam had said. Parts were rented out, but on a daily basis, so no one would be here tonight. Some of the doors were labelled, which was helpful.

T. Spellman, Archives, Kitchen, Ellie's Spot, S&S, Rod.

Viewing Room 1, Editing Suite, Cutting Room, Padded Cell . . .

That one brought her up with a slight twist of amusement.

Misc, Misc, Misc. Watch This Space.

'This is getting surreal,' she said aloud. She tried the door to *Watch This Space* but it was locked.

She found herself looping round past *Ellie's Spot* again. This was going to take forever. She'd be discovered, old and grey, plodding around these corridors in fifty years' time – or when the team came back from filming islands. No. Realistically, she'd be discovered when someone showed up in the morning. There was more to Diamond/Spellman than *In the Rough*.

If I were Jasper's office, where would I be?

Close to Jasper, came the answer, but that was no good. Near the viewing room, perhaps, since he must spend a lot of time in there. She found her way back, and turned left instead of right.

Jasper Diamond.

Easy as blackberry pie.

She had to squint to insert the key in the lock, but the office was partially illuminated by a skylight in the roof. Now *there* was a practical idea . . . She froze, her senses alive as a cat's whisker antenna. There was something in the air, achingly familiar.

'Jasper?' she said uncertainly, and flinched away as a hand touched hers. Her heart thudded wildly, madly in her chest, all her pulses were leaping, and she was drowning in a flood of sparkling sensation.

'What the *hell* are you playing at this time?' she screamed.

'I thought you knew I was here,' he said. 'I can see *you* quite clearly.'

'Bloody *hell*.' She had to sit down, but she couldn't find a chair. She edged around and leaned on the desk instead, her hand barely missing a spun-glass swan.

The room was revolving, she could feel his warmth surrounding her as if she were already in his arms. The weeks of hard-won peace were burned away, the casual conversations went up in flames. Here, in the half-lit office, they were together again on the physical plane and she couldn't bear the tension.

'You spoke to me.' His words fell into the silence, but the desk was between them now and he made no move towards her.

'I didn't see you,' she said with the bitterness of defeat. 'Smelt you, maybe, but I thought – I hoped – it was just the room. I wasn't expecting you.'

'You've had a shock,' he said. 'Sit down. There's a chair behind you.'

'I'm not sitting, I'm going,' she snapped. 'I never should have come!'

'Don't go. Please. I need to talk to you face-to-face for a change.'

'So, you should have come to the house. *Your* house. I couldn't have refused to let you in.' And Ellie and Kate and Dottie would have protected her from herself.

'So I could,' he said reflectively, 'but I didn't want an audience. Not even Kate. How is Kate, by the way?'

'You didn't come back from Thursday Island and lure me here to talk about Kate.'

'I never went to Thursday Island at all. Tam is heading up that segment to balance the stuff I did in Tasmania. And, thanks to your timely inspiration, *Islands – In the Rough* is going to be magic.'

There was a silence, and she made no move to break it. Her muscles were all wound up as tight as the strings of a harp, talking urgently about fight or flight.

352

'It isn't finished yet,' he continued. 'I have one more island and one more segment to film.'

'You'd better get cracking, then,' she said through stiff lips.

'I am. I came to ask you again to marry me.'

She closed her eyes, leaning heavily on the desk as the world spun round once more. 'Jasper –' Why didn't he touch her? Why didn't he hold out his arms?

'Hear me out,' he said. 'There's something you have to know about Jet. He should have told you himself, but he said he'd leave it to me. I think he hoped you'd shoot me.'

Sickening comprehension flooded her. 'If this is about Rusty Green,' she spat, 'forget it. I've known about her since I broke off my engagement.'

'*What?*'

The word came out like the crack of a whip. He was round the desk in three swift strides and she backed away, as desperate to escape as she had been for his embrace. They regarded one another in silence, and the rejected chair was biting into the backs of her legs.

'Why, Aberdeen?' he said in a quiet, deadly voice. 'Why didn't you tell me?'

'I didn't tell anyone,' she said. 'I didn't want to upset Kate.' Her chest was hurting and everything was terribly, terribly wrong. Jet's mocking touch again, though he was far away. 'I had no reason to tell you,' she added.

'You had no reason? You knew I wanted you, you let me beg, but you turned me down because you were engaged to Jet. Now you say that's over, yet you didn't even tell me! All that time on the telephone, all the things we've said, yet you never told me the thing I needed to hear.'

'You didn't tell me you were coming home,' she countered.

'And just as well,' he said coolly. 'You'd have cleared off, wouldn't you?'

'You bet I would!'

'So, how did you find out about Rusty?'

'Jet told me. Pretty naïve, wasn't I? I thought she was just a kid – like Nick and Todd and Tiger.'

'It must have hurt you a lot,' said Jasper more gently.

'It hurt my pride. Here was I, trying to break it to Jet that it wouldn't work, and all the time he'd been grooming a replacement.'

'You'd decided to break it off *before* you heard about Rusty?'

'That's what I just said. It was the night he came back, the night that *you* first rang.' She heard his sharp intake of breath, saw, despite the poor light, the flare of colour along his high cheekbones. '*No*,' she said violently. 'It had nothing to do with that! Jasper, *don't*.'

'I haven't done anything,' he said remotely, but she knew his hands were clenched.

'You were about to.' The sick suspicion grew. 'You knew about Rusty, Jasper. You knew that Jet and I had broken it off.'

'I knew about Rusty. Nothing else.'

'Jet didn't send you to try your luck? He didn't toss me to you as a crumb from his table?'

'No!' he said forcefully.

'Of course he did. It was his idea for you to lend me your house.'

He made a furious gesture and flung away. 'Believe that if you want.'

'I'm not playing your game, Jasper,' she said. 'I'm not playing Jet's game either. I told him I wouldn't marry you, and I told him why.'

'Then tell me,' he said passionately. 'And tell me what you plan to do instead!'

'I'm going to live with Kate at her cottage. We might grow herbs to sell, or run a tea-room.'

'For God's *sake* –'

'No,' she said. 'For Kate's sake – and my own.'

'Kate could live another twenty years or more,' said Jasper. 'Marry me, and Kate can live with us.'

'I can hear Jet's voice again,' she said. 'I won't marry you – or anyone – just to make life easy. I won't be used and I won't use anyone else. And there's no way I'm going to set myself in between two Diamonds. Once was enough, at that party.'

'Nothing happened then.'

'And that was thanks to Jet. *You* would have started something. You were itching to knock him down.'

'Too right I was!' The glass swan shattered to the floor as Jasper's fist struck the desk. 'What the hell are we fighting about?' he demanded, crunching forward over the bits of swan. 'Abbie, *please*. You've got it all so twisted!' His hands closed on her arms at last and she nearly fell over the chair. 'Forget all this,' cried Jasper. 'Forget it and *look* at me.'

'I can't forget,' she said hopelessly. 'Oh Jasper, *Why* –?'

She broke off in a sob as the demons swarmed about her.

'Then tell me what you want,' he said and his voice was suddenly resigned.

'I want to be let *alone*,' she gulped. 'I want to get on with my life. Oh, Lord, I want to forget these last months ever h-happened!'

'Mop yourself up,' he said. 'I'll get you a taxi. Go and live with Kate and grow your herbs. How long do you need to move out of my house?'

'Two or three d-days,' she said, and caught back another sob, bereft and astonished. She could have screamed at him.

'You have three days,' said Jasper. 'I'll move back into the house on Wednesday night. If you're leaving earlier, let me know. If the place is empty Doc would scream the street down and I'll get sued.'

He left the office and she collapsed at last, scrubbing her cheeks with her hands, sick with misery.

He had given Aberdeen a contact number, but he didn't expect her to call. And this time, he told himself harshly, he really had given up. Not like last time, when he had kept in tenuous contact through her tenancy of his house. Jet had left the field, but it made no difference. He had to face the fact that she didn't want his love. He hadn't been rejected in favour of Jet, he'd been rejected in favour of nothing. If Jet knew, he'd be laughing.

He didn't hate Jet. What was the use? He didn't hate Doc for destroying whatever he could lay his beak on and shrieking half the morning. That was Doc's way, his cockatoo nature, and Jasper could forgive him for the sake of his aplomb. Just like Jet. And how strange to think that Jet, after all his city-flat-based blondes, should have finally wound up sharing bed and boat with Rusty Green. And Jet had better tread warily there, for if he mistreated Rusty he would have to face her close-knit family. But the confrontation (if there was one) wouldn't happen yet. Jet had sailed away and taken Rusty with him. What they'd done about *Greensleeves* and the charter business Jasper neither knew nor particularly cared.

One thing he demanded was the chance to say goodbye to Kate.

'I don't care about appearances,' he said remotely to Aberdeen when they met at the house late on Wednesday afternoon, 'but I care about my friends and I won't have Kate thinking I threw you out.'

'I wouldn't let her think that.'

'I've come to say goodbye to her. You owe me that much.'

As soon as he said it he could have bitten his tongue, but she nodded sadly. 'I know what I owe you, Jasper. You've been a great support since Kate was hurt.'

'But you want that support withdrawn.'

'Yes,' she said bleakly. 'I wish I'd never been weak enough to take it up. But never mind that now. I've itemized everything we've used, and there's a box of groceries in the pantry. The same things you left behind, or more or less.'

'Your efficiency stuns me,' he said. 'I wanted you to come and work with me, you know. I wanted your help with *Islands – In the Rough*. I wanted your input in a project that's completely new.'

'Kate's in the courtyard, Jasper, with Dottie and the galahs. I have to finish the packing.'

'I'll tell you about the project while you pack.'

'No!' She said it curtly. 'Go and talk to Kate.'

He hadn't seen Kate for weeks, and he was astonished at the change in her. He had meant to greet her

357

slowly so she wouldn't be confused, but he found himself striding forward with his arms outstretched, tripping over Dottie. He bent to hug her warmly, and she hugged him back. 'Oh, my dear! I didn't think you'd come.'

'Of course I came.' He crouched beside the chair. 'I'd have come before, except I didn't want to be underfoot.'

'Aberdeen didn't want you underfoot,' she corrected, and she sounded so much like the old Kate that he gave her a sudden smile.

'You're thinner,' she added.

He shrugged and patted Dottie, who was grovelling with delight. 'I've been working hard.'

'You should smile more often,' she said. 'It's very attractive. If I were twenty years younger, I'd want you for my toy-boy. Since I'm sixty-eight and disabled, I'm going to be very rude. What happened to your face?'

'My *face*?' he said quizzically. 'Nothing, Kate. I was born like this. Red hair, brown eyes, the lot. It isn't handsome, it isn't even unique, as you know.'

'Your smile, my dear,' she said. 'Is it a scar?'

'Not a scar, exactly.' His voice was dry in his ears. 'It's some kind of nerve damage from a fall I had as a kid.'

'A fall?'

'All right. Jet and I had an altercation and he got lucky – or unlucky.' He shrugged. 'No real harm done, but it couldn't be repaired. Maybe now they could fix it – I don't know. I'm used to it. And at least it's achieved one thing: there's an infallible way of telling Jet and me apart. Just ask us to smile.'

'Jet never stops smiling,' said Kate.

'He did when I knocked him down, but you don't want to know about that.' He took both her hands in his. 'You look so much better, Kate! I can't believe it.'

'Aberdeen doesn't believe it,' said Kate. 'She thinks I'm much more helpless than I am. Seeing me every day, she doesn't really *see* me any more. The legs aren't much but my mind is coming back.' She leaned forward urgently. 'Jasper, I don't want to live with Aberdeen. I don't want her to martyr herself for me, and I *don't* want to be grateful. It might sound harsh, but it's true.'

'I see.' He wondered where this was leading.

'I love Aberdeen,' said Kate. 'She's my only child, unexpected and unplanned. Tom and I married late and we had a lovely semi-detached relationship. If you know what I mean.'

'No,' said Jasper courteously, 'I don't think I do.' He rose to his feet, wincing as his legs protested. 'I must sit down. Shall I wheel you over to the seat?'

'No, give me your arm.' Kate edged forward and then, with an enormous effort, rose from the chair. 'I can't walk,' she said, 'but I can shuffle.' She gave him an irritated glance. 'There's nothing wrong with my legs or back, it's just my blasted brain that won't pass on the messages. I'm trying to jog its memory.'

Carefully, he supported Kate to the rustic seat. Their progress was impeded by Dottie's love and by the old galahs which sidled up and climbed his trouser legs.

'I might as well have had a stroke,' grumbled Kate. 'Since I have to learn to walk all over again.'

Jasper sat beside her, a bird on each shoulder, while he waited for Kate to continue.

'I liked being married,' said Kate. 'I also liked my freedom. Tom and I spent days apart, but we always

359

had a good old gossip when we came together. And then we'd go to bed. It suited us not to live in one another's pockets. Then Aberdeen came along and it was a big adjustment. We rubbed along all right, because I let her alone. There wasn't much point in anything else. She's as stubborn as all get out.'

'Tell me about it!' he said with irony. 'Did you know she's disengaged from Jet?'

'She didn't say,' said Kate. 'But I'm not surprised. She hasn't mentioned weddings in a while. What happened? Did he throw her over? I can hardly blame him.'

'The other way round,' said Jasper. 'She threw *him* over.'

'But it hasn't helped your cause at all?'

Jasper said nothing, but tickled Dottie's jaw so that the dog whined in ecstasy.

'Darn,' said Kate. 'She's stubborn. She sets ideas in concrete. And I, for one, am not ready for death by knitting and daytime telly yet. And that's what will happen to me if I start to see myself as Aberdeen sees me.'

'Have you told her how you feel?'

'Repeatedly,' said Kate. 'She thinks I'm being noble. I'm not the one to get through to her, obviously. It needs some serious persuasion.'

'Hmm,' said Jasper.

'What do you mean, *hmm*?'

'You think *I* should do the persuading,' he said. 'Otherwise you wouldn't have mentioned it.'

'It could backfire on you, you know, in a very serious way.'

'Then perhaps we'd better get something clear. Are you asking me to be underhanded?'

'Yes,' said Kate. 'Would you consider that? In a very good cause?'

'Only on one condition. And to know if the condition applies I'd have to talk to Aberdeen again.'

'Talk,' said Kate tersely. 'Talk to her now.'

'There isn't much time. Your flight is leaving soon.'

'*Make* time, Jasper. Please. Make us a miracle, for all our sakes.'

CHAPTER 20

'The chair,' said Kate. 'It'll have to be returned to the hospital now.'

Aberdeen froze. 'I never thought of that! Lord! We'll have to book another taxi to deliver it.'

'Too late,' said Kate. 'Our taxi's here. Jasper will take it in his van.'

'Jasper has things to do.'

'He won't mind. I'll go in the taxi with Ellie, while you two deal with the chair. Then Jasper will bring you the rest of the way and he can fetch Ellie home.'

'Kate – he isn't a shuttle service.'

'Aberdeen, don't argue,' said Kate querulously. 'You've made enough trouble as it is.'

Aberdeen's mouth opened in a silent mew of protest but she made allowances. 'All right,' she said evenly. 'If Jasper will go to the hospital, I can come with you straight away. Better yet, we'll take the chair to the airport.'

'Ellie's coming with me,' said Kate. 'You can go with Jasper. Then he can come to the airport and fetch Ellie home. The airport has folding wheelchairs for people like me. I *told* you that.'

Aberdeen sighed, but Kate mustn't be upset. She

glanced at Jasper. 'We'd better go,' she said. 'We have to check in half an hour before the flight.'

'There's plenty of time,' he said gravely. 'Kate and Ellie could get your boarding pass if necessary.'

Jasper lifted Kate into the taxi and kissed her affectionately. The interior light gilded his profile, and glinted copper lights from his hair. Aberdeen watched hungrily, storing up impressions for the barren times ahead. Storing up nothing but pain for herself, she knew. Doc squawked, suddenly, and she bit her lip. She'd miss that evil bunch of feathers and the darling old galahs.

Jasper moved away and Ellie got in beside Kate. The cases were piled in the boot and the departing taxi carved a fan of radiance away down the Close.

'Now,' said Jasper, when he and Aberdeen were settled in the van. 'I have to ask you a question.'

Her mouth was dry and her heart began to thud. She glanced sideways and saw his hands were clenched on the wheel. 'We have to get to the hospital,' she said.

'Please, Aberdeen. I have to know. I have to know how you really feel about me.'

She frowned fiercely down at her hands, white-knuckled against her dark blue skirt. 'Jasper, *don't*. It won't do any good.'

'It will do *me* good.'

She sighed, heavily, drew in a breath and sighed again. There was a tightness in her throat and chest that wouldn't go away. 'This isn't fair.'

'I have to know,' he said. 'Otherwise, I can't go on. I know you want me, physically, as much as I want you, but that kind of wanting's empty unless there's something else. Is there nothing else? Is *that* why you wouldn't have me?'

363

He was giving her an easy way out, but to take it would be to tell a lie.

'All right, there *is* something else,' she said. 'I love you. Are you satisfied? I wish I'd met you before I met Jet. I wish I could have known you on equal terms; I wish I had something I could honestly offer you. I didn't and I haven't, so there's nothing more to say. Now let's get rid of this chair so I can go home.'

'Thank you,' he said, and started the engine. 'A fitting epitaph for a might-have-been. Now I can go on.'

She lay back against the seat, and closed her eyes as Jasper drove down the hill. She heard the indicator, and the orientation of the van felt odd.

'This is the wrong way,' she said.

'No,' said Jasper. 'It's getting late, so I'm taking a short-cut. Did I ever tell you much about my island, Aberdeen?'

'Not really,' she said listlessly. 'Only that it has rocks and seabirds.'

'It's where I go, my private place, when I want to forget the world.'

She let his voice wash over her, hearing the tone soften as it always did when he spoke of something close to his heart.

'My courtyard is a kind of island too,' he said. 'An island from wind and storm. Islands are complete in themselves; they have a special magic.'

'I suppose so.' She was looking out the window as the north shore suburbs spangled by. She had loved this city for five years; now it might be a long time before she saw it again. A very long time before she dared to come to Windhill again, for fear of meeting memories.

She glanced at the dashboard clock. 'You'll have to turn back,' she said sharply. 'You'll have to sign the chair in by yourself. My flight leaves in about an hour.'

'Your reservations have been cancelled,' said Jasper.

'*What*?'

'Your reservations have been cancelled.'

'No,' she said positively. 'The airport would have called.'

'I assure you it's true.'

'But Kate's just gone to the airport.'

'No, Aberdeen. Kate and Ellie will be back at the house by now.'

'I don't understand,' she said.

'I don't expect you do.' Jasper indicated and turned off the highway.

'Don't be obscure. I'm not in the mood.'

'It's simple,' he said. 'You are being kidnapped.'

Aberdeen clutched at her head in exasperation. 'You've gone mad. Or I have.'

'I'm taking radical steps to prevent insanity.'

'Stop this van at once!' she said. 'Let me out.'

'I'll let you out when we get there.'

'Get *where*?'

'I'm taking you to Allirra,' he said. 'I hope you have your anti-nausea pills.'

'What if I said no?'

'Then I'll hope you use the bucket.'

'*Jasper*! You can't *do* this. You must see that? It's stupid, it's useless and it's wrong. I could sue you for kidnapping!'

'No doubt you could,' he said, 'and perhaps you will. I did work out a worst-case scenario.'

'A five-year stretch in Long Bay Gaol? And a criminal record?'

365

'The worst case is never having spent an Allirra day with you. Just you.'

It never occurred her to question him on that. His voice was utterly sincere.

'Kate will be going out of her mind,' she ventured after another few kilometres had passed in silence.

'Kate understands the situation.'

'She doesn't know about this, I hope?' asked Aberdeen politely. 'It's a little strange for a woman's mother to connive at her kidnapping.'

'Kate doesn't know the details. She left me to work them out.'

'And how long have you two been hatching this vile plot?'

'Since around five today.'

'It's only six-thirty now.'

'Plots must hatch fast when you're desperate,' he said. 'If they're to hatch at all. Kate and I were desperate, each in our own way. So, Aberdeen, you are spending three days with me.'

'Three days,' she repeated. 'Why three? And what then?'

'Three days can work a miracle,' he said. 'If it can be worked at all. We spend three days on Allirra. No contact with the outside world at all. After that – whatever you want. A ticket to Tasmania, your day in court . . .'

'I'd look really clever in court, explaining why I didn't jump out of the van or the boat. I suppose there *is* a boat.'

'There's a motor boat. The van has central locking and you can't swim.'

She should have been outraged, but all she felt was a magical lightening of her senses, a casting aside of

366

burdens as the Gordian knot unravelled with the road. Only for a while, she reminded herself. This craziness of Jasper's couldn't solve a thing, but at least she could be with him for a time. 'Will Ellie stay with Kate?'

'Of course. They'll stay at the house, looking after the fur and feather brigade.'

Her hand went to her mouth. 'The chair! Jasper, we've got Kate's wheelchair in the back of the van.'

'She'll have to manage without it.'

'No. Listen, we can go to your island, I promise, but I must go back to the house first. I'll make sure Kate's all right, and we can leave the chair with her and –'

'And you'll immediately come up with a thousand reasons not to get back in the van. No, Aberdeen Shawcross, I have kidnapped you, and the victims of kidnappers can't nip home to check on their mothers.'

'You're insane.'

'Are you going to spend all three days telling me something we agreed on months ago?'

'Yes. Probably all three nights as well.' Her own words echoed in her mind as she thought about the implications of that. 'Is there a house on this island?' she asked.

'There's a cabin.'

'Do the doors lock?'

'How else would I keep you in?'

'I was thinking more about keeping you out.'

'You're safe,' he said. 'You know I'd never hurt you.'

She didn't try to argue, for it would do no good. Three days would pass – then afterwards she would book another flight. And this time, she would leave nothing to chance. *She* would telephone the taxi, and warn the airport not to accept any cancellations of her reservation. *She* would return the wheelchair and . . .

She left the rest of it on hold, having quite enough to think about without it.

'At least,' she said, 'it might get you out of my system. And vice versa. After three days of undiluted me, you might look forward to prison.'

Jasper didn't reply to that, so she slid down against the sheepskin seat and turned to watch the far-flung lights of the suburbs on her left. After a while, her neck got tired and she turned to face the other way, seeing Jasper's well-cut profile silhouetted against the window. 'You don't seem very cheerful,' she observed.

'I'm not,' said Jasper.

'But you got your own way. You've kidnapped me. I'm even coming quietly.'

'You're coming too quietly,' he said.

'Making a fuss wouldn't change anything. You talk about kidnapping, but I do believe you'd never do me any harm.'

'I'm going to exert myself.'

'To do what?'

'If I tell you that, you'll take steps to be sure it doesn't work.'

She resented that, but she supposed it was true enough.

'Why do you make things difficult?' he asked. 'Why not take the easy way and give us both some peace?'

'I don't know,' she said. 'But I see what you mean. If I'd taken the easy way at work, done what I knew was wrong, I would have kept my job. Ironic, isn't it?'

'The easy way isn't always wrong,' he said.

'Mostly it is. Otherwise it wouldn't be easy.'

'Then maybe I'll bully you,' he said. 'I'll beat you

and starve you and yell at you. That way you'll know I'm exactly what you want.'

'That makes me sound like a masochist.'

'You are.'

It was late when they turned off the secondary road towards the sea. The van bumped and lurched over a rutted track and Jasper drove right down to a dilapidated building. No beach, no camping places. Just the rough seaside shrubs and jagged-looking rocks.

'Garage-cum-boathouse,' said Jasper. He opened the door and jumped back into the van. 'Deliberately beaten up so no one thinks it worthwhile breaking in. Speaking of which, did they ever catch the vandals at the quay?'

'Yes,' said Aberdeen. 'They got off with good behaviour bonds.'

'Maybe I will too.' He turned off the engine. 'I'll lock the door behind us, but don't be scared, there's a slipway just ahead. Into the boat. I'll bring the supplies in a minute.'

'What supplies?'

'I don't know exactly,' he said. 'I just fetched the box you left in the pantry.'

She stared at him in the dimness. Strange, how many of their encounters seemed to take place by inadequate light.

'I didn't go shopping myself,' he said. 'Unless you count the milk and fruit I had in the fridge in the van. I expected to sleep in my bed at the house tonight.'

The boat was very small. It dipped as she scrambled aboard and she felt a hollowness settle in her stomach. 'How far do we have to go in this thing?'

'Not far,' said Jasper. 'Allirra's in sight of the mainland.'

'That's comforting. I suppose. Couldn't you have kidnapped me to a nice motel?'

'You'd have gone down the fire escape. An hour or so should do it. By the way, the boat is called *Jemima*.'

'What is this place?' she asked, looking about in the darkness. 'Does it qualify for a name on the map? Or is it against the rules to tell me in case I identify it in court?'

'Not much point in hiding information, since you know my face and name. This place is called Quartz Point. There are a few shacks scattered about, and it has a permanent population of eighteen people and about six dogs. None of them would hear you if you yelled from here. Put on your lifejacket now and hold on tight. This stretch of water can be very rough.'

'Wonderful,' she said.

'You faced up to the *Aphrodite* with a better grace than this.'

'That was then.'

'Hold tight,' he said again, and fired the engine.

If the *Aphrodite* was a graceful swan, *Jemima* was a very shabby duckling. She puttered slowly away from the point across the little bay, but as soon as they reached the open water Jasper turned up the throttle. The blunt bows hit the waves head on, and *Jemima* crouched on her tail and scuttered along. The moon laid a silver pathway for them to travel and after a while Aberdeen could make out the huddle of an island in front. To her dismay they seemed set on bucketing past it and if she hadn't been afraid of biting her tongue, she'd have asked what he was doing. As it was, she could only wait.

Their course curved at last, and Jasper throttled back to approach the seaward side of the island. The

370

roar became a purr as *Jemima* nosed in between two rocks and slid along a narrow channel. The bows crunched softly against a wooden landing stage, and Jasper tied up and sprang ashore with the box of stores.

He carried them away without a word, and Aberdeen, deserted, sat in the boat and waited. She supposed she might have tried to return to the mainland, but she had no doubt that Jasper had taken the key.

'The cabin is a few minutes' walk from here,' he said, reappearing.

Aberdeen got on to the landing stage. She could have done with a hand to steady her, but he didn't offer one. Her knees were trembling with reaction and weariness, but she didn't feel ill. Which was odd, really, since she hadn't taken a tablet. Jasper was already disappearing along a rough path, so she hurried in his wake.

The walk through the moonlight was very strange. It seemed that Jasper, having brought her to Allirra, had nothing to say to her. Her spirits, which had been rising and falling like a mad barometer, sank to her shoes.

'I should have been at Kate's cottage in Hobart by now,' she said, to break the silence. 'I should have travelled by plane, not boat. I've had enough of boats.'

'You said you liked sailing.'

'I said a lot of things.'

'So did I,' he said, flinging it over his shoulder. 'The difference is that I meant every one.'

'You lied when you said you wanted that file from your studio computer. And about taking a short-cut to the hospital.'

'Correction,' he said. 'I said there *was* a file in the

studio computer, and I said I was taking a short-cut. You just assumed I wanted the file, and that we were going to the hospital.'

'Prevarication is as bad as lying. You didn't give me a chance.'

'If I had, you would have taken it and run.'

Dark trees lined the path and rock piles loomed over to one side, heaped in amazing wind-sculpted shapes. It was very quiet, but for the hushing of the sea and the scuttle of some small animal. And it was *dark*. Never, in Hobart, Sydney or Melbourne, had she spent time in a place where the darkness reigned unchallenged by anything but stars and moon. She stumbled, and wondered why he didn't take her arm.

The cabin shone dimly through the trees, like something from a folk tale. 'I put the light on,' said Jasper as he opened the door. 'Aberdeen? Will you come in?'

'Oh – yes,' she said numbly. 'I'm coming.' Radiant golden light poured forth and she raised a hand to shield her eyes. 'It's very bright.'

'The lamp's burning high. I'll adjust it now we're here.' He touched her shoulder as if to guide her into the cabin. She shuddered at the contact, and he drew in a sharp breath, bent and scooped her off her feet, stepping over the threshold with Aberdeen high in his arms.

'Jasper!' she gasped, and hooked an arm around his neck for support. Her hand touched the warm flesh above his collar and she gasped again, raggedly, all her senses dissolving in a flood as brilliant as the lamplight.

It was happening again, that thing that overtook her whenever they made contact. It was blinding her, running along her nerve paths as a flame ran along a powder trail. It burned through her resentment, through her resignation, just as it had burned up time when they'd met in the studio office.

Her head was spinning, she supposed her legs were weak, but couldn't tell while she was cradled in Jasper's arms. 'Jasper!' she cried again in protest and in desire. Her hand closed on his collar, then slid inside, her fingertips exploring the warmth of his skin. The other hand rose to touch his hair, that shaggy, vital auburn-coloured thatch that was burning in the golden light. It clung to her fingers like heavy feathers, faintly damp with spray.

'Aberdeen,' he said softly, 'I'm going to put you down.'

She made some sound of protest, but he carried her across the room and shouldered open another door. It was dark in there, but for a band of lamplight which lay across a bed. He laid her on the quilt and let her go, and would have backed away, but she held on, clinging mindlessly. 'Don't leave me again!' she implored, and the words shocked her as much as they must shock him.

'I won't,' he said, and then came down to join her, bringing her fully into his arms. She had both hands against his chest, sliding them inside his shirt, delighting in the rough soft curls of hair and the firm skin beneath. Her stomach was going liquid; she was aching and restless with desire. The hollowness built up within her, and she brought her face against his chest as she had done once before. He had stopped her then, but this time his hands and mouth were equally urgent. Holding her against him, he rolled over so she lay on her back and he was leaning over her. His mouth came gently down on hers, and she tasted the salt of his sweat and the sea and more salt still which she identified as her own sliding tears. She wrapped her arms around his back, trying to pull him closer, to press her aching body against him and assuage the terrible emptiness.

'Abbie,' he murmured, as his mouth drifted sideways across her cheek.

She turned her face blindly, her mouth seeking renewed contact with his, her hands clenched in his shirt. He arched against her, pulling away. 'No!' she cried. She was afraid he'd stop, afraid he'd leave her stranded again.

'Slow down!' he gasped, and his body was arching again. 'I have to catch up with you. Wait!'

He pushed her gently away and brought his hands to her blouse, undoing the top two buttons slowly, giving her time, she realized dimly, to come to her senses. She reached for his shirt and yanked it apart, giving him no time at all. Her blouse peeled away, and her bra was an unbearable constriction. Abruptly, she sat up and dragged it over her head, dropping it somewhere out of sight and opening her arms. 'For God's *sake*, *do* something!' she gasped between gritted teeth. 'I'm going to explode!'

He was bare to the waist now, and he brought her back into his arms, letting her rub against him. She was wearing a skirt which wouldn't be much impediment, but he was still in his old soft jeans. She swept her hands down to his waist and tugged at the belt. It came undone, but she had to let him go to deal with the rest. She kicked off her own shoes and skirt, then her pants. Now she was naked, quivering and exposed, and she reached out for him again. Her hands brushed skin and slid round to grasp his hips, pulling him towards her while her legs strained to wrap around him too.

'Abbie,' he said, and now she caught a breath of laughter and exasperation in his voice, 'don't be in such a *hurry*. After all this time I want to savour the moment.'

'I can't *help* it,' she groaned. 'Please . . .'

He kissed her, stilling her words, taking her eager mouth with his. His tongue traced her lips, and she felt herself opening to him like a flower. She was still twisting and squirming, trying to get closer, but he took hold of her hips and held her still, aligning her with his own body. She was at such a peak of excitement already that the final adjustment spilled her over the edge. She opened her eyes in astonishment as the world spiralled away, drawing her into the vortex and shaking her to her bones. She was aware that he was still kissing her as the startled cry burst from her lips, and she felt him stroking her back and cradling her until the storm had passed.

'What about you?' she gasped when she could speak.

In answer, he moved within her again and again, and she felt his swift relief as an echo of her own. She kissed his neck and shoulder, stroking his damp hair as he gasped against her.

They lay still for a few moments, regaining their breath. Aberdeen could feel her pulses beating in her temples and at her fingertips. She never wanted to move again, but Jasper's fingers were insistent on her shoulders. 'Abbie?'

'Mmm.' Tears still seeped from under her eyelids and she was as limp as a cloth doll, but when he would have moved away she resisted. 'Don't go, Jasper, please.'

'You know who I am, then,' he said in an odd voice.

'Hmm?' She was startled, blinking the tears away. 'Of course I know.'

'That's a relief,' he said. 'I'd hate to think I was just a convenient body.'

'How could you think that? I don't make a habit of . . . of . . .'

'Exploding?'

'Ugh,' she said, and shivered. 'Don't remind me. It was terrifying.'

'You don't make a habit?' he prompted.

'I don't make a habit of begging men to make love to me. In fact, you're the first.'

'I'm sure in your case, it's not so much begging as begged against,' he said.

'I'm afraid I went a bit haywire.' The languor was fading fast and she was near to a fresh burst of tears. She wanted to be loved and cradled, not forced to defend her inexperience.

'A *bit*?' he said.

'Exceedingly haywire, then,' she snapped. 'It's your fault, anyway.'

'For reminding you too much of Jet?'

She sat up then, cold and clammy as the night air touched the surfaces that had been warmed by Jasper. 'That's it!' she said and her voice was chilled with misery. 'You've proved my point. If I married you I'd never be free of this darned, irrational contest between you and Jet!'

'I'm sorry,' he said quietly. 'But you begged me not to leave you again, so I assumed you were thinking of Jet.'

'I was thinking of *you*,' she said. 'You left me that night when I ripped your shirt, you left me in the office. It was my fault then – don't tell me! But I nearly

376

couldn't bear it, and I *really* couldn't bear it again tonight.' She shivered and let herself down beside him. 'What now, Jasper? You've got what you wanted now. It was my fault too, but if you hadn't brought me here it wouldn't have happened.'

'And would you believe it isn't why I brought you?'

'There's not much point in keeping me here for three days now. And for your information, you *don't* remind me of Jet in that department. You're totally, utterly different, and if you ever insult me like that again I'll bite you. Exactly what *did* you bring me here for?'

'To wear you down,' he said. 'To win a breathing space for Kate. I was going to spend the whole three days in wooing you the best way I knew how. Away from other people and distractions, away from the things you think you should be doing. I was going to point up the virtues of loving companionship, mutual respect, and sharing common ground.'

'We certainly shared something, but I don't think it was common ground exactly.' She shivered, resentful because he sounded pensive, and not at all impassioned.

'I was going to spend three days persuading you of the advantages of marriage with me.'

'So start persuading,' she said waspishly. 'Unless you've been put off by my lack of self-control.'

'I was going to take you for moonlit walks and explain to you slowly and carefully the things that Kate explained to me.'

'Explain them.'

'I was going to talk to you, listen to you, walk with you . . . but I wasn't going to touch you once until you asked me to, if you ever did.'

'I'm asking now,' she said. 'Touch me.'

'I'm touching you,' he said. 'I'm trying to believe you're here and holding me at last.' He gathered her gently against him, kissing her hair. 'I'm going to stick to it,' he murmured. 'The rest of the schedule. I won't make the mistake of thinking you're convinced, just because you took a little short-cut.'

'That's good,' she said, and caught her breath. 'I'll need a lot of convincing.' She put her arms around him, her mouth against his chest.

Jasper said nothing, but his hands were stroking her back, curving round her hips, gentle as Jet's had never been, yet raising her to a pitch that frightened her again.

'Maybe now's the time to savour the moment,' she said. 'That's if you feel like trying it again.'

'I feel like it,' he said. 'Maybe we'll even get synchronized this time, since you won't be in quite such a hurry, my lovely.'

She bit her lip, and drew away a little.

'Don't be hurt,' he said. 'It was really a very great compliment to me. It made me feel king of the world, to bring you to that flowering in my arms.'

'I suppose you might take it that way, if you want to be kind.' She was very nervous, for the blinding desire had scattered her inhibitions before and now some of them were back in place. 'I'll try to keep my head this time, I promise.'

She lay against him, and every caress was magnified. His skin under her questing fingers was warm and responsive, she shivered repeatedly under his touch. The shiver built swiftly to fever and she began to struggle against him; his stroking hands brought her gently back to control. 'Jasper?' she gasped. 'Please – I can't hold out much longer.'

'Sssh,' he soothed, and brought her down against him. 'There's so much I don't know about you yet,' he said, 'we have a lot to catch up on.'

'You know – too darned much – already,' she retorted. '*How* do you know where to touch me?'

'I suppose I read your movements. Does it matter?'

'No,' she said. Her back was arching, her body was gathering itself. She could feel his arms close round her, nursing her into his rhythm. She turned her mouth to his. 'I love you, love you, love you,' she whispered desperately, and heard her own name in the gasp which was snatched from him as they toppled together from the mountain they had climbed.

Jasper clung to his hope that the island would work its magic on Aberdeen. 'It's the silence,' he said, as they lay together under the stars on their second night. 'I come here when I need to see things clearly.'

'Did you come here when your German girl took up with Jet?'

'I did not,' he said. 'My pride was bruised, but pride can always mend. It wasn't Grete, you know, whom I regretted. It was Jet.'

She lifted a hand from beneath the quilt to stroke his hair, and he felt it like the caress of the night. 'You must know him better than anyone else.'

'I do,' he said, surprised. 'I know him inside out all over and I often wish I didn't.'

'Why? Isn't that what you want to do with me?'

'I hate to see him being less than he should,' he said, and felt surprise, for he had never put it into words before. 'I look at him and sometimes see myself, but he takes the paths I wouldn't. And I have to stand and wonder why.'

'He's the other side of you,' she said with a shrug. 'But you're not your brother's keeper, Jasper. You're not his conscience, either. You look after your back yard and let him tend to his. And now you can tend to me . . .'

'With pleasure,' he said.

'Where did you get the galahs?' she asked next morning as they walked along the narrow band of beach.

'The *galahs*?' She had the power to disconcert him, again and again.

'Tam says they're over fifty years old, so you can't pretend you brought them up from eggs.'

'They belonged to a friend of my mother's,' he said. 'She died and I took them in. That's all.'

'And what about that Dottie dog of yours?'

'I've had her about five years.'

'Where did you get her?'

'The dog pound. Why the sudden interest in my fur and feather brigade?'

'At a guess,' she said, 'you got Doc from someone who found he screeched too much, and Nyssa from someone who had neglected her. And that's not all. You gave Ellie a job when she badly needed one, and you rescued Kate and tried to rescue me. Why do you do it, Jasper? Why do you take in waifs and strays?'

'I never thought of it like that,' he said. 'I guess you could say I do what I want to do. That's all. I have to live with myself.'

'*And* with the dog and parrots and other strange people.'

'The thought of those dear old birds would have

380

haunted me and I don't like to be haunted. Come and see my rock pile. There's nothing like it, even on Kangaroo Island.'

She climbed through the crazy wind-sculpted caverns and he saw the wonder in her eyes as she touched the bands of sparkling quartz in the darker stone. He touched her cheek and then they were close in one another's arms.

'So,' she said, on the third and final evening, as they sat in a sheltered place and watched the sea. 'I'm another waif or stray for your collection.'

'*You*, a waif or stray?'

'Haven't you rubbed it in that I don't have anything else? Admit it, Jasper, you just don't want to be haunted. You offer a home, you gain another dependent.'

'Now that,' he said, 'is an entirely separate matter. I don't want to *give* you anything. I want to share the things I have. Responsibilities, my down-side and my love. I want someone to depend on, someone whole, to love me best . . . someone who holds herself aloof with others but shares herself with me.' He winced as the words came out. 'So, now you know,' he said. 'The shabby depths of my soul have been revealed.'

'Yes,' she said softly, 'now I know your darkest, deepest secret. It would take some living up to, to be your someone. It would be a worthy challenge.' He felt her fingers on his shirt and hardly dared to breathe. 'You like preserving things,' she said. 'You keep the best and let the rest go by. You see things clearly, most of the time, but you're not the easy path. What have you planned for Kate?'

'Nothing much,' he said. 'She's made her plans herself.'

'Well?'

Aberdeen's voice was astringent, but her hands were trailing streamers of delight along his nerves. He let his own hands drift to her blouse, and found her breasts, cupping them with sensuous pleasure. 'Kate wants to go home,' he said. 'She's planning to take in a lodger, someone who needs a home in exchange for things she can't manage for herself.'

'I see!' she said. 'She'd rather live with a stranger than with me!'

'She'd rather be in the driver's seat,' he said. 'Swallow it, Aberdeen. Take your medicine like a lady. It can't be any worse than the medicine you've often given me.'

Her hands were gentle on his skin. She was learning self-control. 'It will be hard,' she said. 'And Jet might try to make trouble, just because he's Jet.'

'And you might be seasick next time we come to Allirra,' he said, against her breast. 'And Doc will undoubtedly keep our babies awake all day and half the night . . . and he'll certainly want to eat any costumes you conserve.'

'Will I be conserving costumes, then?'

'You bet your doublet and hose!' he said. 'That's what I want to do for my next project. *You* get a museum together, and *I'll* make a film of the way it's done.'

'No, Jasper. I can't believe you want to do that.'

'I do want to,' he said. 'And it won't be a picnic for you. I insist on everything being done in the most meticulous way. I'll want you up to your ears in pins and shattered silk and babies and acid-free tissue, and

382

you're going to marry me in a genuine copy of a nineteenth-century gown.'

'Before or after the babies?' she asked. Her breath was coming quickly now, and he felt like the king of the world.

'Soon,' he said, and brought her gently beneath him. 'I'm sorry, Aberdeen, but I warned you I didn't do any special shopping. I keep a razor here, and a toothbrush, but I've never needed latex goods before. Not on Allirra.'

'Oh,' she said, and her teeth were clenched.

'I'm sorry.'

'Don't be,' she panted. 'This isn't going to be easy at all.'

'No,' he said, 'it's going to be murder.'

'Yes, probably yours. You'll get mixed up in the fuss when the Greens find out that Rusty's sailed off with Jet. Your turn.'

'Tam and Rod could fall apart at any moment,' he said hopefully. 'And *Islands – In the Rough* might never make the screen. Your turn.'

'The whole dashed island might sink like Atlantis beneath the waves, and *I can't swim!*' she gasped and writhed beneath him.

'I'll teach you.'

'Yes, of course you will. And probably make a film of that as well –'

Her voice broke off in a gasp, and for a while there was nothing to say.

'Jasper?'

'Abbie?'

'It won't be just for what I can get, if I marry you.'

'No,' he said gently, 'it won't. So – what's the

383

verdict, my lovely? Are you going to charge me with kidnap and see me sent down for five or seven years?'

'Not five years,' she said, 'not seven. Your sentence will be the term of your natural life.'

'Marry me, Abbie? Please?'

'I'll marry you,' she said.

EPILOGUE

Islands – In the Rough was completed by the end of September, and Jasper arranged for a special preview screening for Kate before she went home.

Aberdeen was sick before they went to the studio. Tam was sick just afterwards.

'Never,' said Tam to Kate, '*never* should I have said yes to this baby. To think I deliberately let myself in for this! It's all Rod's fault. I hate him.'

Rod was holding her close. He winked at Kate but directed his words to Tam; 'Don't you talk about Diamond Spellman Bowen like that! She might be born with a complex!'

Tam sat up abruptly. '*Diamond*?' she said in horror.

'Why not?' said Rod. 'She'll be Daddy's little diamond.'

'Over my dead body,' said Tam. Her teeth appeared to be clenched. 'Next you'll be calling her *Rodmyn* or *Tamney* . . . or even, God save us, *Onyx*.'

'Pipe down,' said Jasper. 'Tam, can you dim the lights?'

Tam did as he asked, the screen flickered with numbers, and the opening credits rolled.

ISLANDS – IN THE ROUGH
A Diamond/Spellman Production.

The title shimmered and broke up into a mass of jagged fragments which sped across the screen and vanished.

There was silence as the team watched the phoenix which had risen from disaster. The islands mixed and matched, a glorious confusion of palms and rocks, yachts, rescues, accidents and fun. Jasper battled devils, Tam and Rod disagreed on Thursday Island, Stew and Steve met an octopus and the dolphins leapt offshore at Kangaroo Island. Tropics, temperate, summer and winter, and the links were cut with the silence of Allirra, on the unnamed shore where Aberdeen sat on the rocks and watched the sea. A very personal hymn to his island, filmed by Jasper himself.

The film cut off, the credits rolled.

'What did you think?' asked Jasper.

'Beautiful,' said Aberdeen, touching his face in the dimness.

'I know I am,' said Jasper, 'but what did you think of the *film*?'

'Jasper, it was – ' She got just three words out, then fell mysteriously silent.

Tam put up the lights, stared transfixed, then put them out again.

'Nobody, *nobody* strike a match,' she said.

THE EXCITING NEW NAME IN WOMEN'S FICTION!

PLEASE HELP ME TO HELP YOU!

Dear *Scarlet* Reader,

I have some wonderful news for you this month – we are beginning a super Prize Draw, which means that you *could win an exclusive sassy Scarlet T-shirt!* Just fill in your questionnaire and return it to us (see addresses at the end of the questionnaire) before 31 November 1998, and we'll do the rest! If you are lucky enough to be one of the first four names out of the hat each month, we will send you this exclusive prize.

So don't delay – return your form straight away!*

Looking forward to hearing from you,

Sally Cooper

Editor-in-Chief, *Scarlet*

QUESTIONNAIRE

Please tick the appropriate boxes to indicate your answers

1 Where did you get this Scarlet title?
Bought in supermarket ☐
Bought at my local bookstore ☐ Bought at chain bookstore ☐
Bought at book exchange or used bookstore ☐
Borrowed from a friend ☐
Other (please indicate) _____

2 Did you enjoy reading it?
A lot ☐   A little ☐   Not at all ☐

3 What did you particularly like about this book?
Believable characters ☐   Easy to read ☐
Good value for money ☐   Enjoyable locations ☐
Interesting story ☐   Modern setting ☐
Other _____

4 What did you particularly dislike about this book?
_____

5 Would you buy another Scarlet book?
Yes ☐   No ☐

6 What other kinds of book do you enjoy reading?
Horror ☐   Puzzle books ☐   Historical fiction ☐
General fiction ☐   Crime/Detective ☐   Cookery ☐
Other (please indicate) _____

7 Which magazines do you enjoy reading?
1. _____
2. _____
3. _____

And now a little about you –
8 How old are you?
Under 25 ☐   25–34 ☐   35–44 ☐
45–54 ☐   55–64 ☐   over 65 ☐

cont.

9 What is your marital status?
Single ☐ Married/living with partner ☐
Widowed ☐ Separated/divorced ☐

10 What is your current occupation?
Employed full-time ☐ Employed part-time ☐
Student ☐ Housewife full-time ☐
Unemployed ☐ Retired ☐

11 Do you have children? If so, how many and how old are they?
_____

_____

12 What is your annual household income?

under $15,000	☐ or	£10,000	☐
$15–25,000	☐ or	£10–20,000	☐
$25–35,000	☐ or	£20–30,000	☐
$35–50,000	☐ or	£30–40,000	☐
over $50,000	☐ or	£40,000	☐

Miss/Mrs/Ms _____

Address _____

_____

_____

Thank you for completing this questionnaire. Now tear it out – put it in an envelope and send it, before 28 February 1999, to:

Sally Cooper, Editor-in-Chief

USA/Can. address
SCARLET c/o London Bridge
85 River Rock Drive
Suite 202
Buffalo
NY 14207
USA

UK address/No stamp required
SCARLET
FREEPOST LON 3335
LONDON W8 4BR
Please use block capitals for address

MIMAT/8/98

Scarlet titles coming next month:

FINDING GOLD Tammy Hilz

In this, our second *Scarlet* hardback, Jackson Dermont is on the trail of a thief! If he doesn't find her he will forfeit the business that he almost lost before, through someone's cunning and deceitful behaviour. Rachel Gold is high on his list of suspects . . . and Jackson is determined to do *anything* to save his beloved company. Anything . . . except fall in love and learn to trust – again!

SEARED SATIN Vickie Mohr

Security guard Tess Reynolds is a woman to be reckoned with. Boss of a successful security firm, she doesn't need any man's help to do her job. Until, that is, she meets gorgeous Ethan Booker who reluctantly joins forces with her to solve a deadly mystery. But isn't the real mystery how he's gonna persuade Tess to stick around once the case is closed?

A WOMAN SCORNED Kathryn Bellamy

Reeling with shock as a man from her past walks into the cafe, Tessa Grant grabs her daughter and makes a run for it – straight into the path of a passing bus! She wakes in hospital to discover that Max is back, and has taken over her life and her daughter. Now that he knows he is the father of her child, will they be able to make a life together? And why is someone else trying to destroy Tessa?

JOIN THE CLUB!

Why not join the *Scarlet* Readers' Club – you can have four exciting new reads delivered to your door every other month for only £9.99, plus TWO FREE BOOKS WITH YOUR FIRST MONTH'S ORDER!

Fill in the form below and tick your two first books from those listed:

1. *Never Say Never* by Tina Leonard ☐
2. *The Sins of Sarah* by Anne Styles ☐
3. *Wicked in Silk* by Andrea Young ☐
4. *Wild Lady* by Liz Fielding ☐
5. *Starstruck* by Lianne Conway ☐
6. *This Time Forever* by Vickie Moore ☐
7. *It Takes Two* by Tina Leonard ☐
8. *The Mistress* by Angela Drake ☐
9. *Come Home Forever* by Jan McDaniel ☐
10. *Deception* by Sophie Weston ☐
11. *Fire and Ice* by Maxine Barry ☐
12. *Caribbean Flame* by Maxine Barry ☐

ORDER FORM

SEND NO MONEY NOW. Just complete and send to **SCARLET READERS' CLUB, FREEPOST, LON 3335, Salisbury SP5 5YW**

Yes, I want to join the *SCARLET* READERS' CLUB* and have the convenience of 4 exciting new novels delivered directly to my door every other month! Please send me my first shipment now for the unbelievable price of £9.99, plus my TWO special offer books absolutely free. I understand that I will be invoiced for this shipment and FOUR further *Scarlet* titles at £9.99 (including postage and packing) every other month unless I cancel my order in writing. I am over 18.

Signed ....

Name (IN BLOCK CAPITALS)...

Address (IN BLOCK CAPITALS)..

....

Town... **Post Code**...............................

Phone Number ....

As a result of this offer your name and address may be passed on to other carefully selected companies. If you do not wish this, please tick this box ☐.

*Please note this offer applies to UK only.